Bridget.

Hope you enjoy
the read!

♡ melina

ps. hope to catch up
one day over
cocktails!

THE
Manhattan
MISHAP

MELINA MARIA MORRY

 FriesenPress

One Printers Way
Altona, MB R0G 0B0
Canada

www.friesenpress.com

Copyright © 2021 by Melina Maria Morry
First Edition — 2021

This novel is a work of fiction. All names, characters, businesses, incidents, and events are either a product of the author's imagination or used in a fictitious manner. Any resemblance to actual persons, living or dead, is purely coincidental.

ISBN
978-1-03-911348-0 (Hardcover)
978-1-03-911347-3 (Paperback)
978-1-03-911349-7 (eBook)

1. Fiction, Contemporary Women

Distributed to the trade by The Ingram Book Company

Andre, thank you for believing in my dreams so fiercely. Without you and a celebratory cocktail, this journey wouldn't have been half as intoxicating.

Chapter One

I'm not saying that my skin-tight, impossibly glossy, black vinyl pants are *not* comfortable—they are, somewhat—but if push came to shove, they could be a teeny bit more so. And quiet. Quiet would be even better. Their incessant squeaking is migraine-inducing, and my temples are threatening to throb. My legs feel like two mile-long chorizos stuffed into a sensational but suffocating casing, and every move I make is accompanied by my own personal soundtrack, played at full volume.

For the love of Britney Spears, it's too early in the day to be tormented by my so-called edgy outfit choices.

Don't get me wrong—I'm dressed to kill. But these pants are not exactly practical; particularly for public transit, as I'm currently discovering. Not that I knew that when I threw them on seconds after brushing my teeth with my bamboo toothbrush, sweeping back my shoulder-skimming walnut hair with a tortoiseshell claw clip, and scooping up my hand-me-down Fendi baguette bag. One speedy glance in the full-length mirror that precariously balances in the entrance of my shoebox apartment and I was bolting out the door.

It wasn't until I'd already reached the sidewalk that I realized that my pants were a total disaster. I'm talking Earth-shattering, bone-shaking, cows-flying-through-the-sky-in-a-tornado kind of disaster. Five o'clock news coverage catastrophe. Chipped nail on the way to a first date debacle. A full-blown fiasco!

Not to be overly dramatic.

Do you think it's possible to grease vintage vinyl pants like you would an old, rusted hinge? Because that's unerringly what they sound like. I've seen Hailey Bieber strut around SoHo on Instagram wearing an almost identical pair to the ones I have on and she didn't look like she needed greasing.

Come on, Margot, I chide myself, *you know you can't believe everything you see online.*

"Can you move?" asks a sizable man to my left, impatiently. For a split second I think he's referring to the tightness of my pants. My biggest wardrobe inspiration is Kate Moss circa the nineties, although, at this very moment, I wish I had considered toning it down just a smidge. I should've safely opted for a pair of woolly, slate-gray, *silent* slacks and not a pair of disobedient, shiny latex leggings. "This is my stop and you're blocking the door in that whale of a jacket," he ridicules. He looks down at me, judging me and my adventurous sense of style over the tip of his bulbous nose.

But there's nowhere for me to move to—aside from the one free seat that's decorated with multicolored blobs of chewing gum. No, thanks.

"Sorry," I automatically respond, even though I'm not sorry in the least. It's a habit. I feel like a slimy sardine squeezed into an overflowing tin can. By the way, do I *smell* someone eating sardines? Gross. Seven forty-five in the morning is an unethical time to be out in public. There are only three situations I willingly get up this early for: flights, ski trips, and when I've stayed up late enough at a fabulous party that it's technically morning when I get home. I know I sound like a spoiled, rich bitch, but I'm far from. The only thing getting me through the abominable A.M. commute is the sneaking suspicion that I'm getting a major promotion today. No one works harder than me—I'm like Jane Villanueva but only half as Hispanic (literally). I just *know* that this is the moment all of my hard work pays off. Finally, I can reward myself by buying a new pair of leather boots, something animal print, or a nude shade of toffee lipstick to celebrate.

Owning thirty different tubes of lipstick—organic and cruelty-free, of course—but only wearing three of them is essentially a prerequisite to a job at La Pêche, the city's Sephora rival in plant-based, environmentally aware products. We don't make or stock anything that can't be completely composted into your favorite houseplant. I'm dead serious about my career so naturally, I invest in new lipstick whenever I can. I swear, Yvette Trémaux, the CEO, thinks she's the Stella McCartney of the beauty industry—minus the sixties sex god dad, as far as I'm aware.

One more stop on this stifling subway and I can get off. Thank *god*. I'm really starting to sweat under my heavy, burnt-marshmallow shearling. My body is perspiring in places I didn't realize were possible to perspire in the winter. And is it just me or is my thong *completely* non-breathable? Actually, that might just be the pants. Nonetheless, whoever invented the G-string should be sent to a maximum-security prison ASAP. And whoever marketed them to the masses should be too. I say, bring back panty lines! They're sexy.

By the time I reach the La Pêche lobby, it's 8:07. I sprint up the stairs, my pants announcing my hasty arrival with every step. *Morning, everyone! Move out of the way! Margot Moss is in the building!* Suddenly I'm slapped with the realization that I forgot about my shoes. There's *no way* I can rock up to this meeting in my scuffed New Balance commuting sneakers. I need my ebony boots. It's okay. My desk is just one more floor up. A quick pit stop and I'll be good as gold. This is better because I can also drop off my sweltering coat, blot my nose, and take a moment to regroup after that treacherous train ride.

When I get to my desk, I exhaustedly take a seat, tucking my feet underneath its smooth, organized surface as I quickly untie my laces. I don't want anyone to see my sneakers; they don't explicitly go with the whole promote-me-I'm-so-smart-and-fashionable look I'm trying to pull off. Plus, they're covered in salt stains from the splotches of slush that are entirely unavoidable on the sidewalk. It's that really awkward time of year in Toronto where there's not enough snow on the ground to confidently wear Sorels but anything else is utterly inadequate. All of the other women who work here show up to the office in sexy stilettos— even during a blizzard—and I honestly don't know how they do it. It's one of the company's many unsolved mysteries. Like, why we go through so many executive assistants or what people claim to accomplish after four P.M. on Fridays.

The delicious, square-toed boots I slip into are *so* much more befitting to my outfit. I got them last year secondhand for $12. They were an absolute steal. Not literally, because I paid for them, but you know what I mean.

Boots on. Shoe problem solved. Easy as pie. My stomach growls at the thought of pie and I realize that in my haste to leave my claustrophobic apartment, I skipped breakfast. I wonder what kind of snacks they'll be serving at the meeting. Muffins? Fruit salad? Warm, toasted bagels with gigantic globs of Philadelphia cream cheese? My stomach growls again. I'm beginning to think it's in competition with my shrieking pants.

The office is so eerily hushed, it's like I'm in a horror movie. The only sounds are my own breathing and the smooth zip of my leather boots. Well, and my pants, but I'm trying to be as still as possible. Everyone must already be downstairs. *Eek!* Only three minutes to spare. I abruptly stand up, anxious to get to the meeting on time. Surely they won't promote someone who's late, no matter how fashionably.

Rip! Something awful pierces my style-sensitive ears. Hesitantly, I look down. To my revulsion, I see that the pocket on my blazer has caught on the arm of my stupid swivel chair and ripped wide open. You've got to be kidding me! There are frayed threads, shreds of lining, and chunks of horsehair facing hanging out of the destroyed seam. It's threatening to unravel further if I don't fix this wreck immediately.

"Margot, is everything okay? You look rather tense," Adam Frank, the *third* executive assistant of the year, asks. He's stopped dead in his tracks and has an amused look on his face. He's always so sickeningly smug, like he thinks he's hotter than Harry Styles or something. So what if he has two hundred thousand followers on TikTok? Who cares! Not me!

If this *were* a horror movie, he would totally be the killer. You know, the one that you don't suspect at first but once he reveals himself it becomes all too obvious? I would be mortified to be murdered by someone as annoying as him. It wouldn't even make a good podcast.

"Everything is great," I beam, attempting to smile through the anguish.

"You sure?" He looks at me quizzically. I nod, slightly flushed. "Well, you might want to hurry up and get down to the board-room. And make sure those filthy sneakers are tucked away. They're bringing down the stature of the office."

I smile tightly until he carries on and then I roll my eyes so hard into my skull that it feels like they might be stuck that way forever. *Ouch.* He is so aggravating. Him and his overly contoured cheekbones; his makeup looks like what Kylie Jenner wears *under* her foundation. Someone should give him a cotton pad and some micellar water, pronto.

Hastily I rummage through my desk drawers, searching for a safety pin. I must have one in here somewhere. How can I be obsessed with fashion and *not* have an emergency kit at the ready? I'm going to be late, but I have to fix this rip. All I have on underneath is a knitted tube top and that's not really going to fly on its own. No luck on the safety pin front. I'll have to use paper clips. Maybe it'll look cool, like a punky Alexander McQueen vibe? I'll pretend I'm Kate Moss at a grunge concert.

As my pants vociferate their way to the boardroom, I rehearse what I call my "Power Woman Mantra" in my mind, trying my best to radiate a façade that's as sleek and sophisticated as a panther. Trust me, manifestation works. I mean, I've been manifesting a promotion to senior communications specialist for the last few months and it's *finally* happening. If that's not proof, I don't know what is. *I am worthy of everything I desire in this world. I attract divine abundance. My power moves me to extraordinary places. I am—*

"Running a bit late, Moss?" Gia Johnson's voice sends a ripple of unfiltered irritation through my full physique. Even just hearing her stevia-sweetened inflection makes my nerves all twitchy. She gets under my skin more than Herbivore's coconut milk body polish, and let me tell you, that stuff is penetrating.

Without missing a beat—or a step—I hit back: "I could say the same about you, Johnson." You know those people who you inexplicably don't like the moment you lay eyes on them? That's me and Gia. She's been a pain in my vinyl-clad ass since the minute I met her. The distaste is mutual between us; it's pretty much the only thing we have in common. She's naturally beautiful, of course, with her pouty lips and hay-field hair, which makes it even harder to hate her because she has the face of an angel.

Literally, she looks like Candice Swanepoel. But it's the angelic ones you have to worry about. She's the devil in a really expensive, on-trend disguise with blemish-free skin, straight teeth, and flawless highlights.

Life really isn't fair—genetically speaking, anyway. "I've already been in," Gia declares. "I just popped over to Cafe Moi for Yvette and myself." She gives me a complacent smirk and pushes past me, not bothering to hold the door as she struts into the room with her extra foam, no fat lattes.

Oh, no. The sans-coffee reality sinks in, and it's more hideous than Margiela Tabi boots. What kind of crack-of-dawn meeting doesn't offer caffeine? What about breakfast? My dream of cream cheese bagels dissipates. Honestly, this should be illegal. Or at the very least, against the company's code of conduct. I become a different person when I'm hangry. I've tried to blame it on being a Gemini, but it's more like James McAvoy in *Split.*

My planned seat in the front row has been snatched up—by Gia, of course, who else?—so instead I tightly squeeze into a spot at the back of the boardroom. *Oh my god.* My pants are totally rambunctious. Every time I so much as *shift* on this pleather couch, they make the most horrific disruption. A few coworkers who I vaguely recognize turn to give me dirty looks. Great. The day has barely begun and I've already been labeled as fashionably ill with no cure in sight. Seriously, how does Hailey Bieber do it?

"Sorry," I whisper. "It's the pants. They're new."

I'm met with more judgemental glares and gestures telling me to zip it. Looks like I'm not the only one who skipped their breakfast and espresso today. Someone should really suggest that we get a Keurig machine installed in here for emergencies as dire as this; these forlorn employees are desperate for a fair trade Italian roast. I patiently sit and wait for my promotion because I know it'll make everything worth my uncomfortable embarrassment. I'm sure of it.

***

Okay. We've been sitting here for what feels like an eternity. My butt is totally numb, my thong is pinching me in places that should *never* be pinched, and my furious digestive system is beginning to eat itself. I hardly have a spare pound to shed so the latter point is troublesome.

I'm trying not to move so my gorgeous, albeit dreadfully noisy, pants don't interrupt. Again. In fact, I'm sitting so still that I've almost convinced myself that I could be pretty good at impersonating one of those metallic-painted people in Times Square that stand motionless and overcharge tourists for photos. I could be *The Hungry Girl in the Black Vinyl Pants*. If I don't get promoted, that's my backup plan. Which, I was totally kidding about when I first thought about it but is unfortunately looking more and more likely.

Yvette is starting to wrap things up and my name hasn't been mentioned once. Not even to praise me for the write-up I did about our new deodorants and their biodegradable packaging that was featured in *Allure*. Okay, so my name wasn't printed beside the blurb—not even in a microscopic, scantily legible font—but *I know* I wrote it, and so does Yvette. I think. I added it to my online portfolio regardless because why not?

There must be some sort of mistake here. Other people have been getting celebrated for their contributions . . . except for me. Why was I even asked to attend this meeting? I could have slept in and then taken my puppy, Lola, the fluffiest and cutest and tiniest two-year-old Maltipoo you've ever seen, for an extra-long walk instead. We could've gone to Jimmy's on Baldwin Street and picked up a single Americano and double fudge brownie.

It's so unfair. I swear, if anyone else gets their career upgraded today, I'm writing a letter of complaint. But to whom? The CEO of the company is the one leading this meeting. Yvette clearly needs to take a step back and reevaluate where she wants this business to go because in my opinion, this direction is totally wrong.

"Last but not least, I'm pleased to announce that Gia is being promoted to senior communications specialist," says Yvette. A round of applause breaks out. She smiles and holds up her latte— the one that Gia brought her—in a makeshift, pre-noon toast. "She will now oversee all copywriting standards, social media initiatives, blog content, and ensure that our brand message is clear across all mediums. Congratulations, Gia!" More applause.

All of the color drains from my face. If it weren't for my rosy W3ll People High Vibrations powder, I'd be paler than Gwen Stefani. This can't be happening. That's the promotion I've been manifesting. Last Wednesday I sat down with Tracy—my boss— and confessed all of my company-driven goals right to her face. She looked me dead in the windows to my soul and promised she'd do everything she could to help me get there. And now this?

Betrayal bubbles up inside of me like a bottle of champagne that's been shaken too quickly. Is this how La Pêche thinks they can treat their employees? Gia has been here for an entire year less than me! I practically slave away my existence for this job. And for what? This just isn't right. I mean—

"Seriously?"

My cheeks begin prickling before I realize what's going on. *Oh my god.* Did I just say that . . . out loud? In front of Yvette and Tracy and half of the company? Judging by all of the appalled expressions gawking at me—except Gia, she's absolutely revelling in this—I'd say so. I don't usually swear but . . . *fuck*. I'm in panic mode. Every last ergonomic chair has swiveled around to face me in complete and utter shock. And am I *standing up?* It all happens so fast I don't even hear my pants protest.

I've never had an "out of body experience" before but let me tell you, I'm not a fan. In fact, they suck. Even the part of me that's supposed to be "out of body" is shrinking away in mortification.

The boardroom is so still, I can hear a computer rebooting from down the hall. Maybe this *really* is a horror movie and the thing that gets brutally murdered at the climax is my decorum. Two dozen perfectly made-up faces are fiercely focused on me. Yes, even the guys are flawlessly beautified—except for Adam, in my humble opinion. Our office is mainly girls and gays and the gays know more about makeup than I do. (Not that it's hard; until last year I was applying eyeshadow with my pinky finger.)

"Margot, if you're finished, please sit down," says Tracy shortly. "Now."

I want to, I really do. There's nothing I'd like more than to just shrink back down and become invisible. If I had a superpower, that would be it—to be spontaneously unseeable. Unfortunately, I'm about as invisible as Drax in *Guardians of the Galaxy*. Much to my chagrin, my legs won't bend either. They're like two gleaming chopsticks at Nobu, holding me bolt upright. I can't sit down while this . . . this injustice is happening right in front of me! And most importantly, to me. This just isn't *lawful* and I have a right as a woman to fight for what I believe in. What would Elle Woods do?

Tracy's steely glare is burning into me hotter than the sun that time I spent Christmas in Los Cabos and only brought SPF15. Why did I have to say anything? But now that I'm up and all attention is on me, I feel like I need to take advantage of it. When life gives you lemons, mix a gin martini, spritz it with citrus, take a massive gulp, and stand up for yourself—especially when you've without a doubt been wronged.

"I'm sorry, Tracy, but I can't sit down," I manage, my voice slightly shaky.

"What's wrong?" Gia pipes up, giving me a supercilious once-over. She snickers, "Pants too tight?"

How is it acceptable to be so openly malicious? Where are the consequences? I scowl at Gia through narrowed eyes before continuing on.

"I'd just like to say . . ." *Come on, Margot, muster up that fierce confidence of yours.* Besides English and very, very conversational Spanish, "fierce" is the only other language I know inside and out. "I'd just like to say that I don't agree with the decisions being made here today." My eyes sweep the room and I summon every ounce of fearlessness I have in my possession. Boldly looking directly at Yvette, I add, "I'm a smart, hardworking woman and I deserve that promotion. Gia, on the other hand, does not." My hands have found their way to my lustrous hips and I'm as empowered as Gisele Bündchen looks on the runway.

Gia laughs mockingly as Tracy shoots daggers in my direction. Yvette apathetically sips her coffee, and I can't tell if she's entertained or enraged. You never quite know with her. It's the Botox. Nonetheless, I carry on before anyone has a chance to stop me or drag me and my too-tight pants out of here kicking and screaming.

"Marg—" begins Tracy but I unintentionally cut her off.

"Did you know that Gia takes three-hour lunch breaks every Wednesday? And she steals from the sample closet. Just last week I saw her smuggle out *three* bottles of the new bumbleberry body scrub that were meant for *Elle*." The room gasps. I'm really on a roll. "I've been working here for over two years and I keep being told that it's not the right time for a promotion. When *will* be the right time? I resent working for a company that suffocates my potential so blatantly. If you can't see the worth that I bring to the brand, then maybe you don't deserve to have me working here at all."

Finally, I inhale, desperate for oxygen. This is *so* unlike me. I am definitely blaming this eruption on hunger pains and claiming plausible deniability if I'm ever asked about it again. I feel slightly out of breath, but I think I really got everything I wanted to say laid out on the reflective lacquer conference table—even things I didn't know I wanted to say.

Everyone is transfixed. Some jaws are on the floor while others look tense and tightly clenched. They should loosen up. What they say is true: it really does help to get your feelings off your chest. My feelings didn't stand a chance to be kept bottled up after this; they drenched the room like a Formula One champagne shower.

What seems like a zillion seconds on the wall clock audibly tick by before Tracy, at long last, speaks. Deep down, I think I'm nervous for what she's about to say but my adrenaline is muting the warning signs.

"Thank you, Ms. Moss, for that captivating outburst-turned-speech. Since you feel miles above where we have you placed, I think, and I'm sure the room would agree, it's safe to assume that this is your verbal resignation?"

Yvette is still dispassionately sipping her latte, Gia looks like she's engrossed in her favorite movie of all time, and everyone else is equally as absorbed.

Resignation? To be honest, I hadn't given much thought to resigning. I had sort of hoped that they'd rush to apologize, tell me that I was right, they'd been unreasonable, and of course there was a promotion waiting for me. *Surprise! It was all a giant misunderstanding!* I really played myself on this one; the unfolding situation is so repulsive I can hardly swallow it.

"Um . . ." I stall, all of a sudden nauseous with humiliation. Should I resign? I feel like I might throw up. This can't be kosher. But can I really face seeing these people every day after what just happened? I'll be the main topic of gossip and the butt of every joke for *months* and I can't stand people—notably, workplace frenemies—in my personal business. "Yes, I guess it is," I reply. I hold my head up high even though my mood is promptly deflating like a rejected balloon from a forgotten soirée. If there's one thing worse than having a conniption in the boardroom, it's following it up with tears and a full-blown panic attack, which I feel ominously approaching like a tsunami that's about to destroy the entire coastline of Japan. Did I really just quit my job? It's not even socially acceptable to start drinking yet. But if you're unemployed, do you have to follow the same social guidelines as everyone else? I'll Google that later.

"Then please have your desk cleared out in the next hour," Tracy says. "We certainly wouldn't want to put you through the trauma of having to be *undervalued* here for the standard two weeks."

"Right. Well, thanks." I know I should get off my high horse and admit I was wrong, but I just can't. What is *with* me today? I turn to leave. Am I PMSing? Did I wake up on the wrong side of the bed? Is this the *Freaky Friday* sequel, and Gia took over my body and is hell-bent on ruining my life before we can switch back? I'm trying my best to maintain a cool, dynamic appearance but it's disgruntling, to say the least. Venturing out of the room as tactfully as I can, my pants betray me, giving the loudest wails imaginable. Have they gotten worse? There's zero chance no one is hearing my strut of shame. It's an orchestra of screeching car tires, feral cats, nails on a chalkboard, and corroded bed springs.

That's it. I am never wearing these pants again. *Never.* Forget how fabulous I look—or think I look. They've just ruined my entire life. They are going straight into the donation pile.

Chapter Two

A ll I want to do in life is write for a fashion magazine, buy vintage clothes, ride horses on the beach, wear leopard prints, ski through fresh powder, drink martinis, swim in the ocean, laugh a lot, live in Manhattan, make money, read books, and be undeniably, ecstatically happy. Is that *really* too much to ask for?

Apparently.

I arrive back at my desk feeling totally dejected. This wasn't my ideal scenario at all. Now, without an income or a reputable job, how will I ever get to the Big Apple? How will I even afford an apple? Or pay my bills? From what I've gathered, being an adult is just surviving in order to pay one endless bill and now I'm not sure I can even do that for very long. My dreams feel like they're floating further and further away like a bottle sent out to sea; except, instead of containing a romantic love letter it contains the shredded remnants of my career. What just happened? One minute I was on my way to a new title and a raise and the next minute I was relinquishing the position I've worked tirelessly for.

Or I was being unceremoniously fired. It's all seeming a bit shady to me now.

I begin gloomily packing up my belongings. I found a tattered cardboard box near the recycling bin that I'm using to stuff everything into. I'm not sure how five pairs of shoes, a stack of magazines as tall as my kneecaps, and my rose gold stationery set are going to fit into it, but that's a problem for later. Right now, I'm focused on not melting into a pathetic puddle of self-pity.

Liao Chung, who is in charge of digital analytics and was somehow exempt from the meeting, saunters over and places two chilled bottles of Perrier on my desk. He's tall, lanky, dark-haired, and handsome in a boyish way. He calls his personal aesthetic "matchstick skinny," which means that his body is thin, he has a big mop of coiffed hair, and he's always on fire. We quickly bonded over fifties cinema and a taste for martinis so strong you're drunk after a single sip when I got hired. He's been with the company since the launch five years ago.

"Morning! It's hot, you're hot, I'm hot. Actually, I'm like a rotisserie chicken under all of these layers. When did the weather become so Cruella de Vil? I'm nostalgic for the negative thirty-degree breeze." He gives me an exaggerated look of exasperation as he slips off his checkered silk-blend scarf, camel cashmere overcoat, and smooth black Yves Saint Laurent blazer, tossing it all over the back of his swiveling chair. His desk is directly beside mine. I've gotten used to the dramatic entrances he makes every morning. I'll miss them.

"Hey, Liao. Do you want any of my snacks? I've got a few bags of sea-salted cashews, dried mango, and what looks like it used to be chocolate-covered almonds but they're all cloudy and gross now. On second thought, I'll toss that last one." Without inspecting further, I promptly throw the almonds in the waste bin. *Where my aspirations presently reside*, I wistfully think.

"Have you seen my frame? Does it look like I indulge in something as careless as snacking?" He puts a hand on his lean waist and rolls his eyes as he takes a sip of the chilled, bottled refreshment. "Not everyone has an abnormally fast metabolism, Margot. Some of us have to *work* for what our mamas attempted to give us. Anyway, let's toast to your promotion in the most fashionable way we can because champagne is definitely frowned upon this early in the day. Or is it? I haven't checked the employee handbook in years."

Liao notices my anxious expression for the first time. "Okay, what's wrong? You look like you've just binged an entire season of *Keeping Up with the Kardashians* and are more confused about life than you were before watching—not that I blame you, that show is pure sedation. And why are you getting rid of your snacks? You know you can't make it past three o'clock without snacking! Who are you right now?"

"I'm a girl who just ruined her life."

"Oh, come on. Don't be so tragic. How did the meeting go? I wish I had been there to see you shine! Are you Ms. Money Margot now? Are we going to put on our best furs, jewels, and drink from real crystal? Please tell me yes, I'm dying to get my Gatsby on after re-watching the movie last night for the *millionth* time. Leonardo makes me feel things I never even knew were possible." Liao's eyes momentarily glaze over. His thoughts are definitely NSFW.

"I wish," I laugh ruefully. "But I definitely did not shine and I'm so glad you weren't there to witness my implosion. The meeting was going alright—or so I thought—and then I was fired. No, I quit. But I didn't want to." I dab at a trickle of wetness in the corner of my eye. "Nobody realizes what an asset I am! My promotion backfired on me and I've been told to pack up all my things, like, right now and leave."

I sigh as my head falls with a gentle thump into my hands. Saying it out loud makes me realize how idiotic my boardroom stunt really was. What was I thinking? This was *so* not the time to stand up for myself at work. Everyone knows you shouldn't leave a job until you have another one lined up. I feel more foolish than Ashanti did in 2002.

"You can't seriously be leaving me alone here? You're so selfish," he says, with the hint of sass that always rounds off his sentences. Okay, I know what's going on. He thinks I'm being overdramatic. He gets all of his social cues from RuPaul and it shows. I've told him a thousand times to watch something other than *Drag Race* once in a while.

"Li, I'm serious. I was *forced* to quit. In front of everyone! Gia was loving it and my pants wouldn't stop squeaking. Tell me again why you said I absolutely had to buy them? I hate them with a fiery passion." I squirm in my chair to give him a proper earful. I notice Lauren on the other side of the office looking around to see where the noise came from; Dave also glances up curiously before resuming his photocopying.

"Sister, don't kid yourself. You wanted them and everyone in that store wanted you to have them too. They look glorious on you and make you look like you have some junk in the trunk. No offense. You know I love your bony booty but a little fattening up now and then isn't such a bad thing." Finally, it seems to have clicked. He stops mid-slosh and sits down on my desk, narrowly avoiding a pair of soft, aubergine ankle boots I haven't had the chance to wear yet. "Wait. What are you saying? You're *actually* leaving? This isn't you just threatening to leave because you didn't get what you wanted?"

"I'm saying that I'm no longer employed here, so, yeah, I guess so." Really, and he thinks that *I'm* dramatic. This is the guy who told me that he called in sick the day that John Galliano lost his job at Dior.

"Well, fuck me. Do you want me to do something about it? Let me put my seniority to good use. I swear on Gucci, I'll storm into Tracy's office right now and demand that she give you your job back. Or I'll go corner Yvette and threaten to expose her Botox addiction online. I'll tell them I can't function without you! I'll lie on my reports and say we had zero conversion with you gone!" He looks at me with such a vehement passion that I don't doubt for a second that he really would do that.

"No, it's fine. I mean, I'd love to see the look on her face if you *did*, but don't. I'd rather just go home, drown my sorrows in some cheap wine, and contemplate my life as a newly jobless and soon-to-be homeless person because I can't afford my rent. Even if my apartment is smaller than a walk-in closet and should technically be rent-free."

"Oh my god, Mar. You've officially gone off the deep end if you're already wallowing in cheap wine territory," he says disapprovingly. We both take lethargic gulps of fizzy Perrier. "And you're not going to be homeless. Do you know how many sugar daddies out there would love to support you? I can give you the numbers of five fabulous fifty-something silver foxes right now. If for nothing else than to stop you from crumpling your unwrinkled forehead by worrying about money. People like us have so many options! Just look at my closet if you need proof. I have a benefactor on every continent. There's Pablo in South America, Frederik in Europe, Jian in Asia ..."

Finally, I genuinely laugh. "Thanks for the optimism. I appreciate it. But me and my sauvignon blanc and forehead wrinkles will be just fine." Eventually. All I want to do right now is curl up with Lola underneath my feathered duvet and watch the episode of *Girlfriends* where Joan quits her job at the law firm, in order to pursue her dreams. I'm not about to start my own tapas restaurant or anything, but I could use the encouragement.

Liao checks his watch for the time even though his phone is right beside him. He's old fashioned like that. "I'm late. Just remember, you really are *that bitch*. Now I've got to get to my meeting—hopefully it won't go as uncivilly as yours did." He gives me a dainty hug and then turns to leave. "This place will be so boring without you."

As he walks away, my phone pings with a new email.

Reminder: The Green Nectar preview is happening today from 3–6 P.M. at our downtown studio. Bites and bubbly will be provided. See you there! XO, Green Nectar.

I totally blanked on that event. Can you blame me? It's been quite a morning. I've been looking forward to it for weeks, but now that I'm out of a job, I'm not in much of a socializing mood. Do I really want to make cheery, meaningless small talk with a bunch of people I only see socially?

Unless . . . that's exactly what I need. It sure would beat moping around my cramped apartment alone. I can always reschedule my pity party for later this evening. After all, pity is one emotion that *always* accepts a rain check. Maybe I could go for one drink? I mean, I was only just fired—or quit, however you want to spin this. News hasn't traveled yet. I wouldn't even have to bring it up if I didn't want to. Plus, organizing a new outfit to wear would definitely take my mind off my tragic state. And a free drink would totally cheer me up. It always does. And canapés. Oh, and a gift bag! Suddenly, my mood feels as light as a slice of tiramisu from Eataly.

"Margot?" Tracy infringes on my reverie. "Are you just about finished? I need to walk you out before my next meeting which is in precisely two minutes."

"Sure," I mumble. The tiramisu collapses into an unappetizing lump. "Just need to put on my coat and grab my things." I shrug on my marshmallow suede, sling my purse into the crook of my elbow, and hoist the overflowing box into my grasp. A bag of dried mango falls to the floor and I'm not sure whether to leave it or pick it up.

"Tracy, would you mind—" I'm about to ask her for help but she's looking at her phone and apparently doesn't hear me. I guess a bag of mango is a fair sacrifice to get out of here sooner. I leave it behind as we start walking towards the tinted-glass double doors. Hopefully Liao will find it later and be reminded of me. Not that he's going to eat it so it's kind of a waste, but whatever. Finally, Tracy clicks her phone off.

"Again, we as a company are *so* guilt-ridden to discover that you've been feeling this way. We had no idea. This constructive dismissal is for the best. Really, it's for your own well-being. Think of it like a fresh start. That being said, perhaps at your next job you can try to be a bit more vocal, although subtle, about your quote-unquote *mistreatment*."

What is wrong with this woman? I've brought it up in at least three of our one-on-one meetings; one of which was less than a week ago! I know she's relatively new around here and we haven't exactly established a super-close working relationship, but still. "You know, Tracy, I did tell you—"

"Anyway," she says as we step into the elevator; it's only three floors but the higher-ups rarely take the stairs. It's bizarre. Another mystery. "I'm sure you'll be much happier elsewhere. You're *so* experienced, Margot, you won't have trouble finding something right up your alley. Maybe an internship to start? You know, to really get the feel of a place before you commit to it. You wouldn't want to fritter away more time figuring out what it is you want.

And maybe take a bath when you get home with some lavender salts? It'll really help ease the edge you're experiencing."

Who does she think she is? Is she implying that I *won't* find somewhere else? Well, she's wrong. I'll get a job in record time. And not an internship. I have a degree; anywhere would be *lucky* to have me. I'm a hard worker, I'm passionate, I take initiative! Truthfully, I deserve better. Although, if I *had* been promoted, I'd be singing a very different tune right now. It would be more upbeat like Mariah Carey's "It's Like That" than "Un-Break My Heart" by Toni Braxton.

"Thanks, Tracy. I appreciate your advice." I give her my best, breezy, I'm-so-cool-with-this-decision smile with just a hint of ill will in my dark-brown eyes. Tracy doesn't say anything else as we awkwardly reach the building entrance—or in my case, exit.

Her phone rings, and she picks it up. "Hi, Yvette. Yes, just walking her out now. All good. Be right there." She mouths "bye" to me and gives a half-ass wave as I'm booted out the door with my teeming box of possessions and what's left of my dignity.

Standing on the sidewalk, I realize that I didn't change back into my New Balance 990s. *Great.* I don't have the mental capacity or strength to deal with the subway again. I set the cardboard box down on the ground and fish my iPhone out of my Fendi. I'm ordering an Uber. It crosses my mind that I should be extra stingy with my money now that I no longer have a steady paycheck, but I'm too deeply depressed to care. Even the inquisitive looks from passersby don't have any effect on me. So what if they assume I was given the boot for plagiarism, tax fraud, or an illicit office affair?

Just as I think things can't get any worse, Gia appears behind me. Why does she insist on torturing me like this? *Just leave me alone!* I want to scream.

"That was quite a stunt you pulled in there. Even I didn't think you'd be moronic enough to do that," she remarks, lighting up a menthol cigarette. (Aren't those banned?) My face is tingling but I'm not sure if it's from the cold, the minty secondhand smoke, or further embarrassment. "Thanks a lot for throwing me under the fucking bus." She exhales in my direction.

"Sorry," I say out of habit. I'll have to break that Canadianism if I truly want to thrive in the States one day. Do you think born and bred New Yorkers habitually apologize to their workplace rivals? No way, José. "How *did* you snake your way into that promotion?"

"Wouldn't you like to know." She gives me a self-satisfied sneer, stubs out her Newport, and heads back inside. Sometimes, it's difficult for my brain to comprehend how one woman can be so brazenly bitchy 24/7. Doesn't she get exhausted?

My Uber arrives and I decide that I've already wasted too much time and effort being upset. As far as I can tell, there are two bright sides. First of all, I never have to see Gia Johnson again, and second, I have a party to get to.

Chapter Three

Even though my morning turned out to be a flaming hot dumpster fire of a disaster, I am determined to make up for it. Choosing my outfit for the Green Nectar party totally cheered me up, just as I predicted. For the moment, I am back to being a fluffy piece of tiramisu.

I swapped out my miserable vinyl pants for faded, straight-leg Lee jeans in ocean blue, paired with a front-tying avocado-green cardigan, faux alligator ankle boots, and my trusty marshmallow shearling coat; it's the only outerwear piece I've been wearing all season. It cost me $35 and is apparently from 1973. Very glamorous.

As I strut up to the weather-worn brick venue, I try telling myself that I look as hot as Zendaya looks on any given day. My life will soon be back on track. For a girl as serious about her career as me, I have faith that everything will work out. It has to. By this time next year I'll probably be mailing out handwritten thank-you cards to the entire La Pêche team, even Gia, thanking them for doing me the biggest favor of my life.

An extremely bored-looking girl with a clipboard, platinum tresses, and a T-shirt that features a plump diamanté plum on the chest takes my name and languidly lets me inside. She couldn't look more blasé if she tried. "Enjoy the event," she says emotionlessly.

I move past her as quickly as I can. Too long in close proximity and I might start to sponge up her negative energy and that is the last thing I need right now. Energy transfer is real. I step into the elevator, pressing the button for the sixth floor. At my destination, its doors glide apart to reveal a sprawling, open-concept loft with mountainous windows overlooking the heart of downtown. The city oozes like melted butter; skyscrapers and boutiques rise in its warm, gooey wake. Dainty dangling fairy lights, strung from the soaring ceiling, punctuate the panoramic view while a jaunty buzz permeates the atmosphere.

"Can I take your coat, miss?" asks a long-haired man in the same glittery T-shirt as the brooding girl downstairs. It must be mandatory. I shudder at the thought of having to wear the same thing as everyone else—uniform or not. Blending into the crowd has never been my strong suit. But strong, structured suits on the other hand . . .

"That would be great." I smile, shrug it off, and hand it over. He's momentarily caught off guard by how heavy it is. It should come with a warning: *lift with your legs!* If I had to guess, I'd say it easily weighs more than *Vogue*'s last September issue.

Servers with silver trays are passing around flutes of champagne and I grab one right away. This is exactly what I need. There's nothing like chilled bubbles to bring out your happy side and your most charming personality—especially in times of despair. A glass of bubbly is unquestionably the best elixir known to womankind. Whoever said champagne was strictly for celebrating was sorely mistaken. I happen to think it's a foolproof beverage for any occasion: brunch, parties, breakups, breakdowns.

All around the bright, airy space, brass peekaboo tables have been set up to showcase each new product, as well as a handful of cult classics and bestsellers. Mariah Carey's infectious hit "Honey" is booming over the sound system, complementing the animated chatter of fabulously dressed beauty bloggers, vloggers, editors, and TikTok sensations alike. (Adam Frank *better* not be here. At least he can't make fun of my shoes this time—this pair is undoubtedly stunning.) What a perfect song to lift my spirits and remind me of the carefree, saucy mood I should be striving to obtain. If anyone knows how to beat a bad situation, it's Mariah.

The party is off to a *très* chic start for a low-key, late-afternoon shindig. My eyes scan the room, mentally absorbing the scene. I want to soak up every scent and sight. I think I'll do a lap and see if I recognize anyone here. Not that I particularly feel like chatting, but I'll look totally freakish if I just hang solo and quaff my melancholy in the corner. As far as these people are concerned, I'm as effervescent as ever. I've got to play the part. My motto? Fake it 'til you make it. And then maybe fake it a little bit more until imposter syndrome subsides.

I barely have time to finish my first prosecco before I hear a familiar voice that sends my soul into high alert. My flight, fight, or freeze response kicks in. But these boots were not made for fighting and I can't flee this *fiesta* until I've tasted every appetizer so I'm completely frozen on the spot. Right away, I know who the disembodied voice belongs to; it can only be one person. Priya Khan.

"Hello, love! How *are* you?" Priya asks, a little too loudly, as she extends her arms and reaches out for me. She's wearing a long-sleeve turtleneck dress in a dusty-rose hue with a sateen bow and sky-high suede pumps. Chunky costume jewelry hangs from her wrists, neck, and ears like she was baptized in a bathtub of disco balls. Her matte pink lipstick is smudged on her front left tooth, but I don't have the heart to tell her. I also don't have the heart to tell her that her hair looks like it has been victim to a violent tornado although it's a calm, albeit cold, sunny day without so much as a gust in the air. This is Priya's normal look. But she rocks it like no one else.

"Hi, Priya," I say as she envelops me in a stiff hug. She smells like potent drugstore body spray. Something that would be called Morning Seduction or Feminine Fantasy. (But not Fantasy by Britney Spears because that was my ultimate preteen go-to— especially the two-in-one roller ball fragrance and lip gloss duo.) I hope, however harshly, that it doesn't rub off on me. I'm more of an *eau de parfum* person these days.

"It's been so long since I last saw you! When was it? The Estée Lauder launch? Let's catch up! You know, us women have to see each other and support each other. It's so important. What's going on in your life? Your job? I want to know everything!" She's smiling at me but all I can see is the smudged lipstick. It takes me two blinks to realize she's asked me several questions.

"Same old," I say, draining my glass. Where's the server with more? This conversation is going to require a dramatically higher level of intoxication—and quick. "What's going on with you?"

"Well, I'm not sure if you heard, but I left *Chatelaine*." She takes a sip of cucumber water. In all of the events we've been to, I've never seen her drink alcohol. "I just wasn't *progressing,* you know? But I am *so* glad I got to meet you during my time there."

She gives me a wide, warm smile and I suddenly feel bad for having thoughts of dread when I saw her. Priya may be all wrong in so many ways, but she really is nice. I've never once thought about being grateful to have met her. To be honest, I don't think of her much at all. And now I feel like a heartless bitch.

"Totally. Happy to have met you too," I fib as I reach for a lavender macaron. The dessert bar, where we've meandered over to, is to die for. I have an insatiable sweet tooth and combined with my enviable metabolism, it's not a problem. Desserts are very high on my never-ending list of weaknesses. Along with leather boots, leopard prints, and pineapple on pizza.

"Last time I saw you, you mentioned an opportunity for growth in your job at La Pêche. Did it go as planned?" Priya remembers *everything*. The last time I saw her was approximately three months ago. She looks at me expectantly through clumpy, overly mascaraed eyelashes. I swipe a second flute from a passing server and take a swig before summoning the courage to give her a truthful response.

"Well, if I'm being honest, I quit my job today." There it is. The truth is out. It's not so bad. No more painful than the time I twisted my ankle while wearing six-inch stilettos in front of the guy I had a major crush on and fell to the ground like Bambi learning to walk. Actually, now that I mention it, I'm not sure which is worse. I had to go to physiotherapy for five weeks after that.

"Oh my gosh. So exciting! Where will you be working now? Tell me you got the job at *Vogue* you've always wanted. I knew you had it in you, love!" She holds out her lipstick-smudged glass to clink with mine. Hot pink is *so* not my color.

"Not exactly. I just sort of . . . quit. No method to my madness. I'm living on the edge!" I nervously laugh and resist the urge to add "of glory." Suddenly, I feel Priya's manicured claws—ballet slipper talons that compete with Cardi B's—grasp my forearm in what I think is meant to be meaningful contact, but feels more like I'm being selected as prey by a bald eagle. *Ouch.* I bruise worse than bananas.

"Margot, if there is anyone in the world who will recover from this, it's you. You got this, love. I'm confident you will bounce back, even more of a hashtag *girl boss* than you were before." She pauses. "It's a new beginning. Take it and run with it, lady."

I smile halfheartedly and mumble some sort of thanks. Maybe she's right. Maybe it *is* a new beginning for me. What have I always wanted to do? Write for *Vogue*. Resell vintage clothing on Depop. Be JoJo's personal stylist. Maybe I could even—

Oh, god. Priya is still talking. She talks *a lot*. I totally zoned out; her voice is like white noise, lost in the babble of the party. I raise the flute back to my lips and try my best to figure out what she's been saying.

"So, are you interested?" Her spiderlike lashes are scurrying up and down at an alarming rate. What is she talking about? I wish I could press pause, rewind, and hear this conversation all over again.

"I'm sorry—I totally just had a brain glitch. Interested in what?"

"Meeting Sidney? Sidney Lalonde."

Why do people only ever repeat the last thing they said? I don't have a clue what she's talking about or who Sidney Lalonde is but I feel bad asking her to explain everything again. The name sounds *vaguely* familiar. "Oh, right," I politely laugh. "Yeah, I'd love to."

"That's great, lady! Sidney asked me just the other day if I knew anyone that would be a good fit, but I didn't know that you were available. Lucky that we ran into each other. It was destiny!"

Ugh. It's my belief that destiny is for people who don't want to get up and work for their dream life. The only destiny I acknowledge is Destiny's Child. Anyway, I give Priya my phone number to pass along to the mysterious Sidney Lalonde. I'm rapidly racking my brain, going through anyone I remember with that name. They probably work at *Chatelaine*. Maybe Priya's old boss? Is she possibly setting me up to take her old position? I think she was the associate lifestyle editor. Okay. Maybe this *is* destiny. Imagine quitting your job with no game plan and then getting offered a new one that same day in the field you're dying to work in? It's implausible! Luck looks good on me.

Priya gives me one last toothy, pink-stained grin and walks away, her size-too-big pumps ricocheting along the hardwood floor. "You'll love Sidney!" she calls, blowing me a kiss. We are definitely not good enough friends for that.

Desperate to wash away Priya's unsightly smooch, I spend the next forty-five minutes consuming more sparkling flutes, shrewdly stuffing my face with bite-size desserts, and chit-chatting ("OMG does every single celebrity have to create their own beauty brand? Everyone just buys Fenty!") with a few women I know through the industry and veritably like. Thankfully, no one has heard about my departure from La Pêche yet.

After saying my good-byes, grabbing my considerably weighted gift bag, and leaving the event, I feel a warm, tingly tipsiness flush through me. It's as desirable as a salted-caramel mocha with extra-whip. My disposition is in direct contradiction with the crisp, evening breeze that convinces me to button my heavyweight coat to the very top. I'm feeling blissfully ignorant of the events of this morning. In my hazy mind I'm wondering: If you don't think about it, did it even occur? Can I just show up at the office tomorrow and pretend it never happened? Not that I want to, I'm just weighing all of my options.

I sneak a peek at my freebies; the bag is full to the brim with everything Green Nectar has ever made. Well, at least I won't have to restock my stash anytime soon. Suddenly, I have an idea. Maybe I can pitch out an article about my time in the beauty industry. Like, the positive effect it's had on my social life and savings account. Both have flourished in the last few years. It could feasibly bring in $250 if it got published in the right magazine. The article can be called: "How to Save Money but Stay Fed & Fabulous" by Margot Moss.

As long as I keep my toes in the water, I'll be fine. Freelancing isn't so bad. And there's still the potential meeting with Sidney Lalonde. Now that I've had some time to think about it, I'm convinced that they're from *Chatelaine*. They have to be. My stomach swirls with sanguineness. Or maybe it's the champagne. Regardless, I must be the most fortuitous woman in the city. Looks like I'll be sending out those handwritten thank-you cards sooner than I anticipated.

***

The second my key slides into the lock on my front door, I hear Lola's little paws clawing at the other side. That scratchy sandpaper sound fills my heart with so much joy I could just burst like the cherry blossoms in High Park. Lola was by far the best thing to come out of my breakup with my ex, Chris. He wasn't a dog person and with 20/20 hindsight, I see that was the first warning sign of him being a soulless tree stump.

It doesn't matter if you're a modern-day version of Cary Grant hot, if you don't like dogs, it's a definite deal breaker. Besides, the real Cary Grant would *never* hate dogs.

I toss my keys into the scalloped dish I have placed on top of an antique brown-sugar table by the door. After languorously slipping out of my considerable coat, I sink to the floor and Lola jumps all over me, her fluffy tail whipping back and forth. It doesn't matter if we've been apart for two minutes or two hours, Lola's greetings are just as ebullient.

My apartment, if you can even call it that, may be diminutive, but it's impossibly stylish. I say *impossibly* because when I first saw it, I thought it would be impossible to transform it into anything I'd want to live in. But I did the best I could decorating on a budget and it's not the worst it could be. I've seen those home improvement shows; it can always be worse. I didn't buy anything *new* per se, but it looks like I did. So what if I had to spend two afternoons and an entire pack of Lysol wipes disinfecting most of the things I brought home via Value Village? It was worth every penny.

Lola and I will move out one day but she's not fussed about it; she's happy wherever there are Milk-Bones and a comfy bed.

"Hi, baby girl," I say to my fetching puppy, scratching her velvety ears. They're softer than vicuña. "Are you hungry? I am. Let's see what there is to eat." Turns out those macarons didn't fill me up at all even though I scarfed seven of them—plus a couple of macadamia cookies and mini vanilla bean cupcakes. I categorically despise empty calories. They're officially my biggest pet peeve. Empty calories, and then pimples, phonies, and being poor.

I hoist myself off of the floor and meander towards the kitchen. This is said with very loose context because it's more like a ship's galley—there is a hot plate, microwave, and a miniature fridge like one you'd find in a hotel room stocked with single-serving bottles of booze. Lola's kibbles make a clanging noise as they tip into her metal bowl. She watches me vigilantly.

While she scarfs down her dinner, I order sushi on UberEats. I'm in no mood for a salad and that seems to be the only possible outcome from the grim selection of produce in my fridge.

Although I'm, for the most part, loving living alone, it does have its downsides. Namely when it comes to the cost of everything. Being a frugal, independent woman who resides by herself has never been more flawlessly put into lyrics than when Ari Lennox sang that she was no longer afraid of the dark as a direct result of a high-priced electricity bill in "New Apartment." I light soy candles every chance I get. However, not even the flicker of romantic flames can cast a flattering light on the fact that I went from 1,400 square feet near St. Lawrence Market to this place— no matter how cute I've made it look. Sometimes, I tell people that I live in Harry Potter's closet under the stairs except on top of a bookstore. Usually they laugh and tell me I'm being overly dramatic. Yeah, *right*.

I saunter towards my single leather armchair, Lola trailing loyally at my heels before plonking herself down on the rumpled cow skin rug. The corpulent chair occupies a corner spot near the colossal arched window that overlooks my Little Italy neighborhood. The sunlight that streams in is ethereal. I swear, I'm solar powered; I can't function without natural light. On the weekends, I like to ensconce myself here and sip my dark-roast café crème as I spy on people out running their morning errands. It makes me feel all giddy inside when I see paper bags from the independent bookshop downstairs, Angelo's, swinging from the crook of an arm.

Sluggishly, I sink into the overstuffed chair and crack open a Stephen King novel that makes me skittish about leaving my house at night. I'm almost finished with the final chapter when my phone rings. Is my sushi here already?

Nope. It's Jessie Browne, my best friend. (And yes, I'm the type of person to have people listed in my phone by first and last name.) I answer right away. I could use someone to vent to and I can talk to her about anything—from period cramps to politics. Jessie and I have known each other since preschool. From the minute we met, we were inseparable. Or so we were told; I don't remember her until we were about five and a half, playing dress up in my mom's extravagant clothes from the eighties. Over the years, people have come to know us as a packaged deal—like Paris and Nicole during *The Simple Life* era.

"Ugh, you won't *believe* the day I've had," I dramatically sigh, tossing my book on top of a stack of vintage *Vogue*s that live on my worn-in wormy maple coffee table.

"Brace yourself. It's about to get worse."

Chapter Four

Have you ever had such a bad week that all you want to do is down a scotch on the rocks and restlessly puff on a slender French cigarette? Preferably in the bathroom at the Met Gala surrounded by supermodels, actresses, and the Olsen twins? These activities are thoroughly out of my realm of expertise but sometimes the craving is just there.

It's finally Saturday. I've been in a darkly sophisticated mood all week long; dark because I've been drinking straight espresso and gravitating towards all-black ensembles, and sophisticated because I've been drinking espresso in top-to-toe black. I may not be surrounded by MK and Ash, but I definitely feel like an honorary sister. Now, if only I could get a *holiday in the sun*.

After savoring a home-brewed cup of caffeine, which today I mixed with a splash of half-and-half so I know I'm on the road to recovery, I decide to pop downstairs to Angelo's Books to see what's new on the $1 rack. It's so reasonable, it's almost better than the library because I get to keep the books. (At this point, my bookshelf is morbidly obese.) I've got an inclination towards murder mysteries and psychological thrillers that scare me so badly, I can only read them during daylight. But in between those heart-pumping paperbacks, I always switch it up with something fluffy and insouciant and romantic.

The morning is dazzling and bright, full of possibilities. Now that I'm no longer as moody as Sarah Michelle Gellar in *Cruel Intentions*, I'm behaving more like myself again. It's virtually impossible for me to stay down for too long. No matter how morose I get, I end up bubblier than Veuve Clicquot in roughly three days flat. The thing I always remember is, being a positive person doesn't mean that you have to be happy 100 percent of the time; that would be *so* monotonous. It means that even on the hardest days you know that better ones are coming. Days that are even better than a silky-smooth skinny-dip in the Caribbean Sea.

When Jessie called me after the Green Nectar party on Tuesday, it sent me spiraling into a very shadowy place—I'm talking Vantablack kind of shadow. I was less prepared for what was coming than I was for being fired in front of all of my coworkers. (Yes, it's still a sore subject.) After instructing me to pour a glass of pinot grigio, open my email, and sit down, she sent over a digital wedding invite from my sexy but dog-despising creep of an ex-boyfriend.

I knew I shouldn't even look at it, but the temptation was too strong. It was akin to the pull I get towards a unique pair of calf-skin boots or a BOGO sale at my favorite consignment store; my heart skips a beat when I see discounted Calvin Klein, Danier, and Levi's beckoning me to buy. But at least with that I end up walking away with a reusable tote full of stylish confidence, not a broken heart weeping into my white wine.

However, I didn't *actually* weep over Chris and his forthcoming nuptials. I have common sense; I know when to waste my mascara and when to stay dry-eyed and luminous. Still, it did sting to see that he was marrying the girl he cheated on me with; a girl who collects Michael Kors bags, solely shops at Fashion Nova, and thinks bandage dresses are Black Tie. As if breaking my heart wasn't bad enough, he also kicked me out of our apartment (the aforementioned 1,400 square feet) and promptly moved *her* in. It's still agony to remember. I sleep with my bed next to my microwave and *she* gets to soak in my clawfoot tub. *Unbelievably* unfair.

All I want is a laid-back, fun, comforting type of love. But at this point, I think I'll just be single forever. Lola and I will be just fine in our pint-sized dwelling with the fabulous view. Jessie says that I dodged a major bullet with Chris, and she's completely right. I lost 194 pounds of dead weight and I've never looked better. How's that for an effective diet?

The invitation was truly horrendous: an obviously staged Walmart Photo Studio-type portrait with the words "true love still exists" written in comic sans. Upon seeing it, Jessie and I simultaneously burst into hysterical laughter, cackling like the witches of Eastwick. (I'm clearly Cher with her badass abs and Jessie is *totally* Michelle Pfeiffer.) I felt a maelstrom of both relief and repulsion swirling inside of me. On one hand, I was annoyed that I spent three years of my youth with Chris before I found out what a snake he is, but on the other, it was a lesson in love.

Even through the phone, Jessie could tell that I needed an ego boost, so she said, "Look, Mar, you keep it realer than real. You're the coolest, most honest human being I've ever met. I might be biased here, but Chris is the real loser in this situation. Don't give him another thought. He wasn't worth your time then, and he isn't worth your time now. You have all the potential in the world waiting for you to just grab it by the balls and take it for a ride."

That sent a surge of aplomb racing through me from my pedicured toes to my choppy hair. However, the feeling was fleeting. My emotions hit rock bottom after we hung up and my jobless, relationship-less status sank in with the same pleasure as sinking into a lukewarm bath. (Although, these days I only have a stall shower.) But that was then. Now, I'm on my way to heal my bibliophilic heart through some fiction retail therapy.

Chantelle Hartman, one of my BFFs since high school, calls me on my way out the door. I switch Lola's leash to the other hand so I can reach into my chestnut suede purse and answer my phone. "How's it going? Not still moping around, are you?" she asks when I pick up. Chantelle is not someone you want to go to if you need emotional support. The only type of crying her shoulder accepts are tears of laughter.

"No," I say. "But thanks for asking … I'm on my way to Angelo's." Lola and I begin to make our way down the precarious flight of stairs that leads to the sidewalk. They're steeper than Everest.

"If there's anything involving architecture, pick it up for me and I'll pay you back," she says. Chantelle is a real estate agent; mostly commercial. "Anyway, I just wanted to check up on you. I'm heading into Saks. I need something to wear to my second cousin's wedding and I want to be the hottest one there." Chantelle is already so hot it's criminal. She has wavy jet-black hair down to her elbows, the straightest nose to ever exist, full lips, emerald eyes, and smooth bronze skin. If Normani, SZA, and Ryan Destiny could somehow make a hybrid of their DNA, it would be Chantelle Hartman.

"Morning, Angelo," I say cheerily as we enter the store. I love the ding of the old-fashioned bell above the door; it reminds me of *It's a Wonderful Life*. I'd probably get sick of it if I had to listen to it all day long but when I pop in, it's charming.

I usually stop by Angelo's once every couple of weeks. I've gotten to know him quite well since I've been living above his business. I think of him like a cheery, adopted grandfather. He's a bright-eyed and bushy-tailed Italian man in his late sixties with a round nose, eyebrows so unruly they resemble feather boas, and an affinity for limoncello; he always keeps a bottle under the front desk, ready to go for a spur-of-the-moment celebration.

"Morning, *cara*," Angelo says with affection. "How is my favorite customer?"

"You say that to everyone," I say with a slight roll of my eyes.

"I was talking to Lola." He gives me a friendly wink and Lola bounds over to him. Besides limoncello, Angelo also keeps teeny bits of cured pepperoni handy.

I begin browsing the endless racks of books. *Murder is Served* by Frances and Richard Lockridge catches my eye. How can you go wrong with venomous prose and New York high society? It's a done deal. I hand Angelo a crumpled $5 bill and tell him to keep the change. Isn't carrying cash *so* vintage?

When I get home with my new novel, I immediately strip down and slither back into bed to start reading. At least being unemployed hasn't affected my weekend routine. Lola and I cuddle up together and the next thing I know, it's getting dim outside and Jessie is on her way over with a bottle of Tanqueray. I didn't exactly invite her over, but my bleakness did. She texted me to say that she wasn't going to let me "squander my Saturday night wallowing" when I could be drinking my dolor watching *Dexter* reruns with my best friend instead.

Two episodes and one and a half martinis each later, the sun has abandoned its post and we haven't had dinner yet. I'm so hungry, I feel like I could pig out at a Las Vegas smorgasbord and still be starving. I open up my fridge to see if there's anything for us to eat but of course, it's slim pickings: a container of hummus, goat cheese, a few shriveled, seedless green grapes, last night's pad thai scraps, and a bottle of wine. That's one of the cons of small, hotel-sized fridges and microscopic kitchenettes—you rarely have the things you need to make what you really want to eat. Actually, I'm not much of a cook even when I do have access to full appliances anyway. Chris was the chef out of the two of us; I prefer takeout and delivery. The way I see it, I'm supporting local businesses, helping the economy, and enjoying a convenient, hassle-free meal. It's a total win, win.

"No luck for food," I say. "Should we order in? Vietnamese? I'd commit manslaughter for a spring roll."

"How about we go out? I think we could both use a night on the town. Let's treat ourselves to some overpriced appies," Jessie suggests.

I regard her skeptically. "I get why *I* might need a night out, but what's your excuse?" Closing the fridge door, I jump up onto the scrawny, immaculate countertop. Say what you will about my tiny kitchen, but it's spotless. I'm something of a clean freak.

"I'm your best friend. Anything that happens to you, automatically happens to me. Or at least it feels like it. And Mar, your life ain't been easy lately. Quitting your job, your ex getting engaged . . ." She exhales heavily, causing her wispy bangs to flutter in her eyelashes. Her sunflower hair hangs below her shoulders in enviable layers and has the texture of corn silk. Jessie has always had this sort of beachy beauty with her oat-milk complexion and bright sapphire eyes, like she should be living in Malibu Barbie's Dreamhouse. She also has the most covetable jewelry collection of all time, thanks to her stylist position at Mejuri. The best part? She gives me a discount.

"Ew! You don't have to remind me so candidly," I laugh while scolding her. "It's the end of March, seasonal depression is still out in full force, and I'm extra susceptible to traumatic memories." If I'm being honest, I *could* use a couple of hours at a vibrant locale. And so could my thrifted leather pants. I got them for a ridiculous $25—every penny counts, especially when you're out of a job— two weeks ago and I've been dying for an excuse to take them for a spin. They're the deepest, most delicious shade of Shiraz with contrasting caramel topstitching and are basically brand new. I'm such a sucker for a good deal; the cheaper, the better—in cost, not quality. More than half of my wardrobe is thrifted but I still think I look as good as Elsa Hosk. My bank account *adores* my frugality.

"Okay, let's go out." I spring down from the counter, grab my phone, and hit shuffle on my favorite, personally curated playlist. "He Wasn't Man Enough" by Toni Braxton starts booming through my Ultimate Ears Bluetooth speakers. Even though this song was released over twenty years ago, I still listen to it at least once a week; it's eternal. And it's wholeheartedly helped me get over every breakup, fling gone wrong, and ruptured *corazón* I've ever had.

I begin rummaging through my soon-to-be-dwindling gifted beauty stash to see if there are any products I can try out tonight; I want to look the best I've ever looked for my reappearance on the social scene. I've been so distraught these past few days, I haven't even bothered to sort through the Green Nectar stuff yet; I dump it out on the floor. Lola lumbers over and sniffs at the scattered products. Analyzing the contents of a gift bag is a fashion girl's way of playing a homicide detective: blood-red lipsticks, wrinkle-slaying primers, pore-murdering masks, criminally insane cleansers, forensic foundation. This one is guilty as charged on all counts.

"I know it was my idea, but I wish we'd known that we were going to go out *before* I came over. I'm a hot mess! But not *literally* hot because I feel like yesterday's garbage and there isn't anything hot about that," Jessie complains, a chafed expression on her face. Currently, she is clothed in a baby-blue angora cardigan with dark-wash jeans and knee-high Stuart Weitzman boots. Her outfit is casual and cute; a far cry from a mess. Although, for nights out, Jessie usually prefers something that shows off her milky décolleté and itty-bitty waist.

"Come on," I say to her. "You look fine! It's not like we're going
to a club or anything. Those days are *so* behind us. We're just going
for food, you don't need to look like Sofia Richie."

"*Fine* doesn't even begin to cut it," she pouts. I think I know
what's coming but I'm trying to block it out of my mind. *Please,
don't let her say it.* "I'm looking through your closet."

There it is: my most dreaded five-word sentence. Our senses of
style are galaxies apart. She's more *The Seven Year Itch* while I'm
more *Funny Face*. Whenever she borrows things from my closet, I
become a furious flurry, racing around behind her like I'm training
for a marathon, seldom managing to catch my delicate chiffon
tops and patterned frocks before they hit the ground. Call me
neurotic, but I just can't stand to see my clothes lumped in a pile
on the floor.

Just as I'm flying across the room to catch another shirt
Jessie has mindlessly tossed over her shoulder, she turns around
and asks, "Why do you have to be so *fashionable?*" She says this
as if fashionable is a dirty word. "Not every piece has to be so
editorial. Where are all of your regular going-out pieces?"
Okay, I'm going to pretend she didn't say that. It's as if she's for-
gotten that my toxic trait is obsessing over and imitating looks
I see on *Vogue Runway*. My styling abilities could rival Maeve
Reilly's. "How about you just borrow one of my coats?" I propose.
There is more desperation in my voice than the housewives of
Wisteria Lane.

"My eyebrows are nearly invisible and need serious rehabili-
tation," Jessie says, scrutinizing her appearance and ignoring my
suggestion. "Why is my natural beauty so ugly tonight? A bold
lip color is the last thing saving me from looking like an intensive
care patient. Do you have one?"

"Jessie! You've got to stop saying things like that. It's offensive," I criticize her. Jessie may look as sweet as a fresh-picked

strawberry but sometimes the things she says really worry me. I suddenly remember that I have a fuchsia lipstick that I'd tossed into my rejected product pile last month. I search for the lustrous tube and hand it to her.

"You're the best," she says as she starts applying the blindingly pink gloss in my circular mirror. With each swipe of the slick wand, I swear her lips get bigger and bigger until they look like a stack of cocktail wieners coated in Malibu Barbie's signature hue.

"Yes, I know. But hurry up. Your lips are done and I'm dying to eat."

"They're not done until they look like two wads of Hubba Bubba," says Jessie matter-of-factly.

At long last, our makeup is perfected, our jewelry is clasped, and our coats are buttoned up—Jessie decided to borrow my powder-blue leather trench that *totally* complements her fuzzy cardigan. I got it last year, out shopping with Liao, for $13 on an ultra-deep discount; it was such a good deal, I practically embezzled it.

Chapter Five

"**A** gin martini with a lemon twist, please," I tell the tattooed bartender. "And a red sangria. Thanks." I start a tab at the bar because I rarely carry enough cash to pay for a round of cocktails—who does anymore?—and wait for mine and Jessie's drinks. The atmosphere is buzzing with more electricity than a high-frequency facial. (I've heard that those are *all the rage* these days for treating acne.)

We decided on our favorite Spanish joint, Bar Lucía, which is just a few minutes' walk down the street from my place. Before I forget, I text Jessie to put in a half-order of grilled octopus and a cheese plate if and when a server comes by. She went to snag our go-to table in the corner beside the stained glass window; it has cushy blue velvet chairs on one side and a faded wooden bench on the other. We sit there every time we come here—that is, when nobody else has claimed it, which usually happens on wildly busy nights like tonight.

I'm reaching for my phone like I always do when I'm waiting for something—a habit I'm trying to discontinue because I'm sure my self-esteem could use a break from seeing double-zero influencers sipping baby coconuts in Morocco all day long—when I feel a tap on my shoulder. Slightly annoyed that I haven't had a chance to senselessly scroll, I turn around, and my jaw goes slack. Well, it's not Jessie telling me she couldn't get our table, so that's good news. But even better news is what I'm staring at with an expression more clueless than Tai Frasier.

Standing in front of me is a tall, toned, and tanned boy—no, *man*—with loosely curled, dirty blond hair and holy smokes, is that a dimple? He speaks and I try my best to concentrate on the words that are escaping his exquisitely kissable lips, but it proves to be very difficult—like I'm watching *Parasite* without the subtitles.

"Excuse me," he says. "I don't mean to be forward but . . ." He has an accent. My guess is Australian, but I could be wrong. Whatever it is, he sounds severely sexy. "Can I just tell you how pretty you are?" He smiles and it's like someone switched on the *good* lighting. I'm melting faster than Sweet Socialism ice cream from Sugar Hill Creamery.

Is he talking to someone behind me? Guys *never* come up to me and tell me I'm pretty. It's not that I'm not pretty, but you know, it just doesn't happen every day. I've always been told that I'm "unconventionally attractive"—whatever that means. Most of the time I don't even want to be pretty anyway, I want to be alluring and exotic and exude the aura of a femme fatale. But tonight, I'll settle for pretty if he's the one saying it.

I find it hilarious that I can be audacious in so many ways but the first time a hot Aussie comes over to talk to me, I forget how. He's so overwhelmingly cute that I'm literally lost for words—which doesn't happen very often. Six-foot-something of devastating opportunity has just come knocking and I'm tongue-tied. What are the odds? Wait a minute. What a *line!* My sauciness comes rushing back in an abundance akin to the signature spaghetti and meatballs at Joanne Trattoria on West 68th Street in Manhattan.

"You can tell me again if you want," I say with a cheeky smirk, while I flirtatiously finger my small gold vermeil hoop earrings. At least, I hope it looks cheeky and flirtatious. After the martinis and lack of dinner, I'm not sure I'm in full control of the muscles in my face anymore.

"Okay," he says, completely serious. "I think you're really pretty. What's your name?"

"Margot." I consider lying for half a second but something about that dimple makes me feel like I'm under oath. I want to preach the truth, the whole truth, and nothing but. *Amen, hallelujah.*

"I'm Oliver. Can I buy you a drink? Or, uh, pay for those you have there?"

The bartender has placed mine and Jessie's drinks down in front of us. "One red sangria and one gin martini with extra olives . . ." I just about have a heart attack. I vehemently despise olives. They're more evil than Blair Waldorf. "Kidding! Lemon twist." He laughs heartily.

"Thanks," I mumble, relieved. The bartender is cute in a Travis Barker kind of way, but he doesn't have anything on this new guy. I turn back to Oliver. As much as I'd love a free drink, I've already handed over my credit card, and it'll look incredibly tacky if I ask for it back now.

"I've got these ones covered, but how about the next round? In case you're wondering, they're not both for me. I'm here with my friend, Jessie. She's waiting for me at a table over there." I point off into the corner past the flocks of deliriously jubilant people.

"Deal," he agrees. "Let me help you with those. Lead the way." He swiftly picks up both cocktails in one of his grippingly large hands and grabs his beer with the other. I do not believe in love at first sight, but I do believe in R-rated thoughts at first glance. When I look at Oliver, I feel like I'm Holly Golightly in *Breakfast at Tiffany's* when she lowers her tinted sunglasses to gawk at the stripper. He's so good-looking I swear my eyes *must* be playing tricks on me.

As we wind through the crowded venue, I catch a few females giving him a look. You know. *The look.* The one that says, "Hey, baby, if it doesn't work out with her, I'm here for you." Well, too bad. He's with me. At least he is for the moment, and I intend to soak it up for as long as I can. I know I look hot in my leather pants. Liao would be proud of the illusion of junk they add to my trunk. Seriously, the best $25 I've ever spent. They make my small-scale glutes look like a round, ripe, juicy nectarine.

Jessie has her head buried in her phone as we approach the table. She's going to be *so* shocked when she sees my steamy stranger. Something she would never admit but I don't have any problem saying is that she's in a rotten relationship. Seriously, she should've thrown her relationship in the compost half a decade ago. I keep encouraging her to audition for *Love is Blind* or *The Bachelor* but she refuses. She's "too comfortable" (her words) to think about "life after Bryce" (my words).

So, instead of dumping Bryce and moving on, she likes to live vicariously through my exploits. Which, if I'm being honest, there were a regrettable amount of them after Chris dumped me. Let me see, there was Jeff from the gym, Pete from the coffee shop that I can no longer frequent, Lamar from the club on King Street West who was—never mind. I've already said too much. I'm strictly living in the moment from this moment on. Oliver places the drinks on the intimate, candlelit table.

"A sangria for you, and a gin martini with a handsome twist for me." I lean in closer to Jessie as I say this last part, so Oliver doesn't hear and think I'm jumping the gun or anything. There's only one gun I'd like to jump and it's—I have to stop. I'm out of control.

She looks up, and after three long seconds of confusion, clicks off her phone and places it facedown on the table. Nothing like the power of a decadent man to make your phone seem like the least important thing in the world.

"Jessie, this is Oliver. We just met at the bar. Oliver, my best friend, Jessie."

"Pleasure to meet you," he says.

"Is that an accent I hear? Wait, don't tell me! Let me guess . . ." Jessie bites her lower lip and squints her eyes like she is really working hard to figure this one out. Her blonde ambition is running overtime. "British?" She's always been *awful* at the accent guessing game. Once, she asked a guy if he was from Ireland and he'd been born and raised down the street from her in Forest Hill. It was mortification central—for me, not her.

"Kind of close," he says politely. "But no dice. Try Melbourne, Australia."

She giggles. "I love how you say that. *Mel-bin.*"

I glance over at Oliver with my best *sorry-my-friend-is-so-weird* look. He doesn't seem to mind. This guy is cool as a cucumber, if cucumbers were smoking hot and as bronzed as a Greek god. We sit down at the table—Jessie and I on the bench and Oliver on one of the plush velvet chairs—and fall into easy conversation. He tells us that he's been in Toronto for three years, works for a tech start-up in Liberty Village that helps connect pet owners with local vets, and he has a soft spot for girls who drink gin martinis. My cheeks instantly flush. He's openly flirting with me *and* he obviously adores dogs.

The server brings us our octopus and cheese plates, which Jessie and I are delighted by and dig into straight away. At this point, I am so starved that it feels like my carcass has already dug into itself in order to survive. *Please, please, please don't eat any fat from my ass,* I think in a panic. I don't want to look like Khloe Kardashian, but I'd rather not be described as concave either. When are flat butts going to be a hot commodity again? Not that I think body parts should follow trends . . .

We offer a fork to Oliver, but he declines. "I haven't been able to do seafood since I left home," he says, shaking his head. "It's just so fresh. Where's the ocean around here?"

"There isn't one," Jessie replies, missing the sarcasm. "Just the lake. But it *kind of* looks like an ocean . . ."

"Exactly," says Oliver.

"Oh, come on. Just try this," I tease. "Guaranteed it's one of the best grilled tentacles you've ever tasted."

He agrees and I stab a bite-sized piece. The sexual tension is palpable as Oliver opens his mouth. He really does have irresistible lips. I'm about to feed the octopus to him when Jessie's phone buzzes, vibrating the entire table, and the moment is lost. Then, his friends motion for him to come join them at the bar. I hadn't even thought about him being here with other people. *Oops.* How greedy of me.

"Excuse me, I'll just check on my mates and be right back." He stands up and from my position, he looks taller than the *Cruz de los Caídos*.

Although annoyed that our flash of intimacy is over, I'm ready to dish about how cute Oliver is, but Jessie looks distracted. She picks up her phone, frowning. I'm honestly worried that if she stays in her relationship much longer, she's going to need an on-call dermatologist. She sighs heavily. "It's Bryce. He won't stop calling and texting me. He wants to know when I'm coming home. I've gotta take this."

"Just let it ring. He knows where you are. Can't he ever just—"

"Margot, it's fine, not now," she says sulkily. "But I should get going. Tell Oliver it was nice to meet him. And be safe! Okay?"

"Aren't I always?"

"When you wanna be . . ." She gets up to leave, but turns back with an amused look on her face. "Don't you think it's ironic that you detest olives but are now flirting with a guy named Oliver? Hopefully he'll taste better." She smiles and winks.

"Fingers crossed," I smirk back. First of all, that was funny and second, right now isn't the time to get involved in her relationship business. Again. Actually, for the zillionth time. It's just that I care about her, and Bryce is her biggest flaw. He's gotta go. Jessie doesn't—or refuses to—see it. He's been suspected of cheating on her, like, seven times, but he somehow, without fail, worms his way back into her fragile heart. Probably because she hasn't witnessed his wretchedness for herself.

I'm plotting how to get her to finally break up with Bryce—an intervention? A scheme? A lie? The truth?—when Oliver gets back to our table. "I reckon it's time for that second round. What'll you be having? Hey, where'd Jessie get off to?"

"She had to leave. Clingy boyfriend." I give a nonchalant shrug. My mood has been slightly dampened like hot pavement after a summertime drizzle.

"Fair enough," he says insincerely as he moves from the seat across from me and slides into the vacant spot to my left. It's a bit of a tight squeeze so our thighs gently touch. There is definitely something happening—we have more chemistry than Walter White. "Truthfully, I've been wishing to have you all to myself."

Sparks are flying. If I'm not careful, they could burn right through my leather pants. But I like where this is heading too much to slam on the brakes. "Let's get out of here," I whisper in his ear. He smells so good. What *is* that? This is what I presume a Tom Ford man smells like: musky and masculine with a hint of leather and a misting of citrus.

"Yeah? You sure? We didn't get that second round . . ."

"Forget the second round. I've got something better in mind."

Okay, who am I right now? I am *never* this gutsy with guys. It's definitely the martinis. My sober brain is trying desperately to keep up with the antics of my drunken desires. But it's too slow, can't catch up, and before I know it, we're closing my tab, putting our coats on, and calling an Uber.

Chapter Six

"**B**y the way, I'm very shy," I confess as I slip my silk camisole over my head. I'm not wearing a bra—I rarely do—and Oliver has definitely noticed. He's sitting on the unkempt bed staring at me with a look that can only be described as raw, unfiltered lust. It's a look I could get used to seeing more often. I feel as though I'm starring in a Savage X Fenty runway show; forget *pretty*, I'm sexy, desired, enticing, and beautiful.

We got our momentum back in the car; we locked lips the whole ride to his apartment. He's a *great* kisser. Almost too good. I'm a bit suspicious because it means that he's had *a lot* of practice. But who am I to be jealous? I only met him an hour ago! Also, I'm a good kisser too, which I'm sure he's noticed. After all, the best advice I learned from Gabrielle Solis when I was fifteen was to never buy a car without taking it for a test drive first. Even though at that age I really did think she was talking about cars.

I unzip my leather pants and wriggle out of them as provocatively as I can. I'm envisioning Jamie Lee Curtis in *True Lies* for inspiration. Oliver is fixated on me; he's famished for it. Next, I start sliding off my sexy lace—

Scratch that: sensible Jockey briefs. This is a *nightmare*.

My inner seductress sprints back into hiding. I must have forgotten to change out of them before we left. This is the type of underwear I wear at home with a raggedy tank top while eating popcorn and watching *Gentlemen Prefer Blondes*, not when I'm trying to seal the deal with a hottie I just met in the bar! Why do I do this to myself? Well, I didn't foresee myself going home with anyone. Although, the condoms in my purse might tell a different story . . .

I'll just have to roll with it. It's darkish in here anyway. And they're black, they blend in. What if Oliver needs glasses? For all I know, he took out his contacts in the bathroom and everything is a big blur to him right now. Let's stick with that theory for the time being. As long as he can find his way to my modest curves it's all good. Smooth sailing.

Supressing my embarrassment, I slip down my granny panties lickety-split and give them a little kick off to the side. Out of sight, out of mind. I make a mental note of where I assume they land for when I inevitably sneak out later on. Before I have time to stress out about my underwear awkwardness any further, Oliver reaches one long, lean arm over and brings me close. His cool palms find their way to my breasts and I readily shiver as he starts kissing them. His hands slither their way down to my ribs, then my hips, causing my silken skin—thanks to a rigorous daily moisturizing routine—to flare with goose bumps. Every inch of my anatomy is howling with anticipation.

He pulls me horizontal on top of the downy dove-gray duvet. He has somehow removed his own boxers without me noticing. Very slick. His kisses are like a warm summer's day and I melt like rich, chocolate fondue. God, the weight of this dangerously handsome guy feels *so* good. It's been too long since I've had sex with someone that wasn't me and, to quote Victoria Monét, my "ten new friends."

"I don't do this . . . often," I say huskily. The white lie just slips out; my breathing is heavy, and my head is tilted all the way back. I'm not sure why I just blurted that out. I'll admit, I've had my fair share of one-night stands, but it's definitely not what I want to talk about *in the middle of one.* I'd rather not talk at all. I need to concentrate on the unfurling scrumptiousness.

"Me neither. But I can't resist you," Oliver breathes. "You're so bloody sexy."

He definitely does do this often. But that's not what's important here. Everything feels too sensational to get caught up on the small stuff. He begins kissing his way further and further down my torso until—oh my *god.* My instincts tell me that this is just the warmup and it's shockingly satisfying. I already feel tingly all over, from my curled toes to my rolled-back eyes. My internal dialogue comes to a standstill when a condom magically materializes as if out of thin air. Oliver begins determinedly crawling his way up my body and then—well, I have to leave something to the imagination.

A perfect, blissful amount of time later, I feel like Aphrodite reincarnated. How have I never had sex this fantastic before? And that's not just the remaining ounces of gin left in my system talking. Maybe I've been sleeping with the wrong men all of my life. Honestly, I wouldn't doubt it. My track record hasn't exactly been stellar.

What time is it? I don't want to leave, but if I don't get up now I never will. I make a halfhearted struggle to get out of bed, but Oliver holds me tighter. I really could stay tangled in these crinkled sheets all night long. But that could be hazardous for my emotional fragility.

"So, I really have to leave, but thanks for . . . that was . . ." I'm speechless. Again. On second thought, I don't *really* have to go. Lola is fed, she has water, and she knows how to use a pee pad. But leaving seems like the right thing to do given that he's a complete stranger. Even if we did just have mind-blowing sex.

"Bummer. Stay for a bit? Just five minutes. Then leave, if you want . . ." He's holding onto my hand and kissing each finger, counting to five in his sexy Australian accent. Is he for real? What kind of guy uses a cheesy pickup line and then wants you to stay longer? I thought he would be hassling me back into an Uber by now. *Great sex, nice to meet you, talk to you never!*

I pretend to contemplate this more than I need to. After all, I can't let on right away that inside I'm screaming *yes, I want to stay until the sun comes up* because that would just be too much, too soon. No one likes a Stage-5 Clinger and I refuse to be the Gloria to his Jeremy—until the second half of *Wedding Crashers* anyway.

"Fine," I say. "But only five minutes. I'm setting my alarm."

***

The last thing I remember is snuggling in closer and laying my head beside Oliver's, my fingers running through his jungle of curly golden-blond chest hairs. Sunlight is piercing my sleepy eyelids and I'm wondering why there aren't any curtains. Did I go home with a curtain-averse psychopath? How can he ever stay asleep with this room being so bright? I wish I had my sleep mask with me. I should keep it in my clutch when I go out, just in case I want to sleep over at . . .

Wait. Sleep over? I scramble to find my phone and see that my alarm has been silently going off all night long. We must have passed out right away. Squinting to read the screen, I see that

I have five texts from Jessie and two missed calls from Liao. Is everyone looking for me?

Hey Mar, sorry I had to leave early. You know how B gets

How was it? Did you go home with him?

Omg ur still there aren't you?

Mar, come on!!! Tell me some details

Ok if ur alive pls write back. NOW or I'm calling 911

I send her a quick text to let her know I'm okay and that I'll fill her in later. I really wish I hadn't fallen asleep. I was hoping to avoid the whole "morning after" thing—questioning if my breath smells bad, if my makeup is smudged all over my face like a raccoon, what I look like in the morning light versus the nighttime, wondering if he's wishing I'd leave, or maybe he's wishing I'd stay. And do we eat breakfast together or say a hasty *adiós, hasta luego*? Did he enjoy last night as much as I did? Does he want to do it again? And most importantly: Where are all of my clothes?

Surreptitiously, I creep out of the bed and start herding my things. I'd rather just leave him a note or something and get out of here before he wakes up. Camisole? Check. Pants? Check. Boots? Check. Where are my Jockeys? I remember kicking them to the side as nonchalantly as I could during my amateur striptease, but they don't seem to be anywhere in sight. I swear, they were right here! I'm on my hands and knees, going through Oliver's heap of last night's discarded clothing when out of the corner of my eye I spot them bunched up underneath the bed. I get down flat on the floor and reach for them, but can't get far enough. How are they *so* far under there? My kick must have been more powerful than I thought. Just a little stretch further. Almost there . . .

"Morning." I start and gasp, bumping my shoulder on the bed frame. *Ouch.* "Are you okay? Didn't mean to scare ya," Oliver sleepily laughs, which turns into a yawn. He's even cuter in the morning glow. No! Focus. *You've got to get out of here.*

"Morning," I say as cheerfully as I can. "I'm okay. Just thought I dropped an earring. But I found it."

Oliver reaches over and pulls me back towards the mattress. Before I can resist, he kisses me fervidly. Who *is* this guy? Doesn't he care that my breath probably smells like fermented octopus and alcohol? This is every hardcore romantic's ideal one-night encounter, but given my history, I've become too cynical to believe it's for real. There must be something wrong with him. Is he a mama's boy? A sex addict? Does he watch disturbingly vulgar porn? Are there dead bodies hidden in the closet?

It takes all of my strength and willpower to pull myself up into a seated position. "Look, Oliver, I had a really good time last night. Better than good. Fantastic. I'd love to stay and . . . But I really have to go. Also, I'm in desperate need of caffeine." I plant a juicy kiss on his lips once more before jumping out of bed. Then, I slip my camisole over my head and step into my leather pants—sans underwear. This is beyond disgusting. Oliver is watching me get dressed but doesn't question my lack of undergarments. Ew. Who calls them undergarments? Apparently, me. And apparently, I am going without them today. *In leather pants.* No one should ever have to experience this. It's appalling and abusive and assaulting towards my most sensitive parts.

Okay. Yes, I know I could just get back down onto the floor and reach with my abnormally long arms and get my underwear. But unlike Shawn Mendes, there *is* something holding me back: my own nagging embarrassment of how profoundly unattractive they are. Also, my teeny tiny white lie about the earrings.

My phone alerts me that Liao has texted.

Hey, sister, checking in to see if you're up yet. Oscar needs a walk with or without his little girlfriend, Lola

I open Apple Maps so I can see exactly where we are. I have a vague idea, but if I recall correctly, we took a couple of turns down some side streets that I don't think I've ever stepped foot on before. Oh, good. I'm only a seven-minute walk from the subway station and just three stops from home. This hookup couldn't have been more convenient if it had happened in my own apartment. Not that I *ever* bring people back there, except for my closest friends.

I text Liao back:

I'm up! Currently having a hot, Aussie rendezvous. Will fill you in later. Usual park in an hour?

"How are you getting home?" Oliver gets out of bed and throws on a T-shirt. I wish he wouldn't. His chiseled physique deserves to be seen. (By my eyes and my eyes only.)

"Just going to take the train," I reply as I zip up my boots. I say a tight-lipped prayer in my head for deciding to wear this pair and not anything with a deadlier heel that would have made my morning-after ordeal even worse than leather pants with no protection for my . . . you get the picture.

"Okay. Let me walk you. I know a great place where we can pick up a coffee, for the road." Turns out, Oliver lives across the street from a café. It's really cute with long metal tables, white-painted brick walls, and plenty of thriving green shrubs. It's early, but it's already packed. There's not a free table in sight. I didn't notice it last night, given that our mouths were essentially suctioned together the whole way here. And in the elevator. And as he unlocked the door . . .

He orders us two iced coffees to go, claiming they're too good to pass up, even in the winter, and we stand in awkward silence waiting for them to be made. Thankfully, the chatter of the place fills the gaps in our lack of conversation. I listen in on a pair of girlfriends, both still in their clubbing clothes, talking about their abhorrent, after-hours experiences. Apparently, some guy asked one of them to have a threesome with him and his roommate once they got back to his place. The nerve! She tells her friend he was a "total pig," and they clink their cappuccinos together in agreement. I'm so glad Oliver doesn't have a roommate. At least, I don't think he does.

After a few moments of bashfully catching each other staring at the other, our coffees are placed on the counter in front of us. We head outside and start walking towards Ossington station. Neither of us seem to know what to talk about besides the weather. This is exactly what I was trying to avoid by sneaking out. Well, this is it, we're here. Although I'm praying that we will see each other again, I realize that I don't even know his last name. I'll have no way to contact him after this. Unless he miraculously asks me for my—

"Can I get your number? If not, fair enough. But I'd love to see you again."

Is he a mind reader? "Yes! I mean, sure. If you want," I say as nonchalantly as I can. "I'd like to see you again too."

"That's good to know," he smiles, amused, or perhaps flattered, by my embarrassing eagerness. He reaches for his phone from the back pocket of his jeans. I can't help but keep my fingers crossed for an iPhone . . . it just doesn't hit the same when you go to send an iMessage and it turns chartreuse instead of that calming cobalt. "So, what're your digits?"

"Here, allow me." I take his phone (made by Apple!) and carefully input my number. I make sure to type my first and last name
into the contact info so that if he wants to stalk me online later, he
has every opportunity. I hand it back and take a slurp of my coffee.
It's *really* delicious. Another bonus for him: he has great taste in
caffeinated beverages.

He studies the screen for a moment before slipping it back into
his pocket. "I'll text you later so you have my number. Have a good
day, Margot." His hands envelop my face, and he kisses me one
last time before he turns to leave. This time, my morning breath
doesn't even cross my mind because I'm too enraptured by his
dimple. "Oh, and for the record, you're not shy. At all."

Once again, I'm stunned into silence. My feet feel like they're
cemented to the sidewalk. I've got to get a move on, or I'll miss
my train. I *definitely* want to see him again. I'd be crazy not to.
Besides, I have to at least *try* to get my underwear back. I start
walking—very uncomfortably—towards the eastbound platform.
A big, goofy grin hijacks my face. I think I *like* this guy. So much
so that I'm momentarily distracted from my commando situation.
Or should I say—*itch*uation?

Ugh. I have to get out of these pants.

***

When I get home, I head straight to the bathroom, strip down,
and take a quick but much needed shower. I am never, ever
wearing leather pants without underwear again. That was beyond
brutal. The parts of myself that are meant to remain delicate
and private have never felt more violated. Even compared to the
time the Venezuelan guy I was dating asked me why I couldn't
have "given myself a haircut" down there before arriving at his

apartment. So insulting. It's ironic because he didn't even have a good *haircut* himself.

What is up with me and my bad luck with pants lately? I can't wait for spring so I can simply pull a slip dress over my head and be fabulous—underwear or not.

I throw on a pair of Puma joggers, a black hoodie, and layer my charcoal wool-cashmere overcoat on top. Cozy, warm, and comfortable. My New Balance runners and an olive-green baseball cap finalize my casual, dog park look. One quick swipe of Glossier's Boy Brow, a dab of vanilla Chapstick, and I'm ready to go. Lola is already waiting by the door, her little tail whipping side to side in excitement. I slip on her harness, clasp her leash, and we're off.

Fifteen minutes later, Lola is charging through the dewy grass with Oscar, Liao's Labradoodle, and we're sitting on a bench dishing about my risqué rendezvous with a couple of takeout drip coffees and mini cinnamon sugar donuts from COPS that Liao picked up on his way.

"Do you think it's horrible that I slept with him the first night I met him? I mean, he could have been a murderer," I say with an anxious furrow of my defined brows. I pop a donut into my mouth; it practically melts. Since Liao is opposed to gratuitous snacking, the burden of finishing them has fallen on my shoulders. I'm not complaining.

"Sister," says Liao, placing a hand on my forearm. "A man could end up being a murderer after a decade together. You never know. Anyway, you're preaching to the wrong choir about sleeping with someone too soon . . ." He smirks and his eyes are practically beaming with cheekiness.

"I know that look. What are you hiding? Tell me!" I demand.

"Well, long before we met, I once challenged myself to see how many men I could sleep with on an overnight furlough in Prague. I was only in the city for twenty-four hours, but I was hoping *it* would be in *me* for longer," he pauses, reminiscing. "I ended up with a total of six Europeans who were very easy on the eyes but so not easy on the body. Lucky number seven was on his way over, but I regretfully had to cancel. I felt like I'd been run over by a Mercedes-Benz."

"Oh my god, you're an animal," I joke. When I think about that many people in one day, I'm exhausted. Already I could use a nap and it's been approximately ten hours since I last had sex. My stamina is not what it used to be in my early twenties. I nibble on another donut for sustenance.

"Sister, you know it. I've lived a very scandalous, drama-filled life and had my fair share of eggplant emojis in my thirty-two years. Now I'm old and insipid."

"You're not old. You're only six years older than me! And you're definitely not insipid." I roll my eyes at him and he continues on.

"Well, I'm glad you think so. In gay years, I'm a relic. Anyway, I've got to fill you in on the office drama since you left last Tuesday."

"Was that only last Tuesday?" I ask sarcastically. "It feels like it's been a century."

"Yes, it was. But if a century had in fact gone by, I'd say we still look pretty fuckable." Liao recounts the news. Nothing too outrageous, just the usual antics. Gia was lightly reprimanded for taking products without permission, Tracy was running around all day asking people if they had any referrals for my now-vacant position, and Yvette was her same old aloof self. Of course, people couldn't get enough of my little outburst. According to Adam Frank, I'll forever be known in the office as *The Crybaby in the Latex Leggings*. I didn't even cry! It's not exactly the title I'd hoped for, but it's better to be remembered than forgotten, right? All publicity is good publicity. That being said, I don't think I can ever ask anyone at La Pêche for a reference.

As we're laughing about my stupid squeaking pants, my phone rings. It's an unknown number. Oh my god, it could be *him*! My dreamy one night—hopefully more—stand. We both freeze. If it's Oliver, I'm going to die. I make him wait a few rings before answering. Gotta keep him guessing. He said he was going to text me later, not call, but this could be even better. It's more personal. Intimate.

"Hello?" I rasp, sexily. My heartbeat thumps below the belt. Who knew I was *that* good? I mean, it's only been a couple of hours since we parted ways. I wonder if he wants to see me again tonight? Tomorrow? This time I'll make sure my outfit is better prepared and my underwear is Agent Provocateur. Correction: something *like* Agent Provocateur because the real deal is way out of my price range.

"Hello? Is this Margot Moss?" It's not Oliver. It's a man's voice, but one I don't recognize. Who is this person? How do they know my full name? My mind goes to dark places: a serial killer, a kidnapper, some random guy I gave my number to the last time I was blackout drunk? Which, come to think of it, was definitely over a year ago so that would be startling if he was just calling now.

"Yes, it is. May I ask who's calling?" My voice does a one-eighty from sexy and raspy to professional and polite.

"Sidney Lalonde, here. The lovely Priya Khan passed along your number. She highly recommended you—a smart, beautiful, young woman—for the position I'm looking to fill. Are you free tomorrow? I'm interested in getting to know you better."

"Oh! Right, hello," I answer, slightly taken aback. I was not expecting it to be Sidney Lalonde—especially on a Sunday morning. I'd almost entirely forgotten about my encounter with Priya. However, I appreciate him looking out so steadfastly for *Chatelaine*'s well-being. They must need someone to start soon.

My adrenaline starts pumping. "I can definitely be free. What time? And where would you like to meet? At the office?"

"Let's do drinks. I'll have a car waiting for you at seven thirty sharp. Text me your address. Wear something eye-catching, conspicuous. Something womanly. I very much look forward to meeting you, Margot."

"Sounds great . . ." I say, perplexed. "See you tomorrow!" I jab the End Call button, and my excitement evaporates only to be replaced by incomprehension. Womanly? Eye-catching? Conspicuous? What does that mean? "That was really weird," I say, turning to Liao. I recap the story of bumping into Priya, confessing my job situation to her, and her pushing this Sidney Lalonde character—who, come to think of it, I was assuming to be a woman—on me while I was zoned out. I missed half of what she was talking about; the most important half. "I think he works for *Chatelaine*," I explain. "But he wants to meet for drinks. Is that normal for a magazine?"

Liao raises his arched eyebrows. "You *think* or you know?"

"Well . . ." I pause. "I'm almost positive. I mean, I looked at the masthead online and didn't see the name Sidney Lalonde on there but he could be some super important, behind-the-scenes guy."

"And he called you beautiful and young and told you to wear something sexy?"

"Womanly."

"Not any better," Liao says with palpable skepticism. "Margot, I hate to break it to you, but I think she's setting you up with a sugar daddy. Trust me, I would know." I almost choke on my coffee. "What?" I sputter, shaking my head. "No. There's no way." Liao is undeterred.

"I'm jealous!" he exclaims. "Go for it. If I could, I would. But Lord knows I don't need another one. How would I keep up?"

"No one would just *assume* someone wanted a sugar daddy." I toss a stick for Lola to fetch and watch her chase after it for about five seconds before getting distracted and going to sniff something else. She has the worst attention span ever.

"Excuse me? Who *wouldn't* assume someone wants one? When are you going to have this opportunity again? I say, go for gold. Or *golden years* if you know what I mean. All cats look the same in the dark . . ." Liao winks while making a wildly inappropriate, tongue-in-cheek gesture. Literally. "As long as it's not a golden shower, you're fine. I've done that once and it was—"

"Liao, stop! I get it. Golden years, not showers." We both laugh and reminisce on that episode of *Sex and the City* when Samantha goes home with the old*er*, unbelievably loaded guy and finds diamond jewelry on her dinner plate. I swear, we relate half of our lives to that show. It's like the Bible to us. I know people say it hasn't "aged well" or whatever, but let's just accept it for what it is: an iconic treasure full of high-fashion and saucy one-liners.

"Margot, that could be you! Don't knock it 'til you try it. Believe me, sister, experience counts for a lot."

"That's what I was thinking about Oliver. He was extremely experienced and more delicious than New York cheesecake. He better text me." Physically, I'm sitting here in the dog park but mentally, I'm back in Oliver's sumptuous sheets.

"Who's Oliver again?"

"Liao! The guy I was with last night." I playfully swat his arm.

"Oh, right. Him. Come on, you've only known him one night. Forget about Oliver and start thinking about what you're going to wear to meet the enigmatic Mr. Lalonde."

As we part ways, with a graceful hug and the dogs clipped onto their respective leashes, I wonder if Liao's right. Did Priya set me up with a sugar daddy? I mean, would she do that? Really? It seems laughable since she is *almost* more career-driven than I am.

The uncalled-for flattery notwithstanding, I still believe Sidney Lalonde is from *Chatelaine*, no matter what Liao is predicting. It just makes sense. Despite a position in traditional media most likely not paying me the big bucks, it's my preeminent vocation. And I'd do almost anything for a paycheck at this point, no matter how meager. The only thing worse than staying in my current apartment is not having an apartment at all.

Hands up if you're invariably torn between wanting to save for a down payment but also craving to work at a job that you're actually passionate about. I thought my professors at university were being facetious when they said that working in the media industry will leave you broke but socially flourishing.

I give Lola a little tug to dissuade her from sniffing at *every* tree trunk, parking meter, and patch of grass along the way. We have to hurry because I need to tear apart my entire wardrobe in an attempt to find something eye-catching, conspicuous, and womanly to wear tomorrow night. Whatever that means. I'll probably just settle on "fashion-forward professional" and call it a day.

Chapter Seven

It's twenty to eight on Monday evening and I'm in the Uber that Sidney Lalonde sent for me. I'm starting to wonder if this is work-related after all. As much as I don't want to admit that Liao is right, it's feeling a lot more like a date than a business meeting. With every passing stoplight, I twinge with newfangled nerves. So, I do what any rationally thinking person would do. I make a list to break down the monsoon of thoughts in my dubious mind.

First of all, he's paying for my transportation. If this were a job interview, wouldn't it be acceptable for me to find my own way there? But maybe he's just being polite. Then, there's his "womanly" outfit criteria; that must mean that my appearance is important to him. And last, but not least, it's after working hours. We're going somewhere called Brussaux Society, and it's apparently a private club. Wouldn't we just go to Starbucks if this were a straight-up meeting? What's wrong with a coffee shop? Or for that matter, a boardroom? (Not that I've fully recuperated from the last time I was in a boardroom.)

What if I misinterpreted the whole situation? Liao certainly is the authority on seducing men for personal gain. But I doubt that Priya Khan advocates for it. Oh, who knows? I'm now at the point of worrying where I'm also anxious about stress zits popping up across my forehead tomorrow. It's so unfair. My complexion shouldn't have to suffer for this surreptitious meeting.

I have no idea what I'm walking into; in every sense. What is this place? I'm standing on the sidewalk, Googling the location. It says the venue is mere steps away but I don't see anything but desertion and a flickering streetlamp. It's spookily quiet. Did the driver get the address right? Terror grips me. I'm about to be murdered; I feel it in my bones! Well, either that or I've been listening to too many episodes of *Casefile*. Anxiety aside, at least I look fabulous. My ghost will live on forever, haunting society in an eerily fierce, translucent ensemble. I wonder if you can change outfits as a ghost? Surely you can't be forced to wear the same thing for eternity? If so, that's the true definition of hell.

Right now, in my living state, I think I've mastered my look. I chose a spaghetti-strap leopard-print midi dress with an oversized chocolate-brown blazer and my knee-high black leather boots. I'm stylish and roar-worthy but also business-y. Side note: I don't trust anyone who doesn't like leopard prints. I mean, *who hurt you?* But anyway, at this moment I'm more concerned about somebody *not* hurting me.

Tucked behind a towering faux palm tree, I spot a glowing sign for Brussaux Society; a fluorescent frond of hope or despair, I can't tell. My heeled boots echo on the desolate pavement. Remind me again why I agreed to meet here? It *better* pay off.

There are two burly bouncers standing guard outside. They're giving me Hobbs and Shaw, but cheap imitations. (Although, can anyone be a *genuine* imitation of The Rock's muscles?) Serpent-like velvet ropes are strung across three separate queues and all of them are empty. Like, tumbleweeds kind of empty. Is this place even open? Maybe these bouncers are here to *stop* anyone from getting *in*. Maybe it's such an awful place that their only job is to prevent people from having to endure the misfortune that inevitably comes with daring to enter the gruesome establishment.

"Hello? Miss? Which line are you supposed to be in?" asks the one who looks like Hobbs. His biceps ripple with every syllable.

"I'm not sure," I admit. "I'm just meeting . . . someone. He should be here already."

"Are you a member?" grunts Shaw.

"No, first time. Are you guys even open? It looks pretty dead."

"Yes, we are. You'll want the guest line. That one on the end, please." He gestures to the line farthest away from where I'm standing. Are these guys for real? I'm the only one outside and they're worried about which line I'm in? This is too funny. They all lead to the same door! Regardless, I obediently step around the suspended rope and enter the correct one.

I can't believe I've lived in this city all my life and I've never heard about this place before. Is Brussaux Society new or just tragically unpopular? Or perhaps excruciatingly exclusive? I mentally note to explore places outside of my usual hangouts every couple of weeks. If I manage to survive tonight, that is.

When I walk through the monstrous, metal—not that I'm an expert but they look like they could be bulletproof—doors, I'm greeted by the intense stares of three peroxide-blondes, each in a different style of bodycon dress, standing in front of, sitting behind, and leaning against a long, varnished desk in an alarming shade of red. Although each of them saw me enter, not a single one makes a move to interact with me. Instead, they continue chatting, as if I'm already a ghost and they just peered right through me.

"But did you see Bella Hadid's latest post?" asks one of them.

"Yes! And she totally had her nose done again."

"Get out," shrieks the third as she flings a finger towards her own sculpted snout.

There are plastic palm trees swaying in the heavy air conditioning and palm-printed wallpaper accenting the area behind the desk. The air is thick with cigar smoke; I could have sworn it's been illegal to smoke indoors since before I was born. I'm not sure what I expected from Brussaux Society but it's definitely not this. It's like someone regurgitated Miami Beach into this room, but it didn't quite come out the same. "Uh . . . hello?" I say to them, cutting short their gossip session. I take a ginger step forward.

"Welcome to Brussaux Society! Can I get your membership card?" asks the one who resembles a Bratz doll, as she synchronously judges my outfit—as if to say it doesn't belong here, which it doesn't. It's not form-fitted enough.

"Actually, I'm not a member. I'm meeting someone. Sidney Lalonde?" The blondes start excitedly whispering amongst themselves. Apparently, the name Sidney Lalonde means something titillating to them, and I'm not sure if that makes me feel better or even more high-strung.

"Oooh, you lucky girl," the blondest of them all coos. Her hair looks like it's made out of stardust. "Mr. Lalonde is one of our favorites. I'll take you right to him. He's at his usual table. We keep it permanently reserved for him. One time, Justin Bieber's manager came in and we weren't even allowed to sit him at that table. It's, like, really special." Her immaculate teeth blind me as she smiles over her shoulder and leads me through a second foyer.

Inside the actual club, there are neon lights everywhere and somewhere hidden away, a smoke machine; its bellowing fog floats around my boots as we walk past gaggles of middle-aged men sipping brandy and discussing either the stock market or which woman they're trying to take home later. Jazzy house music blasts through skillfully unseen speakers as unnaturally augmented servers shimmy their way from table to table in plunging minidresses and crotch-high stiletto boots, all in shades of

Pepto-Bismol pink. It's like I've walked into a cosmetic surgery ad. *Get your overly plump lips, chiseled chins, and cheekbone implants here!* The flavor I'm getting is, in a word, sleazy. And that's me being polite. Is this a member's only strip club? The set of *Hustlers*? Whatever it is, I've officially entered the land of gaudiness, where all the garish taste in the world came to die. Kelly Wearstler would *never*.

We arrive at the table and there sits the infamous Sidney Lalonde, sipping brown liquor on ice. He's a bit older—wrinklier—than I expected. *All cats look the same in the dark.* He's wearing a Hugo Boss polo shirt with navy slacks and suede loafers. He has graying hair, a five o'clock shadow, and is sporting black thick-rimmed glasses. He has a sort of Jeff Goldblum thing going on. Not my type.

"Hey, handsome, I have someone here to see you," says my flaxen escort. "Let me know if you need anything else." Sidney dismisses her with a single wave, adjusts his glasses, and focuses on me. Not that I don't like to be in the spotlight, but that was rude. Is he determined to make a skeevy first impression? He greedily devours my appearance, his prescription lenses lingering on my chest. *Ugh.* We need to normalize telling men—even wealthy mogul types—when they're staring too long for comfort.

"I take it you're Margot Moss? Look at you! You're just what I imagined. Please, have a seat," he offers as he knocks back the last of his syrupy drink.

"That's me," I confirm, hesitantly grinning. Saying I'm stumped by this scenario would be a gross understatement. I'm what he imagined? Is that a compliment? An insult? I don't have a clue. He's not anything like I imagined, and my assumption that he's part of the *Chatelaine* team is beginning to erode—as much as I'm clinging onto it with every inhale.

"What's your poison? Can't have a pretty little thing like you sitting around with no drink in her hand. Let's loosen up those nerves and get comfortable with each other." Okay. I'm officially repulsed. Yes, I'm pretty, but my soul is prettier.

In spite of his cocksure attitude, free alcohol entices me to at least hear him out—whatever his agenda entails. I won't let my wild theories ruin this meeting right off the bat. If you shouldn't judge a book by its cover, then perhaps you also shouldn't judge a man by his deplorable demeanor? *Hmm.* That one's debatable. It's possible that Liao is wrong and planted all of this suspicion in my mind for no reason. However, I've learned from the #MeToo movement that if Mr. Lalonde tries to pull anything inappropriate, I'm sprinting out of here faster than a cheetah. There are plenty of other ways for me to get a job that don't involve *that.*

"I'll take a glass of prosecco? If they have it," I say diffidently. "If not, then a gin martini?"

"If they have it?" Sidney laughs exuberantly. "Forget prosecco! We'll get a whole bottle of the good stuff. Champagne, the real deal. Straight from France. Have you ever been to France, Margot? You'd love it."

"No, I haven't," I admit. "I've always wanted to visit though."

He motions for our bedazzled server. Her name, I learn, is Charisma. She's almost bubblier than our champagne order. That would be a pretty tough name to live up to if you were having a bad day—or on any day really. She briskly returns with a cool, crisp bottle of Moët & Chandon. The cork pops and although I love that lip-smacking sound, it inexplicably makes me tense up. I have to hold my hands in my lap to resist the urge to grab my flute and chug my nerves away in one swift flick.

"So, Margot. What did Priya tell you about me? Good things, I hope?" Sidney winks as he says this. Is it a grotesque predator wink or something harmless? A twitch?

I take a subtle sip before answering. "Oh, you know. She just said that I absolutely *had* to meet you!" Another sip, this time a little bit bigger. I eye him discreetly over the top of the glass.

"She said the same thing about you, but she didn't tell me how attractive you are!" Another wink. I'm starting to (wishfully) think he may just have a muscle spasm and not a predatory habit. "I've known Priya for a long time. I trust her character. So, when she told me that you'd be the perfect fit, I believed her." I'm dying here. Does he think I'm a perfect fit to work at *Chatelaine*? Or is he thinking I'm a perfect fit for something entirely different? He continues on. "Priya mentioned that you like to travel, is that correct?"

I nod as I drain my flute.

"Great, because travel would be an essential part of the deal," he says.

Charisma comes to top up our champagne and I can see Sidney mentally taking *her top down*. Honestly, I can't even blame him for this one. Her boobs are so big, they're like an extension of the table. Even I'm—regretfully—staring. She pats Sidney on the shoulder before turning to leave and did he just *quiver*? He's shaking in his loafers. His lustful eyes come back into focus and he sets them on me.

Now that I've got six ounces of sensually fruity Moët flooding my nervous system, I'm beginning to feel more assured. I need some confirmation: *Chatelaine* or sugar? I try to imagine sleeping with Sidney and am forced to supress a gag. I don't think I could do it. Sidney couldn't even be called a sugar *daddy*; he's more of a sugar *papa*. If he looked more like Paul Rudd, ageless and eternally cute, things would be *so* different. "So, how long have you been working at the magazine?" I casually ask.

Sidney looks bemused. "Me? Oh, no," he chuckles. "I'm not a magazine kind of guy. But it seems like all the women I surround myself with are."

My brows furrow. "You don't work at *Chatelaine*? I thought that's how—" Before I can finish, Sidney lets out a squawking guffaw and slaps his knee in delight.

"*Chatelaine*? No! I work in investments," he says, readjusting his glasses. "Pretty boring stuff. Although, maybe I should switch careers . . . something tells me I could get used to being surrounded by beautiful women every day."

My top lip involuntarily lifts in not-so-veiled distaste. I'm noticeably nonplussed. If he didn't ask me here to take Priya's old position, then what am I doing here? Liao *cannot* have called it. I have to get to the bottom of this before we get to the bottom of the bottle. "Mr. Lalonde, it's getting late. What exactly—"

"Please, call me Sid."

"Okay. Sid, what was it that you wanted to meet with me about tonight? The suspense is killing me." I hope I sound more light-hearted than I feel.

He grins; his mouth is crammed with cigar-stained teeth. "You get straight to the point. I like that in a woman," he says. "Priya was right about you. You've got class, style, beauty, brains." He pauses to take a noisy slurp of his champagne. "My friend Perla Rivera recently launched a travel publication and she's looking for someone to help her out. After meeting you, Ms. Moss, I'd be more than happy to recommend you for the editing position." He leans forward to clink our half-full—not five minutes ago I would have said half-empty—glasses together. "As far as I know, the job is based in New York City with potential travel to Los Angeles, Miami, Buenos Aires . . . so, what do you say? Are you interested?"

Did I hear that right? This is a legitimate job and it's based in New York City? My *dream* city? Like Maya Wilkes said, *oh hell yes*! My eyes sparkle brighter than the Empire State Building on a clear night. A week ago I was convinced that my goal of getting to Manhattan had been rendered impossible. Say no more, Mr. Lalonde. I mean, Sid.

I'm in.

Chapter Eight

Remember when Donatella Versace, with all the conviction in the world, stated that she was very lucky to be Donatella Versace? That's the type of verve I'm currently conveying.

It's as if I'm already the career woman I want to be; I'm the world's most renowned fashion editor—*move over Anna Wintour*—on my way to New York Fashion Week and everyone who's anyone wants to know my innermost thoughts on the season's sexiest sustainable styles, animal prints, and accessories. Life is glorious, and glamor is in abundance.

Except, instead of fashion week, I'm heading to The Rosedale Diner to meet Perla Rivera for the first time. It's her pick, I've never been. Apparently, SPINCO is down the street and she has a midmorning class that she'd never miss, not even if Marc Anthony asked her to. I'm doubtful he ever has—or would—but I like that Perla seems to have high standards in terms of fitness and Latin hunks.

I'm so nervous to meet her, I could hardly choke down my breakfast this morning. Granted, it was five-grain oatmeal or something unbearably healthy like that. I went for a run to sweat out some nerves, but they're once again stabbing at my skin like a thousand acupuncture needles. While the endorphins were still coursing wildly through me, I took on arguably the most important task of the day: picking a first impression outfit. Obviously, I want to look flawless for Perla Rivera, but also for me. My soul glows on a whole new level when I feel good about what I'm wearing.

Additionally, I'm not looking to squeak my way across town in vinyl or be forced to go commando in a pair of leather pants *ever again*. I have to be smart, sophisticated, and savvy.

In the end, I opted for split-hem trousers with a creamy cashmere pullover, a men's blazer, and slouchy mocha boots. I'm carrying my vintage Fendi baguette and have layered an ankle-skimming wool overcoat on top. My hair is slicked back into a low bun, and I'm wearing simple gold hoops in all thirteen of my ear piercings. I thank the universe every day that Jessie works at Mejuri because all of these holes in my lobes can get seriously pricey.

Exiting at Summerhill station, I begin walking south down Yonge Street towards the diner. I arrive precisely on time. Usually, I like to be early but long story short, the subway is repugnant.

The Rosedale Diner is sandwiched between a real estate office and a boulangerie. It's painted a charming pastel pink and features a beckoning neon sign above its glass front, complete with a budding rose. Persistent aromas of bacon grease, hamburger patties, and oversized carafes of coffee hit me like a wrecking ball as soon as I pull open the door. The atmosphere is animated, with clanging cutlery and the vibration of contented patrons. I look around, but when I don't spot Perla, I snag a vacant table for two in the window.

I did a little online stalking of her last night and although her social media accounts were private, I found a few photos on Google, which is a relief. To me, going in blind to a first-time meeting is like getting dressed for a party in the dark.

A waitress in a soup-stained black T-shirt comes over and takes my drip coffee order. When she brings it back not two minutes later, it's weaker than I'm used to, so I flag her down again and ask for honey and extra cream. The combo makes the coffee *just* ingestible. Nonetheless, I sit and wait, sip and wait. My foot is fidgeting, jiggling the table. Where is Perla? I take out my phone and see that I've been here for almost fifteen minutes. I send an urgent text to Jessie.

Perla is so late! Is this a bad sign?

Jessie texts me back right away.

No! You know I'm notoriously late and I never mean it as a bad sign . . . Btw I looked up The Rosedale Diner. Did u know it was on an episode of Diners, Drive-Ins & Dives???

I'm searching for the episode on YouTube when Perla Rivera walks in. I know it's her right away even though she doesn't look anything like her photos online; they must be a decade old. She appears to be in her early forties, although most of her face is covered by a pair of prodigious acetate sunglasses. She's wearing an oversized hoodie that says "Feminist & Proud" on the front with a pair of white leggings, effulgent crucifix earrings, and red, studded ankle boots.

Up until this moment, I believed that the only two women to ever be able to pull off white leggings successfully were Selena and Jennifer Lopez as Selena. I've been proven wrong.

I give her a wave and stand up, ready to shake her hand and introduce myself as she reaches the table. She ignores my out-stretched palm, instead opting to give me a walloping hug and a kiss on both cheeks before sliding the sunglasses onto the top of her head. Her curly, habanero-highlighted hair is in a messy pony-tail, she's not wearing a smear of makeup, and she has more plastic in her cheeks and nose than I do in my wallet. Not judging. Just a fact—no one naturally has a nose like a freestyle aerial ski ramp.

She slides into the empty spot across from me and immediately takes her Surface Book out of a full-grain leather tote. "We don't need to do all that formal handshake crap," she says with a faint accent. "I prefer to keep things casual. What are you having for lunch? Order whatever you want. Everyone knows me here, I'm a regular. The food is amazing! You'll love it." She motions for the waitress, who then makes a beeline towards us.

"How are you doing, *cariño*?" Perla stands up to air kiss the petite girl before turning back to me. "Ready to order?"

"I'll have the salad," I say, handing back the laminated menu. What I really want is the burger with smoked cheddar and fries but that somehow doesn't feel appropriate for a first-time meeting. Especially when you're sitting across from someone who just spent an hour peddling their brains out on a spin bike. Perla doesn't order anything but coffee, and now I feel semi-awkward about being the only one eating. I should've just said I wasn't hungry and stopped at The Burger's Priest on my way home.

"So, give me your elevator pitch," Perla says as she lifts her black coffee to her plumped-up lips. "About yourself. Who *is* Margot Moss?"

"Well, I have a degree in media studies from the University of Toronto and spent the last few years working for La Pêche, the environmental beauty company? But writing for a magazine has been my total dream *forever* and—"

Perla holds up an imperfectly polished hand. She has rouge acrylics but the tip on her left middle finger has snapped off. Was it a spinning accident or just due to frequent use? "But what about *you*? I want to know more about you as a person. As a woman."

She squints her eyes, scrutinizing my facial features. "Are you Latina? European? You have this interesting look about you, but I can't figure it out."

"I get that a lot," I say. "I'm mixed. My dad is British, my mom was from Madrid." *Was.* The past-tense word sends a pang of anxiety rippling through me but I brush it off. "I'm what you get if you cross Penélope Cruz with Lily Collins."

"That makes sense! *Me encanta España.* Madrid is one of my favorite places to party. I have some insane stories I could share with you one day." She laughs wickedly. "I'm Argentinian but my family moved here when I was sixteen. Do you speak Spanish? *Hablas Español,* Margot?"

"No," I admit, embarrassed. "Not really. I understand a lot but I couldn't hold a full conversation on my own. Unless we were speaking *Spanglish.*" I attempt a laugh but it sounds more like I'm choking. Swiftly, I take a sip of honey-sweetened coffee.

"Why not? Didn't your mom teach you?"

"She tried to," I reply. I don't usually get into this when I first meet someone. Sometimes I don't get into it even *years* after I meet someone. But there's something about Perla that makes me feel comfortable enough to dredge up one of the most painful memories of my life. "She passed away when I was eleven. She used to talk to me in Spanish, but after she died, I didn't keep it up." I shrug to give the illusion that I don't care as much as I do. I barely remember my mom's voice. My dad did a heroic job raising me, but I still miss her. Or I miss the thought of her, I suppose, since I've lived most of my life without her now. I miss the idea of having a mom.

"Wow, fuck. I'm so sorry," she says as she places her mug down. Her hazel eyes search me for any signs that I might be about to have a breakdown right here, right now at the table. When she's satisfied that I can keep my composure, she carries on. "Anyway,

I'm really good at reading people and judging their character, and your aura is telling me that you're good shit, Margot. I can feel it. I think we could do some really great work together."

"Thanks," I say. I can't get over how easygoing she is, but I'll take the compliment. So far, I really like Perla. We seem to click. "What about you? How did you start your magazine?"

"Well, it wasn't easy!" She throws her head back in laughter. The glare of her earrings nearly blinds me. "I'm a single mom, my daughter, Paloma, is nine. I started *Roam & Rove* Magazine— *R&R* for short—about a year ago out of my apartment with a digital edition and I'm wanting to get into print as well. I thought I could do it on my own, but it's fucking hard. Long story short, I told a few *amigos* that I was looking for an assistant editor and here you are! You seem to be what I've been looking for. Of course, we will be moving to New York at least part-time in the near future, but Sidney said you're okay with that."

Is this really happening? Am I going to be employed by a magazine? I can see it on my résumé already. *Margot Moss, Assistant Editor at* Roam & Rove *Magazine*. True, I've always wanted to work at a *fashion* magazine, but this is close enough. I'll take gardening, bridal, interior design—whatever gets my name on a vibrant, glossy page.

I lock eyes with her. "I am *exactly* what you've been looking for. And I adore New York."

"Love that tenacity! Can you start on Monday?"

Before we part ways, Perla asks for my email address, social media details, and the URL for my LinkedIn page, which to her is the most valuable profile you can have. She's borderline obsessed. "It's the only page that shows you who someone truly is," she lectures. I don't agree, but don't vocalize that. She tells me that she's "sort of between offices at the moment" and will let me know on the weekend when and where to meet her. It's all good with me because I have a job again. And not just any job—I'm an assistant editor! And soon-to-be part-time New Yorker. I can hardly believe it. My career is back on track.

I have a really good feeling about working with Perla. She seems determined, dedicated, and obviously courageous—not only because of her flashy outfit choice, but because she started a whole magazine as a one-woman show. I think I could learn a lot from her. All of a sudden, my meeting with Sidney Lalonde doesn't seem so raunchy. (I'll have to thank Priya for setting that up next time I see her.) Perla is eccentric, but you have to admire a woman who is a single mother, entrepreneur, and on top of it all, a loud and proud feminist.

As soon as I leave the grease-charred smells of the diner behind, I retrieve my phone from the confines of my handbag. *Eek!* There's a text from Oliver asking how my meeting went. We've sent a couple of messages back and forth over the last few days and every time I see his name pop up, my breath catches in my throat. I'll admit, I had a minor panic attack thinking that he was going to discover my granny panties and immediately block and delete my number. That hasn't happened . . . yet.

Jessie warned me to wait a bare minimum of three days before I even *contemplated* texting him back, but I refused to play those juvenile games. Look where they got her—with loser Bryce. I think, if you like someone, you should go after them. But in a totally non-creepy, non-stalker kind of way. Nothing is worse than an unreciprocated crush.

However, just because we've been texting it doesn't mean that I'm wholly unruffled by it. I've been overthinking every single character I painstakingly type. The thing is, I want to come across as bewitching and confident but not overwhelming. I don't want him to know that I've been consumed with thoughts of him but

I also don't want him to think that I *haven't* been consumed with thoughts of him. *Ugh.* Why is texting so grueling? Here it goes.

Hey! It went well. Got the job! New boss seems really cool. Need to celebrate

Sent. I check my phone a zillion times on my way back to the subway to see if he's responded but he hasn't. To be fair, it's only been a few minutes. I hope he doesn't think I meant I need to celebrate alone, because I was hinting at celebrating with him. In retrospect, it wasn't very obvious. Should I have asked him what he was doing later? No. And I am definitely not texting him again. After all, *he* is the one who reached out to *me.*

When I get home and there's still no text from Oliver, I decide to take Lola for a walk. It's beautiful out. Spring is on its way! The flowers aren't the only things starting to bloom. I have a new job, a new outlook on life, and possibly a new beau—or at least a new body to cuddle up with on lonely nights. You know, if he ever texts me back.

What could go wrong?

***

I take it back. I don't want to know what could go wrong. For the record, that was a rhetorical question. It's just something that people say but don't mean. And I definitely did not mean it. Not in the slightest.

I haven't heard from Perla. Not a word. It's 9:45 on Monday morning and my pantsuit persona has been put on indefinite hold. I'm floating aimlessly around my puny apartment, just waiting for her to reach out, unsure of what to do or where to go. I sent her a text around nine asking where I should meet her but got no response. My intestines are knotted so tightly that I can't even eat the poppy seed bagel I bought in celebration of this momentous occasion.

My entire weekend was spent researching travel publications to prepare for today. On Saturday morning, Lola and I gallivanted down the block to this mom-and-pop magazine shop and picked up every travel magazine they had. It was quite expensive, but I figured it was worth it because I'm investing in my career. By Sunday night, I'd memorized the latest issues of *Travel + Leisure*, *National Geographic*, and *Condé Nast Traveller* from front to back—even the types of ads they print.

It can't have all been a waste. It just *can't*. But what if it was? Perla was cruelly cursory at our meeting. I mean, I didn't even sign a contract or anything. *Oh, god.* Should I have insisted on that? She just seemed so friendly, and she sucked me in her with compliment about my enchanting aura. What if this is what she does—preys on innocent, stylish, smart women and pretends like she's giving them the opportunity of a lifetime and then goes home to her husband or her girlfriends or whoever and cackles about it over a glass of Chardonnay? It's almost too callous to consider.

Just as I'm starting to feel disgustingly mournful for myself, contemplating mass-emailing my résumé to mundane job postings on Indeed, Perla calls. To my surprise, instead of being relieved, my anxiety amplifies.

"Morning, Perla," I answer as composedly as I can.

"*Buenos días*," she breathes. "I'm so glad you're there. You have no idea the kind of morning I've had." She pauses. "Listen, I know I said I would call you on the weekend but unfortunately something came up . . ."

She sounds suspiciously like she wants to tell me more, but it's not like I can just pry into her private affairs. I hardly know her. It would be totally inappropriate. Besides, I'm a very private person myself. Private planes, private islands, private parties. Even if I haven't exactly been on a private plane or island yet, I'm certain I will one day. And I'll probably be so private about it no one will even know I've done it. Posting and deleting is a hobby at this point.

"Oh, that's okay. Don't worry about it," I respond, trying my best to conceal my disappointment. Last night, I rifled through my entire wardrobe, attempting to create a bulls-eye "first day as an editor" outfit. I even steamed my pinstriped suit.

"You're awesome and I really wanted us to start working together today. I have big-time plans for the magazine. It's just that . . . well . . . I'm having a bit of a . . . dilemma."

Okay. She's pretty much begging me to ask her what's up. I have an inkling that I shouldn't get involved, but at the same time, Perla is my new boss—however elusive she acts—and I want her to like me. What's the harm in lending an ear? (Again, a rhetorical question. If there's any harm, which I'm sure there won't be, I do not want to know.)

I balk just slightly. "Is everything okay, Perla?"

"*De verdad*, no," she blurts. "I know this isn't really work-related, but do you think you can come over to my apartment? I'll send an Uber for you. If you want to skip today and start work *mañana*, I completely understand but . . ."

Something in her tone of voice makes me think that she wouldn't "completely understand" if I said no, but this is good. Very good. She just invited me over! It's not technically to start work but maybe she wants to *confide* in me about her predicament, whatever it is. This could be crucial for my job in the future. My new strategy is to become Perla's friend, help her build her business, prove myself, gain invaluable wisdom, and eventually start my own magazine or get hired by one of the publications on Condé Nast's first-rate roster.

"Totally. I can be ready to go in five, if that works?" Brick number one has been laid on the path to my new, fabulous, thriving career.

"Amazing. *Gracias.* Don't dress up. Wear something casual, like you're going to the gym. Text me your address. Thanks again, I really appreciate this." She sounds more relaxed when she clicks off and I'm glad that I'm doing something that will help her out; a shoulder to sob on, an ear to vent to. I'm shook by her gym clothes comment, but she's the boss, she makes the rules. I'll wear my pinstripes another time.

Once I've changed into something that is 95 percent spandex, I leave Lola a handful of mashed blueberries in her dish, and race out the door to my awaiting car. I feel a bit like Cinderella. Except, in this version of the fairy tale, I'm dressed like Sporty Spice and am forgoing the pumpkin carriage for a Toyota Prius.

Just as I'm about to slide into the backseat, I notice a different car with Empire State licence plates parked to the right of my building. I've never seen a car from New York here before. Should I take it as a sign? In an alternate universe a driver would hop out and say, "Hello, Miss Moss, I'm here to take you to your new life!" I'd happily climb inside, settling into the butter-soft leather seats. A chilled grapefruit mimosa would be waiting for me, and I'd slowly sip and savor it while the driver dashed upstairs to grab little Lola, tail wagging and tongue lolling. I'd send for my things later, of course. After all, I could definitely buy new clothes once I got to New York. And then—

My alternate universe fades into oblivion and I'm back on the chilly Toronto sidewalk, tumbling into the Prius with its polyester fabric and no mimosa in sight.

Traffic is blissfully nonexistent as we turn north from College Street and head up Yonge towards midtown. I've spent more time in this neighborhood in the last week than I have in my entire life. We zip by slush-soaked public parks, pricey boutiques, and a handful of restaurants that I add to my "must-try" list. I spot a few people out walking their dogs with tiny rubber booties on and it makes me miss Lola, even though I saw her fifteen minutes ago and she *hates* wearing those little shoes.

I wonder what Perla's place is like? Soon I'll be walking into her home, maybe being offered a cup of coffee, and being *confided* in. What better way to demonstrate my seriousness about my career to my new boss than being there when she really needs me? If Nelly and Kelly can work through their dilemma, I can definitely help Perla with hers. First and foremost, because I won't be texting her on an Excel spreadsheet. Blame it on being a creative person, but I zealously loathe Excel.

I sneak a glance at the driver's GPS. We're almost there. I'm more jittery with every passing kilometer. Imposter syndrome has hijacked my last remaining brain cell. What if I'm a terrible assistant editor? Or what if Perla thinks I'm not up for the challenge and she's calling me over to fire me in person? Even worse, what if today goes so horrendously that she doesn't have me back to prove myself in my actual role?

As we pull up in front of her building, I thank the driver and get out of the car. An SUV behind us honks and I hastily slam the door shut. We're barely a block up from The Rosedale Diner; no wonder Perla is a regular there. The condo is four storeys high and looks very European with its archways and tiny terraces. I'm about to text Perla to let her know that I'm outside when she swings open the lobby door. My eyes take approximately five seconds to adjust to her appearance. She looks *wildly* different than she did the other day in her baggy sweatshirt and calcium-colored leggings.

Today she's wearing a full face of *heavy* makeup—way too heavy for this time of the morning—and her hair looks like it's been expensively blown out, her natural curls almost nowhere to be found. Her plain but professional-looking sheath dress is a vibrant shade of daffodil yellow and she's wearing faux-diamond chandelier earrings. Her feet are strapped into peep-toe stilettos although there are still the odd spots of gray snow on the sidewalk.

Now I'm even more bewildered by her request to come in gym clothes if she was going to be ready to . . . well, I'm not exactly sure what she's ready to do, but it's not lifting weights or hitting the elliptical.

"Thank *Dios* you're here," she puffs. Her eyes are wide as she gestures for me to come inside. "We have to hurry. I need your help with these bags."

"Okay?" I answer, puzzled. Just inside the front door are five, black, extra-large garbage bags. "Are we taking them to the depot or something?" I suspect that this job is going to be anything but conventional; editing with a side of egregious tasks. Who asks their brand-new assistant editor to come help them take out their food scraps and eggshells and dirty paper towels and exfoliating wipes on their first day on the job? Actually, who asks that *ever*? We didn't even make the interns at La Pêche touch the garbage, and everyone knows that interns get the worst assignments. Also, who puts on peep-toes to take out the trash? I have a whole slew of questions that require immediate explanation.

Perla looks at me impassively. "No, we're taking them to my boyfriend's—*ex-boyfriend's*—house."

Okay. Now I'm intrigued.

Chapter Nine

"**P**aul told me that he didn't think I should hire you! Can you believe it?" Perla is craning her neck to look at me while she rants from the front passenger seat of the taxi. Her impassiveness of seven minutes ago has dissipated. It's been replaced with a *Scarface*-like rage.

She continues. "I saw him after we met and he told me I was rushing into things with you, that I should find someone with *more experience*. As if you don't have any! I told him, just because she didn't work at *Vanity* fucking *Fair* it doesn't mean she doesn't have experience!" Perla's current complexion is less Argentinian and more blood orange.

Four of the overstuffed garbage bags are crammed into the trunk and one is sitting beside me in the backseat. We're on our way to her ex's—Paul's—duplex. She fills me in on the intensely dramatic situation along the way as I recline, wondering what I just got myself mixed up in. I know she said today wasn't "technically" about work, but this doesn't have *anything* to do with being an assistant editor. Is this really the reason she called me over? It can't be.

"I caught Paul fucking another woman last night. Well, not *fucking* exactly, but I know that's where things were heading. They walked in together, drunk, holding hands like teenagers, and found me sitting on the couch in my brand-new crotchless lingerie with a glass of scotch. I threw it at her head but she ducked. That sobered them up *muy rápido.* He yelled at me to get out, I yelled back and told *her* to get out. She left, and he chased after her. *Her!* His final words to me were along the lines of *get the fuck out by tomorrow.*" Perla takes a brief pause to fume.

"I waited for him to come back and choose me. I poured myself another scotch from the bar, he likes the expensive shit, and I waited some more. Once my babysitter called and said she couldn't stay overnight, and I realized that he really was picking that *puta* over me, I made the decision to steal everything from his closet. Hence, the bags. And now I'm going to have to go to a double confessional next Sunday. *Dios mío.*" She gestures the sign of the cross, starting at her forehead, top to bottom, left to right.

I consciously unfurrow my brow before I look unsupportive. I'm having trouble processing this information. She *what?* And how is she so freely confessing all of this in front of the driver? This sounds dangerously close to being illegal. If it isn't already. And if not totally illegal, then morally wrong. It's like she's describing the failed plot of a godawful rom-com—a box office flop. The kind of movie that goes straight to streaming services. The kind that I wouldn't even be bothered to watch, and I am obsessed with rom-coms. Okay. Maybe I would watch it, but only if there was a drinking game involved.

"So, what you're saying is—"

"Yes. We're going to put it all back before he gets home. Hotel checkout is around eleven so that means we have almost an hour." She scoffs, rolling her eyes. "Although his parents give him a $10,000 allowance every month, he still has to get his money's worth of everything, down to the last penny—he's *that* type of asshole. Guaranteed that *hijo de puta* will come back home with the entire toiletry collection stuffed in his pockets. Can you believe my daughter had her own *room* at his place?" Perla's throaty voice is bogged down with disgust.

I still haven't been able to form a complete sentence. She just keeps going on. I don't know if she's realized that I haven't verbally agreed to help her or not, but I need to process this. And quick. What should I do? What if he comes home? The last thing I want is to get muddled in Perla's relationship drama. I *barely* even know this woman. This feels unquestionably questionable. However, there's no time left to wrap my mind around it because we're here.

The cab screams to a stop in front of a towering concrete duplex. It's striking. If these were any other circumstances, I'd be looking forward to going inside. The residence is tucked away on a quiet, leafy street, with neighboring homes that don't all look like cookie-cutter suburbia. It reminds me of a Brooklyn brownstone but with less stairs and more metal. Perla is counting loose change to pay the $12 fare.

"There's a key in the mailbox," she says. I'm vaguely aware that she's speaking to me. But why is she telling me that?

"What?"

"Unlock the door. The key is there. I'm trying to find my cash and we have a limited amount of time. We need to get a move on. *¡Por favor, apúrate!*"

My brain is split in a serious moral dichotomy. One side is imploring me to run for the hills while the other half is telling me to just do it. After all, if I say no, she could decide not to hire me and, I don't know, frame me for breaking into Paul's house on my own volition. But would she really do that? Also, is it *technically* breaking and entering if they were in a relationship? From what I've gathered, she practically lived here and they only

officially broke up last night. It's kind of like she's just coming . . .
home? My eyes dart from left to right; I look guiltier than Lindsay
Lohan's mug shots.

Somehow, in spite of my internal turmoil, my feet are working
perfectly fine, and I find myself standing in front of the stainless
steel mailbox. My hands are shaking, but a part of me still doesn't
want to disappoint Perla. She's wounded. Of course she is. I mean,
imagine catching the man you loved with someone else? Wouldn't
that make any normal person behave erratically? I have to help
her. What kind of a woman would I be if I didn't help a fellow
woman in need?

Although, if I'm really honest, I'm not only doing this for her.
I'm doing it for me too. I'm doing it for my career. If I can show
her that I'm a loyal employee, then I'm sure my room for growth
will expand exponentially. (Something that was snuffed out at La
Pêche.) This is a peculiar way of proving myself on my first day
on the job, but if I don't do what she wants it could also be my
last. And I *really* don't want that to be the case. After all, I already
made the biggest mistake of all: not signing a contract.

I roll my shoulders back and attempt to stand as tall as Jourdan
Dunn. I can do this. Reaching into the mailbox, I feel around for
the cold metal of the keys. *Shit*. It's an entire ring. Well, this just
got more complicated. The keys feel like a concrete slab in my
hand, way heavier than they should. It's the guilt weighing me
down. *Do it for your job,* I admonish myself. *Do it for New York.*

I try the first key but it doesn't fit. Onto the second. This one
doesn't fit either. *Come on!* I take a breath so big that my lungs
almost break out from behind my rib cage. It's a no-go for the third
and fourth keys as well, but the fifth one glides right in. Only now
it's stuck, and I can't get it to turn no matter how much I jiggle it. I
am officially the worst partner in crime in history. Well, partner in
literal crime. If we're talking about being a supportive, fun friend,

I'm fantastic at that. I wish that's what I'd been summoned this morning to do. What happened to being a shoulder to sob on?

Suddenly Perla is out of the cab, storming up to the house. "It's not open yet? Oh my god," she shrieks. "*¡Muévete!* Let me try."

"It's really stuck," I snap, dodging out of the way. The lock clicks in one swift motion when Perla tries it. Of course it does. She's unlocked it a thousand times. We drag the plastic bags in through the front door and promptly close it behind us.

Immediately, Perla veers into the open-concept kitchen to the left of the entrance. She heads for the fridge and begins rummaging around. "Are you hungry? Do you want anything to eat? I could make us a salad?"

Is she serious? "No, thanks," I say incredulously.

Perla looks like she's about to scold me on the habits of healthy eating. Then, something falls into place. "I just can't shut off my *mom brain*. Usually the first thing I do when I get here is make my daughter a snack," she explains pitifully. Obviously, Perla's not thinking straight. My guilty conscience is slowly being covered with anger and compassion on Perla's behalf, like a sandy shoreline at high tide. If my boyfriend left me for another woman—which, he did—I wouldn't be acting like myself either. I was a total mess after Chris left me. Granted, I didn't raid his entire closet and shove it into super-sized trash bags. The biggest revenge I got was crunching my way to a banging body, sleeping with a few guys who were infinitely sexier than him, and just being happy within myself. Sounds corny, but it's true.

Okay, back to the burglary! No, wait. We're returning things so technically it's not a burglary anymore. It's a *return*lary. Please let that make sense.

Paul's place is seriously swanky. For a single*ish* man in his forties, he really has excellent taste. I was sensing more of a man-cave vibe—beat-up furniture, a gigantic flatscreen, dirty dishes, maybe even a motorcycle randomly plunked in the middle of the hallway. On the contrary, everything is sparkling clean and white, with brushed chrome accents and artwork that looks like it costs more than my entire yearly salary. A shag rug decorates the living room, anchoring a chubby sectional sofa. I could totally live here. Liao, Jessie, Chantelle, and I could throw some fabulous happy hours with bottomless martinis and Hawaiian pizzas ordered at midnight.

Perla and I start dragging and thumping the obese bags up the single flight of burnished stairs. My heart pounds harder the closer we get to the top. I imagine us entering the bedroom and finding Paul and his mistress sound asleep and waking up to us hauling a bunch of temporarily stolen goods into the walk-in closet. That could get *really* ugly. I'm holding my breath, covertly creeping up to the top stair, when Perla loses her grip on one of the bags and it goes slipping and sliding back downstairs, coming to a crash on the landing.

Well, if anyone was asleep up here, they're not anymore.

The bedroom is *huge*. It's bigger than my entire apartment. And don't even get me started on the closet. You could rent it out as its own separate room. But that's not the point. I'm losing track of why we're here. The closet is essentially bare. Perla took everything except for a pair of golf shoes, a few tacky plastic sunglasses, and six different parkas. I know we're in Canada but who needs that many parkas? Also, how was it possible for Perla to get all of this stuff out of here by herself when it's taking the two of us to put it back now?

A solid forty-five minutes fly by and I've started stress sweating. I know I shouldn't have let myself get dragged into this scandalous situation, but I've wanted to work at a magazine for *so* long. I'm so close. I can't just give up now. Besides, I don't think Perla would have asked me to help her with this if she didn't trust me. I suppress my second thoughts and dump out the last bag; its contents go gliding across the hickory hardwood floor.

I hand Perla a few T-shirts, some socks, a workout top. Then, something sparkly catches my eye. This definitely doesn't look like anything a straight man would own. *Oh my god.* It's a Prada purse! An ugly Prada purse, but still Prada. It's an investment based on its name alone. Any fashion girl would agree in a heartbeat. Buttercup-yellow gemstone studs punctuate its metallic-green exterior; it's completed by a hefty gold chain strap. *Oh, god.* What if it belongs to the other woman? Perla can't see it. It might just send her over the edge to know that she was already leaving her things at Paul's apartment. Where can I hide it? I hopelessly look around the room. My only options are under the bed (too obvious), in the en suite bathroom (too unsanitary), or in the closet (way too obvious).

Under the bed it is.

As I'm about to toss it underneath, Perla catches me holding it. For a suspended moment, I think she's going to have a mental breakdown, which is why I'm confused when she casually asks if I want to keep it.

"It belonged to Paul's fiancée before me. She left it here and never asked him for it back. I don't even remember taking it last night but apparently I did," she snickers. "It's just been hanging out here for years. You want it? He's not going to miss it or even notice that it's gone."

"Really? That feels . . . weird." You could argue that the only difference between being offered a used designer purse and buying one yourself is that the previous has an accompanying backstory. Still, it gives me the creeps.

Perla nonchalantly waves her hand. "It's yours. Consider it a thank-you gift for helping me out."

Would that count as stealing? My sense of right and wrong is becoming increasingly blurred and I've only known this woman for, like, two days. What will happen after two weeks? Two years? And what if I ran into Paul while carrying this bag? It's very distinct. Would he remember that it belonged to his ex? Good investment or not, my gut is telling me not to take it. It's tainted, and hideous.

"It's not really my style," I admit.

"Well, if you don't want it, I'll have it." Perla grabs the purse from me and tucks it under her arm. "Let's get the fuck out of here."

Afterwards, we end up at Goldstruck Coffee on Cumberland Street. I'm emotionally exhausted. Perla orders two iced coffees and a pair of sea salt cookies. We take them across the street to the park. There are two metal chairs and a free table next to The Yorkville Rock. The late-morning sunshine and crisp air feels good on my stressed-out skin. I *better* not have anxiety acne tomorrow.

Perla nibbles at her treat like we didn't just spend the last hour restocking Paul's walk-in wardrobe; like perhaps we just finished a yoga class and are catching up over caffeine and baked goods. Everything about Perla's state is so detached, I can hardly stand it. Usually, the Vanilla Raf from Goldstruck is my favorite coffee in the city but the *return*lary plight has left such a sour taste in my mouth, I can't even properly enjoy it.

Did we *really* just break into her loaded ex's million-dollar home? Well, not technically, because there was a key, but in all seriousness, I can't believe that just happened. My nervousness is rapidly boiling into something that more so resembles rage. How could she put me in that position? And worst of all, how could I let myself be put in that position? I'm furious.

Even so, for reasons beyond me, I can't bring myself to take it out on her. I hazard a guess; part of me must empathize with her. I mean, she was *traumatized*. Also, if I confront her and lose my job opportunity, I would have done this distressing thing for nothing. It *can't* have been for nothing. Especially if I'm going to have to spend the next seventy-two hours guzzling lemon water to flush out my impending blemish outbreak. The deed is done. Instead, I ask Perla why she's so fancy when she specifically told me to come dressed down.

"It's dumb, but just in case Paul returned, I wanted to look good," she explains. "To show him what he's giving up. I thought that if he saw me again, looking all dressed up and *bonita*, he would realize that he wanted to be with me." Perla sighs heavily and swipes a few rogue crumbs from the table. My heart breaks for her. "Thank you for helping me. I didn't know who else to turn to. All of my friends already think Paul *es un desgraciado*. You don't know him, so I figured you'd be the best one to bring along. It won't happen again. I hope this doesn't change the fact that you're interested in working with me? At the magazine."

Relief washes over me like a rainforest shower. She was temporarily insane. She didn't mean to put me in that position. Well, actually she did. But her bullheaded approach to the predicament is no doubt due to her having had to battle a ton of adversity to get to where she is today. A strong woman in a male-dominated field? She wouldn't be such a badass entrepreneur if she wasn't a little bit brazen in going after what she wants. She's not a bad person. She just . . . made a bad decision, had a lapse in judgement. She could easily claim diminished capacity. Besides, I could have said no at any time. It's just as much my fault as hers.

What really matters is that I helped her correct the situation, and that makes me feel good. So good that even my coffee is regaining its syrupy flavor. I take a languorous sip and strive to move on with my day.

Later, when Jessie comes to my apartment with Korean takeout and an ice-cold bottle of Saintly sparkling wine, I bury the truth of the day's events under a giant glob of glass noodles.

"Tell me everything! How was . . . what's her name again?"

"Perla," I offer, picking at a mound of kimchi fries.

"Right! Almost like your birthstone," Jessie says with a grin. "That's how I'll remember her name." She rips off a chunk of steamed beef bun, drenching it in hoisin sauce. "So? How was Perla? What's her place like? Did she have you working like crazy on the first day?"

"It was . . ." I drown my mouth in a swig of peachy wine. "Different than I was expecting but amazing! We definitely got down to business."

"I'm so happy for you, Mar," she burbles. "I mean, an actual magazine! You've been talking about this since we were kids. You *so* deserve this break." Jessie looks so unabashedly happy for me that I don't dare tell her the full story. I don't want to risk her doe-eyed judgement. Today was a one-time thing. It won't happen again, so what's the point of saying anything? I want this job more than I want a closet full of Jacquemus and I'm not going to let anyone, even my best friend, talk me out of it.

"Yeah," I agree. "I sure do."

Chapter Ten

L et me start by saying that I'm not obsessed. Enamored, defi-nitely. But not obsessed. I don't want anyone thinking that Oliver has a John Tucker-style hold over me, because that is *so* not the case.

However, it has been almost two weeks since we had mind-blowing sex, and I want it to happen again. Badly. I'm craving it. It's not like he's the *only* thing I have on my brain. Obviously, I'm focusing intently on my new job but he's taking up a sizable chunk of my thoughts. I feel like a lovesick teen sitting in my bedroom, drooling over posters of Jesse McCartney and Josh Hartnett, meticulously torn from *Tiger Beat*, and pinned to every spare square-inch of wall space.

Every time I look in the top drawer of my dresser and see that I'm missing a pair of black cotton hipsters, I'm reminded of Oliver all over again. I'm starting to wonder if maybe that's why he hasn't asked me out on an actual date yet . . . Maybe he found my granny panties and was so repulsed he decided right then and there he could never be sexually attracted to me. It's a libido-crushing thought. Although, we *have* been texting almost daily and why would he bother if he didn't like me? Even a little bit?

Regardless, what I need to do is get my underwear back so that I'll stop obsessing over them. (And him.) That's the plan: get them back as soon as possible so I can move on from the mortification that's attentively waiting on the sidelines, ready to attack my self-esteem at the first sign of their discovery. *I need* them back. One way or another I *will* get them back. It's just a matter of time.

Dating—or in this case, unattached intimacy—is a sick, twisted game of waiting. And waiting. And, you guessed it, more waiting. Well, I'm over it. I don't care if everyone says I should remain on standby until he asks me out. That is so passé. Why shouldn't a woman ask a guy she likes to go out? I've been waiting to find a good man for longer than I've been waiting for Rihanna and Beyoncé to get their acts together and record that album called *R&B*. Well, no more stalling. Time's up on this game. I'm seeing him tonight and that's all there is to it. Unless he's busy. I really hope he's not. There's only one way to find out. I send him a text before I can change my fickle mind.

Hey, Oliver! Free tonight? My fave sushi spot, Fins, is amazing. I promise it'll change your mind about seafood here . . .

Surprisingly, he writes back instantaneously.

I'm in! I'll reserve for 8? Meet you there?

I reread his text three times to make sure he didn't say no. Once I'm reassured that he in fact said yes, I start calculating my closet. What will I wear? I need something that will make him pray with every shot of sake to take me home and rip my clothes off. I know!

My sexy black halter dress with a pair of pointed knee-high boots and my powder-blue leather trench—the one Jessie borrowed that night—layered on top.

"Is the article almost finished?" asks Perla, glancing at me from the top of her Surface Book. I'm instantly beamed back to reality.

"Yeah," I respond after a short delay. "Just need to schedule the time for tomorrow, hit publish, and it'll be good to go."

I'm currently sitting in Perla's apartment at the lengthy rustic cherry table, our makeshift desk, putting the final touches on a piece about "7 of the World's Most Soothing & Eco-Friendly Spas." Lola is with me, which is beyond amazing. I hate having to leave her alone all day more than I hate finding villainous mushrooms in a supposedly mushroom-free dish. Now she gets to curl up at my feet while I write, edit, and schedule. There's even a little park around the corner from Perla's place that I take her to at lunchtime. In this last week, I feel like I've leveled up so hard that anyone who knew the old me would have to re-meet my new elevated self.

After the casual B&E, things went back to normal. Or they *started to be* normal, I guess, since we didn't really have a normal before that. Most days we work out of Perla's apartment—like she said, she's between offices—and a couple of afternoons we've gone back to The Rosedale Diner or Boxcar Social, which is a little bit further up the street. So far, things are going *really* well. See? I *knew* the incident at Paul's townhouse would be a one-off.

I've been set up with access to all of *Roam & Rove*'s accounts and I feel like a real, robust editor! I have my own bio on the website and everything. I'm also a real writer, social media content creator, and interviewer. Perla says that until she gets a "big-time cash injection" she can't afford to hire much of a team, so the two of us take on a lot of scattered responsibilities. She also has a graphic designer in Ecuador and a tech guy in Vietnam, but I think she pays them a fraction of what it would cost for her to hire them out of North America; she's keeping the costs lower than hip-hugging denim.

However, as it turns out, Perla likes her title of editor-in-chief more than she does the work. So, the lion's share of her tasks fall on me; she is excellent at delegating. I don't mind though because it means that I'm getting a lot of deadline-driven, firsthand experience. It's a lot, but I'm handling it in the fiercest way. Our social stats have already gone up and the clicks on my latest article—a guide to a luxury spa weekend in Montréal—were through the roof. Just imagine my expertise in a year from now. With all of this experience under my Salvatore Ferragamo belt, I'll be able to walk into any publication I want and get my dream job.

The only thing that's giving me pause is Perla's penchant for alcohol. I've become, unwittingly, her daytime drinking buddy. On most days, as soon as the clock hits noon, we're discussing what we want to imbibe later on. It's always posting schedules with a side of sparkling rosé or editorial brainstorming with a light-bodied Beaujolais. I've tried to tell her *no*, but she says things like, "Come on, *cariño*, you're not going to make me drink alone, are you?" And then I tell her of course not and usually opt for a small glass of *vino blanco* that I can slowly sip while she works her way through most of a bottle.

She says that she's still trying to process the whole Paul leaving her situation, and is it so wrong to need a liquid lunch every now and then to help her cope? However, I'm starting to think that these liquid lunches were a pre-Paul thing too.

"Okay, done," I tell Perla, breathing a sigh of relief. "What a week!" I'm about to close my MacBook Air when she stops me.

"Wait . . . Let's go over the weekend posting schedule once more before you go."

Oh my god. I admire Perla's dedication, I really do, but we already went over the schedule after lunch. Twice. There's only seven minutes left on the workday clock and I absolutely, no questions about it, must go home before my date with Oliver to freshen up and change into my dripping-with-sex ensemble. It's like my version of Carrie Bradshaw's naked dress but a little more modest. Just a touch. After all, he already knows what's seductively lurking underneath. And this time it won't be accompanied by full-coverage cotton.

Right now, I'm dressed in high-waisted black jeans with a smocked leopard tank top and faded cowboy boots. Technically I could wear this to dinner, but the dress would be way more satisfying—in more ways than one. Besides, I need to drop off Lola, give her dinner, and hop into a quick shower to ensure I'm buffed, shaved, and polished to my full potential.

"Didn't we already go over it earlier?" I ask innocently, even though I'm well aware that we did. It's hard to keep the blade of annoyance out of my voice.

"Yes, but I want to make sure I have everything written down correctly."

"I have to leave by five thirty, latest," I say firmly. "I have a date with Oliver tonight."

Perla looks at me disapprovingly. Her eyebrows raise as much as they can, which isn't much, but I can imagine the expression she's aiming for. "Margot, don't you think you're rushing into things with him? You only met him a week ago and you're already going on another date? What do you even know about him? My advice: make him wait." All these people with their unsolicited advice and their incessant waiting. I only met Perla a week or so ago, but she has no problem with me rushing things along with her.

"I'm not getting *serious* about him. And it was *two* weeks ago," I say. "Besides, a girl's gotta eat. He invited me for sushi." That's a lie, but she doesn't need to know that I was the one who invited him. She definitely wouldn't understand me asking him out. It goes against all of her macho morals.

"Fine, I get it," she concedes. "You have to use men before they use you. I've been through it one too many times before." She sighs heavily and picks up her phone. "Can you fucking believe that *pendejo* Paul is already posting photos of that *puta*? He just shared another one. Look." She thrusts her phone in my face, the screen bright with a photo of a fake-baked, black-haired woman relaxing on Paul's chubby couch. It's captioned, *Friday nights in with my lady!*

Perla hasn't been able to stop creeping his social media every hour on the hour since the scandal. Honestly, she needs to block him. Or he needs to block her, which I bet he would if he knew how much time she spends reloading his profile. She's completely consumed, stalking and scrolling until she complains to me about sore thumbs and hand cramps. Okay, I'll admit, if Oliver had social media, I'd probably, maybe, be doing the same. But I haven't been able to find it and I don't want to ask Perla for help because she will definitely lecture me again on rushing into things. Plus, in a world as overexposed as the one we live in, I believe that internet anonymity is the coolest thing you can possess. I'm constantly toying with the concept of deleting all of my social apps and going off the grid.

It takes a full thirteen minutes to run through the weekend calendar, refuse a glass of wine, and finally pack up Lola and my laptop. We get home expeditiously, thanks to one of those miracles that happens when transit actually runs on schedule. I strip, shower, scrub, shave, and begin to get ready. Despite my pre-date jitters, I'm oozing with confidence. I admire myself in the mirror as I securely knot the halter dress's ties around my bare neck. "*Hello, gorgeous,*" I purr to my reflection, channeling my best Barbara Streisand in *Funny Girl.*

Oh, baby. I am so ready.

***

Although tucked away in a narrow alley in between two of the busiest downtown avenues, Fins is easy to find. A neon shark lights up the façade in an enticing lapis glow. I walk up three steps to reach a double set of expansive glass doors. The interior is authentic yet modern, with that busy buzz and aromatic deliciousness in the air that all the best restaurants have.

Every time I come here, I feel like I've been transported directly to Kyoto. When I give Oliver's name, the kimono-clad woman at the entrance informs me that "my date" (*eek!*) is already seated at a tucked-away table for two and leads me over. The restaurant is packed—people on dates, business meetings, celebrations, family dinners. A massive open kitchen is the focal point of the bustling restaurant. As we walk by, I admire the chopping skills of one of the chefs, skillfully slicing through a piece of salmon as if it were softened butter. Suddenly it's like I haven't eaten in a decade. Everything looks beyond scrumptious.

"Hi," I breathe, shrugging off my trench. Is it just me or is Oliver even dreamier than before? We have one of those sublime private booths that everyone who's anyone *adores.* I once spent a New Year's Eve sneaking bottles of champagne into a private booth at a Japanese restaurant in Vancouver with Chantelle and a group of friends and flings. It was fabulous—until the next morning when we both ended up purging pieces of shumai. I feel a gag coming on just thinking about it. Not exactly the memory I wanted to reminisce on before my hot date.

Oliver looks up from a leather-bound menu and smiles warmly, his eyes scrunching and his dimple out in full force. "Hey, Margot, how're you going? It's great to see you again."

I'm inches away from sitting down just as he's getting up to give me a hug. We're caught in a sort of limbo, unsure of who should retract their action first. After a few lengthy seconds, he reaches across the table and I lean over, and we have the clumsiest hug of all time. How can we be so awkward here when we worked so flawlessly in bed? It should be mathematically impossible! Or maybe I just *think* we were flawless when in reality we were far from. The only way to find out is to do it again. Tonight.

"Great to see you too," I say with a sexy smile. "How's your week been?" I reach for a menu and begin to browse. His eyes are already feasting on my dress, but we need some real food too. Fashion can't sustain you forever.

"Good, good. Work is nuts. Really busy," he responds, distractedly. "How about you?"

I give him a quizzical but playful look. "Are you sure? You don't sound too thrilled for someone who just had a good, busy week."

"Well . . . Okay, it's been full-on," he admits. He self-consciously wrings his palms together. "I might have to go back to Melbourne for a little bit. Unexpectedly. My parents are getting a divorce. Sorry. I don't know why I'm telling you this." He attempts a laugh, stops, and looks away, flustered. The sounds of searing seafood and clinking glasses of icy cool Sapporo fill the air while I figure out what to say.

"Oh . . . I'm . . . that's . . . terrible," I manage after a pause. Not to discount his feelings or what he's going through, but this is *so* not how I pictured tonight. A therapy session? I don't have much experience in the divorce area, but I always figured that parents tried to keep their kids out of it as much as possible with all of that "it's not your fault" jargon.

"Yeah, I guess it doesn't matter how old you are, it still sucks when your parents split. So, I reckon I'll have to go help my sister sort some things out." He grins and shakes his head, running a hand through his tangle of blond waves. "I just found out about all of this a few hours ago, with the time difference and everything. But I didn't want to bail on you on our first actual date."

First of all, he confirmed this is a date. My heart is scream-ing. And second, we can definitely still salvage it. "It's all good." I smile and place my palm over his hand that's been unconsciously picking at the corner of the menu. "But I'd totally understand if you wanted to call it a night . . ." Please don't let him say he wants to call it a night. Let the record show that I only said that out of politeness.

"Are you joking? Without trying the food? Never."

"You're gonna love it," I gush. My heart is fluttering faster than Twista raps. "As soon as I walked through the door, I felt like I hadn't eaten for ten years. It always smells *so* good in here."

"Let's just focus on proving my theory about fish far from the ocean wrong. My family issues can wait. It's late in Australia anyway. Nothing I can do about it now." We lock eyes, smile, and I know we're having sex later. It's visceral. I have to give some credit to my dress and boots for making me more tempting than the tempura, but once they come off, it's game on. I think Oliver was correct when he said I'm not shy.

"Ready to order?" A waitress in a dark pink kimono with a pear-green sash has materialized at our table with a pen poised expertly over a small white notepad. We break eye contact and promptly pick up our menus again, scanning about five thousand different options. Should we order oysters? Nature's aphrodisiac. Couldn't hurt to have an extra dose of sex hormones coursing through us. Just to make sure.

"Uh—yes. I'll have the assorted spicy sushi set, please," I say. That's always my go-to order. "And a half-dozen oysters?"

"I'll get the teriyaki salmon bento with the sashimi appetizer, edamame, and shrimp tempura basket to share. Thanks," Oliver says as he returns our menus. "Hope you're hungry," he adds to me with a sly smile.

"I'm starving."

Oliver and I are hitting it off better than I could've imagined, even better than at Bar Lucía. We order a round of sake shots and easily flow through conversation, food, and another drink each. I tell him about my new job, conveniently omitting the part about Paul's house, and he fills me in on his Aussie upbringing and how he got the small scar on his temple from a surfing accident in Byron Bay as a reckless teen.

Clearly, he's impressed with the far-from-home fish because we scarf it down in record time. There is obvious sexual tension as we both reach for the last piece of maguro sashimi. It's the octopus tentacle all over again. This is too much to handle. I need this man *now*. In my head, I'm imagining all the things that will go down—including both of us, together, apart—when we get back to his place, but I'm also trying *not* to think about it too much because I have a virulent habit of building things up *way* too much in my head and then being disappointed when they don't come true exactly how I'd pictured it. Like my promotion at La Pêche. I'm desperate not to fall back into that Olsen-approved, espresso-guzzling, all-black outfit rut.

At long last, we've finished eating and are experiencing just the right amount of inebriation. When the bill comes, I offer to pay but Oliver insists—which, if I'm being really honest about, is a relief. I haven't received my first paycheck from *Roam & Rove* yet. I slip back into my trench and we're out the door.

"So, what now?" he asks as we arrive on the sidewalk. Our faces are illuminated by the restaurant's neon-blue mascot.

"I'm not sure . . ." I respond coyly even though I am *so* sure. I've never been more sure about what I want to happen next. I tuck my hair behind my ear and make eye contact with him for three solid seconds before modestly looking away.

"You could come over?" he suggests.

"Do you want me to come over?" I'm holding my breath. Thankfully, he answers well before I become *actually* blue in the face.

"Is that a rhetorical question?"

We lock eyes again, as if challenging each other to . . . I don't know what, but it's definitely a challenge. "Well, let's go then."

***

My not-so-naked dress is discarded on the floor on top of my deadly pointed boots as soon as we walk into Oliver's apartment. We're making out against the door frame, then the wall, and then the cognac-colored couch. It's shocking that we managed to keep our hands to ourselves the whole drive back. It only served to make these moments right now all the more delectable.

I've almost entirely forgotten about the spicy salmon of mere moments before. It must be the oysters. They worked like a charm.

He slips my lace-trimmed panties off and tosses them to the side. This time they remain out in the open, which will make things much easier when rounding up my clothing later on. Oh, who am I kidding? Tomorrow morning.

Oliver writes hit songs with his mouth all over my body. His tongue is seriously skilled, moving from my neck to my breasts, down to my bellybutton and in between my long, smooth legs. I've already gone triple platinum by the time he picks me up and carries me the short distance to the bedroom. I can feel his well-proportioned anticipation—hard, strong, and ready. We tumble down onto the bed, lost in each other's lips and limbs. His kisses feel like a gentle sea breeze and are more addictive than gin martinis. I'd consider giving up animal prints and thrift shopping just to feel his lips on me for the rest of eternity.

A condom appears out of nowhere, escapes its package, and slips onto . . . Well, we're ready to go. Safely. Responsibly.

Afterwards, we lie intertwined on top of the sheets. I think of us like a puzzle, each piece fitting together perfectly. But that's crazy! We barely know each other. I mean, I couldn't tell you if he loves eating mangoes on the beach, is hooked on murder mysteries, or if he sympathizes with Dexter Morgan, like I do. Still, my mind is blissful as Oliver brushes his fingers through my hair; it's such a comforting sensation. It's as if he *knew* all along that I'm a total sucker for that move. He kisses the top of my head, then gets up and pads his way to the bathroom, naked and irresistible. As much as I want to keep laying here, basking in the dewy aftermath, I have to execute my underwear mission.

Clandestinely, I crawl out of the cozy linens and crouch down beside the bed, peering underneath. I don't see them. Where are they? Maybe they're hidden in the shadows. They *have* to be there. Where else could they be? It's not like a pair of underwear can just get up and walk away on their own free will. It would be terrifying if they could.

"What are you doing?" Oliver has soundlessly reappeared in the doorway. He catches me on the floor, butt-naked, hand stretched under the bed, struggling to find my long-lost briefs. My face flushes a vivacious crimson.

"Oliver! I didn't hear you come back," I stammer. Thankfully, this time I don't bump my shoulder; that really hurt.

"Looking for these?" he teases, twirling my Jockeys around his index finger. *Oh my god.* I helplessly blink. I think I might spontaneously combust. Can you die from a shame overdose? Would it be acceptable to just run past him, out the door, and never look back? Who cares about my ludicrous underwear anyway! I can always buy new ones. How did he even find them?

"Um . . . well . . . kind of," I admit after an excruciatingly long pause. My face feels so hot, I swear if I looked in a mirror, I'd see myself engulfed in flames, burning alive like a California forest in the dry season. "How did you . . .?"

"Well," he smiles cheekily, "it's a funny story. You couldn't have known this, but I have a Roomba. So, I was at work one day and I got this notification on my phone telling me that something was caught in the bristles. I was 99 percent sure that I'd picked up my socks from the bathroom floor before I left that morning . . ."

Although I'm still undeniably mortified, I can't help but feel a disbelieving smile spreading across my face.

"I came home," he continues, "to find the Roomba underneath my bed with *these* stuck in it. They're definitely not mine, so I reckoned they must've been yours."

"Oh my god," I blurt, covering my face with my palms. I peek out at him from between my fingers. For a split second, we're both silent, staring at each other. Then, the hilarity of the situation sinks in and we both convulse in raucous fits of giggles. We're hysterical.

"I'm . . . so . . . embarrassed!" I barely manage to get the words out between heaves of laughter. Oliver slingshots my underwear onto the garment-burdened armchair that's stationed across the room. "Hey! Careful with those," I tease. "I don't want to lose them a second time."

"How did you lose them the first time?"

I sag back against the bed frame. "Well, to be honest, I was embarrassed that I'd worn my granny panties, and in the hurriedness of trying to undress, kicked them under your bed to try and save a shred of dignity. The next morning, I went to get them, but they'd somehow gotten too far away. I had to go *sans underwear in leather pants*! Do you know how incredibly painful and uncomfortable that was?"

Oliver laughs, looking so deliciously cute. "No, and I definitely don't want to find out."

"I genuinely thought that you weren't going to ever want to see me again if you happened to find them . . . which, apparently you did."

Oliver confidently takes the room in three strides and I know what's coming. (Me, soon.) He kisses me with abandon and I forget all about my underwear blunder. I like a guy who doesn't need me to squeeze myself into expensive strings like a roast at the butcher. But when I do, like tonight, it'll be better than bottomless mimosas at Sunday brunch and sweeter than a scoop of pralines and cream gelato on a sultry summer evening. Judging by the ferociousness of his kiss, Oliver is craving both.

When I wake up the morning after our sushi-turned-sex date, Oliver is in the kitchen making waffles from scratch with chopped strawberries and whipped cream; the kind from a carton, not an aerosol can. Am I still dreaming? This man is too good to be true. The scent of sizzling batter is intoxicating. Despite the fact that I gluttonized an entire ocean last night, my stomach roars loudly and I'm sure he can hear it over the sputter of the waffle mix hitting the piping-hot skillet.

I gently pinch myself. It's confirmed, I'm wide awake. Lazily, I stretch out of bed, wrap the slinky washed-linen sheet around me, and make my way out of the bedroom. Oliver's honey hair is tousled in the sexiest way ever. He's wearing a pair of soft fleece pants and no shirt. This is going to sound cheesier than a charcuterie board, but I feel like our *souls* were meant to meet. And

I'm not just saying that because he has Ryan Gosling abs. I truly mean it.

"Morning, sexy," he says, placing the breakfast spread on the rounded walnut table that inhabits a nook of the kitchen. I'm melting with hunger and desire. "How'd you sleep?"

"Perfectly. But I could really use a cup of coffee." I'm about to ask if we're going to go downstairs for those infamous iced coffees again when he envelops me in a sappy smooch and my sheet falls smoothly to the floor. Half of the whipped cream ends up on us, not the food, but I'm not complaining. On the contrary, I'm completely satisfied. Forget caffeine, waffles, and fresh fruit.

No one has ever tasted better.

***

On Sundays as devastatingly gorgeous as this, it's impossible for me to stay cooped up inside. I want to hear the birds chirping and the cars chugging along and Lola's almost inaudible sniffles as we mosey past patisseries and pasta specials. A nice, relaxing walk is just what we need. My phone vibrates in my back pocket with a text from Chantelle.

I'm returning a key to a building near your place. Lavender lattes at Empire?

I text her back that I'm on my way to meet Liao at Bickford Park and to join us there. And if she wants to pick up the lattes on her way, I'd be forever grateful.

"What did you do this weekend?" Liao asks me as he unclips Oscar. "Or should I say *who*?"

"Who else? Oliver," I say. Liao is the kind of person who expects you to move onto different men quickly and often. I've tried to remind him that heterosexual dating doesn't always work like that but he doesn't believe me.

He wrinkles his nose. "Still? Don't you get bored? When it comes to men, I have the focus of a fruit fly."

"Yes, still. I think it could be serious . . ."

Before Liao can retort with what I'm sure is very unsound advice, Chantelle appears with a cardboard tray of takeout cups. "Morning, babes," she sings. "I come with reinforcements."

We huddle under the dappled shade of a towering maple tree. I keep one eye on Lola while she frolics nearby. She begins to dizzy herself by swirling in circles a dozen times over; she's a peculiar pup. I reach into my coat pocket and prepare the biodegradable poop bags for the inevitable. Chantelle and Liao are itching to know everything about my new job and my first official week as an assistant editor. Just as I did with Jessie, I jazz things up a teensy bit and omit the unseemly details.

"You're working out of her condo? Why? Doesn't she have an office?" asks Chantelle.

"That's what I was wondering," Liao chips in. "She's paying you pennies and still can't afford to get a proper workspace? That seems like a red flag."

"It's not that she *can't* afford an office," I retort, a bit defensively. "It's just that she's looking for the right one. Besides, the goal is to move the company to New York. At least, part-time. That's what Perla and that Sidney Lalonde guy told me." Chantelle and Liao exchange dubious glances.

"Well, if she's serious, give her my card," offers Chantelle. "I have half a dozen really cute spaces available right now all across the city—*this* city—that would be suitable for Perla's magazine." She reaches into her embossed leather briefcase and pulls out a matte black business card with gold foil lettering.

As I tuck it into my coat pocket, I feel a surge of achievement that tastes almost as good as my lavender latte. Surely Perla will be impressed that I'm taking the initiative to find us a fabulous office—even if it is in Toronto. I'm feeling more a part of this publication every day. After all, *Roam & Rove*'s future is my future.

Chapter Eleven

After my conversation with Liao and Chantelle, I can't stop thinking about Perla's financial standing. How *is* she paying for everything? Can she really not afford an office? Is that why we're, three and a half weeks later, *still* working out of her apartment?

I gave her Chantelle's card but as far as I know, she hasn't called. When I handed it to her over a glass of sparkling rosé one evening, she coolly took it from me and placed it on the bookshelf in the living room without so much as a second glance. Every weekday since I've checked and sure enough it's still there in the exact same spot, collecting dust and uncertainty.

I've become a bit of a private investigator, inconspicuously gathering as much information as I can about *Roam & Rove's* behind-the-scenes action. So far, it's not much. I've discovered that we don't have a single paid ad campaign and the talks with investors that Perla has been having are just that—*talks*. Nothing is concrete and no one has handed over any sort of monetary life-boat. However, Perla's payments to me arrive on schedule. If she has no income, and she isn't a bona fide billionaire or trust fund baby like Paul, then how is the magazine still alive? How is she able to continue paying me? I can't figure it out. Although, as long as my dismal direct deposits—she pays me $3.50 above minimum wage—keep clearing, should I even bother with the details?

Perla twists the cap off of a bottle of blush-pink wine. "Let's toast to a productive week," she says jovially. It's just after six o'clock and her daughter, Paloma, is at a playdate until eight, so she wants to take advantage of her parental freedom. She sloshes the *vino rosado* into two long-stemmed glasses and hands me one. "*Salud, amiga.*"

We clink and take thirsty gulps; Perla finishes her first glass in a single swig and goes back for a refill. It's been a wild week—and we've still got tomorrow to go. I'd really rather head home and clamber into bed, but I'm determined to ask Perla about the magazine's office situation, and this is the most opportune time because I'll need a bit of liquid courage first. I meander over to the bookshelf. Lola, who had been sleeping at my feet, lifts her head curiously and follows me with her puppy-eyed gaze.

"Have you had a chance to call Chantelle yet?" I ask, picking up the business card and flipping it between my fingers.

Perla's demeanor hardens. "No, I haven't."

"Do you want me to set something up? I know how busy you are," I offer.

"It's fine," she says. "You don't have to."

"It's no problem at all. I talk to her all the time!" Lola bounds over to me. I crouch down to let her lick my free hand. "Wouldn't it be fun to go check out some brand-new offices together? *Roam & Rove* would be like a totally legitimate—"

"*Roam & Rove* already *is* totally legitimate," she counters, reaching for the wine bottle. I'm halfway through my first glass while Perla is heading for her third. I swallow a full mouthful in a feeble attempt to catch up.

"Yeah, I get that," I nod. "But I mean, having our own office would be—"

"Enough!" Perla roars, capriciously. Her face is mottled with contempt. "I already said no, so will you stop fucking pestering me about it? *Por el amor de Dios.* I already told you that I needed a big-time cash injection into the business before we can grow. How many ways do I need to say it? I'm not rolling around in disposable income here! I have *una hija* to take care of."

"Okay . . ." I say, slightly shaken. Why is she yelling at me? What did I do to provoke her? Lola is shivering behind my ankles; she's not used to loud, sound-barrier breaking voices. I pick her up, mostly to comfort her, but also to comfort me. The silence in the condo is heavy and awkward after Perla's frantic freak-out. Clearly, the money situation is more furtive than I thought. I'm relieved I didn't just ask her flat out or I might not live to reap the benefits of a career in the media that I'm so desperately seeking.

"You know," Perla says at last. "If we don't get an investment soon, I'll have to let you go." She looks at me with haughty disdain.

A jolt of panic sprints down my spine. You don't quite realize how tipsy you are until your boss threatens to fire you during a hazardous happy hour. My legs feel like spiralized zucchini. Are my ears playing tricks on me? She *can't* let me go! I'm so stunned, I can barely form an adequate response.

"Let me go? But . . ." Instinctively, I reach for my left lobe and begin fiddling with my gold hoops.

"Yes, Margot. Let you go." There's a sardonic tone in her voice. "As you might be aware, without a steady stream of something called *revenue*, I won't be able to pay your salary for long—let alone rent out an office! I was doing just fine on my own, and I'll do just fine without you and your ridiculous recommendations. Don't think you're not disposable, *cariño*." How Perla managed to make a candy-coated word like "cariño" sound like a death threat is beyond me. I feel like an invisible switch has been flipped and turned Perla from friend to ferocious foe, ready to bite my head off and cook me for lunch. "You can let yourself out," she says venomously.

Piping-hot perplexion prickles at my eyes. I do *not* want to cry in front of Perla but my salty tears feel like they're about to rebelliously burn their way out regardless of what I want. I grab my stuff and wordlessly make my exit. I'm about to dial Jessie's number, but decide against it. Should I call Oliver? No. Instead, I internally go over and over Perla's explosive behavior, wondering what I did wrong. Or if it was even my fault in the first place.

Life lesson #311: pay attention to how people make you feel about yourself.

The next morning, I wake up with what I conclude to be a watermelon of apprehension ripening in my abdomen. If I could stay tucked into the safety of my squishy bed and watch *Girlfriends* reruns all day, I would. But I can't. There's no way. I have to go and talk with Perla, now that she's hopefully sober and levelheaded. I have to convince her not to fire me—or "let me go" as she so blandly put it; like she was giving me permission to move onto bigger and better things without her.

Lola is thoroughly zonked after walking around the block five times, so I decide to leave her at home today. I grab a baby carrot from the fridge and hold it out in my hand for her. She sniffs at it before gently taking it into her tiny mouth. "Just don't chew it on the cow skin rug," I warn. As if she completely understands me, she patters away, fully content, and plops down on her bed. Good girl.

I take my time walking the couple of blocks from Summerhill station to Perla's apartment because the warmth of the early May morning is so luxurious—and I'm working out what I want to say when I see her. How should I bring it up? I don't want to seem accusatory, but what she said to me last night wasn't cool. I don't want to work for someone who dangles my career over my head like she's fishing for a Broadway-style reaction.

Speaking of Broadway . . . When are we going to New York anyway? For a job that's supposedly based in Manhattan, I spend a lot of time commuting between mine and Perla's Toronto addresses. Where's all of the travel that Sidney Lalonde boasted about? Los Angeles? Buenos Aires? Those trips seem as likely as Lauren Conrad and Heidi Montag actually moving on and making up.

After reciting my "Power Woman Mantra" seven times in a row, and feeling sufficiently reinvigorated, I enter Perla's buzzer code. No answer. I wait about a minute, then dial again. Still nothing. Where is she? Did I forget that today was a SPINCO morning? No. Maybe I should call her. The phone rings more than five times before she eventually picks up. "Morning, Perla! I'm downstairs. Buzz me up?"

"*Buenos días*, Margot. I'm not home at the moment," she explains. "I'll be back in ten minutes. You don't mind waiting, do you? I'll hurry. I lost track of time."

"It's all good. See you soon!" In order to efficiently murder ten minutes, I pop across the street to Nadège and pick up two Americanos and a box of assorted macarons. Parisian confections are sure to remedy Perla's drunken decision. I give the buzzer another go when I get back to her building but again, there's no answer.

Loitering outside like a fashion-forward creep, a woman wearing a fleece zip-up takes pity on me and lets me inside as she leaves to walk her chocolate Labrador. I head over to the plush sofa that lives in the corner of the lobby and wait. Where *is* Perla? Ten measly minutes turn into twenty and then thirty. My coffee is a dribble away from extinction and I briefly contemplate downing the one I got for Perla. See? This is why I am adamant about the office idea. If we had an official workplace, I could use my own electronic swipe card, let myself in, and get down to business.

You know, I consider myself to be a punctual person. I'm not talking about going to a party or for cocktails with your friends when it's acceptable and even *expected* to arrive fashionably late. But when it comes to my job, punctuality is key. In hindsight, showing up late to our first meeting was a strong indication of how seriously Perla takes her own business, not to mention, my time.

Irritation has since replaced my watermelon-sized apprehension of earlier when Perla, at long last, shows up. A papaya-colored Porsche zips up to the curb, perfectly in view from the lobby's glass door. Even through the glare of the windows, I can see Perla poised in the front seat. I squint harder, trying to make out the driver. Oh my *god*. Is that . . .? Sidney Lalonde? Perla leans over to kiss him and I choke. He seizes the opportunity to feel her up, clawing her lower back with animalistic longing.

Perla slithers out of the peppy two-door car and teeters into the lobby on her classic peep-toe stilts. "*¡Hola!* I'm a bit behind schedule. Did you have a chance to get any work done? Give me an update. Where are we at with social? And the 'Undiscovered Beaches of Venezuela' article?" She heads straight to the elevator.

I sling my tote over my shoulder, fumble for the macarons, and follow her inside. She jabs the button for the second floor. We could already be working if we took the stairs, but she always insists on the elevator. "Get work done?" I ask, puzzled. "No, I didn't have any internet . . . I figured we'd start once we got upstairs."

She gives me a look that makes me want to shrink back into the lobby. "You're not really telling me you just sat there for the last however many minutes and did nothing? What am I paying you for? *¡Dios mío!* Where's your initiative?" she says harshly.

It feels like she just knocked the wind out of me. Or at the very least, the sassiness. I should have drank her coffee. She doesn't deserve it. "Well . . ." I say cautiously. "You said you'd be here in ten minutes and I didn't want to get set up somewhere else and then have to pack up and come right back. Sorry." *Dammit, Margot*, I berate myself. *Stop saying you're sorry!*

"So now it's *my* fault?" Perla throws her hands in the air like she's swatting away a pesky mosquito.

"What? No. It's no one's fault," I backtrack. Maybe I should try and lighten the mood. "Was that Sidney I saw dropping you off? He is definitely looking to be seen in a car that color. Very snazzy," I giggle.

Perla doesn't join in. Instead, she turns away from me with the expression of someone who has been caught doing something mischievous. "*Sí*. It was. We had some . . . business details to work out. Over breakfast. I'm trying to get him to invest in the magazine. You know how badly we could use it . . ." She looks at me guiltily from the corner of her pink-shadowed eyes as we enter her apartment. "I think Sid could help us get to the level we need to be at."

Although it *clearly* wasn't just breakfast considering she's wearing the exact same thing she was when I left her place last night, I don't call her bluff. We're on shaky grounds and I still need to delicately confront her about the things she said.

"Speaking of investments . . . there's something I need to talk to you about," I say. "About last night."

Perla's posture becomes rigid. "What about last night?"

"What you said to me . . . about letting me go if we don't get an investment ASAP?" I search her face for any recognition of what I'm talking about, but she remains as blank as a leaf of printer paper.

"I never said that," she says. Seriously? Her memory flip-flops more than the $3 sandals I bought to wear to the laundromat.

"Yes, you did," I insist. "You don't remember?"

"Honestly, Margot," she says, moving to the kitchen and opening the fully stocked pharmaceutical cabinet. "How can I remember something that never happened?" She rubs her temples in circles, groaning. "I have a massive headache and need several Advils. I'm going to take a shower. You good to start on that social campaign we talked about? The one for the top five places to get a pisco sour in Lima?"

Perla Rivera, my ambiguous boss, is undoubtedly gaslighting me. But why? Why not just admit that she didn't mean what she said rather than deny the whole thing? Figuring out her motives is like trying to crack the Da Vinci Code. Does she really not remember? Ominously, I feel a massive headache coming on as well, but not from a rosé hangover—from the bludgeoning my mental health just took.

Sometimes, I think I *might* even miss the banality of working at La Pêche. Imagine that. At least Liao and I could spend every three o'clock snack time debating whether Versace's high-octane satin platforms are cute or crude.

Ten minutes later—a precise ten minutes, not thirty-three—I hear the shower turn off. *Eek!* I barely got anything done. I scramble to finish captioning the campaign images. *Dying for a seaside aperitif? This thatch-roofed locale has potent cocktails and panoramic views!*

"Progress check?" calls Perla from behind the bathroom door.

"Just captioning the photos," I respond. "Almost done."

"What?"

"Captioning the photos, but I'm almost done," I repeat, a little louder this time.

"Huh?"

"Just captioning the—" I turn around to yell in the direction of the bathroom and stop midsentence. *Oh my god.* Perla has emerged in a cloud of dispersing steam, and she is nude from her augmented nose to her ankles. Stark-*naked.* She has a towel wrapped around her head in a makeshift turban-like thing that looks *so* glam when Sophia Loren does it but that's about it. She's like Anna Faris in *The House Bunny*—tanned, taut, and exposed—but even more disrobed.

I'm fixated. Perla is a ghastly car crash and my eyes are glued to the wreckage. I fear that her nakedness will be burned into my retinas well into the afterlife, but at the same time, I can't look away. Remind me to start joining her at spin class if this is the body it achieves. She's *definitely* had her boobs done. Before, I thought it might just look like it because they're constantly in really supportive push-up bras, but now that they're out and free, they're just as perky as ever. Perkier.

Perla registers my flabbergasted look and waves a hand from her chin to her upper thighs. "You don't mind, do you? I need to do a load of laundry and wash my towels. This one is the only one I have left," she says, smirking and tapping the looped terry on top of her head.

I consciously pick my jaw up from my lap. "No, it's fine," I manage. "I was saying before that I'm almost done with the captions."

"Amazing. Let's go for lunch. Terroni? My treat. *Tengo hambre* and they have the best paninis. Paloma will be back soon anyway with the babysitter because it's only a half day at school. We have to leave now or she'll never let us get out of here."

***

I've come to appreciate my weekends more than I appreciate Kate Moss's weakness for leopard-print coats. The two dreamy days that I am away from Perla Rivera's apartment are just the elixir I need to make it through the next week.

Tonight, I helped—if you call sitting on a bar stool gorging myself on gin martinis and cheese cubes helping—Oliver cook a mouth-watering, semi-farewell dinner at his apartment. We started off with tomato basil bruschetta, and then his favorite dish, eggplant parmigiana, and for dessert? My body. No, I'm just kidding. We had ridiculously melty chocolate chip cookies from Le Gourmand.

The last few weeks together have flown by in a fiery, sexual, lust-filled haze, topped with just the right amount of romance, intellect, and whipped dairy. Homemade waffles are now just as much of a weekend tradition as meeting Liao at the dog park. Each day is more delicious than the last. I'm eating *well* and haven't gained a single pound. (Much to the disillusionment of my non-existent backside.) Thanks, in part, to our vigorous "workout" schedule.

Oliver and I have spent every possible minute we can in each other's company. Like Mýa said on *Moodring*, we have totally *fallen*. Dare I say . . . I think I could *love* him. One day. My grammy used to say to me that "when you know, you know," and I think I *know*. If that makes any sense at all. It's not like I'm trying to rush things or anything, but didn't every heroine in classic cinema fall in love with the leading man after, like, one day of knowing each other? Love affairs seemed so simple back then. Forgoing the sexist plotlines, of course.

According to my friends it's disgustingly cliché, but I feel like we've known each other for many meaningful months or years. I can even wear my Jockeys over to his place now and it actually makes him want me *more*. I'm not sure what that means on a scale of one to weirdo, but I'm not worried. The whole "Roomba

Ate My Underwear" scandal has become a kind of running joke between us. Sometimes I randomly think about it on the subway or at the grocery store and have to wolf down my giggles. My new mindset is, "You can't be embarrassed if you choose not to be." I'd ten out of ten recommend it.

I even let Oliver come over to my miniscule apartment one night—something I never thought I'd let any guy do. We ordered copious amounts of carb-saturated takeout from Trattoria Taverniti and ate it sitting on the floor in front of my coffee table while sharing a bottle of cabernet sauvignon. He said he loved my place, and even though I'm convinced he just said that to be nice, I appreciated it anyway. It must have been all of the Diptyque candles.

But now it's the night before he leaves back to Melbourne to sort out his parents' divorce. I still don't fully understand why he has to go . . . especially when his sister lives there. I'm chalking it up to him being the best son on the planet. Which makes me even more fond of him. He puts his family first and that's a fantastic quality for a man in this day and age to have.

"I wish you didn't have a flight to catch tomorrow," I pout, sliding the last plate into the dishwasher. My fingertips are covered in leftover tomato sauce and I rinse them under the kitchen faucet.

"I know, babe," Oliver says, coming up behind me and sliding his arms around my waist. "But it's only for a few weeks. I'll be back in no time." He plants a smooch on my earlobe, skillfully avoiding my chunky, geometric hoops.

We take our drinks—a third and final martini for me and a Boneshaker brew for him—to the living room and collapse onto the couch.

"What do you think I should do about Perla?" I ask him.

"About her midday streak or her shameless gaslighting?" He laughs.

"It's not funny!" I jokingly jab his bicep. "I'm serious. I'm worried about my job . . . if we don't get this investment from Sidney or whoever else, she could let me go. Although, maybe it was just something she said in the heat of the moment. Besides, she did say that she didn't remember it at all." I shrug.

"Do you honestly believe that she doesn't remember saying that to you? It's a pretty big threat to feign ignorance about."

"No," I admit, after a pause. "I don't."

"Well, there's your answer. How can you work with someone you don't trust?"

Chapter Twelve

In the two weeks since Oliver's been gone, I've visualized, manifested, and worked harder for my dream life than Emily Charlton worked for the Paris trip. Perla has been on her best behavior; like she's a new graduate from reform school. There have been no threats, no outbursts, no randomly popping out of the shower as naked as the day she was born. I can't explain it—and I'm not looking to try. It's a miracle, but I'm treading lightly. If I'm not careful, I could unknowingly step a sandal-clad foot on a secret landmine.

The back patio at The Rosedale Diner is thriving this afternoon. I've nibbled my way through the smoky cheeseburger and am washing it back with a heavily honeyed cup of joe. No matter how grisly I find the coffee, I *need* it. I was up *muy tarde anoche*—look, my Spanish is improving!—video chatting with Oliver. The colossal time difference between Melbourne and Toronto is detrimental to my beauty rest. Remind me to send him a bill for my eye serums and brightening potions. Once I run out of my freebie stash, that is.

What I'm yearning for right now is a tropical vacation. I'm editing an article about the best things to do in South Beach from one of our unpaid contributors, and all I can think about is how fabulous it would be to soak up the balmy Florida fervor beneath a rustling palapa while wearing a tiny triangle bikini and nursing a piña colada. The last thing I took resembling a vacation was a weekend with Jessie and Chantelle in Niagara Falls. In the winter. It was the most un-vacation vacation ever. The falls were essentially frozen, we lost money in that stupid casino, and there wasn't a hot guy as far as the eye could see. Not even on the New York side.

"Can I ask you a favor," Perla implores. Her forehead is as creased as I've ever seen it. Which isn't much. But I can tell that if she hadn't had a dose of fillers last Wednesday, she'd look somewhere between concerned and uneasy. Perhaps bordering on panicked.

I stop reading mid-sentence, yanked from my feverish reverie, and glance up from my laptop screen. "Sure. What's up?"

"You know how Chase, Paloma's dad, pays for her babysitter?" I nod. "Well, the truth is, that *hijo de puta* has to see receipts before he'll cough up anything. Like, lighten up. You're richer than Mario Lopez." She takes a sip of her black coffee and I'm wondering where this is going. "Usually, I get the babysitter to fluff the numbers *un poco* so that we can both make *más dinero*. While the magazine is still developing its long-term revenue stream, I need some additional cash to get by." She pauses, exasperated. I'm engrossed in the telenovela-style theatrics, but also wary.

"All of a sudden, Paloma's babysitter doesn't want to help me with the invoices anymore. She doesn't get how badly this *fucks* me! And after all I've done for her!" She continues. "So, I was wondering if you'd help me out this month? What I'd need from you is an invoice saying you babysat Paloma all week and charge a big, fat rate. Let's say, $50 an hour? Then, Chase will transfer the money to your account, and we can go to the bank together, pull out the cash for me, and skim a bit for you. It would just help me out *mucho*."

Is it just me, or is Perla seriously Machiavellian? I've never met anyone more devious. Her morals are looser than culottes. My brows are deeply knitted together, and my slicked lips are half-bitten in distress. To buy time, I bury my mouth in the safety of my mug. Can't you go to jail for creating fake invoices? Isn't it fraud? The closest thing I've ever done to committing fraud was repeating an outfit top-to-bottom that Kendall Jenner wore shopping on Rodeo Drive. I have to stand my ground. This is *not* going to be The *Return*lary Part II. I refuse to help Perla with her scandalous schemes.

I try desperately to adopt a sympathetic tone. "That's terrible," I say with as much 24-carat emotion as I can muster. "I'm just not sure that I'm completely comfortable . . . I mean, I feel bad . . . but I don't think I can . . ." My features are twisted in anticipation of a rude remark or a public debacle. However, Perla remains tactfully composed. She indulges in another sip of coffee before becoming reabsorbed in her computer.

"Just think about it," she says. "Anyway, let's wrap up this day so we can go out on the town. Sidney texted me earlier and said he wants to take us for dinner at this private, member's only lounge he belongs to. Are you free to come along?"

A night with Sidney Lalonde isn't exactly my idea of a night on the town, but I don't have any other plans. Plus, things are going so well with Perla lately—the invoice scam notwithstanding—and she's fun when she's not clothed in catastrophe. I just pray that we're not going back to Brussaux Society. "Yeah, sure. But I have to go home to feed and walk Lola first. I'll meet you there? Where is it?"

"Oh, I think it's off Bay Street somewhere. I'll just come with you. Paloma is sleeping over at friend's tonight anyway so I don't need to cook dinner for her. Besides, I want to see where you live."

My cheeks pulsate as if I've been slapped. I *do not* want her to see my place. After spending so much time at hers, mine is going to look worse than solitary confinement. Bringing Oliver there was scary enough. "Are you sure? I mean, don't you want to get changed or something? You'll be bored to death at my place! Really, it's easy enough for me just to meet you there. My neighborhood is on the polar opposite side of town from Bay Street anyway."

"Margot, don't be silly," Perla says as she starts packing away her Surface Book. "We'll Uber there and back. Your place could be in Buffalo and it would be just as convenient. Ready? *Vamanos.*"

What can I say? Prickles of embarrassment sting from my temples to my toes like I just swam through a reef of poisonous jellyfish. There's no way I can avoid going home and I can't think of a good enough excuse for her not to come with me.

We arrive at my apartment in record time. Isn't that always the way it is when you *don't* want things to speed up? If I could freeze time, I would. Nerves are thumping through my veins as we climb the Kilimanjaro stairs and approach my front door. My heart slows a pace once I hear Lola's padded footsteps dashing towards the entrance. Her eager pitter-patter is enough to calm even the most severe anxiety attacks.

"*Dios mío. . .* How do you *live* here?" We've barely stepped inside and that's Perla's immediate reaction. This is explicitly why I didn't want her to come over. Lola bathes my face with kisses while Perla showers me in shame. "Margot, I don't understand? This is the size of a decent walk-in closet, not an apartment!" Her unbelieving eyes dart around in horror, absorbing the coffee table, scattered houseplants, and bedside kitchen appliances. I know her place is ten times bigger and nicer, but she doesn't have to rub it in so ruthlessly.

"I don't live here because I want to, I live here because I have to," I answer, annoyed, scratching Lola's fluffy belly before loading up her dish with kibbles and refilling her water bowl. I've told Perla the story of Chris kicking me out a thousand times. This was all I could afford on a single person's salary in this city! I didn't want roommates, and this was the compromise I was forced to make. "It's not so bad once you get used to it. I like to think of it as . . . intimate." I only recently started to think of it as intimate after Oliver came over and that was only because *we* were intimate.

Suddenly, Perla is beside me, running her ruby-red acrylics over the metallic microwave. "Is this how you cook? *Dios mío.* I'm not letting you leave my house ever again without leftovers. You can heat things up, right? Are you eating okay? You can stay for dinner any time you want. *Pobrecita.*" Perla's demeanor gives me whiplash; she goes from insulting and judgemental one minute to motherly and nurturing the next. She's more unpredictable than Keshia Chanté's 2004 smash single.

"Thanks, Perla," I say. "I really appreciate that. But you know, even with a restaurant-grade kitchen, I wouldn't be much of a chef."

"Of course, you're like a daughter to me." Perla wraps her arms around me in a cloud of Escada's Flor del Sol perfume. I hug her tightly back. Embarrassingly, I feel a lump forming in my throat. She thinks of me like a daughter? Maybe it's the decade-old agony of losing my mom, but suddenly I feel a tidal wave of tenderness for Perla. She's not perfect, by any means, but I think she's *trying* to be a decent, hard-working woman. Well, most of the time.

I unhook Lola's harness from the wall and slip into my running shoes. "I just need to take Lola for a walk and then I can get ready to go."

"I'll take her," Perla offers. "You focus on getting changed. Wear something sexy!"

Now that the panic of Perla coming to my apartment has subsided, I'm feeling heady and positively fancy for tonight. I strip off my work clothes and toss them into my wicker laundry basket. Rifling through my wardrobe, I end up selecting a chiffon tank top with a silk—like Oscar de la Renta said, "silk does for the body what diamonds do for the hand"—midi skirt that's as white as the moon; the look is topped off by a calf-skimming pistachio coat. Even though it's almost late spring, there's still a bite in the breeze.

The front door opens just as I'm putting on a swipe of maroon lip stain. Lola comes bounding in, heading straight for her dinner dish to see if I've added anything else. She's out of luck. Perla hangs her leash while I glide into my square-toed mules.

"Ready when you are," I say.

***

The Dagmar Club is at the tail end of happy hour when we walk through the soaring oak doors. We're immediately met with a distinct, musky scent and dim lighting. Cathedral-style ceilings soar overhead while intricate crown mouldings anchor them to gold-painted baroque walls. We have to give our names to a perky redhead in a full tweed suit at the front desk and sign in before we can go any further. These members-only clubs are a world of their own.

I spot Sidney Lalonde as soon as we step into the opulent dining area; he's difficult to miss. He's sitting alone, smoking a cigar, and nursing a glass of brown liquor. (Similar to how I found him the first time we met.) Beside him, a bottle of Mumm Cordon

Rouge Brut has been plonked into a silver ice bucket, little beads of condensation dripping down onto a crisp white cloth napkin.

"Ladies, welcome," he greets us, spreading his palms out to either side of his bulky midsection which today is cloaked in a paisley-patterned Etro blazer, woven with a mélange of metallic threads. "I took the liberty of ordering us a bottle of the *very* good stuff. If I remember correctly, both of you gals are suckers for champagne."

"Big-time," Perla confirms.

Strictly based on first impressions, The Dagmar Club is members, men, and misogyny only. Looking around in bewilderment, I get the hunch that we're back in the 1800s and I should be wearing a corset cinched so tight my lungs could pop. Women are welcome as guests, but become a member? As if. I wouldn't want to join this club even if I could. It's stuffy, dated, and reeks of centuries-old, long-expired Creed cologne. The small amount of sunlight that manages to stream in past the heavy crimson velvet curtains sets the floating dust particles ablaze. Who would *pay* to come here?

I could think of a million things I'd rather spend my money on. For starters—structured blazers, books, a trip to Italy. Mark my words, one day I *will* drive a retro convertible along the Amalfi Coast while wearing a leopard scarf in my hair, mini sunglasses shielding my eyes, and my summer playlist filling the salt-infused air. Can you *imagine* Snoh Aalegra's creamy voice with a turquoise coastal backdrop? Suddenly, I'm annoyed to be here at the oppressive Dagmar Club instead of drinking martinis, getting a tan, and savoring spaghetti carbonara in Venice. But whatever, I digress. At least there's champagne.

As if peering into my thoughts but reading them completely wrong, Sidney asks, "Admiring the beauty of the lounge? Let's toast, to the two beauties sitting in front of me. I'm the luckiest guy here!" Luckiest creep, more like it.

Pop! The champagne cork goes flying in the direction of a man who's wearing a three-piece suit and a monocle over his left eye. He grimaces in our direction before turning back to his newspaper. Have I died and gone to Sherlock Holmes-era London? Sidney fills up our flutes and we clink them together in the center of the table.

"*¡Salud!*" Perla shrieks, taking a behemoth gulp as a server comes by and places three menus on the table. "We're starving," Perla announces. "Should we order?"

"Order whatever you want, girls," Sidney offers. I shudder at his use of *girls*. Perla is a middle-aged mother and I am a power *woman*! It's just as bad as Priya Khan's use of *girl boss*. Once, at a party *FASHION* Magazine was throwing for their latest issue, I heard her refer to Natalie Massenet as a *She-E-O* and I wanted to propel myself over the ledge of The Rooftop at Broadview Hotel. Luckily, the lure of the crispy crab cakes and miniature sundaes kept me from doing anything rash.

"Two cobb salads, a side of truffle fries, and more champagne," Perla demands as she winks at me and refills our flutes with practiced ease.

An hour later, we've finished eating and are slipping further and further into a bubbly bliss. We're well into our second bottle of Mumm and I sense that a third one will be procured. I'm feeling buoyant but critically close to going overboard. (Cue: Goldie Hawn and her fabulous zebra bathing suit.) I wonder if we can get some sparkling water?

Perla and Sidney have become quite openly touchy-feely. Which is odd since she looked so sheepish the last time I caught her kissing him in the papaya Porsche. I'm very much a third wheel.

"You really are something else, Perla Rivera," slurs Sidney, his glasses slipping slightly down his nose. After all, his happy hour started well before ours did and who knows how many brandies he tossed back before we arrived. "My *reina*. Did I say that right?"

"Yes, *mi amor*," Perla smiles as much as the fillers in her cheeks and lips will allow. Surprisingly, it's a pretty big and cheeky grin. "Sidney, you always know what to say to make me blush," she coos. She glances at me with a look that says, *watch and learn*. She twirls a lock of Sidney's peppery hair with her index finger. "Not to discuss business in the middle of a great time, but I have a favor to ask you. *Roam & Rove* is ready to take the next step, but we need an investment. You know I hate to ask, but . . ."

"Yes, Perla? You know I like a woman who gets straight to the point," he says. "How much were you thinking?"

Perla pretends to contemplate this. Of course, she's not the type of woman to give an exact sum and limit herself. "As much as you're willing to give. Obviously, the magazine will look great in your portfolio. Supporting small businesses *never* goes out of style." She smiles coyly, brazenly sliding her hand underneath the table to squeeze Sidney's thigh. I'm sure her lacquered nails are resting provocatively close to his . . .

She could be tossed out of The Dagmar Club for such suggestive behavior! I'm thirstily watching this scene unfold. What will happen next? Sidney's eyes roll back in anticipation. He's putty in her hands. But not really because something tells me he's getting *harder* than putty could ever dream of. I truly cannot believe what I'm seeing. Sidney fumbles, reaching into the interior pocket of his eccentric blazer. He's visibly shaken—and not in a bad way. But then he jerkily comes back to reality.

"Wait," says Sidney. "I have a proposal." There's a glimmer of rapid calculation going on behind his heavy spectacles. "If Margot agrees to go on a date with my son Julian, I'll give you as much money as you want. Within reason, naturally. I suppose I'll want to see some numbers—statistics, conversion, estimated return on investment, that kind of thing—before I sign anything as well. But that can wait until after. What do you say?"

I freeze, except for my eyeballs which flicker from Perla to Sidney and back again. They're both watching me fixedly. First of all, *Roam & Rove*'s "numbers" are crap. Second, I loathe setups. And I'm with Oliver. Sort of. Technically, we haven't had the "what are we" talk but I think it's safe to assume what we are: sexily and happily going with the flow.

"Margot?" Perla prompts.

Sidney refills my flute. "Just a date, you don't have to marry him," he chortles. "My son has been so depressed since his last girlfriend broke up with him, and I'm sure that wining and dining someone as pretty as you would do him good."

"Um . . ." I simultaneously luxuriate in the pale yellow bubbles and weigh the pros and cons of this *date*. Pro: it'll help us get an investment for *Roam & Rove*. Con: I have to go for dinner with someone other than Oliver. Pro: I'll be able to keep my job safe and make up for not helping Perla commit invoice fraud. Con: it's dinner with someone other than the guy I *really* like, possibly *love*. Pro: a girl's gotta eat and it would be a free meal . . . What's the harm in eating dinner in male company? I can just think of it like a business meeting. Strictly business. Risky business.

Sidney reaches back into his interior pocket and brandishes his checkbook. He lays it down on the table but doesn't acknowledge it further. Perla looks at the rectangular, leather-bound object longingly and then at me with supplicating eyes.

"Okay. I might be willing to go," I say hesitantly. "But I have a few ground rules."

"Atta girl," Sidney chuckles. "You should always, always lay ground rules before agreeing to anything in life." He turns to

Perla. "She's feisty, this one. I like her. But before we continue, I have to visit the little boys' room. Excuse me."

I wait until Sidney is out of earshot before turning to Perla. "This *date* with Julian has to be strictly business," I say firmly. "I am not going home with him, kissing him, or doing anything to compromise my relationship with Oliver."

"Of course, Margot, I totally understand. I don't want you to be uncomfortable, but this would *really* help us—and you—out, big-time," she says almost threateningly. "And to think, I was willing to fuck Sidney for the investment, but I guess I'm off the hook." I stare at her, bewildered. "I'm kidding!" She laughs gutturally, but something in her champagne-doused irises tells me that she wasn't. At all.

Chapter Thirteen

Sotto Sotto is humming. A purr of flirtatious chatter, overpriced intoxication, and background music fill the air with an infectious, upscale ambiance. I've never been here before—as if anyone on a budget has—and despite my reservations about attending this dinner, I'm excited to try somewhere new; somewhere that Oprah, Drake, and Brad Pitt have all dined before me. So glam.

Even if this restaurant is rich with old-world charm, at least Julian Lalonde doesn't have an affinity for private clubs like his dad. I'd take the deep-fried scents of McDonald's over the dankness of The Dagmar Club any day. Or the sleaziness of Brussaux Society.

Perla showed me a few photos of Julian on LinkedIn, so I'd know what I was walking into. You know me, I like to be prepared. From what I saw, I figured out three things about him: he uses Crest Whitestrips religiously, he's solely responsible for keeping American Crew hair products in business, and he must spend six days a week at the gym. Although he did look pretty cute in his pics—in a high-maintenance kind of way—I'm not interested in him *like that*. This is strictly business. Get in, get out, get an investment.

Oliver knows I'm meeting Julian tonight. I told him, not to get his permission, but to be totally transparent about the whole thing. He said that he reckons I bend too much to Perla's will, but that if I needed to do this for my job, then it was my decision. So, here I am. Perla is thrilled that I'm meeting Julian. She's already begun crunching numbers to let Sidney know what amount to make the check out for.

I'm fashionably late as the hostess leads me to the table. I feel a seed of anxiety begin to grow in the pit of my pelvis and I wobble just slightly on my pointed-toe leopard sandals. The idea of pimping myself out for an investment is growing increasingly grotesque, but at the same time, it's not like I'm *doing* anything—even if Julian is handsome in an Adrian Grenier type of way. Besides, any chance of a meaningless fling has been tainted by the fact that I'm here on business and I have a *sort of* boyfriend. Not that I'm even entertaining the idea whatsoever. The only thing that's troubling me is not knowing if Julian knows this isn't a real date . . .

He's wearing an immaculately tailored suit—my guess is Tiger of Sweden—with a crisp white shirt unbuttoned just a touch too low. His swept-back hair is so black it's almost blue and he has the cerulean eyes to match. Splotchy stubble covers his sharp jaw and his skin exudes the kind of glow you get from sunbathing on a yacht.

"Julian?" I ask as I plop my miniature purse on the table. He sets his glass of red wine down and gets up to greet me.

"You must be Margaret," he says. "My dad has told me so much about you."

"Margot," I correct him. His comment piques my curiosity. What did Sidney say? I can't imagine it being anything other than, "she's a feisty but pretty little thing!"

Julian winces. "I'm sorry. I'm the worst with names." He eyes my exaggerated sleeves—they remind me of fluffy fashion clouds, like the ones that Lauren Bacall wears in *Designing Woman* but a little less humongous—before appraising the rest of my ruched minidress with approval. "Great dress," he says. "Nordstrom?"

"Oh, thanks," I say. "No, thrifted, like, a zillion years ago." His compliment sounded quite natural and not creepy at all; I'm not getting much of a resemblance to Sidney. This apple fell so far from the tree, it ended up in a fresh-baked crumble. *Yum.*

"Merlot?" he asks, reaching for the wine list. "We could share a bottle?"

"Actually, I'd love a gin martini."

We order drinks and enough cheese, meat, and sourdough appetizers to feed a table of twelve. I'm pleasantly surprised at how effortless it is to talk to Julian. My posture is relaxed, I have an easy smile on my face, and by some miracle I've managed *not* to get the assorted fruit mustards on my voluminous sleeves. We're discussing our favorite Julia Roberts rom-coms and when I bring up *Pretty Woman*, Julian gets an amused look on his face.

"That movie always reminds me of my dad and Perla Rivera," he says.

"Why?" I ask, spearing a hunk of Parmesan with a toothpick.

"Just how they met," he explains with a raised brow. "Perla was a lot worse off than Vivian when she blundered upon my dad . . ."

I accidentally inhale my martini and it whorls down the wrong way. I lapse into a coughing fit. Classy restaurant-goers gawk at me. I like being the center of attention, but not for sputtering into a platter of cured chorizo.

"Here," Julian offers, pouring from the bottle of mineral water. "Have some of this."

I take a substantial swig and clear my throat. "Sorry," I apologize. "That just . . . caught me off guard." I don't know why I'm surprised. I've come to realize that in order to date—or even be seen with—Perla, a man must fit into one out of three categories, preferably all of the above: disgustingly rich, over the age of sixty, or owns an expensive sports car and/or summerhouse. Sidney Lalonde has it all. Check, check, and checkbook, please.

"Perla dated my dad for a while," Julian continues. "Right after my parents split. I always thought she might have been the reason it didn't work out between them, but my dad would never admit it. He is completely infatuated by her. He's got a thing for Latin women."

Well, that I could've told you.

"Anyway," says Julian. "I know my dad set this whole thing up for Perla's magazine or whatever."

"You *know*?" I'll admit, I'm relieved.

Julian laughs. "Yeah, it's not the first time he's tried to send me on a blind date with ulterior motives."

"He said that your girlfriend broke up with you and you've been depressed ever since." Then, feeling insensitive, I add, "Sorry . . ."

Julian shakes his head. "I haven't been depressed, I've been footloose and fancy-free!" He engluts his red wine. "I'm gay but my dad either doesn't know or doesn't want to know. He probably wishes I was a better wingman."

Wait, what? He's gay? I mentally rewind the evening; his impeccable appearance, complimenting my dress, knowing Julia Roberts's filmography better than I do. My *gay*dar has completely failed me. As a matter of fact, it's pretty nonexistent even on a good day. The first time I met Liao I thought he was straight. He laughed so hard he almost gave himself an aneurism when I confessed that to him a few months later. Suddenly, it's like a lightbulb has gone off inside my brain. Maybe I could set Julian up with Liao! They would make such an attractive couple; the envy of gay men everywhere.

Julian's phone rings. "I'm really sorry," he says. "But it's business. I've gotta take it." He excuses himself from the table and makes his way outside. I snatch this opportunity to soak another slice of bread in olive oil and indulge in the last chunk of smoked *queso*. I think this might be the best non-date I've ever had.

When he returns, Julian has an apologetic crease across his forehead. "I hate to cut the evening short, but I've gotta run. I hope everything goes well with the magazine! I've taken care of the bill, so take your time." He bends down to peck me on the cheek. "And Margot? Just a word of advice: watch your step with Perla. From what I've heard, she can be pretty ruthless when necessary and you seem like a good person."

His words haunt me as I finish my second martini. Part of me thinks he's being overdramatic, but deep down I know that he's not. I've seen glimpses of her ruthlessness up close and personal. But if I continue showing up as my best self, working hard, and helping to grow *Roam & Rove*, I think I'll be safe.

Weaving my way to the exit, I'm so distracted by my thoughts that I almost don't notice the new hostess. She must have just come on shift. Is that ...? No. Way. It can't be ... But I'd recognize that hay-field hair anywhere. Slicker than an oil spill, the overhead lighting casts an ethereal halo on top of her head.

I stop dead in my tracks. "Gia?"

Gia Johnson turns her head and I swear, she's in slow motion like a Pantene Pro-V commercial. It really is her. Her snooty demeanor says *guest* but her uniform screams *staff*. "Margot," she gapes. "What are you doing here?"

"Well, I just finished having the most fabulous dinner and cocktails with a gorgeous guy," I boast. Gay or not, she'll never know. "The real question is, what are *you* doing here?" I give her a Manhattan once-over, like she's done to me on countless occasions.

Her cheeks flush scarlet, overpowering the dusting of bronzer she has on. This might be more shocking than my non-date's perilous warning. I don't think I've ever seen Gia blush or be at a loss for words before. This is all the dessert I need—but do I feel like having the chocolate mousse or a sliver of homemade cheesecake? Before I have the chance to fully revel in my choice, her embarrassment evaporates.

"What does it look like I'm doing here? I'm working. Obviously. You still aren't that perceptive, are you?" Ring the alarms, the bitch is back.

I dodge her venom like I'm auditioning for *The Matrix*. "What happened to your promotion?"

Her eyes narrow. "Your little stunt that you pulled, that's what," she hisses. "Your comment about the bumbleberry scrub and the extended lunch breaks really screwed me. They didn't have proof of course, but they found other reasons to fire me. Not that it's any of your business. We're not even friends, what do you care?"

I don't care. Not really. Gia has been so awful to me, to everyone, over the years that I'm reciting a silent invocation that maybe, just maybe, she's finally getting a taste of her own medicine. I'm not a vengeful person, but enough is enough. Although, it seems that when Gia fell from grace, she brought her signature, spiteful vernacular in a carry-on suitcase. She hasn't been humbled in the slightest.

"I know you don't believe me," I say. "But I'm sorry to hear that. I didn't want them to fire you too. I just wanted that promotion."

"Too? You weren't fired," she spits. "You quit. There's a glaring difference." Her angelic features morph into something monstrous, like the vampires in *Buffy*. What I wouldn't give to slay Gia once and for all. "That was your own stupid, reckless choice. That, and those heinous pants you were wearing. I hope you trashed them along with your career."

Of course she had to bring up the pants. Just when I'd finally deleted them from my recent memories. "Well, that's not exactly what—"

"Are we done here? I have a job to do." Gia straightens a stack of menus and blows a tuft of hair from her face.

There's nothing left to say so I push through the door and make my way down to the sidewalk. As much as I want to completely ignore Gia's remarks, I can't help but wonder if she's right. Did I senselessly sabotage my own career? Toss it into the trash? Not only did I ruin my promotion, I ruined Gia's too. Does that make me just as bad as her? I always held myself to higher standards than she did, but now I'm not so sure I succeeded in being the bigger person. I must have been given the wrong directions to the high road.

I'm strolling down Bloor Street, seeking comfort in the cacophony of the city, when Jessie calls. I don't really feel like answering but I've been neglecting our friendship lately. Things have just been so wild with Perla that when I have free time, all I want to do is take Lola for a walk and people watch from my ginormous window. I haven't even been to Angelo's in over a month! This weekend, Chantelle has planned a mandatory brunch date for our foursome, and I'm very much looking forward to spending quality time with my friends.

"Hi, Jess," I say. "Guess what? I just went on a fake date with a really hot gay guy."

"Pardon me?" She sounds authentically shocked. "Do you mean Liao?"

"I'll explain at brunch. This story will do better with a full audience," I laugh. There's a long pause. Long enough for me to wonder if the call got disconnected. "Jessie?" I remove my phone from my ear to check. Still connected.

"Bryce and I had a major fight," she says miserably. "The kind that I don't know if it's possible to recover from." It's awful of me, but I can't help the tiny prick of excitement that jolts me to full captivation. I've known for years that Bryce is as desirable as rancid breath. But if Jessie finally sees that too, I'll be over the moon with joy. She trusts him to a fault. The sooner she can get rid of him, the sooner she can start to live her best life.

"Do you want to stay the night at mine? I'm heading there now," I offer.

"I'm already downstairs," she admits. "I'll see you soon."

As I scan my metro card and head down into the dingy depths of St. George Station, I've all but forgotten about Julian's warning and Gia's cattish remarks. My sole focus now is my best friend and her splintered heart.

***

Jessie ends up staying at my place for two nights. Which is fine by me; I've missed our hangouts more than I initially realized. We order Vietnamese takeout, belt out the lyrics to "The Boy is Mine," and mix the meanest martinis of all time. Bryce has been calling nonstop but I've hidden Jessie's phone in a pair of my snakeskin boots so she can't be tempted to answer.

We've developed a new "Power Woman Mantra" of her very own. It goes like this: *You are worthy of someone other than a brute like Bryce. When you open yourself up to new possibilities, you will attract someone hotter than Regé-Jean Page. You are meant for more than Bryce's lying, cheating ass.* So far, I can't tell if it's been effective or not, but it did get a laugh out of her between sobs.

When she told me what happened between them, I felt like a fashionista about to sit front row at a Givenchy show for the first time. The excitement was *real*. Relief pulsed through my arteries, but I tried to mask my merriment under a veil of sympathy because Jessie has been there for me through all of my Chris drama, my mom's untimely death, and everything else I've gone through since the days when we were both obsessed with *The Proud Family* and Dunkaroos.

Long story short, Bryce was so overprotective of Jessie all of these years, accusing her of things she didn't do, because *he* was the one doing them himself. She found a sordid thread of messages on his computer with racy photos, illicit texts, and vulgar videos. Apparently, Bryce liked to keep digital souvenirs of all of his conquests. It was the cold, hard proof she needed to finally be as convinced as I've been since the very beginning. They had a hurricane-sized blowout and Bryce punched a hole through the wall. Thankfully, the lease is under his name so he'll be responsible for that damage.

We're due to meet Liao and Chantelle for brunch in two hours, but Jessie has sworn me to secrecy about the breakup; she's not ready to get into the details in public yet.

She's currently sprawled across my bed, slurping a turmeric lemonade and flipping through a stack of gossip magazines she bought yesterday afternoon. I'm more of a *Harper's Bazaar* person than *HELLO! Canada*, but even I'm finding it entertaining to discover how celebs are "just like us"—Meghan Markle holding her baby sans nanny, Rosie Huntington-Whiteley at a farmer's market, Jessica Simpson picking a wedgie.

The buzz of my oscillating fan and Lola's rhythmic snores are the only sounds until Jessie yelps. She sits bolt upright, holding a copy of *People* an inch from her face. "Margot! What is Oliver's last name? Tell me immediately!"

I look up from painting my toenails with OPI's Big Apple Red. "Thompson. Why?" She leaps from the bed and excitedly thrusts the magazine in my face. A headline reads: DRAMA DOWN UNDER FOR THOMPSON TYCOON. I quickly skim the article like I'm doing a word search puzzle, noticing certain text popping out at me: nasty, net worth, divorce, millions, prenup, void. It all sounds very scandalous, but I don't know what this has to do with Oliver.

"How could you not tell me that your Oliver is also Oliver Thompson, son of Peter and Sherry Thompson, the Australian mega-millionaires?" Jessie shrieks.

She's not making any sense. Obviously, there's some mistake. I turn my concentration back to my shimmering red nails and glide the polish brush over my big toe. "Are you sure it's even the same Thompsons? I'm sure there are tons of Thompsons in the world."

Jessie wordlessly flips the page and points to an inset photo showing three people caught walking up a sprawling set of steps. I read the caption: *Sherry Thompson arrived at the courthouse on Monday alongside her son Oliver, 30, and daughter Joanna, 24.* Okay. There's no denying that. Gossip magazine or not, that's an undeniable fact.

"Oh my god," I say, agog. "I didn't know!" My whole body tingles and I feel quite breathless. This is *massive.* Why wouldn't Oliver tell me about his family? Were there any clues? His apartment is nice, but I just assumed that most people who work in tech with six-figure salaries had nice apartments. His wardrobe is normal—plain T-shirts, jeans, sneakers, sometimes a knit beanie when it's cold—nothing that screams, *Look at me, I grew up rich!* He always offers to pay when we order in or go out, but I thought that was him being chivalrous.

"Mar, come on," pleads Jessie. "You're dating the son of one of the top one-hundred richest men in the world and you didn't know? He never casually dropped it in? You guys are more inseparable than Gigi and Zayn. No pillow talk?"

"What do you expect him to say? 'Hey, babe, how are you? FYI, my family is so rich I don't know how to spend it all. Think you can help?'" I roll my eyes skyward.

But seriously . . . How did I not know? Was I supposed to guess? Suddenly, heading home for the divorce drama makes more sense; particularly if they're as high-profile as *People* is making them out to be. Is this why I couldn't find him on social media? I take a closer look at the photo of him at the courthouse. He looks so dreamy, even in a pixelated thumbnail. I feel a pang of longing. I miss him. Thankfully, he's back next week.

"What are you going to do?" Jessie asks. She's taken the magazine back to my bed. "You *have* to ask him about it."

"What would I say?" I suddenly feel restless—like I need to go for a run. Maybe there's a reason he doesn't want me to know. Does he think I'm too . . . poor? That I wouldn't understand? Or that I would try to gold dig him? Newsflash: I chase *goals* not GICs.

Jessie shrugs. "Just text him and say you saw him in *People*."

"No way," I say, horrified. "I don't want him to think that I'm stalking him!"

Jessie looks at me through hooded eyes. "Okay . . . but someone on that level most likely has Margot Robbie on speed dial . . . just saying."

My mind swirls with images of supermodels, caviar, and 1 percent tax brackets. How can I possibly compete with that?

***

Lady Marmalade is on the complete opposite side of town from my apartment, so Jessie and I are sweating off our scrupulously applied makeup on a fossilized streetcar, traversing along Queen Street East. I reach for a tissue inside of my woven pearl purse and blot a bead of moisture from my forehead. It's only the end of May but this heat is more like the middle of August. The humidity is giving me more of a glow than I bargained for.

Liao and Chantelle are already cackling over fresh peach bellinis when we walk in the door. "They better have preordered two
of those for us," I whisper to Jessie as we sidle up to the table. The
four of us embrace, clamor about our head-turning outfits, and
perch on the edge of our respective chairs. Liao snaps his fingers
and another round of drinks appear. He's been sleeping with our
server on-and-off for the last year. Apparently, today, they're *on*
but we're not supposed to know that.

"You guys will not believe what happened with Perla . . ." I start.

"Sister, please. You just got here, and you already want to start
talking about that damsel in distress?" Liao quips.

I eyeball him, unimpressed. "Liao . . . come on. She's my boss.
And this is really juicy."

"Well, spill it already," demands Chantelle, sassily tapping her
lengthy maroon-colored nails on the table. "As if we have all afternoon." Actually, we have nothing *but* all afternoon, but I decide
not to correct her.

I recount the story of The Dagmar Club, Perla reaching
underneath the table to feel Sidney up, and then asking him for
an investment. I told Jessie earlier so she just sits and listens. "So
then," I say. "Just as he's about to write her a check, he says that he
has a proposal."

"A marriage proposal?" Liao snorts. "Tell me he did *not* put a
ring on that conniving woman's greedy finger!"

"No . . . he said that he would only give her the investment if
I went on a date with his son! Can you believe it?" I reach for my
fizzy bellini.

"What about Oliver?" Chantelle asks. "Aren't you guys, like, the
real deal?"

Jessie gives me a look and I know she's dying to tell them about
Oliver's millionaire status, but she's going to have to wait. "Well,
I had some conditions. And I talked about it with Oliver and he

said if it was for work, then I should do what I thought was best,"
I say. "But he also said I do too much for Perla."

"You do!" Liao and Chantelle say in unison. Did they plan
that? Jessie nods, as if to agree with them, but stays taciturn.

"Guys, it's my *job*," I counter. "Anyway, I *did* go on the date but
it turns out—"

"Ready to order?" asks Liao's current conquest. I swear, servers
always come to the table when you're either in the middle of a
really buzzy story or you've just taken a massive mouthful and
can only enthusiastically nod when they ask how everything is
tasting. "What can I get you?" Jessie and I settle on peameal bacon
Benedicts, Chantelle orders blueberry pancakes, and Liao sticks
with his go-to spinach omelette. We also request another round of
bellinis; heavy on the bubbles, light on the peach purée.

"Hold up," says Chantelle. "You're dating Oliver, but went for
dinner with this Sidney guy's son so that he would give money
to Perla for her raggedy magazine? Help me make sense of that.
She's a textbook *user*."

"And abuser," adds Jessie. "She's really not paying you enough
to put up with her shenanigans."

"Was the guy cute?" Liao inquires. "Cute enough to make up
for Perla's instability?"

Chantelle scowls. "Li, that's not the point. Perla is essentially
treating her like an escort."

"No, she's not," I say defensively.

"She is," Chantelle reiterates. "She's totally unstable! And she
still hasn't called me about an office. Honestly, I don't think she's
interested. Which is why I wanted to let you know . . . I just leased
a pop-up space to someone from *Toronto Life*. I can put you in
contact, if you want? Maybe they have a lead on a job opening?"

No way. *Toronto Life* is tempting, but I didn't work this hard
just to jump ship now and go work somewhere else. It's precisely

because I've put up with all of the antics that I need to stay at *Roam & Rove*. What is my next job going to think if I have a three-month blip on my résumé? No, I have to stay with Perla for at least a year. I swallow. *Oh, god.* Just saying it in my mind makes me wary. A whole year of bizarre behavior and flagrant favors? Perla Rivera makes Jack Torrance seem even-tempered.

"Thanks," I say. "I'll think about it. Anyway, let me finish the story." After taking a sip of my nectarous cocktail, I continue. "My so-called date, Julian, told me some wild things about Perla and his dad—like how he thinks she might be the reason his parents separated . . . but in the end, it was very much a non-date because he turned out to be gay!"

Liao comes to full attention. "Did you get his number?"

"Yes . . ." Really, is that all he is thinking about? And with his lover across the room?

"She literally broke up his parents? She's more trifling than I thought," muses Chantelle.

I ignore her comment. "But it's what happened afterwards that is so outlandish . . ." I pause to let everyone marinate in the suspense. "Gia was working there as a hostess! I thought the martinis had gone to my head and I was seeing a mirage of lip gloss and gilded hair. But it was really her."

"Oh, this is too good," says Jessie. I'm not sure if she's talking about the drama or our food, which has just been placed on the table. It does look exceptionally good.

"The one from your old work?" asks Chantelle. She looks at me, then Liao. "Well, your current work," she adds to him.

"That's the one," I confirm before facing Liao. "How come you didn't tell me she was fired—which she claimed was all my fault. Also, she insulted my pants. Again! I scarcely made it out of there unscathed."

"I rarely look in her direction," he says with a shrug. "She's like a solar eclipse—you can't look right at her or you'll go blind, and I have too much beauty in the world left to discover. Yvette must have kept everything reticent. I had no idea she wasn't around." He turns pensive. "Now that I think about it, I guess it has been rather scandal-free around there. I miss the drama."

"Well, go make yourself a reservation at Sotto Sotto then because she hasn't changed a bit. She was still as bitchy as ever." I stab my fork into my poached egg and its gooey center floods the accompanying home fries.

"A leopard doesn't change its spots," jokes Chantelle.

"I resent that. Leopards are beautiful," I say, lifting a heaping forkful to my mouth. "Gia is . . . more of a . . . tarantula! Or a snake."

"How about, snakes don't change their scales?" offers Jessie. If we were the Plastics, she would unquestionably be Karen Smith. Thank *god* she doesn't have any cousins.

"Except that they do," points out Chantelle, laughing. "This is hopeless!"

We all try to come up with an accurate analogy to describe Gia's unrelenting bitchiness, but in the end decide that we're wasting too much time on her. Today is about us, day drinking, and brunch. I'm relieved to have moved on from discussing Perla's fast and free moral compass—it's always pointing directly south towards sin, schemes, and shameless trickery.

I drain my flute, putting my skepticism out of my mind. "Who wants another bellini? I'm parched."

Chapter Fourteen

June is the most delicious month. It tastes like juicy mangoes and icy martinis. Not only is it the best part of the Gemini season, but it's the initiation of poolside prosecco, strapless tops, and ceviche on the patio in Kensington Market. Of course, my birthday is also in June, but that's not the only reason why I love it—I swear. Even if I am brimming with excitement that my friends are finally going to meet both Perla and Oliver at my birthday drinks.

By the way, Oliver is back! He arrived late last night. Once again, I have a brand-new lease on life. I'm emphatically itching to ask him about his riches-to-rags bluff, but first . . . sex. I ingest my daily vitamins, hop into a borderline tepid shower, moisturize, and head over to his apartment with Lola bouncing in tow. She almost seems more elated than I am.

In the time since Sidney Lalonde became the sole investor in *Roam & Rove*, Perla has shed any rancorous rumblings about revenue and has been as effervescent as a cloud of champagne. We've worked hard, and celebrated harder. Whoever said money doesn't buy happiness obviously never wrote Perla Rivera a check.

We went for lavish libations at Leña immediately after she deposited the money and I felt like we were both relieved to be once again thriving career-wise. Perla has been so easygoing that I've come to terms with sticking around with her for a full year. Maybe longer.

I mean, if *W* Magazine came knocking, I wouldn't falter to open the door and invite them in for a martini. However, the chances of that happening seem slimmer than the linguine straps on my cowl-neck dress—but it would be wonderful.

A single step through the door is all it takes for Oliver to fasten his luscious lips to mine. *God*, I've missed them. My pelvic floor spasms with readiness. I resolve to make my heart grow fonder with short, sweet absences more often. But not *too* often because I still have needs. Lola sprints to the couch, jumps up, and promptly goes to sleep. We continue to the bedroom and close the door. I have a hang-up about Lola witnessing anything . . . indecent. And we are about to get outrageously indecent.

Subsequently, I'm glowing with a translucent layer of sweat. I imagine if I tried to get up at this very moment, I might collapse to the ground like an overcooked soufflé. So, I think I'll just stay put. Can we normalize being quiet post-sex? It's so delicious to just lay here and stare at Oliver's devastating profile. We stay like this, lolling in the residual heat, for a solid five minutes before Oliver breaks the silence.

"I missed you heaps, Mar." His scratchy chin is nuzzled into my neck.

"I missed you too." I run my fingers through his labyrinth of chest hairs. I love doing that. "I'm so happy we exist at the same time."

He chuckles. "You're weird. But I am too."

We leisurely force ourselves from the bed. I slip on my underwear and one of Oliver's T-shirts before sliding onto the couch beside Lola. She stirs, slowly blinking her eyes open, and begins to lick my dampened skin. Oliver moves to the kitchen and after looking in the barren fridge, suggests we order pizza for dinner. I wholeheartedly agree, but only if we get extra pineapple and a side of cilantro garlic dipping sauce.

"So, how did everything go? Back home?"

"It was . . . interesting," he says ambiguously. "Not exactly my idea of a happy trip, but it was good to see my family."

"Speaking of your family," I say, taking the reins of the situation. *Giddyup, Margot.* "I have to tell you something." Oliver looks mildly concerned but he's fixated on me. I wonder if he has a hunch of what's coming. "I saw you in *People* with your mom and sister. There was this whole write-up. Jessie showed me."

Oliver runs a hand through his Bondi Beach-style waves. He comes to sit beside me. "I hate gossip magazines," he says with slumped shoulders.

"Same," I agree. There's a nanosecond respite. "But why didn't you tell me . . .?"

He sighs. "To be honest, when I first moved over here, I was on a sort of family sabbatical, I guess you could call it." He looks at once culpable and relieved that the cat's finally out of the bag. "I was trying to work things out for myself—forgoing the silver spoon that my parents have been intent on feeding me with my entire life. I wanted to achieve something on my own. So, I mentally left all of that behind in Melbourne."

"I get that," I say. What I get is that if we were in *Roman Holiday*, he'd be Audrey Hepburn and I'd be Gregory Peck. "Still, there's nothing wrong with accepting help from the people that love you."

"Fair enough. It's just that when I've tried to date in the past, I've never known if women like me for me or for my dad's burgeoning portfolio," he admits.

"Well, if it's any comfort to you, I fell in lo—" I halt myself. *Oh my god.* Was I just about to tell him that I'm *in love* with him? A surge of adrenaline swells inside of me. What is wrong with me? My spine straightens and I quickly look away, distracting myself by scratching Lola's doughy belly.

"What's that?" Oliver says, a smile as long as the Gold Coast stretching across his face. "Were you just about to . . ."

"Stop!" I screech. "I wasn't about to say anything. Just that I liked you for you without having a clue about your dad's influence on the Dow Jones."

Oliver being rich doesn't have any bearing on my affection for him. That part is just the icing on top. And lucky for me, icing is my favorite part of any dessert.

***

"Refill?" Perla asks, flaunting a half-empty bottle.

We're sitting in her living room sipping flutes of sickly floral-scented rosé. It reminds me of melted Jolly Ranchers and the thought makes me gag. It stenches of old-fashioned perfume; the kind my great grandmother kept in a decant on her antique dresser. "No, thanks," I say. "I'll be drinking later, so I don't want to have too much now." Thankfully, I'm meeting Jessie and Chantelle for cocktails and live music at Mrs. Robinson tonight.

"*Más para mí,*" Perla sings. She's in an exceptionally good mood. I'm suspicious. With every sip of rosé, she becomes more animated. "So . . . I have a big-time proposition for you."

My thoughts immediately go to break-ins, babysitting scams, and non-dates. What could she possibly ask me to do this time? Rob a bank? Murder someone's self-esteem? Have a threesome with her and Sidney Lalonde? (Ew. I would *never*.) Hesitant but curious, I say, "Oh, yeah? Tell me more."

"Now that Sidney has given us that *muy grande* cash injection, I think it's time . . ." She pauses. "To start looking for offices in New York City! Will you go with me? *¿Por favor?*"

All of a sudden, this nauseating rosé is the best thing I've ever tasted. I can't help but beam with excitement. *Finally!* I was beginning to think that the whole "based out of New York" thing was just a marketing tactic for the magazine; something to impress readers and potential investors. My mind flashes back to that car I saw all of those months ago with the Empire State licence plates outside of my place. Is the alternate universe coming back to pick me up and take me to my fantasy city? Did I finally manifest this into existence? It's taken long enough.

"Are you serious?"

"*Muy serio,*" says Perla. "I've been giving it a lot of thought. I know you gave me your realtor friend's card ages ago, and I'm sorry I never called her, but it just didn't feel right to look for an office here. Who wants to be a Canadian business? Not me. We need to establish the brand in Manhattan. It's the only place to be!"

"I couldn't agree more," I say ecstatically.

"We'll have so much fun," Perla continues, refilling her flute for the second time. "Just you and me, businesswomen in the big city. I was thinking we could rent an apartment, work during the day, party at night. You know I lived there for almost ten years, right? I have a lot of friends who would love to show us a good time. Of course, *Roam & Rove* will pay for everything. *Todo incluido.*"

I feel a mist of elation spreading over me. You can't just *tease* this kind of stuff to me. My hopes are already higher than the Rockies. Mentally, I'm sorting through my wardrobe, highlighting any ultra-cool outfits that I should pack. I have to emulate an aesthetic as fierce as Chloe Bailey looks on any given day. *Fiercer.* What about my off-the-shoulder mauve minidress? Also, elongated palazzo pants for a casual day. Definitely some kind of power suit and my pinstriped trousers, criss-cross sandals, and chunky leopard belt.

"Count me in," I say. I drain the rest of the flamingo-colored liquid that fills my glass. It was *almost* worth the empty calories.

"Amazing! I'll start looking into flights."

"I'm so excited, Perla!" I unstick myself from the sofa, and grab my oversized, double-breasted blazer from the rack by the entrance. "Thanks for the happy hour—made even happier by our new plans." I sling my canvas tote containing my laptop, cardholder, and matte black LARQ water bottle (best hydration investment, *ever*) over my shoulder. Lola is soundly sleeping in her fuzzy little bed and I bend down to tenderly scoop her up.

Without warning, the front door swings open and I jump back, startled. Lola squirms in my arms, rudely awoken. It's Paloma, home from her after-school care. It must be after six thirty already. I lost track of time with the excitement of Manhattan and my internal wardrobe prep.

"*Margot,*" she cries, hurling her backpack onto the floor and tossing her coat in the opposite direction. Paloma is the definition of boisterous. "I'm sooo happy you're here! Can I play with Lola? Hi, Mom. What's for dinner? Can I play with her now?" Paloma loves me, but she loves Lola even more—much to Lola's loathing. She's one Maltipoo that despises children; she's too delicate and sophisticated.

"*Hola, mi hija preciosa,*" Perla coos. "How was your—"

"Fine, Mom, whatever," Paloma interrupts before turning her focus back to Lola who is now trying to paw her way up my chest and onto my shoulder. Any little bit to get away from the busy hands of this grabby child.

"Paloma Estrella Rivera, don't you *ever* interrupt me like that again!" Perla's face is suddenly raspberry red. "I was asking you a question. If you keep up this attitude, I'm throwing your iPad out the window and you're never going to see it again." The tendons in her neck are throbbing and her breathing is heavy. She's like a bull, ready to charge. And it all happened in a mere millisecond.

Both Paloma and I freeze. Even Lola stops wriggling. Paloma's eyes instantly well up with tears and I feel hopelessly bad for her. Even if her response was pretty bratty, she's just a kid. Perla should try more placid parenting. There must be another way to adequately punish Paloma's attitude. A time-out? No television? Grounding?

"Mom, no! You can't! You wouldn't," she shrieks, her eyes bigger than Alexandra Daddario's. She spins around to look at me, pleadingly, as if I have any control over what her mom does.

"You think I'm joking?" Perla whips around and beelines for Paloma's bedroom. She rips the iPad from the charger, almost knocking a porcelain Virgin Mary statue off the shelf at the same time. "*¡Por el amor de Dios!*"

"I think she's kidding," I whisper to Paloma, but I'm not sure she hears me over her wails. I know they say holding onto anger is like drinking poison or whatever, but there's something sinister about unleashing your fury on your kid. Poor Paloma. I contemplate giving her Lola to play with but quickly squash that thought. There's no sense in punishing Lola as well.

Perla is now at the sliding glass balcony door, fumbling with the lock. She's ranting in Spanish and this is another example of a time I wish I knew how to speak the language fluently. It's like I'm watching the climax of *Las Juanas*. This situation is escalating *muy rápido*.

I fake a cough. "Perla? Not to interfere, but I really need to head out . . ."

Abruptly, she snaps back to reality, stopping in her tracks, halfway outside between the living room and the balcony. She turns around, a pained expression is spanning her taut face. "Come here, *mi Palomita*. Mom is sorry. What do you want for dinner? *¿Qué quieres?* Anything you want, *preciosa*. Margot, do you want to stay and eat with us?"

"I'd love to," I lie, crossing my fingers behind my back. Although I'd like to be able to console Paloma, this scene was far too tense for me and I'm dying to escape. "But I have drinks with my girlfriends, remember?"

"Of course. Get out of here! Have fun." Perla's complexion is slowly fading back to its typical unbleached-silk hue.

Paloma looks like she might burst into hysterics again. "No! But I didn't get to play with Lola! I really wanted to play with her! Mom, you promised me this morning." Fat drops pool in the corners of her eyes.

"Next time, *mi amor*," Perla assures her, handing her the iPad.

I awkwardly inch towards the front door, holding Lola tight. Thankfully, Paloma is immediately engrossed and she doesn't put up any more of a fuss about us leaving.

"See you on Monday, Perla. Have a great weekend."

"*Ciao, cariño*," she says. "And start thinking about *Nueva York*—where you want to go, what you want to do. We'll be there before you know it."

We couldn't get there soon enough even if we arrived yesterday. I can't wait to tell Jessie and Chantelle about this new development.

***

My head almost explodes with excitement every time I think about *finally* going to New York.

The first thing I'm going to do when we land is seek out the city's best Manhattan cocktail; they're not my favorite, but I figure, *when in Rome!* Then, I'm going to pop into Grimaldi's for a slice of pepperoni pizza, browse as many secondhand shops as I can find, and snap an exorbitant amount of photos. My camera roll will rival @badgalriri's. And I'm going to do loads of work, of course. Work is why we're going. Obviously.

Even though my friends have all tried to warn me about establishing more than a "working relationship" with Perla, I hope they'll understand why I can't just turn down an all-expenses-paid trip to Manhattan. It's not like we're going on vacation together. This is a *work* trip. The truth is, they just don't understand Perla and everything she's had to go through to get to where she is today. I don't think either of them could fathom how hard it is to start a magazine from scratch while raising a daughter on your own.

Strutting down College Street, I feel just like Kate Moss looks on any given catwalk. My kitten heels whack the pavement with every sassy step. I contentedly swing my beaded wrist-bag around a couple of times and narrowly avoid hitting an elderly woman to my right. Okay. Time to reign in the overexcitement.

Mrs. Robinson is livelier than Coachella; sixties funk is ricocheting off the gold and emerald art-deco décor. I squeeze and squish my way in through the entrance and search for my friends, buried amongst the throngs of stylish revelers. There! I see Chantelle, sitting on a blood-red, crushed velvet booth near the middle of the lounge. Hundreds of vintage records fill the shelves from her shoulders to the ceiling.

"Hey, girlfriend," she says as I reach her. She's swathed in magenta silk from head to toe and looks unequivocally confectionary; especially against the venue's vivid jewel tones. Chantelle's taste in fashion is valiant and expensive. "Jessie says she's running five minutes late, which we all know means fifteen."

"How did you miraculously snag a table? It's insane in here."

"I may have slept with the owner once or twice," she winks. "Before you judge, just know he is *very* hot."

We peruse the drinks menu. I settle on a Dancing Queen while Chantelle chooses the Smooth Criminal. We order a Rose Red Sangria for Jessie's imminent arrival. A waiter boogies towards us and takes our order.

"Hey," says Jessie, breathlessly. "I'm here!" She ensconces herself in the booth, and immediately reaches for her sangria. "You guys know me so well," she moans, lifting the glass to her bubblegum lips.

Now that they're both here, it's time to reveal my big news. I recount the story of the invitation to New York and Perla's plan to officially rent an office there. I throw in the iPad incident for shock value, which, in hindsight, was a terrible idea. My nearest and dearest don't think this trip is good news at all; I can feel it. They haven't said as much—yet—but judging by how quickly they guzzle their drinks, it's what they're thinking.

"Okay, let me hear it," I prod. "What aren't you saying?"

"It's just that . . . I mean, how well do you really know Perla? Besides just the regular work stuff," questions Jessie. "Is she someone you'd really want to travel with? Just you and her?"

"You know my thoughts already," adds Chantelle. "She's a pain in the Brazilian-lifted derriere, who abuses the shit out of you and subjects you to her anger outbursts on the regular. I'm calling it now, you're going to regret going away with her—business, pleasure, or otherwise."

I'm about to protest but Chantelle continues. "First it was asking you to scam her baby's father with fraudulent invoices. Then it was sending you out on a 'non-date' with her sugar daddy's son. Now, she tried to throw her daughter's iPad off a freaking balcony? She's instability personified."

"Why don't we go to Manhattan together in the fall?" offers Jessie. "It would be so much more fun to not have to be there for work anyway."

I gape at my girlfriends with furrowed brows. They totally are not seeing things the way I see them. "Come on," I plead. "Forget about those small things for a second. It's New York. My favorite city on the planet. Don't you think I'd be a fool not to take a free trip?"

"I think you'd be a fool to go," says Chantelle bluntly.

Jessie tries to soften the blow. "You have to do what feels right for you. But I think you'll go crazy after twenty-four hours with her. Usually by five o'clock you're exhausted and dying to get out of her apartment. If you're staying together, you won't have anywhere to escape to."

"I know that. But this is different. It's a good opportunity. It could be a fantastic learning experience for me."

"Yeah, to teach you that things are going to get wild, scary, and scandalous before that plane even lifts its wheels from the tarmac," Chantelle warns. She finishes her drink and gives me a cautionary look over the top of the glass. "And what about a work visa? Is she sponsoring that? How are you going to legally work from there?"

"She's right, Mar," chimes in Jessie. "And what about Lola? Is she going too?"

Guilt chews me up and swallows me whole. I hadn't even considered what would happen with Lola. I feel like the worst dog mom ever. "Lola is small enough to be carried on a flight so I'm sure it'd be okay for her to come." I desperately hope. "As for the work visa . . . I'm sure Perla has a plan. We're only working there part-time anyway. We probably don't even need one. You guys just don't know the whole story," I attempt to convince them. "You only know what I've told you, which is usually the drama because it's saucier to explain and makes for a better happy hour tale. I rarely tell you about all of Perla's good qualities and all of the things she does for me."

Chantelle gives me the skeptical look that she's mastered down to an art. "Okay then, tell us. What has she done? Because all we know is that she's a short-fused, raggedy ass psychopath with a blatant disregard for manners of any kind."

"You guys are being really harsh," I mope. "I don't want to talk about it anymore. I'm going, and that's all there is to it." I start fidgeting in my seat, all of a sudden uncomfortable in my tiger-striped sundress. I could tell them that Perla sees me like a daughter and that I'm becoming attached to the idea of having a pseudo-mom in my life. Or I could tell them that she makes sure I have food when I'm at her apartment and more often than not sends me home with leftovers. But my lips remain sealed. I don't want them to hack apart every shred of positivity I'm clinging to.

"Mar," pleads Jessie. "We're just trying to be honest."

"I think I've filled my honesty quota for the day." I know I sound immature, but they're annoying me now. Why don't they see that this trip will be the best thing that's happened to me since I grew out my bangs? It's an all-expenses-paid foray to the city of my dreams! That should cancel out any and all red flags. This trip is an investment in my future. I'm vigorously building the life I want to live so that I can kick back with a lemon-twisted martini and enjoy it later. Isn't that obvious?

Manhattan, here I come. Whether my friends like it or not.

Deep down, buried under my foolhardy optimism, I have a tingling feeling that they might be on to something . . . But, like I said, they just don't know Perla like I do. She's had a tough life. Not to mention the fact that she's a single, working mother! Of course things are going to be hectic every now and then. My girl-friends just don't have enough compassion for the struggles she's fought tooth and nail to crawl her way through.

"Well," I begin. "Perla is coming to my birthday drinks next week so you guys can get to know her in-person."

Chantelle raises a flawlessly threaded eyebrow and Jessie sips her sangria in tacit compliance. I hope inviting Perla wasn't a mistake, but it's too late to uninvite her now.

***

It's safe to assume that I'm fully under the spell of intoxication. I've consumed two and a half martinis and nearly a third of the Mother of Pearl platter which materialized in front of us over-flowing with oysters, shrimp, smoked salmon, lobster, snow crab biceps . . . I could go on. But I'd rather resume my party.

Things are going swimmingly. We have a coveted corner slot on the rooftop at The Chase and a canvas umbrella is shielding us from the . . . oh, wait. Where did the sun go? It must be later than I thought. The city has taken on a tangerine glow and the wispy breeze ruffles my white wrap skirt. I have a lilac leopard tank top on and thin-strapped sandals in the same hue; the kind with the little loop around your big toe and enough height to get me *that much* closer to Oliver's kissable pout.

I'm dreamily looking over the glass balcony at the sprawling city. We're quite literally lost in a concrete jungle. But I love it. I don't think I could live anywhere with less than 2.93 million people. One of my worst nightmares is to be a big fish in a small pond. I'm wincing just thinking about it. I'm also reaching for another slippery oyster. I plop it into my mouth and it glides down my esophagus with ease.

Every move I make is setting me up for my future move to Manhattan—which is why I feel lightheaded every time I think about mine and Perla's upcoming trip. We're leaving in just under three weeks and we're staying for one month. A whole month! I can hardly believe it. The only catch is that the apartment Perla rented isn't dog friendly. I was devastated when she told me, but

Liao offered to look after Lola. He said it will give Oscar a stern glimpse into life outside of being a spoiled only child.

Well, there's another catch too: Oliver and I will be apart, again. He only *just* got back. But it's okay. He might pop down for a couple of weekends. I refuse to be the kind of woman who would give up an opportunity as enormous as this one to stay home and fret about a man. Oliver understands that about me.

"Who do I have to fuck to get another drink around here?" Perla spreads her arms apart, sloshing her sparkling rosé on Liao's beige chinos. He grimaces. Jessie hastily hands him a napkin. How long have I been dreamily gazing at the view? The previously swimming ambiance seems to be sinking faster than an anchor tossed overboard.

"What?" Perla flouts, looking around at my friends and their aghast faces. "I'm only kidding. *¡Dios!* When did this generation get so serious?"

"So," Chantelle says. Her mossy eyes are pinpointed on Perla. "It seems like Margot is doing a lot more for your magazine than she originally anticipated."

Oh my god. I can't believe she just said that. I'm catapulted into high-alert. "She just means that I've got lots of interesting responsibilities," I explain to Perla. I emit a high-pitched laugh and englut my martini. This is bad. I should have known the two of them together would be a disaster—Chantelle's prior disdain for Perla notwithstanding. Neither of them have the kind of personality to back down in a confrontation.

"Are you saying she's overworked?" asks Perla, glowering at Chantelle. "That she can't handle it? That I'm too tough on her?"

"No, I'm saying that—"

"She's saying that I'm learning more than I thought and it's been great!" I prematurely add. I'm like Chantelle's personal translator—from accusatory to acutely sorry.

Perla softens like a leather jacket after years of wear. "What about you, Jessica? What do you do?"

"It's just Jessie," she says. "I work for Mejuri. The jewelry company?"

"Right," says Perla. "Well maybe we can think of a strategic partnership between that brand and my magazine. Something like . . ." She drifts off. "Travel-ready accessories?"

"Arrive at your destination ready to slay?" Liao offers.

Jessie looks sheepishly at me and then Perla. "Yeah, that could be cool . . . it's just that I don't really have a lot of say over what collaborations happen and stuff. That's a different team."

Perla narrows her eyes. "If you don't want to be a part of my magazine, you can just say so. You don't need to make excuses. I can handle it."

"No," gulps Jessie. "It's not that, it's just . . ."

Oliver diffuses the tension. "So, who wants cake?" He nods towards the bar and a waitress is heading our way with a creamy mango cheesecake, set ablaze with half a dozen sparklers. I'm salivating. "It's your favorite," he whispers in my ear. He kisses my cheek and I feel a pang of appreciation for him. Velvety slices are divided between us and the thorniness is extinguished. By the end of the night, Perla's ability to function has deteriorated—thanks to three too many rosés—and she launches herself into an Uber without saying good-bye. No one grieves over her sudden departure.

Later, when Oliver and I get back to his apartment, he unwraps me from my clothing (the power of miniskirts) and I unwrap a present from him: *Kate: The Kate Moss Book*. I'm so excited I could faint. It's only been a few months but he knows me so well already. It's going to look incredible on my coffee table with my vintage *Vogue*s. "Thank you so much," I gush, slinging my arms around him. "I love it more than I loved my birthday cake and those squishy oysters and the martinis!" He paid for the entire night, as part of my gift.

Shyness washes over Oliver's face. He takes a deep breath. "I love you."

It feels like any tangible emotion has been knocked right out of me. For a second, I can hardly breathe. Then, I relive the moment at Bar Lucía when he first told me I was pretty. "Can you repeat that, please? I don't think I heard you correctly," I say with a smirk.

"Okay," he smiles. *Ugh, those dimples!* He's definitely remembering that moment too. "I love you, Mar."

"I love you too."

That night when we have sex—or *make love*, whatever you want to call it—it's like angels are singing, we're skinny-dipping in the ocean in our own secluded cove, and all of the galaxies in the universe are twinkling in rhythm with our every move. Oliver tastes like citrus groves and salted caramel. I never want to leave this bed.

***

"I think you should be *cuidado* with those friends of yours," Perla warns me the next time I see her after my birthday. "They don't seem too thrilled with your recent success. I think they're jealous. And jealousy can be *muy feo*."

I am agog. Be careful with my friends? I agree that jealousy is ugly, but what is she talking about? My friends aren't jealous of me, they're the most supportive people I know. Plus, they always tell me the brutal truth, even when I don't want to hear it. "What do you mean they're jealous?" I ask.

"Chantelle was giving me off-putting glares and Jessica spoke *dos palabras* to me all night. They're rude. As for Owen . . . or was it Omar?"

It's not lost on me that she doesn't answer my question. But my naked curiosity about what she's going to say about my beau keeps me from pointing that out. "Oliver. And what about him?" My defense mechanisms are revving up. Now that we're openly in love, I feel more protective of him. Jessie, Chantelle, and Liao had nothing but rave reviews for Oliver. He's been fully anointed into our close-knit circle. (Perla, on the other hand, not so much.) Liao even wept that "all the sexiest singles are straight" and that I am a very fortuitous female for finding him. Technically, he found me, but whatever. That's not the point.

"Be careful of him," Perla says. "I know his type."

"His type? What? The thoughtful, romantic, ultra-sexy type?"

Perla scoffs. "I have more experience with this than you do, Margot. Or do you think that you know better because you're young and carefree?" Her tone of voice indicates that she wants a challenge. "Do I need to remind you about my *desgraciado* ex? And I don't mean Paul."

She's referring to Chase, Paloma's dad. I'm not arguing that he's a sad sack loser because he totally is. Apparently, she didn't know until she was eight months pregnant that he was married. And if that's not bad enough, it gets even more deplorable. He refused to meet Paloma until she was five years old because, after having three kids with his wife, he didn't want to have to deal with diapers again. He sickens me to my core. Poor little Paloma.

However, just because Perla had a truly horrible experience with *one* (maybe two or three) guys, she thinks that all men are instant trash. Ultimately, I think that's why she chose Glade bags for Paul's clothes . . .

Oliver is *nothing* like Paul or Chase. Or Chris, for that matter. Or Bryce! Oliver is the kind of guy that I wish I could have introduced my mom to. I was hoping for a more maternal evaluation from Perla, but what can you do? My friends adore him.

And I hold their opinions higher than the Statue of Liberty holds her torch.

Chapter Fifteen

Mark my words: it's going to be a sexy *señorita* summer of self-care, affluence, and success.

I've always aspired to be a woman who wakes up every morning and loves what she does for a living—and now I do. Or at least I have these past few days, knowing that New York City was beckoning me with every sleep. Manhattan is the oyster I've always daydreamed about, and I can't help but give into carbonated feelings of ecstasy.

I'm a glittering champagne bubble as I reach for the door at Angelo's. One thing I have missed from my old life is having the time and energy to read multiple books per week. I've been so inundated with interviews and blog posts and social media campaigns since I started working for Perla that I've only just finished the novel I bought the last time I was here. The old-fashioned bell dings and I feel a burst of nostalgia.

"She returns!" Angelo booms, heaving himself from his rickety stool behind the desk. He envelopes me in a hug as tender as cannoli. "Where have you been, *cara*? It's July! I haven't seen you for many months! I've begun to worry."

"Well," I start, a glimmer in my eyes. "I got a new job! It's been *insane*. I started working at a travel magazine and I've been swamped every single second. I'm heading to New York later on today. I came to get a book for the flight."

"A new job! And going to New York!" Angelo's feather-boa eyebrows shoot up towards his salt-speckled hair. "That's great news! We must celebrate." He fills two tulip-shaped glasses with smooth, tangy limoncello. We clink before sipping and the intense lemon flavor of the liquor makes my jaw tingle. I choose a novel that showcases a cloaked assailant across the front and bold red text. It screams *intrigue* and *suspense*. Just my kind of book.

"It's on the house," says Angelo with a smile. "And next time, bring Lola with you! All of this pepperoni isn't good for my waistline."

To get back to my place from Angelo's, I only have to be outside for thirty seconds; out the door, turn to the left, and voilà, I'm home. So, I'm completely amazed that in this microscopic window of time, I hear my name being called.

"Margot! Hey! Margot, wait up, love!"

I easily could pretend that I didn't hear and duck into the safety of my steep stairwell. However, this time, I'm glad to see Priya Khan. After all, I have a lot to thank her for. If it weren't for our chance encounter back on that disaster of a day, I might not be where I am now. Actually, I know I wouldn't be. "Priya," I say with a smile. "How are you?" I keep my arms crossed in front of my chest, clutching my new book and my purse. Just because I want to thank her, it doesn't mean I want to make physical contact.

Instead of her customary stiff-as-a-board embrace, she runs her hand down my tricep and pulls off her bejeweled sunglasses. Her hair is in its usual disarray and she's smiling as if she just heard that she won a year's supply of hot-pink lipstick. "I'm great, love. Ever since I started working for myself I've felt like such a *fempreneur*! Boss babes, forever, right? Hey! So what happened with Sidney? I know you two met at Brussaux Society. Isn't that place fun? I'm thinking of becoming a member."

I almost dry-heave at the mention of Brussaux Society, boss babes, and *fempreneurs* in the same breath. Miraculously, I recover faster than Speedy Gonzales. "Actually, I've been hoping to bump into you," I say. "Thanks a zillion for setting me up with him. I've started working at *Roam & Rove* Magazine and love it."

Priya whoops in delight. "Congratulations! You're such a boss lady. I knew you'd take that new opportunity and strut with it."

"Thanks, Priya," I smile. "Anyway, I'm heading to New York today and I've gotta run. It was nice to see you!" Before she can swoop me up into a hug or blow me another unsightly smooch, I wave and duck into my building.

***

Billy Bishop Airport is bustling. You'd think it was Hartsfield-Jackson Atlanta—the world's busiest airport—with the swarms of frenzied jet-setters.

I've sent Perla a series of "where are you?" texts but have yet to receive an answer. I know how much she favors being tardy but this is cutting it close. Really close. The plane boards in thirty minutes! I decide to call her. If she doesn't pick up, I'll still go to New York. As if I *wouldn't* go. I'm already here and have been through security hell. I deserve to go. Besides, I know where the Airbnb apartment she rented is (Upper West Side) and where the key is kept (at some random pharmacy on Amsterdam). It's most likely Perla's own fault that she's late anyway. I'll have a fabulous time on my own for a night or two until she arrives.

On the last possible ring, she answers.

"Margot? *Hola.* I know you've been texting. I'm here, but I lost my passport," she explains. "I'm really panicking. I can't find it anywhere!" I hear the contents of her purse scatter and bounce across the well-used terminal floor. "Paloma is ready and anxious to see you though so I'm sending her through. Where are you?"

For a moment I can't speak. I feel as if I've just been punched in the vital organs. Maybe I didn't hear her right. Although, I know I did. Paloma? Coming with us? To New York? No way. This is supposed to be—how did she describe it?—just me and her, businesswomen in the big city. Perla *never* mentioned that Paloma was coming. Not even a slight possibility that she might be coming. The last time we spoke about the trip she said that Paloma was staying with her *abuela* and going to theater camp! What happened to that?

"Paloma?" I echo, stupidly.

"Yes. My daughter," Perla snaps. "Remember her?" She's still frantically searching through her scattered possessions. I hear Paloma singing a Taylor Swift song at an ear-shattering decibel in the background. Oh, boy. Here we go. It's not that I'm not fond of Paloma, it's just that the whole dynamic of the trip changes if there's a kid along.

"Yes, I remember her. I just don't remember you mentioning her coming with us."

"Margot, please," she huffs. "I definitely told you." The fact that Perla did *not* tell me is less than meaningless. Once she's committed something to memory, however false, it's impossible to convince her otherwise; like her threat to "let me go" over the lack of investments. "Hi? Hello? I have to find my passport or I'm not going to be able to get through security. Can you come get Paloma? *¿Por favor?*" Her voice sounds off. And not just from impatience. Almost like she's lisping or out of breath.

"I'll be right there," I say, crestfallen.

"Great, *gracias*. Paloma get over—" *Click.*

Chantelle predicted that things would torpedo out of control as soon as we got on the plane. Well, that timeline just moved up. I'm trying not to think of this like a bad omen. I zip my cell phone into my purse, drink down the final drop of my sparkling water, and make my way back towards the security guards with the monotone accents and poker-faced expressions. I see Paloma right away. She's sitting on the floor with a Roblox backpack carelessly tossed to the side and is totally engrossed by some loud and obnoxious video on her iPad.

She doesn't notice me when I walk up to her. "Hi, Paloma," I say. It takes her a full three seconds to break free from her digital hypnotization. She promptly jumps up, discarding her iPad along the way, to tackle me in a humongous hug. She's stronger than she looks. I'm on the brink of suffocation when she eventually lets go.

"Margot, I missed you, I missed you, I missed you!" she squeals, bouncing up and down more than Lola does when I get home from a long day.

"Missed you too. Now let's get your bag and head over to the gate to wait for your mom." Paloma swivels around to grab her stuff, which is sprawled all over the place. One of the customs officers gives me a disapproving eye and I have the urge to murmur "she's not my kid" but resist the temptation.

"Uh-oh . . ." Paloma looks up at me through drenched eyes. "My iPad broke! Look, it's all cracked. My mom is going to kill me! Please don't tell her. You *can't* tell her," she beseeches. "Please, Margot. I'm begging you!"

"Paloma, she's going to notice. It's pretty obvious . . ." That's an understatement. The screen looks like it's been attacked by Spider-Man.

"But not right away. Please don't tell her. *Please!*" She's on her knees, hands clasped.

"Okay. But the longer you wait, the worse it's going to be. Remember the time you broke her favorite wineglass and tried to cover it up?"

"Yes . . ." Paloma's eyes go from sad to scared; I think mine do too. I'll never forget that night. Perla and I were sitting on the balcony having a glass of sparkling rosé (typical) when we heard this enormous crash from the kitchen vicinity. We raced inside and found Paloma tossing a tea towel on top of the mess. She had accidentally knocked a glass off of the shelf and it shattered into a million microscopic shards on the tiled floor. Perla screamed at her, then Paloma tried to pick up one of the pieces and cut herself. She said she was just trying to be a "grown-up lady" like Perla and I, sipping from our stemmed goblets. I want to avoid a repeat of that situation at all costs.

"Paging passenger Perla Rivera," booms the airport speakers. "Please come to Guest Services to claim your passport. Perla Rivera, please make your way to Guest Services for a lost passport."

Not long afterwards, Perla is scurrying towards us, left arm flailing in some sort of wild wave while her right drags two carry-on suitcases alongside. "¡Hola! Can you believe I lost my passport? What the fuck," she cackles. "I'm a mess."

"Mommy! Swear jar," says Paloma. "You owe me an ice cream."

"Are you okay?" I give Perla an up-and-down assessment. She appears unwashed, uncouth, and perhaps under the influence. Her eyeliner is smudged, her lips are swollen like she just spent the last twenty-four hours locking lips with Sidney Lalonde, and her curly mane resembles a rat's nest; I *know* she owns a hairbrush. Her teal blouse is half untucked from her skin-tight jeans, and she's teetering on her signature peep-toe stilettos. I take a closer look. Maybe she had her lips filled? That would explain her minor lisp.

"What do you mean?" Perla asks, swiping away a rogue blotch of eyeliner.

"Well, it's just that you look a bit . . ."

"Mommy was drinking lots this morning," Paloma pipes up. "She was sooo drunk!"

"Paloma! It wasn't this morning, it was early afternoon," Perla scolds her. Turning to me, she explains, "And I wasn't *drunk*. I had some *amigas* over for brunch and they all brought a bottle of wine. I was going to invite you . . ."

"Mom, you drank *a lot*. Almost as much as that time when you threw up in the—"

"Paloma Estrella Rivera! That's enough," Perla interrupts. "Mommy needs to rest her head, so just watch your screen and let the grown-ups talk."

Paloma and I look at each other, silently agreeing that she shouldn't let Perla know about the cracked screen yet. It's not the right time. She pulls the iPad out of her backpack and keeps it stealthily hidden from her mom.

"My head is pounding," Perla tells me as she rubs her temples. "*Me siento mal y* hungover already. *Gracias a Dios* this flight is only an hour long."

Mine is pounding too, but with the fear that my friends were right about this trip after all. Why would Perla think it was smart to get drunk before we took a flight? What was she thinking? I just hope that this isn't going to be the tone for the whole trip.

By the time we board, take our seats, and accept a glass of complimentary wine, my trepidation has begun to thaw. Perla advocated for taking advantage of the free alcohol and I agreed without equivocation. If it makes her stop grumbling about her headache, then I'm game. Paloma is sitting a few rows ahead of us. I assume with her last-minute ticket, there wasn't anything adjacent.

"So, what happened to Paloma's camp?" I ask, nonchalantly. "I thought she was really looking forward to it."

"My mom broke her wrist in the garden this week," Perla says between sips of Chardonnay. "Paloma wasn't able to stay with her after all. That fucking theater camp didn't want to give me back my deposit since it was past their cancellation period. I was *furiosa!* The nerve. Anyway, I found a different camp for her to go to near Madison Square Park. Camp Broadway? I'd rather her start making friends in Manhattan anyway."

Perla beckons over the flight attendant. *"Uno más, por favor,"* she commands, gesturing to our nearly empty glasses. She then unstraps her feet from the confines of her stilettos and wiggles them off. Reclining back, she places her naked, clammy feet on the back of the seat in front of her. I feel a deep-rooted embarrassment coming on, licking at my cheeks. I don't care how expensive her pedicure is, bare feet on an airplane should *never* be allowed. It's grotesque. Perla and her lack of public decency don't think anything of it.

By the time the wheels touch down at Newark Airport, I feel a rude awakening in my skull. I'm not sure if it's the change in air pressure, Perla's foot funk, or Paloma's shrieks of excitement, but I need an ice-cold glass of lemon water and a *siesta.* Unfortunately, both seem cruelly out of reach.

"I *love* New York," Paloma exclaims, catching the flight attendant's arm as she attempts to walk by. "Did you know? I've been to New York four times. This is my fifth! I'm going to camp there for a whole month. It's true! You can ask my mom. She's right there. She's with our friend Margot. They're having wine. Really! You can ask her."

"That's lovely, sweetheart," the flight attendant says, wriggling out of Paloma's surprisingly solid grasp.

The doors open wide and people begin anxiously preparing to disembark. I take a second to reapply my lip gloss, tighten my ponytail, and double check that my passport is still securely in my purse. I'm disappointed I didn't get a chance to start the book I bought at Angelo's, but I have all month to read it anyway.

I know we're only in New Jersey, but I don't care. My excitement is temporarily blocking out my slow-spreading headache and I'm feeling almost fabulous. Looking fabulous too, if I do say so myself in my halter top, vintage jeans, and cowboy boots.

When Perla turns towards me, a teary look in her eyes, and takes my hand, I imagine that she's going to say something mushy to commemorate our first trip together. Something like "there's no one I'd rather be here with than you" or "I'm so grateful for your support." Then I notice the swampy tinge to her complexion.

"I think I'm going to be sick," she spews, before reaching past me to grab the barf bag from the back of the seat.

***

False alarm.

Thank *god*. If Perla had actually puked on—or over—me, I would have been totally convinced that this trip had soured beyond anything remotely enjoyable, like expired coconut water. However, her haggard stomach still proved to be useful. Since she didn't want to risk throwing up on the train into Penn Station, we're now in a taxi from the airport heading to our rental apartment near West 70th and Broadway.

None of us have spoken a word. Except for the driver, who has pursued, unsuccessfully, small talk with Perla. I don't know what it is about her, but men are always vying for her undivided attention. She'll give it to them if their tax return places them on the *Forbes* list, but since this guy doesn't fit her money-hungry standards, she's less than interested. She's presumably also preoccupied with trying to keep her waves of nausea at bay. Paloma is plugged into her device, oblivious to anything else.

Meanwhile, I'm staring out the window in the backseat pretending I'm Serena van der Woodsen returning home from a year at boarding school. Wow. If I permanently lived in New York City, I'd be unstoppable. Can you believe that there are women who are just *born* here and can freely choose to continue living their fiercest lives here? The luck they possess is almost unfathomable to me. For the next four weeks, I get to be one of them. Still myself, of course; who else could I be? But nonetheless, a Manhattanite.

"Margot, you *have* to live here," Perla says, looking back over her shoulder at me. "When I did, it was the best experience of my life," she brags. "Not including having you, *Palomita*." Paloma ignores her.

"It's my ultimate goal. But it's not that easy," I reply. "I can't just, like, stay here and start a life with no plans and no official documentation."

"Why not? Come on, take a risk!"

That's so unfair. I *do* take risks! I'll try or do anything once. Well, almost anything. There are some things I won't do unless someone offers to pay me $1.3 million dollars. For example: staying in a country illegally, eating fish with its face still on, or wearing vests. I hate vests more than I hate the ending of *Dexter*. Once, my high school boyfriend wore a suit vest overtop of a Hollister V-neck to English AP and I ran in the other direction.

"For starters, because getting arrested for staying in the U.S. without a visa isn't really on my top list of priorities right now." Truthfully, I think I'd thrive in New York. I'm *going* to thrive in New York. But the whole icky immigration process has thus far stopped me. I've briefly wondered how Perla intends to set up shop here, even part-time, if she's not a citizen and doesn't have any official sponsorship that I know of, but I've pushed those concerns to the back of my mind for the time being. She must have a plan.

"You worry too much," Perla lectures. "You just need to decide if this is the life you want. Do you want to be successful? Then stay. If you don't, get on a plane with me in a month and come home. It's as simple as that." The funny thing is, Perla really does believe it's that simple. I nod in agreement and say it's an interesting approach to immigration and that I'll definitely think about it. Not. At least not yet. One day, for sure, but not without my things and of course my little Lola. I miss her—and Oliver—already.

After a long battle with New York traffic, our taxi finally pulls up outside a block of apartments on a quiet tree-lined street, each property with its own wrought-iron gate separating it from the common sidewalk. Paloma starts hollering "we're here" over and over, causing my headache to flare up. I'm as excited as she is to be here, but oh my god, my frontal lobe is assassinating my patience. The driver gets out to help us unload the luggage from the trunk.

Perla must have paid a fortune for hers because she has five suitcases between her and Paloma, only two of which could be carried onboard. It makes my one measly carry-on look pathetic—even if I did bundle everything in with Marie Kondo's suitcase-packing efficiency. Did I bring enough clothes? Will I have enough outfits? This is every fashion girl's nightmare.

We strain to get them through the gate and to the front door as the taxi zooms away. He didn't get tipped enough to help us bring them all the way in and up six flights of steep city stairs. Plus, I'm sure that Perla's impassiveness towards him didn't help either. On the bright side, I'll consider this my workout of the day. Perla and I lug the suitcases upstairs while Paloma skips along ahead, her backpack hanging on for dear life. If and when I have kids, they are *definitely* helping with the luggage.

My forehead, chest, and armpits are damp by the time we finish. The pounding in my head is here with a vengeance and I feel as dehydrated as the residents of hell must be. I toss my suitcase into the smaller of the two bedrooms and head to the kitchen for a glass of water. The apartment is petite, but comfortable. The kitchen bleeds into the dining area which is connected to the living room. Floor-to-ceiling windows look out onto the surrounding buildings and crops of leafy trees sprout in the gaps. Through a sliding glass door, a balcony is furnished with a round table and four metal chairs.

"What the fuck?" Perla shrieks as she opens up her suitcases. She's pink in the face and looks utterly stunned, gaping down into the disorganized contents. (She definitely did not pack with the help of Marie Kondo.) Perla's startled tone is enough to make Paloma momentarily glance up from her iPad and for me to jump right out of my boots.

"What's the matter?" I ask with dread.

"I didn't bring any shoes with me. Not a single pair," she panics. "All I have are my high heels. And all of my clothes are dirty! I must have dumped the laundry into these suitcases by mistake."

"I thought you meant to do that, Mommy," says Paloma innocently.

Perla whips around, hands on hips, to glare at Paloma. "You thought I'd do this on purpose? Who would do this on purpose?" She gestures wildly towards the soiled lump of clothing. "Why didn't you say something?"

"I don't know," she shrugs. Paloma returns her concentration to the cracked screen.

I have to intervene before Perla erupts any further. I did not sign up for four straight weeks of Perla berating her daughter. When I was little, I vaguely remember my mom having fiery fits of fury towards me, but I don't remember them being this frightful or frequent. "Well, now we have an excuse to start shopping right away! What about those stores you told me about? The ones you used to go to all the time? Why don't we check them out before dinner?"

Perla stops to contemplate my suggestion. Her features relax. "You're right. Why spend time worrying when I can just buy my way out of this crisis instead?"

The fresh city air does us all good. Not that it's really *that* fresh. We've been outside for five minutes and I've already had a mouthful of exhaust and inhaled a strong whiff of rotting debris. But do I really care? I feel so New York already. But *what* version of New York do I want to be? I know! The Kaia Gerber wearing oversized blazers and carrying books around Lower Manhattan version. Now, that is a vibe I'd like to emulate every day.

After all, it's better to have your nose in a book than in someone else's business. Unless that business is *Roam & Rove*. I'm ready to stick my nose right in, find the perfect office space, and start scheming my permanent move to the city that never sleeps.

Chapter Sixteen

"**F**rom here, you'll have views of Hell's Kitchen and a glimpse of the Hudson. It's a *stunning* perspective come nightfall. And with Times Square a hop, skip, and a jump away, you'll never be short on entertainment."

"This *is* hell," Perla says to the realtor. Her name is Veronica and she has limp blonde hair, cat-eye glasses, and a peculiarly passive personality. It baffles me that she's apparently one of the city's top real estate agents. I would've thought she'd be a bit . . . grittier? More persuasive? More like Chantelle? Honestly, I think she's intimidated by Perla. I don't blame her. "Don't you have anything *más* . . . civilized to show us? *Dios.* How could we have prospective investors to this dump? No one would take us seriously." Perla glances around in unveiled disgust. A water jug from a long-forgotten cooler is sitting in the middle of the room and exposed wires dangle from the ceiling. I could have sworn that I saw a rat scurry across the floor when we walked in, but I'm choosing to believe it was a dust bunny. A *huge* dust bunny.

"Well, it's just that with your budget . . ." Veronica pushes her glasses up her nose and trails off. The insinuation hangs thick in the dilapidated suite. Perla's stingy budget isn't getting us any-where. I respect that she's trying to stretch Sidney's dollar to its fullest extent, but come on. This is Manhattan! When she lived here almost a decade ago, perhaps things were different? More economical? Although it's hard to imagine that she wouldn't have done a bit of research on rentals before we hopped on a flight.

This is the third office we've seen this week and Perla has found fault with all of them. I'm better than she is at looking at things through a pair of rose-colored Marc Jacobs glasses—a little paint here, a new light fixture there, and we could have an office that might not resemble Ugly Betty's but would inexorably stand up against Harvey Specter's.

"Why don't we just think about it?" I say to Perla. "Let's look at a few others and then we can compare them. I really feel that one of them will be what we're looking for, even if we have to do a few renovations on the cheap . . ." After all, I turned my impossible apartment into impossibly stylish without putting so much as a dent in the bank, let alone breaking it. If I could do it once, I can do it again.

"This place is worse than the other two combined," Perla sneers. "But maybe you're right, Margot. *De todas maneras*, we're going to be late to pick up Paloma." She turns to Veronica, who has been standing meekly off to the side. "We need to see at least a dozen more spaces before we can make up our minds. I'll email you later."

"Thanks," I add. Veronica gives me a cautious smile as I follow Perla out the door.

It takes us less than fifteen minutes in a cab to get to Paloma's musical theater camp. It's a miracle for New York's typical traffic congestion. Perla still owes Paloma ice cream for swearing at the airport and about fifty times at the apartment, so we saunter down West 25th Street and across Broadway to Madison Square Park.

The towering trees cast dappled shadows along the paved pathway as we weave towards Shake Shack. We're surrounded by verdant greenery and the slight, murmurous breeze provides a hint of relief from the humid summer heat, much to my perspiration's delight. My soul is more alive than it's ever been; it's electric. This city feels like home to me, like I'm finally where I belong. Staying here illegally is sounding *almost* appealing . . .

We sit down at the only vacant table. Luckily, it's one with ample shade. The park is Madison Square Garden kind of packed, so it was all systems go when I spotted a family getting up to leave. Paloma dutifully sprinted over to stake a claim.

"Can we go to Union Square Park?" she asks between hearty slurps of her chocolate shake. "I want to climb that big metal ball thing!"

"No, not today," Perla says.

"Please, Mommy? I really, really, really want to go!" Paloma curls her bottom lip under in a puppy-dog frown.

"No. Your babysitter will be at the apartment soon because Margot and I have an important date tonight." Perla whips out her cell phone and begins furiously texting. "I'm confirming the dinner with Esther," she says to me. "My very good friend Richard Neuman will also be joining us. He's a big-time player in the media industry here. He's a *crucial* connection. *Muy importante.* He works for Advance Publications. They own Condé Nast . . ."

On the way back to the apartment, we make a detour towards Trader Joe's on the corner of Broadway and West 72nd. Perla wants to pick up a bottle of wine to drink on the balcony before we begin beautifying ourselves. A part of me is reluctant to start drinking with her *before* we go out for more drinks with her friends; her track record for remaining cool, calm, and collected post-libations isn't exactly stellar and unlike back home, I don't have anywhere to escape to if she flies completely off the handle—like the time she threatened to fire me. I'm completely and hopelessly stuck with her.

Paloma's babysitter is waiting outside on the steps when we arrive back home. I know it's her because as soon as Paloma sees her, she races ahead of us squealing like a curly-tailed piglet. She's a rotund woman, approaching senior status, with a butterscotch complexion, and the biggest, friendliest smile I've ever seen. I like her straight away.

"*Hola*, Floramaria. *Perdón por llegar tarde*," Perla profusely apologizes. Either my Spanish has improved exponentially, or I just know in my heart that Perla is apologizing for being late. I'm going with the latter.

"*Está bien*, Miss Perla," says Floramaria in a creamy Cuban accent.

"Take Paloma to the movies, to the park, wherever," instructs Perla. "Just let her tire herself out before you bring her home. We should be gone *en un par de horas*."

Upstairs, I languidly take a seat on the balcony, close my eyes, and bask in the glorious early evening sunlight. I could totally get used to coming home to this place every day. I can hear the sounds of cars driving by a couple of streets over, horns honking, and pedestrians shouting. I feel in tune with it all; these sounds are like a lullaby to me. I blame my dad—he used to listen to *Beautiful Noise* by Neil Diamond on repeat when I was a kid and it had long-term hypnotizing effects.

Perla joins me, setting the wine bottle down on the table. She twists the corkscrew, yanks, and the cork makes its signature smack as it escapes the neck. Her curly hair is falling across her face and, in the soft, apricot lighting, she looks quite beautiful. For someone who's survived so many struggles—and quick cosmetic procedures—I admire that she still has so much zest for the

day-to-day grind. She pours us two glasses that might seem exces-
sive to the average person, but seem perfectly on point for Perla.

"Well, I'd say that this trip is off to a fabulous start," I announce,
without a sliver of insincerity. As of this moment, I truly mean it.

"*Si*, if you don't count me losing my passport, my lack of shoes,
or dirty laundry fiascos, then yes," Perla laughs, knocking back a
long, smooth mouthful.

"Those don't count. Let's just focus on the positives," I say. I
thrust my wineglass into the balmy air. "May we drink, laugh, and
get a breathtaking office for *Roam & Rove*."

"And the next investment," Perla quickly adds.

***

We're totally buzzed by the time our yellow taxi drops us off at
the Murray Hill locale. It's called Sashaymi and apparently it's a
sushi-slash-live jazz restaurant. I'm beyond excited. I'm also bossy,
glossy, and ready to get saucy—that's the wine talking.

I've never been anywhere like this before. Well, not including
Brussaux Society. It was *sort of* similar. Still, I want to burn that
from my mind like a chef does to the top layer of a crème brûlée.

The vibrant atmosphere penetrates my entire body the second
we step through the doors; lively would be an understatement.
Perla coyly asks for Kenneth Cedarwood at the hostess station.
Eventually, a man wearing dark khaki cargo pants, a black Off-
White T-shirt featuring the *Mona Lisa*, and yellow-tinted sunglasses makes his way from the back of the restaurant to greet
us. His—ironically—cedarwood hair is loaded with pomade and
looks like it could withstand any natural disaster.

"Perla, my darling! How long has it been? When did you get
to town? You're skinnier? No, did you get something done? You
look tremendous!" His hands wildly gesticulate through the air.

"Welcome to my main squeeze, my baby, my brand-new operation. Sashay-mi, sashimi, sashay with me! Isn't it *brilliant*?"

They kiss on each cheek before stepping back to absorb each other's appearances. I'm totally overwhelmed by Kenneth's superfluous presence but at the same time, I'm very much intrigued. He's theatrical in a way that makes me miss Liao. Actually, they'd make a dynamic duo—depending on how many men Liao has in rotation.

"We arrived a few days ago! And keep your voice down, I don't want every woman in here asking me for Dr. Grant's info," she says in a stage whisper. They both throw their heads back in rowdy ripples of laughter. "Before I forget, Kenny, this is my new assistant, Margot Moss."

My smile droops like week-old wildflowers. Assistant? I'm the assistant *editor*! Surely, that was a mistake. I'm about to correct Perla, but Kenneth turns to me with wide eyes, lowering his saffron sunglasses.

"Moss? Far-fetched question, but . . . any relation to Kate?"

"Sadly, not that I'm aware of," I admit, sewing a brand-new smile onto my lips. You'd think that being half British would count for something more than a taste for golden-crusted scones, clotted cream, and marmalade.

He leans in and air kisses me on both cheeks. He smells faintly of Tobacco Vanille cologne; of course, mixed with raw fish, rice vinegar, and a spritz of sesame oil. "Oh, well, I bet you're even more fabulous. And you'll eat my food. Skinny tastes good, but I promise you, the creations that come from my kitchen are even more delectable!" He makes an exaggerated chef's kiss gesture.

Kenneth leads us over to a table for four at the back of the restaurant with an unobstructed view of the stage. Three singers, wearing the most ornate crimson gowns, are crooning to a slowed down, jukebox rendition of "Jumpin' Jumpin'" by Destiny's Child.

Behind them, a band consisting of half a dozen dapperly dressed men are giving Tuxedo Mask a run for his money. The whole atmosphere of this place gives me glamorous goose bumps.

"Make yourselves comfortable," says Kenneth. "I'll send out some beverages. What's your demon drink?"

"Johnny Walker for me," says Perla. "Margot?"

"Gin martini? With a lemon twist."

"Done and done," Kenneth replies. "And don't worry about anything tonight, it's all on the house. I'll create a menu of chef's favorites for you to indulge your flawless taste buds in. Mwah!" And with that, he disappears behind a heavy red curtain that must lead to the kitchen.

Once he's out of earshot, I ask Perla about the introduction she made. "Hey, Perla? Why did you say I was your assistant? That makes it sound like I'm your secretary or something, not your editor."

"Did I?" Perla says, examining her nails. She frowns slightly. "It was a slipup, I guess. I meant nothing by it. Let's not allow that to ruin *la noche*." She smiles at me but I sense that there's something lurking beneath her semi-apologetic veneer. I chalk it up to the bottle of wine and push it out of my mind.

Moments later, Richard shows up. "Perla?" he asks, skeptically. Has her appearance really changed *that much* since the last time they saw each other? But if Kenneth recognized her right away, why doesn't Richard?

"*Hola*," Perla breathes, glancing up at him through fluttering lashes. "I'm *so* happy you were able to join us." She gets up to kiss his cheeks; he has to bend almost in half for her to be able to reach.

He's George Clooney handsome—tailored shirt with the top button tactfully undone, a casual blazer and complementing trousers, and a confident, but not arrogant, aura about him. The crows-feet detailing his eyes lend him a masculine attractive-ness with a pinch of gravitas. Judging by appearances only, he is someone who knows what he wants and gets it. It also looks like Perla knows that she wants *him*. I can't blame her; he *is* pretty suave.

"Of course," he says. "Happy to finally meet you in person." Wait, what? This is the first time they're meeting in person? I'm confused. Perla said earlier that they were "very good friends"—or did I mishear her? Are they online-only friends? Dating app friends? Not even friends at all? Perla is too lost in lust to introduce me, so I do it myself.

"Hi, I'm Margot Moss," I say, extending my hand.

"Richard Neuman," he replies, engaging me in a firm shake.

"She's my assistant," Perla sneaks a peek at me, "editor at the magazine. I'm not sure if you remember, but I mentioned my new travel endeavor, *Roam & Rove*, last time we spoke? Margot has been essential in helping me get my business off the ground."

"Of course, I remember," Richard says genuinely. "So, how are you two enjoying the city? You came in from Toronto, right?"

"Technically, yes." Perla tilts her head in self-deprecating laughter. "However, I'm only there temporarily. I'm much more of a New Yorker at heart. Always have been. I lived here for about ten years, up until my daughter was born." As a last-minute thought, she adds, "But Margot is from there."

It's obvious that she's trying to distance herself from Toronto, like she's ashamed that she lives there. Nonetheless, Richard seems intrigued.

"I love Toronto," he says, turning away from Perla and towards me. "I've been there quite a few times on business. I always try to tack on a couple of extra days so I can explore all of the local joints."

"Really? What are your favorite places to visit?" I ask him, eagerly. I love meeting people who've been to my city and comparing notes. Especially people from New York so that I can compare notes about their city too.

Before Richard can answer, Perla shrieks and jumps to her feet. No, wobbles is more accurate considering the wine, Johnny Walker, and her Jimmy Choos with their skinnier than kindling heel. I see now where Paloma gets her excitable nature. "Essie! Over here!" Perla waves like she's directing airport traffic. She told me earlier that her and Essie—real name, Esther—used to be roommates when she was crashing on Pottery Barn couches and ducking immigration.

"Perla, honey! It's been too long. Where the absolute fuck have you been?" Esther is uproarious, to say the least. Her sleek black hair is giving me serious Vera Wang vibes and she's wearing a skin-tight T-shirt with "Miss Independent" written across the chest. I feel like I've seen that shirt, but I can't quite recall where. This is going to drive me nuts; like when you see an actor and you know you've seen them before and can't remember their name or what it was that you saw them in.

Perla envelops Esther in a tenacious embrace before introducing her to Richard and me. "Margot, Richard, this is my best friend, Esther Yi. She owns her own workout brand, Move by Essie, and handcrafts everything here in the city. Margot, you might remember my proud feminist sweatshirt? That's Essie's! I'm thinking of doing an editorial featuring the clothes and how amazing they are as travel leisurewear."

I knew I recognized the aesthetic from somewhere. Not my cup of tea, but then again, I prefer coffee. "That's awesome," I say ebulliently. "Nice to meet you."

Esther gives me a cool smile before turning back to Perla. She seems as interested in me as she would be to find out she stepped in dog diarrhea on the way here. And just like that, I've lost my appetite.

"So, how do you and Perla know each other?" I ask Richard after he requests a whiskey on the rocks from a passing server. Perla and Esther are animatedly chatting away and I don't think there's any risk of me getting caught prying a little bit into Perla's vague affairs and explanations. Plus, it's loud enough in here to have to lean in close to hear what the other person is really saying. The glamorous band has sunk their teeth into Mariah's "We Belong Together" and it's so good I need it on every playlist, pronto.

"Well, we don't really," says Richard bluntly.

"Oh? I thought you were close friends?" It's conclusive that they're not, but I hope my face looks convincing.

"Close friends?" Richard smirks. "She reached out to me on LinkedIn last year. I think she was trying to pitch an investment opportunity. It wasn't clear." He takes a swig of his newly obtained drink. "What about you? How long have you been working with Perla?"

"Just over four months," I say. "I left a job and then this one kind of just fell into my lap. I was lucky, really."

"Sounds like it," Richard says. His eyes are wide, interested. "What was it that you did before?"

"I worked in beauty—copywriting, social media, marketing. Similar to what I'm doing now but with more highlighters than highfliers." I laugh and Richard does too.

"One of my close friends, an actual close friend," he smiles wittingly, "is the beauty editor at *Vogue*. She was able to snag me some Armani colognes last week. I have to say, I don't think I'll ever go back to Axe again," he jokes. He does not emanate the character of anyone who has ever worn Axe—or anything that costs less than $150 per ounce.

But . . . did he just say . . . *Vogue*? Over the hum of fellow diners, snapping chopsticks, and Perla's shrill guffaws, I can't be sure that I heard Richard correctly. I feel like I've just met Kate Moss and realized that I'm standing in front of her naked, asking for an autograph, in the middle of Times Square. Then, it clicks. Perla said earlier that he works for Advance . . . the owners of Condé Nast . . . the publishers of *Vogue* Magazine. Oh my god.

"I'm sorry," my voice trembles. "Did you say *Vogue*?" Richard nods. I'm sure that my face is stuck somewhere between awe and paralyzation. "It's been my dream since I was an awkward preteen to work there. I had *The Teen Vogue Handbook*—a guide to a career in fashion—and everything," I say with perhaps a pinch too much fervor.

"Really?" Richard sounds impressed. "Well, how long are you in the city for? I can try and set up a meeting for you? It would be good to establish some kind of contact with someone at *Vogue* if you're serious about wanting to work there. My friend, Amisha Chowdhury, is always looking for contributors."

"I've never been more serious about anything," I breathlessly burst. "We're here until the beginning of August." Internally, I am freaking out. Could this really be my chance to work at *Vogue*? When Priya asked me at the Green Nectar party if I'd gotten my dream job there, it felt like she was dousing my wounds in pink Himalayan salt. Now, it feels so close I can almost reach out, grab it, and securely tuck it into my mini crocodile-embossed bag.

I'm getting way ahead of myself, considering Richard only said he could "try and set up" a meeting for me. Still, my mind is barreling full speed ahead and it's finally reached the Perla pit stop. What will she think about this? How will it affect my job with *Roam & Rove*? Is it a conflict of interest to do both? I have my doubts that Perla would be in such high spirits if she knew what Richard and I were discussing right across the table. At the same time, if I don't jump all over this chance, I'll be even more brokenhearted than Brandy sang about on her début album. *Remember, Margot,* I encourage myself, *almost doesn't count.*

By the time I finish giving Richard my contact info, a waiter has appeared tableside with a gluttonous trolley of food. It looks sublime; I'm frothing. It's like the Seven Seas have been placed before us. I'm ready to dive right in, salivating—scuba gear or not. The four of us start piling our plates to the ceiling and yakking about how absurdly appetizing everything appears.

"*Buen provecho*," Perla says. "Isn't Kenneth the best?" Everyone nods in agreement, mouths stuffed to their fullest capacity.

The band has started performing a jazzed-up version of "My Love Is Like . . .Wo" and I feel like I've died and gone back to 2003. I'm not complaining.

Everything about Sashaymi is so extravagant and unexpected, I wish I could come here every night. Although, I'm sure that the prices are also what my budget would describe as "extravagant and unexpected" so I'll happily take this free meal and keep my memory of it preserved without the fear of going into debt over veggie gyozas.

"Richard, let's talk," Perla coos, laying her hand gently on his forearm. She maneuvers her chair closer to him, snuggling up a touch too close for comfort. She has turned up the charm to critical levels. Esther reluctantly swivels to face me as she forces a full forkful of udon noodles towards her lips.

"So, what are you?" she asks. Esther doesn't hesitate to continue chatting while chewing. "Perla's new intern or something?"

"No, I'm her assistant editor," I answer with conviction.

"And what does that entail? Grabbing her coffee and proofreading her texts?" she questions sardonically. "Aren't you a little old to be someone's errand bitch?"

"That's not what I—"

"Whatever," Esther gives me a pitying look and engrosses herself in her phone.

What's her problem? Imagine being rude to someone you just met and has been nothing but nice to you. It's unfathomable to me. I excuse myself to the bathroom, as politely as possible, so I can hit the refresh button before I let this woman irk me further.

When I return to the table, I find someone I don't know sitting in my spot, talking to Esther. "Excuse me?" I say pleasantly, smiling with my glossed pout. "You're in my seat."

"So?" she snickers. "Not my problem, chica. Find another one."

"Well," I gesture around. "There are no other ones and I've been sitting here all night . . ." Seriously. Who is this woman? Perla never mentioned that anyone else would be joining us.

"Yeah, but you weren't around when I got here. So, how is that my issue?" She looks at Esther with an expression that says, who is this moron?

Esther looks at me and laughs. "She's with me, sweetheart. Calm down. Just find another chair. It's not that big of a deal."

My posture stiffens. I hate being called "sweetheart"—principally by people who are using it mockingly. Perla is too busy cozying up to Richard to notice this confrontation between me, Esther, and the mystery woman. I wish she'd just look up and see me hovering here. A server is speed-walking by.

"Excuse me," I call urgently. "Would you happen to have an extra chair you could bring out?"

"Sorry! We're totally booked up tonight," he replies over his shoulder while running a tray of sake shots to a table across the room. I sigh. I wish I was back at Fins doing sake shots with Oliver in my naked dress. My spirit is languishing. I feel like a total outcast, not part of the group at all. Why doesn't Perla say something? Why is she friends with Esther anyway? She's a total bitch. Dare I say . . . worse than Gia. They're two edamames in a pod.

I'm beginning to regret wearing my YSL Opyum stilettos. (The only good birthday gift that Chris ever bought me.) Turns out, not only are they not made for walking, they're not made for awkwardly standing off to the side at a sushi-slash-jazz bar after your seat gets stolen right from under you. My baby toes are pinched to the point of turning ghostly white and I'm swaying back and forth on the monikered heels.

I'm about to text Jessie for some moral support before realizing that there's no WiFi here. Great. Now I really don't have anyone to talk to. I'm stewing in my somber situation, mesmerized by the band and their version of Lizzo's "Good as Hell," when I feel a hand on my shoulder. It's Richard.

"Margot, would you like to take my seat?"

For a moment, I consider it, but then where would he sit? "Thanks, but it's okay. I've heard that standing is better for you anyway. Sitting is the new smoking."

"I'm sure whoever said that didn't mean in that kind of shoe," he chuckles, alluding to my unsupportive footwear. "Please, take my seat."

"No, it's—"

"I insist," he smiles warmly.

"Well, okay. Thank you." I can't say no, the man is insisting. Richard meanders off in search of another chair. I hold my head high, slightly embarrassed but refusing to look over in Esther's direction, and lower myself with immense relief. Perla leans over and I smell the pungent Johnny Walker thick on her breath; I'm surprised she ordered that since she's usually such a bona fide rosé addict.

"I just had the best talk with Rich," she murmurs. "I think things are really going to turn around for us. We need to celebrate. Want another drink?"

I feel my previous humiliation gradually liquifying like an icicle at the finale of winter. Who cares about Esther and her friend anyway? She might be able to steal my seat but I'm not going to let her steal my mood. She doesn't deserve it. "I'd love another drink," I say with a nod.

We're collectively tipsy and completely satisfied as we step onto the cracked gray sidewalk. The midnight air feels as refreshing as Boscia's honeydew eye gels plucked straight from the fridge. I whimsically glance around at the dispersed trees, a gently flapping American flag, and the impressive brick buildings. Is it just me or does New York get more mesmerizing by the minute? Perla takes her time gossiping with Esther and her ruder than rude friend while I say good-bye to Richard.

"I'll email you," he says. "No promises, but I'll try my best."

"For *Vogue*? I'll take whatever I can get," I giggle. "Thanks again! It was great to meet you." Richard shakes my hand and then slides into the back of a black town car. He's a real-life Mr. Big. My imagination runs wild with visions of *Vogue*. The best part? They already have an office space. All I need now is a visa sponsorship and a rent-controlled apartment in Chelsea.

"Perla, honey!" Kenneth bursts from the restaurant. "I'm glad I caught you. I'm so sorry I didn't have a chance to visit at all. Orders were up to my knees!" He overzealously flails his arms to his waist and juts out his hip.

As if she's walking a tightrope, Perla shimmies her way to Kenneth and latches onto his elbow—more for balance than affection. I have no clue where Esther slithered off to, but I also don't care. "Everything was *riquísimo*."

"Lunch when you're free?" he asks. "Call me! Enchanted to have met you, Miss Moss."

Perla and I walk towards Lexington to hail a cab. This time, she loops her arm through my elbow before Johnny Walker topples her.

"So," Perla says as we slip into our taxi. "Esther said some not so favorable things about you . . ." She gives me a mildly accusatory side-eye.

My face contorts into a look of pure confusion. What could Esther possibly have said? She doesn't know anything about me; she didn't even try to get to know anything about me. "What do you mean? I barely spoke to her." I try my hardest not to sound too defensive.

"Just that you acted like a total drama queen about her friend sitting in your chair or something? *En realidad*, Margot. It sounds completely juvenile. I'd expect more of you when I introduce you to my friends."

And what about when I introduced you to mine? I feel like retorting. *You were on your absolute worst behavior!* Picking fights with Chantelle, calling Jessie by the wrong name, ignoring Oliver, spilling a drink on Liao's pants. She was sloshed, snarky, and surly all night long. "I didn't make a big deal about it. But I thought it was rude . . ." My forehead creases in a small frown. *Stop frowning and use your jade roller tonight,* I advise myself. "I was far from a drama queen and I don't appreciate her saying those things about me when they're obviously untrue," I say robustly.

"Well, whatever." Perla waves her hand, as if to say that this case is closed. Just call her Judge Rivera. "Let's forget about it. I guess Esther can be a bit possessive of me. She always is when I bring new *amigas* around." She looks at me with moist eyes. "But I hope you know, Margot, that I've come to think of myself like a mother to you." She reaches a hand out to me, resting it on my bare shoulder.

I feel a sudden swell of emotion. Despite all of her wrongdo-
ings and offbeat misconduct, I let her words blanket me like a
supremely soft chenille throw. They feel comforting. Soothing.

"However, Esther's workout brand is still big-time *bueno* so I'm
going to set up a time for us to go to her studio next week," Perla
continues. "You'll need to try the clothes before we feature them.
You'll love them."

The thought of trying on tacky T-shirts at Esther's studio fills
me with bleak misery. I'm already plotting my excuse as to why I
can't go. I'd rather stab a fork into my eye than spend one more
second in the scurrilous presence of Esther Yi.

Chapter Seventeen

I'm feeling increasingly sorry for Veronica. Her listless bob is beginning to frazzle and with the thin layer of moisture that's glistening across her face, her glasses are having a hard time staying in place. She repeatedly pushes them up the bridge of her nose, just to have them slip and slide down again. Dealing with Perla must be the hardest commission she's ever had to work for.

Veronica called earlier this morning and said she had another couple of "rare" listings to show us; one on the Lower East Side and one in Greenwich Village. Perla turned her ski jump nose up at the former, and we're currently traipsing around the latter. I love it. Yes, it's only 478 square feet, but the ceilings are enormous and there are two east-facing windows which give us sprawling city views. It totally helps to open up the space. And the best part? It's renting for $2,082 per month which is a complete steal compared to the other places we've seen. No wonder it's rare. I snap a few photos on my phone for later review.

"This is squalor! *Más peor* than your apartment," Perla says to me. Excuse me? It's okay for me to make jokes about my apartment but it's quite another thing to hear Perla say it. And in front

of Veronica! Talk about insensitive. I give her an appalled look—
behind her back—and then roll my eyes at Veronica as if to say,
this woman, am I right? She rapidly nods. Her glasses almost break
free from her face.

Perla and I leave, undecided about the rental, and meander
over to one of the city's signature coffee carts. I can't get enough of
the blue, white, and gold Greek-themed cups. Why don't we have
any cool cups like this in Toronto?

"You know, if I'm going to have to up the lease budget," Perla
says, "then I'm going to have to cut costs in other places." She rips
open a packet of Splenda and shakes it into her coffee.

"In what other places?" I'm struggling to see where she can cut
costs. Besides the rent money, the only other costs are my salary,
her salary, and however many nickels and dimes she spends on her
underpaid international contractors.

"Well, for starters, I may have to let my graphic designer go . . .
but you can work Photoshop, right?"

"Sort of," I say, blowing into my coffee. Steam bellows away
before evaporating. I can add text and shakily cut out images but
I'm nowhere near body-morphing good. I'd never get hired anywhere based on my graphic design skills alone.

We leisurely walk up Sixth, Avenue of the Americas. Cars
honk and whiz past us, exhaust flitting behind them in smoggy
trails. I can see why a lot of city dwellers head to the Hamptons or
Montauk during the summer; the air is ripe with humidity, body
odor, and sunbaked litter that somehow escaped the confines of
the mesh-metal trash cans. However, I'm unbothered by it all.
I'm eager to take a fat bite out of the Big Apple—even if it is
slightly bruised.

Perla sighs heavily. "I don't want to have to cut into your salary,
but if it comes down to it . . ."

Wait. Cut into my salary? Is she demoting me? She barely pays me anything as it is! At the rate I'm able to save, Lola and I won't be able to afford to move to a bigger apartment until I'm well into my thirties. Not that I'm planning on staying with *Roam & Rove* that long. Especially not if *Vogue* comes through. (Eek!) And besides, it's likely I'll have moved in with Oliver way before that. Nevertheless, making less money than I do now is not a goal of mine. It would be like taking a step backwards in Charlotte Olympia pumps—dizzying and dangerous for my net worth and my well-being.

"Perla, that's not really . . ." I'm searching for a word stronger than "fair" but she starts speaking again.

"It's just something to consider. Unless I can get another investment *muy pronto*," she adds. She checks her phone. "That reminds me. What were you and Richard whispering about at dinner?"

"Whispering about?" I say, as casually as possible. Shouting over the chatter and infectious music, more like it. Out of habit, I finger my chunky gold hoops.

"Yes," Perla eyes me leerily. "You two were getting pretty close. When I was talking with Esther."

Oh my god. She knows. She knows we were talking about her. Is she embarrassed that I found out her and Richard aren't "really close friends" or is she mad that I was having a conversation with him at all? Does she know about *Vogue*? Against my better judgement, I decide to be honest. I must have given my intuition the day off.

"Oh, right," I say. "That night was such a blur! We were talking about . . ." I hesitate just slightly. "About how I used to work in the beauty industry. Apparently, one of his friends is the beauty editor at *Vogue*. He said he could make an intro." I shrug to give the illusion that it's less of a massive deal than it really is.

Perla stops walking. She turns to face me with a mutinous grimace. Even though I'm a solid six inches taller than her, I feel intimidation sizzle up the length of my spine. Or was that a trickle of sweat running underneath my baby-blue slip dress?

"So, I take you out to a nice restaurant, introduce you to someone who was supposed to be helping us with the magazine, not your own agenda, and all you want to do is betray me? Go work for someone else? Leave me high and dry?"

"It's just an intro, Perla. I never said anything about leaving. I'd just like to dip my toes back into the beauty world every now and then. I could easily handle doing both." She's still glaring at me, so I try another tactic. "We'd never have to buy makeup or skincare again with all of the free products we'd get. Think about it. Wouldn't that be great?"

Perla's demeanor changes like she's just spent the last half an hour soaking in a lavender-infused Jacuzzi. "You know, I could use some anti-aging serums—when I'm between Botox appointments. And it could be *bueno* for my magazine, if we could work on a collaboration."

Phew. That quelled her overactive emotions for now, but I don't know how many more of these mood swings I can take. *Vogue* is my life raft. My sleek, on-trend life raft—if Richard is able to make the introduction, that is. *Vogue* can save me from Perla and her fraudulent, flip-flopping ways. I'm starting to think that having no mother was better than having a mother figure as erratic as Perla. I feel unbearably shameful for saying that, but it's true.

"I think we need a bit of fun," Perla says gleefully. "After all of this office hunting, we need a break. Let's go thrifting!" I'm freaked out by how Jekyll and Hyde she can be at any given moment but thrift shopping is my kryptonite.

We hook a sharp right onto West 13th Street and head towards Beacon's Closet. My pulse quickens the second I catch sight of the flirty Nicole Miller dresses, discounted Donna Karan trousers, and mint-condition Dior blouses laid out like calorie-free candy. The only drug I do is designer and I'm as high as a private jet. I rapidly scan the store, taking in every detail, wondering where to begin my fashion feast. It's consignment nirvana. Perla and I split off into separate sections.

I've always been under the impression that women who have the ability to buy their outfits completely thrifted and still manage to be the best dressed person in the room are truly iconic and have limitless power. I don't want to be completely conceited, but that's me. I'm in possession of that power. Suddenly, my eyes come to rest on the coolest leather jacket I've ever seen and I feel like I've met my outerwear soulmate. That is not an exaggeration. My heartbeat races. It's as dark as a shadow with the faintest animal print embossing that you can only see at particular angles. A snap placket runs down the front while long fringe trims detail the sleeves, chest, and back. It's *muy* Megan Thee Stallion. It has me in a chokehold and I absolutely have to buy it. Yee-haw!

Where is Perla? I have to show her my fabulous find. I glance around and glimpse her standing in the shoe section, furiously typing on her phone. I sidle up to her. "Check out what I just found," I boast.

Perla jumps and almost drops her phone. "Margot, you scared the shit out of me!" She clutches at her chest. "Don't sneak up on me like that."

"What? Were you doing something you weren't supposed to?" I tease.

Perla flushes. "No," she blurts. "It was just Veronica . . . texting about another listing."

I hold out the jacket to her. "What do you think? I'm obsessed."

"Love it," she says. I shrug it on and give a little twirl, the fringe trim flying in all directions. "Tell me you're buying it. Actually, tell you what, I'll buy it for you, *cariño*. You have to have it."

"Oh my god," I gasp. "Are you sure? Thanks, Perla." Now I'm certain beyond any reasonable doubt that my intuition is on vacation because I don't second-guess her sudden generosity in the slightest. "I'm going to do a bit more browsing."

As I drift from rack to rack, I repeatedly catch Perla compulsively checking her phone. She must be really anxious about finding an office space. We still have another three weeks in the city so I wouldn't be worrying myself sick, if I were her. Yet.

I'm so heady with my purchase that I decline a shopping bag and decide to wear it right away; that's just how dedicated I am to its undeniable beauty. However, the scalding New York summer hits me like a slap in the face the second I step onto the sidewalk. I instantly regret putting on the jacket. It's like sliding myself into a zillion-degree oven. What was I thinking? I'm going for haute not hot.

Perla checks her phone for the hundredth time as we hail a taxi. "Any news?" I ask her. Maybe if we can squeeze in a couple more viewings today, it could abate Perla's obvious uneasiness.

"Huh?" She looks up from her screen, confused.

"With the listing?" She stares back at me blankly. "Veronica? You said she was texting you about a new listing."

"No, I was talking to Esther." Her eyes shift slightly. I know she said it was Veronica before. My mind is replaying the conversation as we slide into the backseat of the yellow cab. I'm sure she said Veronica. I'd bet my Kate Moss coffee table book on it.

***

When we step through the apartment door, it's blissfully silent. Paloma is at camp and Floramaria is picking her up there later on and taking her back to Shake Shack for dinner. So far, having Paloma with us hasn't really affected our "businesswomen in the big city" sentiment. Probably because she's seldom around. Perla's penny-pinching baby daddy is going to have a field day when he gets these babysitting invoices . . .

Perla and I order half a dozen Argentinian empanadas from Libertador and two pear and arugula salads. We organize the spread on the terrace table and bring our laptops outside. It's a working lunch. The city foliage rustles around us in a flimsy breeze. Above, the sky is as blue as a field of hydrangeas. The warmth of the sun is giving my creamed-honey complexion the glow it desires. I wouldn't be upset if *this* became our new office space. It's such a delicious setting. Although, in the winter it would be nice to have somewhere indoors to seek shelter from the snow. I can definitely envision myself working full-time out of New York. Being remote-enabled, Oliver can essentially work from anywhere, so he could be here with me too. And Lola would adore bouncing along the Manhattan sidewalks; there's an insurmountable number of new scents for her to discover at every turn.

Mid-bite on a spinach-cheese empanada, my email pings. I almost snort the flaky crust down the wrong way when I see it's from Richard. I didn't expect to hear from him so soon! People function at the speed of light in New York.

Unable to control it—because this is *Vogue* we're talking about and Richard has CC'd the beauty editor!—I inhale audibly and Perla looks up from her computer. I can tell that she's curious by the way she's inspecting me over the top of her screen. "Don't tell me you find the treehouse hotel guide so interesting you're willing to choke on your empanada for it?" she says sarcastically.

"Not exactly . . ." I reply, scanning the email for a second time. Holy *smokes*. Richard introduced me to someone from *Vogue*! An actual living, breathing human being that works for my favorite magazine is now in my inbox. I take a screenshot and swiftly send it to my group chat.

Guess who is maybe, possibly having a meeting with someone at Vogue!!!

The replies flood in.

Jessie: OMG your dream!!

Chantelle: Happy for you, babe

Liao: Can you introduce me to Hamish Bowles?

Chantelle: Liao, this isn't about you!

Jessie: LOL

"Then what's up?" Perla persists. She lowers her laptop screen just slightly to show that she's ready to listen; she's all ears. Her curiosity has unsurprisingly taken over her work ethic. Do I tell her the truth? She wasn't expressly enthralled by the *Vogue* news earlier, but I think I won her over with the quip about the free samples. (Whether we'll actually get free samples or not is to be determined.) Also, what if Richard tells her? If she's going to find out that this whole *Vogue* thing is moving ahead, it might as well be from me.

"I got an email from Richard," I cautiously admit.

"And?" Perla seems to be waiting with bated breath. Maybe she's happier about this recent development than I gave her credit for.

"He made the introduction," I say, unable to stop my giddy smile from widening. "I can't believe it."

"Neither can I," Perla says, scantily audible. Louder, she adds, "So, that's still happening?"

"Seems to be." Pulling my salad closer, I stab a piece of succulent pear and delicately chew it. But as its juices flow down my throat, I begin to feel a slimy fishiness about this interaction. Why would Perla wonder if it was still happening? I only told her about it this morning. What could have possibly changed in the last few hours? I have to ask. "Hold on . . . Why wouldn't it still be happening?"

"No reason! I just wasn't sure if Richard would come through or not." She spreads her hands apart and lifts her shoulders to her ears. "I mean, yes, he's a close friend, but we don't really know him that well. He could be *loco!*" She bugs her eyes out at me, as if it's comprehensively obvious that he is, in fact, *loco*. Her voice gets an octave higher and I have a sneaking suspicion that she knows something I don't. However, it's going to take the sharpest pin she can find to burst my bubble, not just the allusion that he's crazy.

Perla reaches for another empanada. "You know, Margot. There's something I've been meaning to discuss with you." The thick tone in her voice implies something unpleasant.

I stop typing. Is this treehouse hotel guide ever going to get finished? "That sounds alarming . . ." I say.

"It is," she confirms, nodding. "I had a long, hard look at your social media. You're going to need to ramp it up big-time if you ever want to get anywhere. You have seventy-three posts on your Instagram! I post that many in a single week." She stops to gauge my reaction. Which, at this point, is undiluted confusion. What is she getting at? I like being low-key on social media. The idea of random people being able to totally capture me online gives me the creeps.

"You need to put yourself out there," she maintains. "If nobody knows about you and who you are, how will they want to work with us? We need to be leaders in the travel space. And that means a religious posting schedule. And what about . . ." Her top lip appears to somewhat snarl. "*Vogue?*" She makes *Vogue* sound like vomit. "Don't you want them to be impressed with your content?"

"I . . . hadn't really thought about it," I admit, shrugging. Should I have? Now I'm a bit worried. I thought my portfolio and writing samples would stand on their own. Should I have a more rigorous routine for sharing tidbits of my life? We share three posts per day on *Roam & Rove's* accounts. To me, it feels like overkill but Perla always says it's never enough; we should be doing more! Saturating the space.

"If you want," she says. Her voice is as sugar-coated as *una manzana de caramelo*. "I can help you out. Just give me your log-in and I can start posting some things that are relevant to you and your audience."

"No," I exclaim. "I mean, no, thank you. I'll think about what you said and come up with a strategy. It'll feel more authentic that way . . . I don't want too many cooks in the kitchen or whatever." I attempt a lighthearted laugh and chomp down on my empanada.

Perla's face goes from smiling to seething. "Are you insulting my skills? My ideas? I'm just trying to help you—"

"What? No, not at all," I backtrack, accidentally snipping off the end of Perla's pugnacious sentence. When did a simple idiom turn into an insult?

"Do I need to remind you that I've completed Hootsuite's social media marketing course and DVF's MasterClass on using social?" She slams her laptop shut—with a force not unlike

Paloma's dropping of her iPad that resulted in the smashed screen; like mother, like daughter—and stands up so fast that her chair makes a screeching noise on the balcony floor.

"I know," I say, attempting to mollify Perla's acrimony. "I just think that if both of us are posting stuff, it could start to look inconsistent. That's all I meant." Not to mention, having Perla post on my behalf would just be bizarre. Who does that? Why would she want access to my accounts? I may not have the strongest, hack-proof passwords but I still know not to just give them out willy-nilly.

"Oh," she says, her features thawing like a Creamsicle left uneaten in the sun; she's a gooey pond of docility. "I get it now. It must be coming to my time of the month." She cackles. "Anyway, I'm going to take a shower. Let me know when the post is done." She scoops up her laptop and heads inside. Once I hear the thundering of the water, I call Oliver on FaceTime.

"Hey, babe," he answers. "How're you going?"

Just hearing his voice slows my blood pressure and brings me back to reality. Sometimes, in the throes of Perla's personal world, where common sense goes out the window and nasty remarks are customary, I can start to feel desperately lost. It's like I'm wandering in the woods at night with 3 percent battery left on my phone, no reception, and no clue how to get home.

"Hi," I breathe. "I'm good, but mentally drained. It's been, what? Five days? And I'm already a shell of the woman I used to be . . ."

"A sexy shell though," Oliver says.

"Oh, always a sexy shell," I reply. "That's a given." We both laugh. I absorb his digital appearance. His devastating dimple becomes more pronounced with each smile and it makes my chest explode with yearning.

"Hang in there, Mar. Do you want me to look into flights for next weekend? We can get a hotel so you can get some respite from Perla? And the kid?"

"Yes, please," I cry in relief. "I miss you."

"Miss you too. Let me know if you want me to book a hotel for you sooner . . . get you out of there."

We hang up and I feel a million times calmer. Although I'd love to stay in a hotel all week—actually, all month—I feel bad having Oliver pay for it. As someone who doesn't have $200 per night (that's next to nothing for New York, I've Googled it) to waste on hotel rooms, I feel guilty having someone else foot the bill. Even if that someone else loves me. I'll be fine. Just one more week and he'll be here to rescue me from the undulating events of what I thought would be the trip of a lifetime. I can do this.

Chantelle's words emerge from the dungeons of my mind where I've been happily keeping them locked up: *you'd be a fool to go.*

I may have let Oliver in on my less-than-desirable scenario, but I am not ready to admit defeat to my friends. I just have to make it through seven dramatic days and my sanity will be restored to its original glory. Even if it's just for a weekend. I can't wait.

Chapter Eighteen

I'm still in slight disbelief. I've gone back and forth with Amisha Chowdhury, the *Vogue* beauty editor, a few times over the last couple of days and she suggested meeting at Culture Espresso tomorrow afternoon. This is *really* happening.

My insides are loosely braided thinking about how Perla might react when I tell her the news. She's been semi-normal since the "cooks in the kitchen" explosion and she seemed thrilled that I'm going to spend the weekend with Oliver; she said Paloma has been incessant about going to FAO Schwarz anyway. However, I'm more determined than ever to make this work with *Vogue*. I'll get down on my knees and beg Amisha to hire me if I have to. Well, okay, I won't get that cinematic, but I'll strongly convey my desire to work with her through my brains, my charm, and my wit.

As much as I don't want to admit it, Perla's unpredictability is finally and ferociously negating my positive experience with *Roam & Rove*. It doesn't matter how much firsthand experience I get, if I wake up with an ulcer every morning because I don't know if I'm walking into a minefield or a strawberry patch, that's a problem. If she's not threatening to fire me, then she's dangling a demotion over my head. And when she isn't coming unhinged over something that she misinterpreted, she's accusing me of being rude to her friends or insulting her knowledge of social media.

And it's all under the guise of being my mother figure. *With a mother like that, who wants one?* I think, pessimistically.

Ever since the airport, I feel like I've been in a never-ending game of squash, frantically racing to smack back Perla's missile-style freak-outs before they explode and destroy everything I've worked so hard for. Were things really this bad back home and I just turned a legally-but-not-totally-blind eye?

We need to normalize leaving jobs that no longer serve you. However, I'm determined not to leave *Roam & Rove* until I have something else securely in place. I don't want to go through the stress of being jobless again. It was almost as bad for me as Perla's temperament. Almost. So, I've decided that no matter how belligerent Perla decides to behave, I am going to suck it up, tough it out, and power through this like the smart, capable, fierce woman that I am. It's only for a few more weeks anyway.

Now, for the most pressing issue at hand: What to wear to meet Amisha Chowdhury?

I'm in my room, carefully going through my singular suitcase. My hands gravitate towards the structured linen skirt suit I tossed in at the last minute. It's almost like I predicted I'd have a fashionable meeting to go to that would require something with a showy checkered pattern. You could say I have a sixth sense—except instead of seeing phantoms, I see fabulous opportunities.

"Margot?" Perla calls. She yanks my door open without knocking and I'm relieved that I wasn't nude. Although, I already know Perla doesn't have any *problema* with nakedness. "We have an appointment with Esther at her studio tomorrow at three." I must have a dumbfounded expression on my face because Perla eyes me quizzically and says, "Is there a problem?"

Only the problem of the century, I think to myself. "Well . . ." I start. "I thought you said you were getting your nails done tomorrow afternoon? So I told Amisha, from *Vogue*, that I was okay to meet her for coffee." I brace myself for a hailstorm.

"Can't you reschedule? This is important for the magazine." Perla crosses her arms challengingly.

My mind whirls. I'll look unprofessional and flaky if I cancel. But Perla could unleash demons I haven't yet seen if I don't. (She seems to keep them on standby.) This is futile. Then, a different approach strikes me. "I probably could," I say, my face creasing in faux guilt. "But wouldn't it be nice for you and Esther to have some time to catch up together without me around? Her and I didn't exactly get along the other night and I don't want things to be awkward. I know it was all a misunderstanding . . ." I'm crossing all of my fingers and all of my toes.

There's a Rockefeller Center-sized pause while Perla ponders. "Are you sure you'll be able to write an adequate post without seeing the clothes in person?"

"Of course!" I say a little too quickly. "Besides, we're still here for a while. If we need to, we could pop into her studio another time?"

"Okay," Perla concedes. "It would be nice to see my amiga without you there . . . no offense." There's a shrill ringing from her phone and she dashes to the kitchen to pick it up. She returns a minute later. "Paloma isn't feeling well. I have to go pick her up. Why don't you take the afternoon off? Just be back before seven. Floramaria is coming to look after Paloma and we have drinks with some of my friends. Don't worry," she smirks, "Esther won't be there."

***

Be right back. I'm in my prime and *loving* it.

Prancing east on West 69th, I pretend I'm in the opening scene of a stylish, romantic film, relishing my complete anonymity. Only a handful of people in the city know who I am; I could be anyone! A socialite? An aspiring actress? The fiercest new addition to the *Vogue* masthead?

I'm exuberantly swinging my metallic pleated purse with every sandaled step. I jaunt towards Columbus Avenue; rustling shrubs, canary cabs, and native New Yorkers pass me on all sides. The sky's the color of the sea and the sun feels like my own personal spotlight. My AirPods are blasting Brandy's "Top of the World" into my ears and I've never felt the lyrics more powerfully. I am on top of the world.

Across the street, Magnolia Bakery catches my eye. The sugary aroma of red velvet, buttercream, and cream cheese infiltrates my nostrils as soon as I open the door. My eyes come to rest on the last confetti cupcake. "Excuse me?" I ask. "Can I grab that cupcake, please?"

"I don't know, can you?" The woman behind the counter stares at me deadpan. When she doesn't flinch—or even blink—I become aware that she's waiting for me to answer. Except, I'm not sure what to say. "Just kidding! Of course you can," she snorts. "Let me wrap that up for you." What a freakish sense of humor.

After plopping myself down on a luscious patch of lawn beneath an imposing elm in Central Park, I prepare to take a lavish, icing-rich bite. I'm so content that I don't even balk over grass stains on my off-the-shoulder mauve mini. Before I can successfully chow-down, I see two pavement-skimming black trench coats and dark sunglasses passing by in an enormous puff of cigarette smoke. My jaw goes slack and a chunk of icing rolls down the front of my dress. Is that . . .? Could it be . . .? There are only two people in the world who would wear inky trench coats in the summertime: the Olsen twins.

They're the epitome of cool. (Except for the smoking part. I'm even regretting my one-time craving for French cigarettes. That was a serious low point for me.) Thinking rapidly, I decide to snap a sneaky photo. After all, I have to get some proof that I was in the vicinity of Mary-Kate and Ashley, the unrivaled teen-queens. They're essentially just a plume of secondhand Marlboro Gold from where I'm sitting. I slyly take my phone from my bag and snap photographic evidence of the apathetic sisters.

"Loved *Passport to Paris*," I whisper in their general direction as I scurry away to find a Starbucks. I need internet access ASAP so I can gush to my friends about my Central Park celebrity spotting. I order a grande cold brew with sweet cream, situate myself at a table near the back, and reconnect to the modern world. The photo I took is a bit blurry and on the nondescript side, but I text it to our group chat anyway.

Jessie: MK AND ASH? I'm checking @olsenoracle on Insta right now

Chantelle: Please tell me you talked to them #goals

Liao: FaceTime? Calling now

"They're so tiny! So gaunt," I blab, adjusting my AirPods. "Their vintage coats looked like they were still hanging off the rack that they bought them from."

Chantelle sighs contentedly. "I'd die if I met them. Also, Elizabeth."

"Same," agrees Liao. "Front row at The Row is my lifelong goal. Then we could see who's more of a matchstick . . . me or them."

"When is your *Vogue* meeting?" asks Jessie animatedly. I can just imagine her living my excitement vicariously. Although, she'd probably be even more amped if I had a meeting with *Us Weekly* or *Page Six*. Jessie could die happy knowing she had access to all of the hottest Hollywood gossip before anyone else.

"Tomorrow!" I shriek. My eyes quickly scan the coffeehouse. Thankfully, no one is glaring at me for talking too loudly. "I'm meeting her—Amisha—for coffee."

"Oh my god," Chantelle gushes. "I guess we were wrong about the trip being a complete shit show. It sounds like New York is the best thing that could've happened to you." I swallow guiltily and pray that my smile comes across as genuine.

"But what about Perla?" Liao asks. "Has she been keeping herself in check?"

I shift in my seat, recrossing my legs. I contemplate being completely honest. But where would I start? With Perla's drunkenness at the airport? The dirty laundry packing blunder? Her threatening to slash my salary? Not standing up for me in front of Esther? Skydiving to the worst conclusions of simple things I say? I promise that I'll tell them everything in excruciating detail one day but I don't think now is the right time. There's no way I can sit through a symphony of "we told you so" and still enjoy my cold brew.

"She's been . . ." I struggle to find the words. Buying time, I slurp my coffee. "Pretty much the same. But I'm handling it." I attempt a laugh. "But what about you guys? What's happening? How is Lola? I miss her."

"Lola misses you too," Liao says, turning his camera to show her snoring softly on the couch. My heart seizures with deep affection for her and her perpetually exhausted self. "As you can tell . . ."

"Guess what?" prompts Chantelle. "I'm taking Jessie out tonight to find a sexy rebound. Hopefully one with a small brain and big muscles."

"Don't remind me," Jessie groans. "I haven't dated anyone in so long I'm practically revirginized. What do people even do to get over someone? Not that I'm not over Bryce, because I am. So over him."

Burbling with my friends, I feel a small jolt of renewed vitality. (Or is it just the caffeine rush?) No matter how funky things are with Perla, there are three things getting me through: Oliver's impending arrival this weekend, the very real possibility of *Vogue*, and my *amigos*.

***

My limbs feel like cement as I reach our six-floor walk-up. It's feasible that I might collapse before I can open the door. All I want to do is tuck myself away on the balcony and pick through the latest issue of *Vogue* with a fine-toothed comb. I passed a newsstand on my walk back and grabbed it, along with the fall fashion edition of *New York* Magazine and *Glamour* because the cover featured a model I didn't recognize and I want to be on top of all the latest sensations before I meet Amisha.

"Margot! Where the fuck have you been? We're going to be late!" Perla's shrill tone snakes out from behind her bedroom door.

"Swear jar!" blares Paloma from the couch. Her and Floramaria are watching *The Magic School Bus* in Spanish—*El Autobús Mágico*.

Late? I'm back fifteen minutes before she told me to be. Honestly, all I'm asking for is one tranquil day. I'll even settle for a single tranquil moment. I never thought I'd long for my pocket-sized apartment, but here I am. At least it's all mine and no one is waiting to bark orders at me when I walk in the door. I kick off my sandals and stroll towards Perla's room.

"Didn't you get my texts?" she asks in a panic. "I sent you *cinco*."

She knows my phone only works here when it's connected to the internet. Regardless, I check my recent messages. There are no texts from her so I check my email as well, just to be safe. Nothing. I wouldn't be surprised if she just thought she'd sent them. "I don't see anything. When did you send them?"

"An hour ago!" she exclaims as she zips herself into a flaming-red lace dress; it's sleeveless with a scalloped hem that ends about three inches too high. "My friends want to meet us earlier."

"Maybe check your phone?" I suggest. "Do the texts say they were sent? I don't have a single one from you. The last one was—"

Perla exhales sharply. "It doesn't matter. Let's just hurry up and get out of here."

"Would you hate me if I sat this one out?" I slump against the door frame. "I kind of feel like just chilling tonight, and flipping through these magazines. I'm exhausted."

Mid-swipe on her mascara, Perla stops. She adopts a sympathetic simper. "Come on, *cariño*! Don't be like that," she pleads. "It's a new place to check out, a new place to say you've been to! We won't go for long but we've been working so hard, we deserve this night of fun. Besides, you'll love these guys."

I let her appeal simmer for a moment. She's right. Did I come to New York to sit at home every night? No. I can always study the magazines tomorrow morning. "Okay, fine," I say. "But just a drink or two." Perla resumes her makeup and I head to my room to change. Slipping into a slinky black dress as fast as I can, I add a rosewood lip and sharp, winged liner. A spritz of travel-sized Maison Margiela Whispers in the Library perfume enlivens me and I'm ready to go.

Twenty-seven minutes later, we're stepping out of a taxi in front of Hotel 50 Bowery. Its sophisticated glass-fronted exterior soars above us. Pedestrians flutter by while an encumbered set of tourists drag their luggage through the revolving doors.

"*¡Chicos!* We've arrived," Perla sings, sashaying towards two men who, unless they're just hopeless with skincare, appear to be existing in the latter half of a century. They both feature softened grandfather bodies, receding hairlines, gray stubble, and a troop of wrinkles. I suppose they might have been heartthrobs at one point in time, but that sexiness apparently got left behind at Studio 54.

Perla smooches both of them on the cheek, a little close to the lips for a strictly platonic relationship. "Rocco, Joe, I'd like you both to meet my assistant editor, Margot Moss." She turns to me. "Rocco is my former lawyer. He helped me out of a big-time immigration bind when I used to live here. And Joe is a former fling."

"Just a fling? Perla, baby, I thought we had more than that," Joe jokes, clasping a hand over his heart.

"The fling was with me, remember?" Rocco cracks. "You liked him more. That was your biggest mistake." He wags a meaty finger at her. Perla gives him a playful push. Turning his head toward the modern venue, he jeers. "What has the city turned into? Gentrification! But dollars to donuts, you want that obnoxious, overpriced New York City experience." He's talking to me. To be honest, that's the last thing I want, but we're here now. Besides, it looks pretty swanky. I'm more excited than I thought I'd be.

"Let's go get our table," Perla says, taking them both by the arm and strutting inside. Their trio makes a very convincing sugar daddy sandwich.

Inside, it's a vibrant embodiment of Manhattan's vivacious energy. We take an elevator to the twenty-first floor. As we exit, we're met with throngs of trendy people, perched on velvet couches and leather chairs, each with a classy cocktail in hand. Joe and Rocco look wildly out of place; practically comical against the glamorous, youthful backdrop. The music booms and I subconsciously walk to the beat. We have two love seats reserved on the terrace and when I catch a glimpse of the unparalleled views of Manhattan, I think I forget to breathe. This is incredible! Imagine, I was going to stay home tonight. Looking out at the sweeping cityscape, it seems laughable that I would almost miss this.

"Dirty martinis all around?" Rocco asks. With a sly look, he adds, "The dirtier, the better. If you know what I mean."

"I'll take mine with a lemon twist," I instruct.

"Seriously?" he asks. Disapproval has contorted his features.

I nod. "I hate olives more than I hate people who clip their toenails on the subway."

"*Dios*, Margot," Perla laughs awkwardly. "We're about to eat. I don't want to be thinking about toenails."

We order an assortment of dumplings, bao, grilled cheese, and blue corn tortillas with guacamole. It's an eclectic food selection, but I'm starving. The cupcake from earlier is not enough to sustain me while drinking.

"These prices are a travesty," Rocco states. "Lucky me, I'm rich."

"Yeah, that's 'cause you don't have a wife and kids Roc," says Joe. "Aren't ya lonely yet? Nobody to cuddle up with at night?"

"Not for a second," Rocco retorts. "That sounds like a 'you' problem, Joe. Unless Perla will finally agree to make an honest man out of me . . ."

"You can't afford me," Perla shamelessly flirts. "I've leveled up since the old days." Our first round of drinks are placed on the stumpy table in front of us and we all reach for our respective martinis. Mine is the only one with citrus.

"So, Perla," starts Joe. "How did you and Margot meet?"

Perla knocks back a hefty slug of her filthy, olive-saturated martini before answering. "Well, Margot was an unemployed, struggling writer and I brought her on to help grow my company and in turn, changed her life."

What? That's so not what happened. I wasn't struggling! Too much. And I had only been unemployed for just over a week when I met her. "Perla, that's not entirely true—" I start, fully intending to set the record straight.

"*Cariño*, essentially that's the story. I saved you from *Dios* only knows what." She smacks her hands down on the couch cushion for dramatic effect. "You guys should see where Margot lives, her apartment. It's bad. Rocco, tell her the advice you told me when I was young. She needs to hear it. Joe, *quieres* another drink? Let's go to the bar." As Perla and Joe get up from the table, our food arrives. I load a couple of shrimp dumplings and a handful of tortillas onto a small plate and dig in.

"Are you ready for the best lesson of your life?" Rocco asks, his voice thick with egotism. It feels too impolite to flat out say no, so I nod my head, and lose myself in the rooftop's infectious ambiance. As the sun sluggishly dips behind the crop of skyscrapers, the patio takes on a bittersweet, cantaloupe afterglow. I wish Jessie were here to snap a few photos of me; she's memorized all of my best angles.

Rocco drones on and on until his voice becomes part of the DJ's beat. I don't know what I imagined his ground-breaking life lesson would be, but I didn't think it would simply be about sleeping with the richest men you can find until you get what you want from them. Of course, I should have guessed as much since that seems to be Perla's only rule in life.

Her entire existence feels like a scam against rich men: Sidney, Richard, seemingly Rocco, and plausibly Joe. Who knows how many others there have been? Is she even capable of having male friends who wouldn't qualify for a discount on senior's day? This trip has confirmed all of my suspicions: Perla feeds off well-to-do men in the same way that Megan Fox fed off boys in *Jennifer's Body*. It keeps her young.

"You don't want a purse or a car. You want real estate," Rocco is drunkenly lecturing. He's now two martinis ahead of me. "Real estate is what you're after. What good is a car if you got nowhere to park it? Know what I mean?"

"Yeah, I got your point," I mutter, reaching for the last pork bao. "The first seven hundred times you made it."

Rocco is inching closer to me on the couch, close enough for me to smell his loathsome aftershave. It's making me queasy. Perla and Joe are so lost in their own conversation, Rocco and I might as well not even exist. I excuse myself to the bathroom just before Rocco stretches a beefy palm towards my exposed thigh. Phew. Close call.

Once I'm safely locked in the privacy of the stall, I log onto the WiFi to check my texts. Chantelle sent a mirror selfie of her and Jessie before heading out and a couple of updates regarding the attempt to break Jessie out of her Bryce bubble. So far, she's said "excuse me" to one guy and "I like your belt" to another. She's evidently out of practice. I touch up my lips and smooth down my hair with my fingertips. I'm ready to go home. Two martinis was my limit tonight. I need to be fresh-faced and as alluring as possible tomorrow and I already feel the gin hacking into my brain. I wander over to the bar to request a glass of water.

"Another drink?" Rocco is suddenly beside me. For a man of his age and lumpiness, he moves quickly.

"No, thanks," I decline. "I've reached my max. They were deadly. I'm just getting a glass of—"

Before I have time to register what's going on, Rocco's sour, olive-pickled tongue is worming its way towards my larynx. It only took a fraction of a second. He's flopping around inside of my mouth like a fish out of water. He's got to be the worst kisser in Manhattan, perhaps all of New York State. Scratch that—the universe! My determined hands find their way to his puffy suit-clad shoulders and with all my strength, I shove him off me. Drool spills down my chin, dragging my mattifying powder and newly applied lipstick with it.

"What's the p-p-problem?" he drunkenly stutters. "Didn't you learn anything from my lesson on r-real estate?"

"Yeah, and your tongue isn't a down payment," I retort, reaching across the bar for a napkin. I roughly wipe my face. After shooting Rocco a sneer of disgust, I beeline to the elevator. I text Perla that I'm leaving and to say good-bye to Joe for me. I'm too disgusted and violated to uphold any sort of socially acceptable façade.

If it weren't for my meeting with *Vogue* tomorrow and Oliver's visit this weekend, I'd be taking a taxi directly to JFK and getting out of here faster than you can spell Balenciaga. Out loud. While screaming at the top of your lungs.

Chapter Nineteen

My mouth feels drier than the Sahara Desert. I try to swallow, but all I get is a measly drop of bitter saliva. It tastes like someone stuffed my throat full of dandelions while I was sleeping.

I only had *two* martinis! This is preposterous. My tolerance really isn't what it used to be. Dumplings, lectures about sleeping with well-heeled financiers, groping—it's coming back to me as hard as I felt Rocco against my thigh last night. I shudder at the thought of his grubby paws, the way his prickly face stabbed mine, and the sheer force of which he bombarded me with his tongue. I think I'm going to be sick.

From the kitchen, I hear the sporadic gurgling of the coffee-maker working its roasted magic. I need a coffee more than I need a memory transplant right now. I take a deep breath, inhaling the caffeinated aroma that's wafting underneath my bedroom door.

"*Buenos días,*" Perla calls cheerfully. "Are you awake?"

"Barely," I grumble. I flip the comforter off of me and pad my way to the couch. I sink down, yawning and stretching my arms overhead.

"How did you sleep?" Perla pours two coffees and hands me a mug. How is she already awake and making coffee? I heard her finally lumber in just after two this morning. I wonder what she was doing out alone with Rocco and Joe for an extra five hours after I left . . . On second thought, I don't want to know. "Let's sit outside."

I sleepily follow her out the sliding door, squinting against the sunlight. Our west seventies neighborhood is alive with the sounds of birds, the scent of toasted bagels, and the awkwardness of a couple bickering on the street below.

"I slept fine," I say. "Sorry for leaving so abruptly last night . . ."

Perla looks at me guiltily. "I heard what Rocco did. What a *perro!*" She shakes her head in faux incredulity. Her hands are both wrapped around her mug as she lifts it to her lips. "Please, let me take you out to lunch today? My treat. Kenneth will pick us up. He suggested somewhere downtown. I just feel so bad . . ."

"I have that meeting with *Vogue* today," I remind her. "I kind of just want to study the latest issue and prepare myself."

"Study now and we'll go for lunch after? An early one. Brunch! Besides, I'm seeing Esther today too, so we both have to be out of there *muy rápido.*" Apparently this is the end of the conversation because Perla gets up, goes back inside, and I don't see her again until she tells me that we're leaving in twenty minutes. I don't bother arguing because I don't want to risk doing anything to set her off before *Vogue*. I'm tiptoeing on macarons. If all goes well, I'll be free of the drama and onto the next chapter of my life before summer's end.

Kenneth picks us up in a sporty two-seater Corvette at five minutes to eleven. It's a tight squeeze for three adults, but he insists that we arrive at the restaurant in style. "My publicist would *strangle me* if she caught wind of me arriving anywhere by metro," he says. "The underground is for the hoi polloi." He wrinkles his nose and makes a precipitous turn, causing me to press hard enough against the passenger door that I fear it might pop open and leave me stranded in the middle of Greenwich Avenue.

Style or not, my wide-leg trousers are getting more wrinkled with every bumper-to-bumper red light. Perla is half sitting on my left thigh, which is now completely asleep and stinging with pins and needles. From our Upper West Side apartment, it's supposed to be a twenty-two-minute drive to the Marlton Hotel on West 8th but between the traffic and finding parking, it's more than double. Hoi polloi or not, the subway makes the most sense in Manhattan, if you ask me.

We have almost the entire back terrace at Margaux to ourselves. We're seated at a mahogany table with moss-leather seats that quiver just slightly on the tiled floor. The roof is thatched, allowing thin strips of light to ignite the space, and the ceiling is fringed by rows of terracotta-potted foliage. It's greenhouse chic. Straight out of *House & Garden.*

Right away, Perla enquires after a bottle of sparkling rosé.

"Perrier-Jouët, if you have it," requests Kenneth.

A silver bucket of ice, a frosted forest-green and blush-pink bottle, and three slender flutes appear almost instantaneously. It dawns on me that in the last four months, I've consumed more sparkling beverages than I have in my twenty-six—no, I'm twenty-seven now—years. Kenneth expertly pops the bottle open and its soft bubbles make that exhilarating whisper. He fills our glasses and we clink them together at the center of the table.

"Here's to forgetting about Rocco," Perla says contritely. I cringe. I wish she'd just let me delete those memories. "Although, he *probablemente* just had too much to drink."

"You're not talking about Rocco Gianni are you?" asks Kenneth with heightened curiosity.

Perla slaps her hand on the table and exudes a flicker of amuse-
ment. "I forgot you know him! Do you ever see him? Without me,
I mean."

Kenneth looks appalled. "Of course not. He's vile! I'm offended
on Margot's behalf that you brought her around him. Shame on
you, Perla Rivera," he scolds with a tsk-tsk.

Perla's jaw stiffens momentarily before she casually shrugs. "*Me
olvidé.* It's been years since I last saw him."

"Saying you forgot what Rocco's like is akin to saying you've
forgotten that you quite literally survived on his cash flow for
over two years." Kenneth pivots to face me dead-on. "He used to
call her *La Perla* because that's the only thing he'd accept seeing
her in."

"Back when my body looked like Kate del Castillo's,"
Perla muses.

"She was broke, trying to find her way in the big city—illegally.
The whole situation was quite sticky . . ." His eyes widen and he
leans in closer. I get the feeling that he means "sticky" in more
than one way. "Rocco gave her about a thousand dollars a month
in exchange for—"

"Kenneth!" Perla sternly interrupts. She's almost as pink as
the champagne. "Those days are in the past . . . let's leave them
there. *¿Comprendes?*"

Kenneth looks slightly taken aback, like a scolded puppy.
"Alright, well, are we hungry?" He waves for a server. We place
our orders and then Perla and Kenneth make a hard-exit towards
memory lane, conveniently leaving out anything scandalous that
Perla did in La Perla.

"Do you remember that awful apartment I used to have in
Borough Park?" Kenneth asks, grabbing Perla's hand for emphasis.
"The one with the loft and the rickety ladder?"

"How could I forget?" she cackles. "It was a fucking suicide mission! I almost died every time I crawled up and down that thing . . ."

My attention drifts from their conversation. The patio has started to liven up. On the far side, there's a couple who looks to be on a first date—they're all jittery and blushing. The guy clumsily knocks over a glass of water and a few drops land on the woman's—*oh my god is that suede?*—handbag. Another man in his late-thirties in a navy-blue piqué polo is sitting alone reading *To Have and Have Not* and sipping an iced tea. What interests me most is a mother and daughter duo sitting kitty-corner to us. I allow myself to eavesdrop as I imbibe my fizzy flute.

"I'm so proud of you, gumdrop," says the older woman. I can't see her face, but I can tell that she means what she said. "I love you so much."

"Thanks, Mom," the girl responds. She reddens like she's embarrassed that her mom called her gumdrop in public, but she's also secretly happy about it. "Love you too."

"You're going to do so well at Columbia in the fall. Hey, do you think we should start with dessert? To celebrate?"

"You read my mind!" says the girl. She smiles, a big toothy grin, as her mom motions for the server to bring the dessert menu.

I take a sip of my drink and feel my posture slipping. *That's* what I envision when I think of mothers and daughters. I understand that it's not always smiles, roses, and dessert first, but I don't know *for sure.* The last thing my mom got to celebrate with me was . . . I barely remember. I think it was the short story award I got in the fifth grade. Imagine if she knew I was writing for websites and magazines now and going on a coffee date with someone from one of the world's most prestigious publications. What would her reaction be? Profiteroles for breakfast? Cheesecake for lunch?

An uneasy ache seeps into my bloodstream; a longing for something I'll never truly have. The urge to cry strikes me. If I were alone, I'd allow myself to drown in a puddle of tears. Perla saying that she thinks of me like a daughter and actually acting like it are totally different. (Although, I've seen how she behaves towards her own flesh and it's not much better.) I realize now that I've been craving something from Perla that she can never give me. And it's not profiteroles or cheesecake. I can't believe I ever thought she could be that type of figure for me. How could I be so naïve? She doesn't love me. Chantelle was right; Perla is a textbook user.

"*Hola*, Margot? You're a million miles away," Perla says, breaking me free from my turbulent thoughts. I smile mirthlessly. "Unless you're thinking about the article we need to write about the must-try restaurants in San Francisco, come back to us!"

Our food arrives and I'm glad for the distraction. My plate is piled harrowingly high with shoestring fries and a spicy chicken sandwich on brioche. I wash my first bite down with a swill of rosé. It's outrageously delicious. What I need to do is finish my lunch, politely excuse myself, and head back to the apartment to get ready for my meeting with Amisha. All of my energy needs to be focused on that. It's *technically* just coffee and not a job interview, but if I've learned anything since working in the media industry, it's to talk to everyone because you never know where one conversation might lead you. If Amisha doesn't have an opening for me, perhaps one of her colleagues does? Or she might know someone over at *The Cut* or *Vanity Fair* or even *Bon Appétit*.

"I'll be back, *baño*." Perla excuses herself to the washroom. Kenneth and I are left alone and I realize that now I'm going to have to get out of my head and participate in a conversation.

"So, Miss Moss, no relation to Kate, how do you like working for Perla?" Kenneth asks me as he dips a chunk of lamb meatball in saffron yogurt.

"It's great," I smile. "I'm learning a lot and getting some fabulous firsthand experience."

Kenneth raises a single eyebrow. He doesn't believe me. "That's interesting . . ." he says suspiciously.

"Why?" My voice is a little too high-pitched.

His eyes swim with suspense. "I'll let you in on a little secret... but like the Pussycat Dolls said, you have to keep this *hush-hush*. Perla is one of my oldest and best friends, but it doesn't mean I don't love basking in her drama." I nod my head in agreement and he continues. "So, back when she lived here, she tried to start her *first* magazine; it was to be a *Time Out New York* competitor. Although, it was doomed from the very beginning if you ask me," he whistles. "Anyway, Perla hired this girl from Long Island—she seemed nice enough—and they began working together out of a corner of Rocco's law firm. They were inseparable. I mean, Rachel and Monica kind of inseparable. But then . . . *every*thing went to hell."

My eyes are wide. I had no idea Perla started a magazine before *Roam & Rove*; she never mentioned it, not even in passing. "What happened?" I ask, intrigued and spooked.

"I'm a little fuzzy on the *exact* details, but the gist of it is," he leans across the table, "the two of them had some sort of skirmish and Perla sent letters around to every publication in Manhattan telling them not to hire the poor thing. She attached her photo and everything! And then, all of a sudden Perla was on the run from immigration! Rocco gave her money to leave the country and head back to Toronto before she was officially deported." He leans back in his seat and reaches for his flute. "I think the girl reported her, but there's no proof. Honey, it was mayhem."

My jaw is sitting in the pile of shoestrings. Given that messy situation, I can't believe Perla would be so flippant about *me* staying here illegally. That's something else Perla didn't mention. What other potentially reputation-ruining things isn't she telling me? Suddenly I'm zinging with nerves. If Kenneth is telling the truth, she's more poisonous than a Deathstalker scorpion, an Asian tiger snake, and a Spanish fly combined. Is working at *Roam & Rove* worth risking career suicide? For the second time today, I feel like I'm going to be sick.

"Are you two talking about me?" Perla asks slyly as she sidles up to the table and squeezes back into her spot beside Kenneth. My spine goes rigid from top to bottom. She picks up her lipstick-marked flute and drains its bubbly contents in one fell swoop.

Kenneth skillfully changes the subject. "Have either of you seen *Page Six*?" I shake my head. "Well, if you do, don't believe a word of it. You can't trust anything you read. My publicist is trying to have me seen on the scene with every socialite in Manhattan to create buzz around my restaurant. It's all for show! New York will attempt to hoodwink you like that. But then again, so will L.A., Miami—anywhere worth living."

"Look at you, *guapo*!" Perla says. "Should we get another bottle? To celebrate?"

"I'd love to stay but I should go get ready for my meeting," I say, trying to sound more disappointed than I feel about bailing. "I want to stop by the apartment and freshen up."

"Margot has a meeting with somebody from *Vogue*," Perla drawls to Kenneth with a slight flick of her wrist.

Kenneth beams. "A job interview? You go, honey! You'll be on *Page Six* before we know it, walking arm-in-arm with all of the models-of-the-moment. If you see Joan Smalls, tell her I'd adore to host her at Sashaymi for dinner."

"It's not an interview," Perla interjects before I can say anything. She looks right at me with steely eyes. "Just coffee. Margot is full-time with me, but she might pick up a few assignments from *Vogue* so she can get us free products. I'm fully encouraging her to go after her lifelong goals. I would never want to jeopardize her career path." Her smile gives me an involuntary shiver.

"Nothing wrong with that," says Kenneth. "Where are you meeting?"

"Culture Espresso," I reply. "On West 38th Street?"

"Oh, I was going to say if you love iced matcha, you should go to Black Fox. It's just a stone's throw from the *Vogue* offices."

"Next time!" I say confidently—because I'm confident that I already want there to be a next time. "Well, I'm off . . ." I get to my feet, slinging my purse over my shoulder in the process, and lean in to give Kenneth a one-armed hug. "Thanks for lunch and everything. Wish me luck! See you later, Perla? I'll be back at the apartment before dinner."

"Wait," Perla says, reaching for my arm. "Do you want me to pop by your meeting? It could be good for me to meet this Amelia person too. Who knows your work ethic better than I do? I'm sure that my meeting with Esther won't go all day and if it really came down to it, I could reschedule with her. She'd understand."

My breath flounders in my lungs. Kenneth's eyeballs flick back and forth between me and Perla like he's flipping through a real page-turner. He catches my unnerved eye long enough to give me a look that says, remember what I told you. How could I forget? Perla's volatility has been seared into my brain like a ribeye steak. That's why I feel so desperate now; I'm charred on the outside but rare inside.

"Oh . . ." I pause. "Thanks, Perla. But I think I've got it covered. I don't want to ambush her or anything." I attempt a nonchalant smile but I no doubt look more *American Psycho* than *Miss Congeniality.*

"Are you sure? I think you're underestimating the power of an in-person referral."

"Yes," I practically exclaim. *Take a deep breath,* I instruct myself. *Don't seem ungrateful or who knows what grenade Perla will toss onto the terrace.* "It's totally fine. I don't want you to have to cancel your meeting with Esther. Seriously. Enjoy catching up with her."

Kenneth comes to my rescue before Perla can answer. "Honey, let's grab that second bottle now. I'm thirsty! And you have yet to tell me anything about your little Paloma! How is she? Taking after her mother? Show me a photo!"

Perla releases her grasp on my forearm and it takes every ounce of strength I have not to sprint to the exit before she makes another argument. Current status: working tirelessly to be a woman I'm proud of and that means controlling my composure in public.

***

The flood of adrenaline that's flowing through me right now is as powerful as the Amazon River. My lips are more reflective than my polarized sunglasses, my frame of mind is fearless, and my confidence has been reactivated to its full potential. When it comes to fashion, fun, and flaunting my talents, I'm as fierce as they come.

I arrive at the coffee shop very early. Like, *way* early. I allotted an extra ten minutes for getting lost, another ten for getting *really* lost, and yet another ten just to be safe. Luckily, I didn't need any of them. But now I'm almost thirty minutes ahead of schedule and I can't just sit here loitering. Even though, for a loiterer, I look pretty fabulous. My structured linen blazer is draped over my shoulders on top of a pale-spruce poplin blouse; the matching skirt's hem is ending at the perfect length between my thighs and kneecaps—not short enough to be scandalous but not long enough to make me look like a nun. The suit's oversized gingham pattern is giving me a splash of *Clueless*. But instead of sunshine yellow, mine is stone blue and ready to rule. Usually I'd say I'm more of a Cher, but today I'm definitely Dionne. I'm monochromatic professionalism personified.

The café is buzzing and just as aesthetically-pleasing as Margaux. It's all floral wallpaper, distressed wood, abstract artwork. Intricate chandeliers dangle overhead for a touch of elegance. Scanning the black-and-white letterboard behind the cash, I contemplate what to order; I think I'll have a coffee now and then another when Amisha arrives. I opt for a simple drip dark roast. I pour a substantial splash of cream and then settle into a free space in the ceiling-to-sidewalk windows. Luckily, there are two free stools together; I toss my purse onto the other one to reserve it for Amisha. I check my phone; there's still a solid twenty minutes to wait.

I pass the time people-watching as I sip. First up: a family of tourists wearing matching I <3 NY T-shirts, Bermuda shorts, and sensible sneakers. I imagine they're visiting from one of the Southern states—Alabama? Georgia? South Carolina?—and it's their first time in as bustling a metropolis as Manhattan. I feel a flash of excitement for them. Next up, a gang of girls no more than fourteen skipping down the sidewalk clasping a variety of bags from Forever 21, Zara, and H&M. I remember, with a hint of regret, the days when I thought those were the coolest places to shop. Now that I'm older, I realize the importance of investing in quality over quantity. Whether it makes sense to my (nonexistent) financial advisor or not, spending a couple of hundred dollars on a dress from a local brand is way more satisfying than shoveling fast fashion into my overburdened closet. Still, thrift shopping is the best option for my wallet, wardrobe, and the world.

I'm just beginning to lose interest in people-watching when a woman with a velvet curtain of black hair, a skin tone as delectable as pecan pie, and flawless bone structure struts past the window. She's exclusively wearing Chanel—including a double *C* chain belt—and has a certain *je ne sais quoi* to her walk that only a nineties supermodel could possibly possess. I'd recognize that glamor anywhere.

"Margot Moss?"

I snap back to the present moment and see that Amisha Chowdhury is standing beside me, smiling beguilingly and extending one purple-polished hand. Her auburn hair is tied up in a bun on top of her head with a few strategically styled wisps framing her heart-shaped face. Her thick, bold brows anchor her features and her curved lips are painted a deep, emphatic shade of wine red. She's unblemished in every way. Well, she does work in the beauty department at *Vogue* after all. I can't imagine that she goes anywhere—not even Trader Joe's or Staten Island—without looking ready for a Grace Coddington editorial.

"Hi," I say, standing up to shake her hand. I quickly swipe my purse from the bar stool so she can sit down. "So great to meet you!"

"You too," she says with a broad smile. "Love your last name. As you know, it's very coveted in this industry: Kate, Lila Grace, even Carrie-Anne back in the day."

I flush slightly. "Not to be off topic but, just before you arrived, walking by the window, was that . . ."

"Naomi Campbell? Yeah, we just had a meeting with Pat McGrath down the street. This is *very much* on the down-low but . . ." Her voice is smoother than YSL's Touche Éclat Blur Primer.

"Naomi is creating a capsule collection for her! It's all golden hues and sunset palettes. It's drop-dead ravishing."

"Oh my god," I gush. "She's even more perfect in person."

Amisha laughs heartily. "Tell me about it. There's nothing like standing beside a supermodel all day to make you feel your most confident. But Naomi is so lovely, you can't help but feel elevated in her presence." She hoists her pudgy purse onto the countertop. "Should we order? What can I get you?"

"I'm leaning towards an Americano," I say.

"Good choice," she responds. "Their coffee is the best I've had outside of Europe. And you *have* to try a cookie. They're so gooey it should be illegal."

"Done deal," I say. "But let me get them, as a thank-you for meeting up with me." I unzip my purse and rummage around for my cheetah cardholder.

"Put that away," Amisha instructs. "I have a company card. It's on *Vogue*."

Now that's something I could get used to saying. This can of mango Diet Coke? It's on *Vogue*. A boozy lunch? It's on *Vogue*. Pad thai with extra spring rolls? Not very *en vogue* but you guessed it—on *Vogue*! I know Perla just bought me lunch, technically at the expense of *Roam & Rove*, but this feels different. There aren't any strings attached.

"Richard tells me that you used to work for La Pêche," Amisha says as we sit down with our coffees and cookies. "I'm beyond obsessed with their cold-pressed deodorant. I can't imagine my life without it. I read about it in *Allure* and just had to try it."

"Oh my god," I gasp. "I wrote that blurb!"

"You're kidding! Well, you're certainly persuasive with your copy." Amisha looks impressed. She rips off a chunk of her cookie, leaving an oozing trail of chocolate behind.

I feel a spirited sense of achievement coming over me. Even if Yvette or Tracy didn't recognize me for writing that, someone from *Vogue* did. And that means more to me than all of the leather boots and leopard prints in the world combined. For the first time since my failed promotion, I don't feel like a fool for leaving La Pêche. Maybe for the way it happened, but not for actually doing it, because it led me here, to Culture Espresso, with Amisha Chowdhury, who just complimented my copywriting skills. Inside, I'm doing Katherine Heigl's happy dance from *The Ugly Truth*.

"You know," Amisha says. "Richard doesn't just recommend anyone to me. The fact that he set up this introduction means a lot. He must see something really special in you—in a totally platonic way," she quickly adds. "He's the nicest guy in New York. Cutthroat, but nice. If that makes sense."

As we get to talking, I make sure that I'm maintaining eye contact and that my posture is as upright and poised as Misty Copeland's. It takes a conscious effort to ensure that my arms don't habitually fall into a crossed position; I don't want to risk exuding any kind of vapid mannerisms. So far, our conversation is easy-breezy. I'm glad I spent the morning studying the latest *Vogue* because when Amisha brings up the beauty editorial—shot on a ranch in Connecticut—I immediately applaud the use of alfalfa-green eyeshadow to complement the rolling patches of farmland and she's even more impressed about that than with my blurb in *Allure*.

"You've got a great eye," she says.

I insatiably gobble up the compliment. However, I didn't envisage it coming back to bite me harder than a bear trap not two minutes later. Out of the corner of my "great eye" I see a wobbling blur of highlighter yellow. I almost sprain my neck doing a double take. If I wasn't already sitting down, I think I might crash to the floor in a heap of impending humiliation.

In typical Perla fashion, she is teetering towards the door of the coffee shop on dizzyingly high peep-toe stilettos; this pair is studded and obviously from Valentino's Rockstud repertoire. She's changed since lunch and is now decked out in coordinating Move by Essie garb. *More like garbage*, I think crudely. Her biker shorts are so tight they look vacuum sealed; her hips don't lie and they sure are suffocating. As for her Lilliputian top, it's almost nonexistent; it looks like it was made for Paloma, not a forty-something businesswoman. I swear on Roberto Cavalli, it's one of the most offensive outfits I've ever witnessed.

Amisha is still chatting away and I'm trying to follow along and nod at all the right moments, but my mind is frantically roiling. The café is even busier than it was before and there are no vacant seats in sight. What will Perla do when she bursts through the door? Awkwardly stand behind us? Maybe I can pretend that I don't know her? I'm tempted to grab Amisha by the elbow and whisk her out the back for a quick escape. Assuming there is a back exit. *Oh, god.* What am I going to do? I can't have Perla dragging me down into her dark depths of purgatory. Not today. Not now. Not ever.

It's impossible to breathe as Perla pushes her way inside; her vociferous personality entering before she does. "Margot! *Hola*," she calls. There's no way I can pretend not to know her now. "What are the chances? I just popped in to grab a cappuccino. I didn't realize this is where you were having your big meeting. When you said Culture Espresso, my mind went to the location on 36th!" She shakes her head comically.

Amisha looks at Perla, rouged lips askew, absorbing her outrageous appearance and then back at me with a look of unmitigated confusion. I look back at her, mystified, as if she just asked me to explain the theory of quantum mechanics.

"*Hola*, I'm Perla Rivera." She thrusts her hand at Amisha, who is almost too stunned to accept it. "I'm also a *very* close friend of Richard's. It was me who introduced him to Margot. Isn't she a big-time star?"

After what feels like an entire lifetime, Amisha takes Perla's hand. "Amisha Chowdhury," she says. "And yes, she seems to be." She flashes her extra-white teeth at me, but by the look of her furrowed brows, she's going to require a whole pot of La Mer's Crème de la Mer tonight.

"Perla is the editor of the travel magazine I work for," I say, almost unwillingly. I seem to have lost my proficiency in fierceness. I feel more like Laney Boggs pre-makeover than Cher Horowitz *or* Dionne Davenport right now.

"It's called *Roam & Rove*," Perla adds. "*R&R* for short— because what else is travel for besides a little rest and recuperation? Margot and I report on everything from the most environmental hotels to the best spots to get a hot-stone treatment."

"That's witty," says Amisha politely. "So, Margot—"

Perla cuts her off. "Let me get you a business card." She fishes around in her oversized tote. Eventually, she grasps a crumpled card and hands it over. "Don't mind the appearance," she laughs. "My design team is working on having new cards printed. All of the info is correct though!" *What* design team? Did she forget that earlier this week she asked *me* if I could take over Photoshop duties?

"Thanks," Amisha smiles. "I'll definitely give your site a browse. I mean, I love to travel and I'd love to read some more of Margot's articles."

"*Si*, Margot is a great writer. Of course, I *have* mentored her *mucho* since she started working for me. We are so busy, I don't know how Margot will find the time for *Vogue*!" Perla blathers, placing her palm on my shoulder blade. It takes every fiber of my being not to swat her away. "You know, I think of Margot like a daughter. *Una hija.*"

Without warning, Perla's phone starts blaring at full volume. "It's my daughter," she explains. "My actual *hija.* But be sure to check out my magazine. Do it right away! I'd love to figure out a way to work together. Travel-sized beauty? We could review some products? Margot promised me anti-aging creams! Think about it. Margot, I'll meet you in Bryant Park? *Ciao, cariño.*" She air-kisses us both and then turns on her studded pumps and clomps away, leaving me to erase the last five minutes of Amisha's memory.

"I'm so sorry about that," I say with compunction. "I had no idea that she was going to show up here." My face is so wrinkled with worry that I'm going to be forced to ask Amisha to share her La Mer with me later on. The Americano is unsettled in my stomach; I feel like retching. Did Perla just do to my career what Kenneth said she did to that other poor girl before me? Is egregious behavior and fatal word-vomit today's equivalent of sending out letters to every publication on the island? If my standing in the media industry has been jeopardized because of Perla and her atrocious antics, I'll *never* forgive her. The industry isn't *that* big! How long will it take me to recover? Can I even recover?

"She's certainly . . . magnetic," Amisha says with an uncertain giggle. "I can't imagine dealing with that kind of energy every day."

"Tell me about it," I laugh and roll my eyes. I'm trying my best to smother the raging fire that's burning in my belly. "But seriously, I really can't apologize enough."

"Don't worry about it," Amisha shrugs. "These things happen." She reaches for her phone to check the time. "Yikes—after four already! I've gotta run to another meeting but it was great to meet you, Margot, truly. I'm glad Richard set this up."

"Same! Loved hearing about *Vogue* and your job and . . . just everything!"

We stand up and shake hands. "I'll email you in a couple of weeks. Things are disgustingly swamped right now ramping up for the September release. You have *zero* idea how much work goes into social posts these days!"

Amisha swans out of the coffee shop and across the street. Now that she's gone, I'm free to fume. I sit back down, praying to any and every powerful being in the universe that Perla didn't just fuck this up for me irreparably. How could she just burst in on my meeting like that? Did she *really* confuse the locations or was that just one of many lies in her web of treachery?

I leap to my strappy sandals. I'm ready to confront her. Straightening my skirt, I drape the coordinating blazer over my arm, and head towards Bryant Park. I find Perla leaning against the park fence, near the Nikola Tesla Corner sign, rapidly tapping at her phone. I'm really going to give her a piece of my mind this time. She deserves it. How *dare* she abolish my one chance at getting my dream job! My fluted heels indignantly slap the sidewalk as I storm up to her.

"Perla," I call, ferociously. She looks up and gives me a wide, unsuspecting grin. "What were you doing? Why did you just burst in on my meeting like that?" I'm only vaguely aware of the hordes of ogling pedestrians.

"What?" she asks innocently. "My meeting with Esther finished early so I thought I'd come by to support you . . . Are you mad? Because I came for *you*." For me? To support me? More like ruin the one chance I had to work for the magazine I've been envisioning since I was wearing butterfly barrettes and shopping at Claire's! I have to be honest. At this point, I don't care if we're having a spat in the middle of Manhattan. I've given up on trying to be *the bigger person*; I'll deal with this how I see fit.

"Mad? Yes, I'm mad. I'm furious," I retort. My blazer almost falls to the ground but I catch it just in time.

Perla shrugs. "*No entiendo.* I thought *Vogue* was important to you."

Is she for real? My hands curl into fists and I exasperatedly look at the sky. "It is! That's what I'm trying to tell you. And don't even pretend like you came for *me*, you came for *you* and *your* publication."

A guy with hair down to his lower back wearing Birkenstocks walks by and yells "couple's therapy for the win!" at us. I'm embarrassed, but Perla doesn't seem to notice.

"Margot," she says. "I didn't come for you or for me . . . I told you, I got the locations mixed up." She tries to reach out for me but I flinch. "It was a simple mix-up! What did you want me to do? Pretend not to know you?" She scoffs.

Is Perla even aware that she's just told me two completely opposite excuses in the span of one green light? "You just said that you came to support me, and now you're saying that it was all a mix-up and you just happened to get the locations wrong. Which one is it?"

For a moment, she's like a deer caught in the headlights. But the thing about Perla Rivera is, once she recovers, she serves harder than Serena Williams. "Are you saying that you wish I didn't show up? That I didn't give you a *glowing* recommendation? That I shouldn't have taken time out of my *extremely busy* day to come and support you?" She pauses to give me a look as dirty as the New York subway. "Because that would be very low of you, Margot. After everything I've done for you. I've supported you, paid your way to be here!"

"My *god*," I say. My head shakes back and forth in disbelief. Is she drunk? Or just dense? "Have you heard a single thing I've said? Not everything is about you."

"I don't have time for this! I'm late to pick up Paloma," she spits. "Find your own way back to the apartment." Perla lurches

to the edge of Sixth Avenue, flags down a taxi, and thunderously
slams the door before I even have time to blink.

Chapter Twenty

I'm not sure what's more crushing—the heat or Perla's obvious contradictions. I've been aimlessly walking for nineteen blocks; my forehead is prickling with perspiration, my deodorant is failing me, and my swollen feet don't even feel like they belong to my corpse anymore. My criss-cross sandals, although gorgeous, are veraciously agonizing.

Taxis whir all around me, horns blare, and the faint smell of city smog clogs my nostrils. It's astonishing how Manhattan transforms from pleasant to pungent based on my mood. Still, simmering with ripe emotions or not, I'll take what the city gives me.

Any rationally thinking woman in as much anguish as I am would sit down, take a break, jump in a cab, or retreat to the depths of the underground transit system. Me? I am not thinking rationally. I'm still reeling over the confrontation with Perla and I seem to be under the impression that hobbling off my anger is a good idea. My mind is becoming more muddled with each arduous step.

"Cute shoes," drones a brunette sauntering past me with a scruffy black and brown dog. I feel an immense longing for Lola.

"Thanks," I mumble, lackadaisically. It takes a full New York minute before I register that it was Emily Ratajkowski with her Husky-German-Shepherd mix, Colombo—but not even that challenges my semi-permanent scowl. Similarly, a lone sandwich board that reads "Less drama, more guac!" isn't enough to break my spell either. (Although, somewhere deep down in my soul I giggle.)

Did Perla honestly get the locations mixed up? Was she really there for my benefit and no hidden agenda of her own? Amisha *did* seem to understand. Am I . . . maybe . . . possibly . . . overreacting? No. I know *me*. I wouldn't get this worked up over nothing. It's just, how can Perla possibly think she's blameless in *every single scenario*? She could be standing over a bleeding cadaver with the murder weapon still in her hand and find a way to absolve herself from the crime entirely.

Without quite realizing how, I've turned up outside of Joanne Trattoria. My tortured feet must have been acting on muscle memory; I come here every time I'm in New York. Except for the ultra-gooey cookie, I haven't eaten since Margaux. I request a table for one and am seated on the patio. My feet throb with temporary relief as I collapse into a cushioned wicker chair. I peek down to assess my foot situation. It's beyond bad. My toes look like a tortured version of the Canadian flag—red and raw on the edges, white and pinched in the middle. I order eggplant parmesan because it reminds me of Oliver, and a glass of house red. Just two more days and Oliver will be here. I just need to make it through *two more days* and then he can comfort me in a king-sized bed with room service, robes, and best of all? No Perla Rivera.

I savor each drop of wine like it might be my last. How long is it appropriate to stay seated at a restaurant after you've finished your meal? I've eaten as slowly as possible but short of licking the plate, there's nothing left. I'm dreading going back to the apartment, but it's not like I can avoid it all night. Where would I sleep? Plus, my laptop and all of my clothes are there and it's crossed my mind that Perla might do something; perhaps toss them off the balcony or stuff everything into a garbage bag and leave it on the curb. I pray it's not pick-up day.

For sixty more seconds, I allow myself to remain at the table, avoiding the inevitable. Then, I work up the courage to hold up my weight on my damaged feet and begin the murderous six-block walk back. The closer I get to the apartment, the harder my heart palpitates. It's all I can hear. I swear, it's so loud that it's echoing off of the stairwell walls as I cautiously make my ascent. I have an irrational fear that at any moment, a neighbor might throw open their door and tell me to keep it down. This is why I hate explosive showdowns so much; I can't handle the aftermath. Fruitlessly, I experiment with inhaling, exhaling, repeating my "Power Woman Mantra"—but nothing works. At this point my apprehension is my most dominant personality trait.

One more flight to go. I'm concentrating so hard on forcing myself up the stairs that I hardly register when I'm nose-diving towards them. *Thump!* I'm a tangle of limbs with aching feet and now carpet burns on my knees. My body slides down a few steps and I make no attempt to stop until the landing irons me out. *What is wrong with you, Margot? How did you go from a meeting with* Vogue *to allowing yourself to flop down a flight of stairs?* Shakily, I stand myself up and slide my key into the lock. I creak the door open as softly as I can. To my relief, the apartment is pitch-black and blissfully empty—no Perla, no Paloma, and no Floramaria. My phone begins flashing with texts and voicemails from Oliver and my friends, all of them asking anxiously about the meeting. I have no idea what to tell them. It went swimmingly? It was cataclysmic? I can hardly wrap my mind around it.

To the group chat:

Still can't believe I met with Vogue! Just getting home now. So tired. Will catch you up tmrw!

To Oliver:

Let's just say, I can't wait until you arrive this weekend. Miss you xoxo

Then, I expeditiously wash my face, brush my teeth, and tuck myself into bed before anyone gets home. I fall asleep within seconds. Who knew hours of overthinking and stress worked better on me than a dose of melatonin?

***

The next morning, I stay in bed until I'm convinced that if I don't go to the bathroom immediately, I'll be left with permanent bladder damage. And I definitely do not want to be stuck with that on top of a hefty hospital bill in the United States.

Lifting the blankets off of me takes extreme effort; it feels like I'm bench-pressing three hundred pounds. Somehow I manage, and make it to the bathroom unseen. Splashing cold water on my face, I consider my options: talk with Perla about the Bryant Park blowout, quit my job and run away, or zip my lips and stay quiet about the whole thing. This is harder than deciding which Britney Spears albums are in my top three. (Actually, now that I think about it—In the Zone, Blackout, and Britney obviously. Currently, I feel like I'm a Slave 4 . . . this job.)

As I emerge, Paloma looks up from watching cartoons and spots me. Well, in an apartment this small, I couldn't expect to stay inconspicuous forever. No matter how much I'd hoped to become invisible and skulk through the rest of the day.

"Morning, Margot," she gleefully squeals. "I'm so happy you're finally awake! Guess what? I got to stay home from camp today!"

"Morning, Paloma," I say, with as much enthusiasm as I can muster. "That's exciting. Was it cancelled or something?"

"No, Mommy just said that I don't have to go. I get to hang out with you instead. I'm so excited." She vigorously pats the spot beside her on the sofa. "Come watch *Carmen Sandiego* with me!" I hesitantly start walking towards her. Where is Perla? I'm nervous to see her, but it makes me even more nervous not to; she's too skilled at hiding in the shadows like an elusive jaguar, waiting to pounce.

"*Buenos días*, Margot," Perla suddenly calls from the kitchen. "Are you hungry? I'm toasting bagels. *Quieres* one or two?" My gut clenches when I hear her voice but . . . she sounds normal. Nice, even? Cheerful. Yesterday, we had a spicy argument on a very public street corner and now she's offering me a bagel? I know I shouldn't be surprised. I've been on the receiving end of her roller-coaster moods one too many times before. Yet, it still catches me off guard. Doesn't she get exhausted? It's exhausting enough for me to keep up with which version of herself she's emulating— supportive boss, motherly mentor, or apex predator.

"Morning," I say cautiously. "I'll have one, thanks." I may be stressed, but my manners haven't slipped. I lower myself onto the couch beside Paloma. She snuggles closer, beams up at me, and grabs my hand in her small, soft palm. My heart spasms with guilt. It's impossible for me to keep gripping my anger towards Perla when this poor little girl is here, craving tender loving care. I rarely see Perla giving that to her. I've seen her yell, berate, and gesture berserkly at least fifty times more often than I've seen her comfort Paloma in any way.

A heaviness weaves through my ribs and balloons in my chest cavity. My mind is made up; I have to ingurgitate my feelings towards Perla. It would be unfair to Paloma to put her through yet another explosive scene. I can only assume she's been through enough of those without me instigating another one. Who knows how many outbursts she's had to endure when I'm not around? I feel a primal need to protect her.

I slip on my imaginary Marc Jacobs rose-colored glasses (they're not only good for seeing office spaces in a new light) and endeavor to believe Perla. Let's say, for argument's sake, that she genuinely did get the locations mixed up. Or perhaps she really did mean well and had my best interests at heart. After all, she has been in the media industry for about a decade longer than me. She could have been trying to help me with *Vogue*; an in-person recommendation does sound good, in theory. Although, I wish she'd been dressed in Theory instead of her neon spandex ensemble. But whatever. That's part of the past now.

Bagels on plates, we set up our "home office" on the balcony. Paloma brings out a pad of paper and a pack of pencil crayons and joins us. Truthfully, I'm glad that she's home today and can act as a sort of buffer between Perla and I.

"I'm going to be a grown-up lady like you today," she says to me. "Mommy, what should I work on?"

"How about . . ." Perla pretends to think about it. "The best ice cream flavors in *Nueva York*?"

"You're an expert on that subject," I add.

"Okay!" Paloma exclaims. She begins drawing ice cream cones and scribbling them in with a rainbow of colors.

Burying my head in my laptop, I begin working on a budget-friendly guide to Manhattan. It's called "Sightsee NYC on the Cheap" and features visiting the public library, strolling the High Line, browsing the Chelsea Markets, reading a book in Central

Park, absorbing the wackiness of Times Square, window shopping in SoHo, and enjoying a frugal food-truck lunch in Petrosino Square. I'm definitely going to take my own sightseeing advice; Oliver and I will make our way through the list this weekend. I'm typing wildly when Perla's voice startles me.

"Margot," she says with a sympathetic expression. "*Cariño*, you've done so much for me on this trip. And I feel terrible about yesterday's misunderstanding. Can I please make it up to you? I want to take you out—just us. Don't ask me how, but I managed to get reservations at one of the most exclusive places in the city . . ."

"What happened yesterday?" asks Paloma with curious, round eyes. Perla doesn't answer, she just continues staring at me, waiting for an answer.

"Umm . . ." My mouth is slightly agape. I begin tensely thumbing my earrings. The thought of spending an evening alone with Perla is as appetizing as a browned avocado; at first glance it looks disgusting but if I scrape off the top layer, there might be something salvageable underneath. I crunch the pros and cons. If I say yes, it'll probably keep Perla's unpredictability at bay, especially now in front of Paloma. If I say no, she could decide to reserve my dignity and self-esteem for dinner instead. "Yeah, sure," I agree listlessly.

"Seriously, what happened?" Paloma repeats. "Hellooo?"

"Amazing," Perla says, ignoring her child. "You're going to love this place. Wear the fanciest thing you packed."

"Mommy?"

"Yes?" Perla's attention is back on her computer screen.

"What happened yesterday?"

"Nothing, Palomita." Perla glances over at me but it's impossible to read her expression. "Nothing at all."

***

We have a table smack-dab in the middle of Il Mulino. I feel exceptionally elite. Didn't President Obama eat here one time? I've only heard rumors about this quintessentially Upper East Side establishment, and they all revolve around how upscale and inaccessible it is to anyone who falls beneath the crème de la crème of the city. As an afterthought, I wonder how Perla managed to make a reservation on such short notice?

My animosity towards her hasn't altogether disappeared but I've decided to put it on hold until Oliver gets here tomorrow and I can really talk things through with him. I know he will tell me to put every ounce of endurance I have left into getting hired at *Vogue*, which is already my lasered-focused aim, but I need to hear it from someone else. (By the way, dating someone who pushes you to be a better version of yourself is invaluable. I love him so much.)

A dapperly dressed waiter glides over to our table and asks if we would prefer sparkling or still? "Sparkling, of course," orders Perla. "And can we see a wine list?"

"It is my absolute pleasure," he answers, smoothly pulling out a menu from behind him. "I'll be back with your sparkling refreshments." He bows his head and swishes away.

My giddiness dissipates like soda gone flat. A single glass of sparkling wine costs more than my entire outfit. (I slipped into a satiny leopard wrap dress and tied my locks back into a bun with a couple of loose strands framing my face à la Amisha Chowdhury. My feet are beyond blistered from walking the length of Manhattan in strappy sandals yesterday, so I was forced to bandage them up and shove them into my cowboy boots.) Unless these prices are in pesos, how can Perla afford this place? Sidney's investment is going to be gone after tonight if we order anything more than a garden salad and tap water.

"Perla," I start, nervously. "Have you seen the prices? I'm not sure that—"

"Margot, stop. I have a plan. Just order whatever you want. We're celebrating!" As an afterthought she adds, "And I'm apologizing." I'm far from ready to accept an apology from Perla but I do feel like a celebration will help lift my spirits. Champagne is the Band-Aid I need to make it through the next twenty-four hours.

I'm at the point in my recovery process where I'm ready to chastise myself for not saying something more interesting to Emily Ratajkowski and her dog yesterday than my pathetically mumbled "thanks." Cultivating a crop of blisters was no excuse to be so jaded. Maybe I'll get to make up for it when I see her around the *Vogue* offices. I'm going to begin fiercely manifesting that now.

By the time the mounds of carbonara start tingling my taste buds, I've fully resolved to just enjoy the evening. I'm still on guard, but slowly melting like the baked clams do when they touch my tongue. I've *almost* brainwashed myself into believing that Perla's actions weren't malicious. She *must* have had her reasons for doing what she did and it feels too sinister and negative to think that she would show up solely to sabotage me. It's so . . . immature! Toxic. She's a grown woman with a business and a child, for crying out loud.

We wash everything back with a bottle of Dom Pérignon; it's bursting with the softest bubbles I've ever experienced. We order more marinated zucchini, grilled octopus, and a caprese salad to split. I think this is the most relaxed we've been all trip. Either that or I'm heavily under the influence of the exorbitant libation we're guzzling like water.

"*Salud, cariño*," Perla says as we clink glasses. "I'm so proud of you for going after the *Vogue* opportunity. I'll admit, it *did* cross my mind that you might be choosing them over *Roam & Rove*, but nonetheless, I've accepted that you can do both." She takes a lengthy sip. "You remind me of myself when I was your age. Determined, stubborn, and vicious."

I wouldn't say that I'm *vicious* but I assume she means that as a compliment. The champagne causes sensations of elation to fizzle through my bloodstream. I decide to give Perla the benefit of the doubt; maybe she is happy for me. Besides, it can't be good for my mental health to spend so much time deciphering her murky motives.

"Shall we order dessert?" Perla asks, beckoning for the waiter.

Even though I'm practically bursting at the seams—my wrap-around belt is digging into my waist—I can't turn down something *dulce*. It would be wrong to dine at Il Mulino for the first time and skip dessert. I settle on the cheesecake while Perla opts for panna cotta. It's so good that I feel like ordering a second slice for the road.

"I'll be back," Perla announces. She gets up, adjusting her ruffled BCBG Max Azria dress and flounces towards the restrooms. I have to admit, this is the best I've seen her look in a while. Definitely better than yesterday. Her curly hair is swept to the side, and her layers wrap gingerly around her plumped-up cheekbones. She's wearing a silver cross on a thin chain with matching earrings, and her makeup isn't overly done. Dare I say, she looks . . . almost as delicate as the vase of red roses on our white-clothed table.

Happily intoxicated, I fumble for my phone and connect to the free WiFi; it spasms with a text from Oliver.

Hey, babe, call me when you get a chance. I have some bad news . . .

My intoxication fizzles out. Bad news? My mind immediately goes to something wrong with Lola. Did she get attacked by a bigger dog at the park? No, because surely Liao would be the one to let me know. Did something happen to Oliver? Did he hurt himself? Hastily, I select FaceTime Audio and my saliva dries up; I reach for my sparkling water.

"Hey," I blurt the second I hear the call connect. "Is everything okay? Are you okay?"

"Hi," he laughs. "Yeah, I'm fine. All good. It's just work . . ."

My shoulders return to their normal place down my back and my breathing calms. "Okay, thank *god*. You have no idea the places my mind went." I exhale a giggle of relief. "What's up with work?"

"Don't kill me," he says. "But . . ." I get the feeling I want to kill him already. "There's been a mammoth fuck-up with the app. We're supposed to have the vertical slice ready to go by tomorrow and as of right now, it's solidly broken. No one knows what the fuck happened and I'm the only one not on bloody vacation so it's up to me to figure it out. The whole company could go up in flames like Digg v3." The tech lingo and references go over my coiffed head, but I know what he's getting at. My elbows drop to the table and I rest my cheek onto my fist.

"You can't come, can you?" I ask, unable to keep the disappointment from my voice.

"I'm so sorry babe . . . but unless I get this sorted by tomorrow afternoon, which I'm not so sure I will, then I can't." He sounds legitimately distressed. "But I could fly in on Saturday? Stay the night? Or what about next weekend?"

"Okay, let's talk about it tomorrow. Good luck, love you."

We hang up and I feel like someone just reached into my chest and plucked out my heart. It's not his fault, and I admire his dedication to his job, but it still feels like a devastating setback to my weekend of bliss. Am I really going to be stuck at the apartment with no reprieve? Up until this point, my bubbling savoir faire has been based off of the plan to escape for two whole, peaceful days with Oliver. The flock of butterflies that I usually have after talking to him have morphed into moths, searching for any glimmer of light to shed on the situation. So, he's not coming this weekend. My head feels on the verge of vertigo. Well, he *might* come if he gets the project done. Although, that didn't sound optimistic. What am I going to do? My champagne Band-Aid is coming unstuck.

I look up to see Perla approaching our table. A gentleman of perhaps seventy or seventy-five is trailing behind her. If I thought Rocco and Joe looked old, this guy could be their father. He has snowy hair, a maze of deep-set wrinkles, and is wearing what looks like an understated but extraordinarily expensive Brunello Cucinelli suit. He reeks of old money.

"Margot, I want you to meet George Gilbert," Perla says, smoothing down her dress. George pulls back her chair and she graciously takes a seat. "I slipped on my way to the washroom, and George helped me get back up. It was so embarrassing!" She doesn't look an iota embarrassed. In fact, she looks rather pleased. She emits a burst of laughter while eyeing George flirtatiously.

"Are you okay?" I ask. Falling from heels her height is like freefalling from a helicopter. "Hi, George. Nice to meet you." We shake hands—his is quite leathery—and he gives me a warm, veneer-filled smile.

"George is going to join us for a drink. He says he might have a lead on an office space here in the city. Isn't that incredible?"

George smiles proudly and says, "It's nothing, really. I dabble in real estate."

Even through my distorted intoxication, my alarm bells start ringing like church on Sunday. There's zero chance of Perla innocently asking this George character to join us for a harmless drink.

She's going to stick him with the tab! So *this* was her tactic all along. No wonder she didn't bat a mascaraed lash before requesting the Dom Pérignon. For someone who claims to be such a feminist, she spends a lot of time buttering up old men. She's a first-class freeloader.

George tells us about his investments in Texas oil and his summer house in the Hamptons, but I'm hardly listening. Perla, on the other hand, is hanging onto every word as if her life depends on it. Or the payment of our million-dollar check depends on it.

"We'd love to spend a few days in the Hamptons. Wouldn't we, Margot?" Perla asks, turning to me and giving me a look that tells me that there's only one acceptable answer. She carefully caresses George's forearm. Ew. I don't think I'll ever get used to reaching into the pockets of total strangers.

I nod, shifting uncomfortably in my seat. I would love to go to the Hamptons, but not with Perla and George. He seems nice enough, but that's not the point. The only place I want to be right now is home—my home, in Toronto. My optimism is strapped to a luge, recklessly riding down an icy track towards rock bottom. I can't believe I've waited all week for Oliver and now he might not show up.

"I'd love to host you, ladies," George says, beaming at Perla. "I have a fifty-seven-foot yacht we can take out and I know the best place to get shellfish. Do you like lobster rolls?"

"Like?" Perla chortles. "Try, love! *Me encantan.*"

George is the last one to finish his drink and thankfully, when the waiter asks if we want another one, Perla declines. Before the check reaches the table, George swoops in and snaps it up. His reflexes are impressive. "Please, allow me," he asserts. "It's been such a pleasure to be in the company of two beautiful women."

Perla makes a false move towards her purse. "Nonsense, I couldn't allow you to pay for us! We only just met."

"An independent woman," he chuckles. *If only you knew*, I think mordantly. "Still, I have to insist."

There's a short pause while Perla bluffs contemplation. "Only if you're sure . . ." Her hand caresses his cheek and it's like I can already see him liquifying his assets for her. This whole exchange makes me writhe. "Margot, why don't you go flag down a taxi?"

Just steps from Madison Avenue, hailing a taxi requires almost no effort. I flick my wrist and one comes to a grinding halt in front of the restaurant. The meter is just under $5 when Perla staggers into the backseat. Her eyelids droop and she rests her head against the window. Did she do a round of shots or something? Her alcohol tolerance is shockingly low for someone who steadfastly consumes eight glasses per day.

"Pull over here!" Perla hollers to the driver. He yanks the car over to the curb without so much as a glance in the rearview mirror. My knees slide and bang against the seat ahead of me. *God*, driving in New York is aggressive. It's the equivalent of a Chanel sample sale for socialites—you have to have your eye on where you want to go and you don't stop for anyone or anything until you get there. Specifically if your eye is on a pair of quilted two-tone boots.

Perla heaves herself out of the taxi, her phone plummeting to the pavement in the process. Unsteadily she bends down in slow-motion to pick it up. "Here," she slurs, tossing it back to me. There's a lightning bolt of cracks on the screen. "Hold onto this. I'm getting pizza. Those portions were *muy chiquito* and I'm fucking starving." The portions were so gargantuan that we could hardly finish it all, but I don't remind her of that. I watch her stumble away in mild irritation. She's drunker than Kristin Wiig in *Bridesmaids*.

Three dollars and forty cents have flashed by on the meter and there's still no sign of her. Where is she? And what time is it? I stifle a yawn. Since Perla's phone is still in my lap, I don't bother fumbling around in my beaded purse for mine. Instead, I tap hers. When it doesn't light up, thanks to the recent damage, I tap it again. When nothing happens still, I tap harder and accidentally swipe up. Her phone not only comes to life, but it unlocks and opens to her email app. I can't believe she doesn't have a passcode. As I'm squinting to read the time stamp in the top left-hand corner, my own name catches my eye.

What? I blink a few times, trying to make sense of what I'm seeing. There's an email to Richard with a "follow up?" nudge beside it, and my name is the subject line. Why is my name the subject line? Who sent the email first? Could it be about the meeting with Amisha? I have to find out.

I check over my shoulder and then peek in the side mirror. No sign of Perla returning with a greasy pizza slice. The coast is clear. I feel a dart of foreboding; I know it's wrong to look through someone's email, but I'm blaming the Dom Pérignon—if it wasn't so easy to polish off, I wouldn't have had as much and my inhibitions wouldn't be on bed rest for the night. Also, Perla has done so much *shit* to me that it feels almost obligatory to look. It would be wrong *not* to look.

My stomach somersaults as I open the email; it feels like I ingested a pound of rocks. They were definitely talking about me—or at least Perla was; there's no reply from Richard. But still, it's not good. It's not good at all, and it's wordy. I carefully read the date; it's from last Friday. I do a mental calculation . . .

That was the day we went to see a couple of offices and then went thrift shopping. I told Perla about Richard setting up the *Vogue* meeting that morning. A flashback of her compulsively checking her phone and furiously typing at Beacon's Closet comes to mind; first she said it was Veronica, and then she said she was talking to Esther. I knew something seemed off. Is *this* what she was sending? My eyes devour the message in its entirety eleven times over.

To: r.neuman@advance.com

From: perlarivera@roamrovetravel.com

Subject: Margot

Richard,

It was great to see you. I enjoyed our conversation . . . Margot mentioned that you're putting her in touch with someone at Vogue? This might be out of place but I think that would be a big-time mistake on your part. She's nowhere near ready for an opportunity like that. Do not risk your reputation for someone who isn't going to make you look good in the long run. I practically invented her and I'm ashamed to admit that she's not even as good as I would have hoped, after so much effort. Sad. I'm thinking of getting rid of her myself. Replace her with someone more up to the level I'm at. Anyway, I thought you should know. I hope this doesn't affect our working relationship!

Besos,

Perla Rivera xxxxx

Every excuse I've ever made for Perla's bad behavior and her verbal attacks and overall *fucking* offensive existence pops in my face like a piece of bubble gum, leaving me in a sticky mess of hurt and mistrust. I'm thinking back on every despicable thing she's done from the very beginning of our relationship—the break-in, the lies, the manipulation, the invoice fraud, the threats, the demeaning remarks. It's a horrific montage. Has Perla *ever* truly apologized to me for any of that? She brushes things off and rationalizes them away, but has she ever looked me in the eye and actually said she's sorry? And meant it?

I feel like a bottle of champagne that's been left in the freezer and finally, this is the moment that the cork has been forced out, exploding everywhere. It's one thing to downplay Perla's maliciousness to my friends, but I've been doing it to myself too; lying to myself. How could I be so stupid? So unsophisticated and gullible?

I've deemphasized every single thing about Perla and blamed it on her past traumas, her single mother status, her struggles . . . I've made more excuses for her than Joan Clayton made for Toni Childs—and if their twenty-plus-year friendship couldn't survive, our tepid one won't. I need to accept that sometimes bad things happen, not because of the situation, but because of the person. And Perla Rivera is bad to the core.

How could she tell Richard that I'm not *up for the opportunity*? That she *invented* me? That she's thinking of *getting rid of me*? I feel the Dom Pérignon and Italian cuisine churning in my belly like a witch's cauldron. Reflexively I whip open the taxi door and retch onto the pavement.

"Hey, just not in the cab, kid," says the taxi driver in a thick New York accent. "You needa get some water?" It sounds like *wattah*.

Shaking my head, I smile wanly and wipe my mouth on the back of my hand, leaving a trail of lipstick. My gut feels disembowelled. The Band-Aid that was holding me together through dinner has vanished. My face is burning with a blaze of anxiety, my palms are slippery with sweat, and blood is pumping through my veins harder than the drums in Beyoncé's *Homecoming* documentary.

I can't believe I let myself get duped *this* badly. All for a job at a magazine that doesn't even break a thousand readers per month and still, after all of this time, doesn't have a single advertiser! If love is blind, careers are suicidal. I'm starting to think that the whole "magazine" is just a front for Perla to take "investments" from her wealthy suitors. The thought makes me want to puke again.

I need to set the record straight with Richard. A terrifying need to explain myself chews at my bones until I think I might just irreparably shatter. But I don't have any cell reception! *Fuck.* I curse my useless phone. With trembling fingers, I forward the email to myself and then delete it from Perla's sent messages. I need to have proof of this sleazy ploy to ruin my career, my connections, my reputation. This has gone revoltingly past anything forgivable. Perla has made a threat to my livelihood and I'm ready to sue her for all she's worth. *Fuck. This. Job.*

Desperately, I wish I could push a button and be instantly teleported back to Oliver, Lola, and a triple martini. I'd even take it with olives.

Chapter Twenty-One

Perla was too consumed by drunkenly Hoovering her greasy slice of supreme to talk to me for the rest of the cab ride. Which was fine by me because I wasn't sure what would slip off my tongue if I'd been forced to converse. When we got back to the apartment, she kicked off her peep-toes and went to bed without brushing her teeth or removing her makeup.

It's now six thirty in the morning and I've had the worst sleep of my life. The only "sleep" I got was between the hours of two and five when my eyes miraculously managed to stay closed. So much for my stress-induced melatonin; it's adjourned production. I haven't told anyone about the email yet—not my friends, not Oliver. I've drafted nine different versions of an explanatory text to Richard but deleted them all. It seemed wrong to send him a panicked message in the middle of the night.

I'm frantically Googling flights back to Toronto. As much as I hate to leave the city of my dreams, I have to escape Manhattan. It would be impossible to stay here another two weeks and however many days with Perla. I'd leave right now if I could, but I'm not seeing anything available until tonight. I've triple checked every airline: Porter, WestJet, and Air Canada are all full. *Shit.* I think my best bet is to just go to LaGuardia, and await a cancellation. Even if the ticket costs more than my monthly rent, I have to get out of here. I'll just cut back on groceries for the next while. I'll survive on mangoes and drip coffee.

Fleeing before sunrise, although cowardly, feels infinitely more tempting than seeking an explanation from Perla; the urge to channel my inner *Runaway Bride* is powerful. However, I know that I have to confront her. Paloma wasn't home when we got back last night, so I assume she spent the night at Floramaria's and will go straight to camp from there. Facing Perla will be easier if Paloma isn't there to witness any nastiness.

When I hear the toilet flush, my neck tenses. Perla is up. My breathing comes in stunted bursts; I don't want her to know that I'm awake yet. She pads to the kitchen and I hear her rummaging around in the fridge, placing ingredients on the counter. Will she be chopping things? I don't want to confront her if she's holding a knife. Not that I *really* believe she would try to stab me, but who knows? Interacting with Perla is like pressing shuffle on a playlist; whether you get murderous or mellow is completely up to chance. I need to be strategic.

Last night, I was so full of rage and disgust and incredulity but slowly, over the course of the last few sleepless hours, my emotions have morphed into pure and simple dread. I'm so exhausted, so worn out, and my strength to handle Perla's absurdity has conclusively depleted. If I don't get out of this situation today, I'll develop either permanent insomnia, depression, or chronic dizziness. Perhaps all of the above. At least, those are some of the symptoms that popped up when I Googled the side effects of severe, unmanaged stress.

My anxieties are whirring faster than the Vitamix; its gurgles ricochet through the apartment. Creeping out of the bedroom,

I feel lightheaded. I pause in the doorway to catch my breath and balance. *You can do this, Margot! Don't let Perla get away with another sabotage. This is your career we're talking about here.*

"Margot?" Perla calls. "Are you up? I made us strawberry smoothies."

My internal organs are as pulverized as a strawberry smoothie. My throat clenches at the thought of drinking one; I'm sure I'd choke if I tried. Like a patch of unruly weeds, my thoughts are tangled. They need pruning. Where do I start? How do I start? Whatever I do, this is total self-annihilation. *Look out, Manhattan, take cover, I'm about to detonate Perla Rivera!*

"I need to talk to you about something," I manage, walking into the dining area. I tensely take a seat at the table. Perla is still in the kitchen, dividing the blender's thick pink contents between two glasses. She whips around and I recoil. The makeup she didn't remove before bed has become an homage to the Joker. The resemblance is uncanny.

"About last night? Wasn't George amazing?" She joins me at the table, sliding one of the glasses in my direction. "Don't worry, we'll go to the Hamptons after your weekend with—what's his name? Oliver? It won't affect anything."

"It's about last night," I say in a fatigued voice. "But not about George. It's something else." My fingertips fly to my earlobe. I apprehensively maul my piercings.

"Oh?" Perla's brows scrunch together as she dives into her drink.

"I saw the email you sent to Richard." When she shows no signs of recognition, I add, "The one about me."

"What email? What are you talking about?" She *almost* sounds rattled but keeps a blank expression—with the help of her cosmetic surgeon. The fact that she can lie so callously about something she veritably did is deeply disturbing. However, the unnerved edge in her voice gives me a boost of confidence. She knows she's guilty.

I know she's guilty. There's no way she can deny it this time. I have proof.

"Perla, please . . ." It takes every fiber of my being to maintain eye contact; even though her blackened eyes are giving me chills. "I saw the email in your phone. The one where you told Richard not to introduce me to *Vogue*? And that you're ashamed I'm not *good enough* and you're thinking of *getting rid of me* . . ."

Perla's bewildered denial lasts no longer than a breath mint. Her skin color is becoming increasingly rouge. Her fist cracks down on the table. "Are you saying you went through my fucking emails? *¡Mis mensajes privados!* What the *fuck*?"

"That's not the point—"

"That's the *whole* point!" She gets to her feet, grabs her smoothie glass, and chucks it across the room. It smashes against the wall and begins dripping down to the floor, leaving a seed-filled trail of goop. It's dramatic, even for her. "You had no right to look through my private messages! How can I ever trust you again? After all I've done for you? *Desagradecida.*"

My eyes feel like they might pop out of my skull. I scoff, an ugly, hoarse noise fleeing my throat, and fold my arms across my chest. "After all you've *done for me*? That's hysterical. You must be joking."

"What else did you see?" Her arms motion with a mind of their own while beads of saliva flee her gaping mouth. "What were you looking for? When have I ever made you question my intentions?"

Has she lost her mind? Her recent memory? I suddenly feel whiter than meringue and am physically shaking. Now, I abruptly stand up; I tower over her. "I helped you break into your ex's apartment! I went on a date with Sidney's son for *your* investment! I worked tirelessly for months to dodge your threats and lies and freak-outs!" My voice comes out more frenzied than I'd anticipated. "And you're seriously asking me why I would question your intentions?" My chest is heaving. I'm struggling to bring my heightened hysteria back down to earth. Although, as wild as this dispute is, I'm quite empowered. "Were you trying to subvert my entire career or just the opportunity with *Vogue*?" I ask, as evenly as possible.

Perla is gnarled in fury. A bulging vein in the middle of her forehead is throbbing angrily. (Fun fact: a spiteful attitude can do more to reverse your skincare efforts than binge drinking and sleeping with your makeup on—in Perla's case anyway.) "You don't get to ask the questions around here, *cariño*. You looked through my *private* emails!"

I exhale strenuously. My fists clench. A sudden ferocity takes control of my composure. This is going nowhere—but I'm not. I storm from the dining room and head straight to my bedroom. I bustle around in a cyclonic state of indignation and haphazardly cram my belongings into my suitcase. Forget Marie Kondo, I'm packing like the Tasmanian Devil and I don't care what my clothes will look like when I get home.

Perla follows me into the room. "*¿Qué estás haciendo?* Where do you think you're going?"

"Home," I grunt, pushing past her to grab my laptop. Since she's throwing more and more Spanish into the mix, I revise my reply. "*Mi casa.*"

"You're not going anywhere," she hisses. "You're on my payroll. I *own* you."

I stop mid-zip on my suitcase. "No, Perla, you don't. I'd rather go take my chances at the airport than spend another minute here with you. You're poison."

"Well you're fucking fired then!" she roars. She continues yelling at me but I'm too busy brusquely checking the apartment to make sure I'm not leaving anything behind. I don't want to risk having to come back here. Perla's stentorian shouts echo off the walls. As she's in the middle of a sentence so vulgar it wouldn't even be allowed to be played for a jury uncensored, Paloma walks through the door. She freezes on the spot, a flood of tears instantaneously pooling in her eyes.

"Perla . . ." I say sharply.

"*¡Vete a la mierda!*" she screams. "You know that you'll never have as good of an opportunity as this again. *Egoísta*, I gave you *everything*!"

"Perla!" I shout, more forcefully this time.

She stares fixedly at me, her face full of contempt. "What?" she snaps. I nod towards the door. Perla spins around and finally notices her whimpering daughter. But instead of comforting her, she only grows more incensed. "What are you doing here? Why aren't you at camp? *¿Dónde está Floramaria?* What am I paying her for?"

Paloma bawls. She can hardly speak through her sobs. "She's . . . downstairs . . . I forgot . . . my backpack." She points to the corner of the living room near the balcony door. I pounce for it and hurry to hand it to her. The sooner she gets to camp, the better.

"Paloma, stop it," Perla instructs. "Stop crying or I'll give you something to cry about. You need to say good-bye to Margot. This is the last time you're ever going to see her. She's going home."

"What?" Paloma blubbers. A glob of snot dangles from her nose. "What do you mean?" She looks from Perla, to me, to the smoothie mess, and back again, eyes wide. "Margot? Why are you going? Will I get to play with Lola again?" She runs over to me and wraps her arms around my waist. "Don't go, Margot, please don't go."

"I wish I didn't have to," I say. I kneel down on the floor so that we're closer in height. Perla watches us in incomprehension. "I'm sorry . . . I'll miss you—"

"Paloma! Floramaria is waiting," Perla says. Her hands are firmly on her hips. Paloma squeezes me so hard that I think I might die by strangulation. Then, she solemnly walks to the door. She gives me one last tearful glance over her shoulder and my chest explodes with sorrow. I wish with my whole being there was more I could do for her.

Perla watches Paloma walk down the first flight of stairs before turning back to me. Her facial features are violently twisted. She looks like someone who has just bitten down on a handful of severely sour candies. "*¿Sabes qué?* You've been nothing but a big-time *dolor en mi culo*. Paul was right, I never should've hired you." Her voice is vindictively triumphant. She truly feels like she's won this battle. "Mark my words, *cariño*, you'll never work in the media industry in New York again. I'll make sure of it. Now get the fuck out of this apartment."

Her words hang stale in the air, slowly evaporating. A sliver of my brain wonders how she plans on crippling my career this time. But other than that, I don't dignify her venomous remarks with a response. Minus the fact that I feel like I could vomit at any second, I feel better than I have in the last two weeks. I finally told Perla how I feel. It's like I've just cleansed myself from a pool of toxic (intoxicated) waste.

All of the justifications I've made for her and her egregiousness since the minute we met are bursting like popcorn kernels, one by one. All I need is some melted butter and sea salt and I can truly begin to relish in her downfall. Perla can't help but fill in the gaps in our conversation—or argument. "Good luck getting hired anywhere without me to back you up. You're nothing without me," she spits, acidly. "*Estúpida*."

As if I haven't heard a word she's said, I robotically slide my feet into my cowboy boots, pick up my suitcase, and traipse towards the front door. There, I pause. I flip my hair over my shoulder for dramatic flair. It's a bit short, but who cares? I've always wanted to do that. I take a deep breath and say, "No, Perla, I'm nothing with you." Narrowing my eyes, I add, "And be nicer to your daughter. She deserves more."

And then I'm gone.

***

It's not until I'm in the cab on my way to the airport that I realize I'm still in my nightgown. However, it's black, charmeuse, and except for the sheer panels with tonally embroidered flowers, looks like it could pass as a slip dress. I'm too shocked to feel self-conscious.

As triumphant as my exit was, I'm slowly fading to black. I have no plane ticket. How am I going to get out of this country? What if there isn't a flight back? Can I hitchhike to Toronto? I lay my head back on the seat, reminiscing on the whirlwind trip, and watching the Hudson River racing alongside the taxi. What a disaster. I didn't even survive two whole weeks. I am a blob of self-pity and disappointment.

"Which terminal?" asks the taxi driver.

"Umm . . ." Stress sweat begins prickling my armpits. "Air Canada departures?"

When we pull up outside of the airport, I hoist myself and my single piece of luggage out of the cab and wander aimlessly inside. I've never been to the airport without a ticket before. What do I do? I find myself standing at the Air Canada service desk.

"Excuse me?" I say. "I'm looking for a ticket to Toronto. One-way. I checked earlier this morning but didn't see anything. Can you tell me if there's been a cancellation?" I'm holding my breath as the perky airline agent in the silky scarf taps away at the computer.

"You're in luck," she beams. "It's going to be quite a wait, but there's one available ticket on a nonstop flight to Toronto, departing at five thirty this evening. Would you like me to reserve that for you?"

"How much is it?" I gulp. Not that it really matters, whatever it costs, I have to get home.

"It comes to $535, including taxes and fees." She smiles as if that's a steal of a price. Shakily, I hand over my credit card. I make it through customs unscathed and seek out a spot away from other travelers. Slumping to the ground, I connect to the WiFi. A text from Oliver comes in.

I'm up early powering through this bloody project so I can make it to NYC today!

Oh, god. I dial his number right away. "There's been a change of plans . . ."

"Don't tell me you want to spend the weekend with Perla instead?" he feigns surprise. "I can't say I'm not hurt . . ."

"No," I sigh. "I quit my job after a huge fight with Perla. I'm at LaGuardia, sitting on the floor in my nightgown. I left the apartment in such a rush, I forgot to change into actual clothes. Anyway, I'm coming home but my flight isn't until tonight."

"Shit, babe," he groans. "Things got that bad, huh? I'm sorry— but I'm glad you're out of there. Is there anything I can do?"

"Finish your project and then meet me for brunch tomorrow?" He agrees and says that, if I want, he will make me eggs Benedict on waffles with "heaps of from-scratch hollandaise." It's exactly what I want.

Next, I call Jessie. "Hey, weird news. I'm coming home on a last-minute flight. Can you come stay the night? And maybe . . . pick up Lola on your way?"

"Stop," she exclaims. "What happened? Of course I can. I work in the morning but not until ten."

"It's a full-marathon-length story and Perla is the villain, of course. I'll tell you details in-person."

"I hope you told her to go to hell," says Jessie. "Which wouldn't be much of a stretch considering that's where she came from."

"Not in those exact words, but essentially, yeah. I'm frazzled to the bone. I just need to chill in a drama-free environment." I also need a deep-tissue massage, a seaweed wrap, and an extra-strong drink.

As if I sent that thought telepathically, Jessie says, "When do you land? I'll be at your place ready to mix a mean martini and queue up *Girlfriends*."

Boarding my flight some eight hours later, I feel like the epitome of failure. My career is in the dumps for the second time in a year, my friendship—or whatever you want to call it—with Perla, my supposed mother figure, is over, and the opportunity with *Vogue* that I've been working for my entire life went up in clouds of smoke bigger than Mary-Kate's languorous exhales. Life feels worse than wearing leather pants with no underwear.

Back at my apartment, Jessie is waiting in the "kitchen"; there's a spread of Korean take-out on the counter as well as two lemon martinis. She is the best friend ever.

"I don't know what I'd do without you," I cry. At the sound of my voice, Lola comes bounding over; all I can see is a blurry ball of light brown fur. She jumps at my feet, drool flying and ears flapping. My chest expands with more love for her than I thought possible. "Lola!" I drop to the floor, scratching her in between sopping wet licks and a jumble of paws.

Jessie joins us, handing me a drink. "First, take a sip of this. Then, let's grab our food. And then, you have to tell me everything. And I want all of the dirty details. Be honest. What happened to make you cut the trip short by a whole two and a half weeks? It must have been bad for you to leave your—"

"Favorite city in the world? Yeah, it was brutal," I say.

"I mean," Jessie starts. She gets a mischievous glint in her sapphire eyes. "I don't want to say we told you so, but . . ."

"Then don't. Just eat your bibimbap and listen." I eye her fiercely and Jessie throws up her hands in surrender.

Between forkfuls of bulgogi on rice, I tell Jessie every sordid detail of the trip. Now that Perla's out of my life, I don't feel the need to cover up her actions or downplay her behavior. I tell it like it is, and it's worse than I'd allowed myself to imagine while I was living through it. I begin with Perla losing her passport and showing up to the airport drunk-slash-hungover. Then, I move onto her not sticking up for me in front of Esther, threatening to demote me if she had to rent a more expensive office, trying to torpedo my meeting with *Vogue*, the screaming match on the street, the nefarious email to Richard, and finally, the volcanic detonation of it all this morning. I even confess about the return-lary to Paul's apartment way back on my first day. I've never told anyone about that before and it makes me nauseous with nerves. I feel like even Lola is judging me with her unwavering puppy gaze.

By the time I wrap up, we're both emotionally exhausted. Jessie is laying on my bed, staring up at the ceiling; her face is frozen with an unbelieving expression. I listen closely to make sure she's still breathing. Good, she's alive.

"You went through all of that and you didn't tell me?" She rolls over and props herself up on her elbow. "Mar, I'm your best friend. You can tell me anything. I don't want you to ever have to go through something like that again." She reaches her hand out, placing it on top of mine.

"Trust me, neither do I," I halfheartedly laugh. "I just wanted everything to work out so badly. Perla seemed great at first glance, but it wasn't until I really got to know her that I saw she was just as flawed as anyone."

"More!" Jessie exclaims. "She's demonic." She bolts upright. "You don't think Perla's going to contact you again, do you? Try to force you to come back to work for her? Or send out defaming letters like she did to that other girl way back when?"

"I hope not," I say, stroking Lola's bushy back. "Knowing her, she'll cool down by tomorrow and ask to take me out to lunch or for a fancy dinner to apologize. Or maybe she's still waiting for me to get back to the apartment." I roll my eyes and we both laugh at the thought.

Jessie and I fall asleep on top of the covers—it's seriously equatorial in here—with Lola resting her teeny head between our pillows. I imagine that I'm back in New York. But this time, there's no Perla, no drama, and no explosive encounters—just me, a suitcase full of fashion, and a second chance at success in the city of my dreams. Literally.

After Jessie leaves the next morning, I throw on a stretchy camisole with vintage jeans and amble down my perilous flight of stairs towards Angelo's; buying books is therapeutic and the universe knows I could use some extra therapy after the Manhattan mishap. Lola bounces along beside me on her retractable leash.

"Look who it is," Angelo says fondly as we enter the bookstore. I walk Lola over to the desk. He bends down under the guise that he's simply scratching her ears, but I see him feed her a bigger than usual chunk of pepperoni. I let it slide; it's been a while since he's indulged her. "How was New York? I wasn't expecting you back for weeks!"

I shrug ambiguously. I love Angelo, but I don't want to get into the drama. Again. Living it—and telling it—once was enough. "It was fabulous! But I was starting to miss home. And your store, of course. There's no Angelo's Books in Manhattan." I grin.

"No," he agrees. "There's not. Oh! I have something for you . . ."
Angelo reaches underneath the desk. The limoncello bottle
clinks against a couple of glasses as he grabs around it on the
bottom shelf. He places a stack of three novels wrapped in twine
in front of me. On top, there's a card that reads, "For the Mar to
my tini. Welcome back, babe." My knees feel as sturdy as kelp.

"These are for you," he explains. "A gift from Signor Oliver."
His eyes crinkle into a warm smile. "He is a good man. He loves
books and he loves you!"

"Oh my god," I gush. "When did he do this?" I loosen the bow
and toss the twine to the side. Staring back at me are three of my
favorite books: *Breakfast at Tiffany's*, *Shopaholic Takes Manhattan*,
and *The Shining*. The fact that Oliver came in here, picked out
these books, and left them for me makes me want to howl about
our love from the top of the CN Tower.

"Yesterday afternoon. He said you might stop by soon, *cara*."

I give Angelo a tight squeeze before slipping the novels into
my reusable tote. For the first time in months, I get the feeling
that I'm on the right path. Things are going to be okay. I'll find
work, my career will thrive, and my fluency in fierceness will pass
any proficiency test. The familiar bell chimes as we leave the store
and head home (sweet, home). I'm meeting Oliver for brunch at
his apartment in a little while, but first, I want to settle into my
glorious seat in the window and start reading.

***

Is there anything more delicious than a hot shell massage? Let
me rephrase—is there anything more delicious than a hot shell
massage with the person you're madly in love with? Oliver and I
are spending the weekend in Montréal. We're currently at Bota
Bota; I never want to leave.

A man who is in touch with his feminine side is so sexy. None of my other boyfriends would have *ever* gone to a spa with me. Not that I even have time to think of previous boyfriends with being so enraptured with my current one. And it was Oliver's suggestion! To help me fully relax, unwind, and decompress. No more stress sweats or anxiety acne for me. *Hmm.* I wonder if I can get a high-frequency facial?

It's been two weeks since the carnage of—what Liao has so aptly named—the Rivera Riots. I haven't spoken to Perla since that dramatic day and I don't ever want to again. She was pure, unfiltered toxicity. My heart convulses when I think about the last time I saw Paloma and the way she gripped me and stared at me through teary eyes, but there's little I can do about that. Perla tried spamming my phone about thirteen hundred times over the next few days—calls, texts, voicemails, emails, you name it. She even tried messaging Jessie on Instagram to get a hold of me. As *if* Jessie would betray me for Perla Rivera. I blocked her on every social media platform and deleted her number. She's out of my life and she would need a sledgehammer, a block of dynamite, and a shred of common decency to get back in. She was a temporary blip. But isn't everything in life? Temporary, I mean.

I feel like a brand-new woman; a better, more elevated version of myself. And it's divine. I'm much sexier now that I'm not revolving my life around Perla and her malevolent agendas. What I'm focused on is reaching my goals, my personal growth, finding inner self-love, and surrounding myself with people who make me feel safe. I am visualizing my dream woman and becoming her with every move I make in my burnt-orange flip-flop sandals—this summer's fiercest fashion statement.

Oh my *god*, these hot shells are heaven on earth. Laying facedown on a massage table, you almost forget about all of your problems. I am so deliciously relaxed I think I might completely melt into the diffused ylang-ylang oil. I'd let it absorb me, if it weren't for the hypnotic pull of Oliver's lips. I am powerless to their pucker. Okay, that sounded totally cringe, but it's true. We are certifiably crazy about each other—like Kate Moss and Johnny Depp were in the nineties.

When we get back to our sumptuous room at Gault Hotel, Lola wakes from a nap but doesn't make any effort to leave the comfort of the astronomical, cloud-like bed; she barely lifts her head from the duvet. You'd think *she'd* just had a hot shell massage with how relaxed she is. I strip naked and wrap myself in a French terry robe; I look and feel like a soft, squishy marshmallow.

"Room service?" I ask Oliver, knotting my robe.

"You read my mind," he says, picking up the menu. "What're you craving?"

"Pizza? But no mushrooms. Please." That's the one downside to this relationship; I discovered that he adores fungi of all varieties. Ew. I'm still learning to control my gag reflex.

"Fair enough," he laughs. "It's your weekend."

"*Merci, monsieur,*" I say.

Adjusting a down-stuffed pillow against the exposed brick wall, I lay down beside Lola and grab my phone from the bedside table. She lifts her head in annoyance as I wiggle around to get comfy. Unlocking my phone, my breath catches in my throat. *Holy smokes.* Did I just see what I thought I did?

"Oliver!" I shriek, even though he's only a few steps away. "Come here. I need you to look at something." He pads over to my side of the bed, twisting the cap off of a bottle of water. "What does this name say?" I thrust my phone in his face, open to my email inbox.

"Amisha Chowdhury?"

"Yes! She's the one I met with, the *Vogue* editor." My phone feels like a thirty-five-pound weight. I've hardly allowed myself to think about the meeting with Amisha; it was too torturous, refreshing my email every hour on the hour. I tried to bury it under all of the other atrocities that went on in Manhattan. I didn't want to get my hopes higher than the Central Park Tower just to have them collapse, as they so often do. But now here she is, in my inbox! Again.

"Well, what does it say?" He tilts the water bottle back and finishes half of it in one go. Say what you want, but spas can be very dehydrating.

I stare at him incredulously. "I haven't read it yet. I'm too terrified. What if it's horrible? What if she's emailing to say that she can't get over how unprofessional it was to have Perla show up and vandalize our meeting?"

"Come on, Mar. I reckon it's gotta be good news. She wouldn't email you to say that she *didn't* want to work with you. Do you want me to look at it first?"

"Let's look together."

He crawls into bed beside me. "On the count of three . . ."

I click into the email before he even has a chance to start counting. My eyes voraciously scan the text. Amisha apologizes for not getting back to me sooner, says she's had a chance to look at my online portfolio, and thinks my expertise would be an excellent addition to the team. Am I reading this right? I read the next part out loud.

"As luck would have it, one of my contributors just gave her notice. Want to start with a digital piece on Halle Berry's best on-screen beauty looks? It's a tight turnaround—her birthday is in August—but if you're up for it, I'll send you the details." As vile as Perla turned out to be, I guess her coming into my life was worth it because without her, I would never have met Richard, and in turn, never have met Amisha.

"Babe! That's awesome," Oliver exclaims. His dimples still get me every time; I'll never get sick of them.

"This is the best weekend," I say effusively. "I think this is going to be the best year of my life. Not counting the blip known as—"

"Don't say her name!" Oliver jokes.

"You're right. I'm not going to waste even a second longer acknowledging her." I hold my chin high. I've worked long and hard for *Vogue*. I deserve this opportunity. Let it be known: I am capable of anything.

"Anyway, you did this without her," he says. "Despite her best efforts to ruin it. I'm so proud of you, Martini." Everyone deserves a man who isn't threatened by their girlfriend's success; he makes me want to be better. And his nickname for me is just too adorable. *Martini*. Speaking of martinis, I'd adore one.

"I'm flourishing! Like a blossoming flower." My smile is as luminous as a pair of pavé diamond hoops.

Oliver kisses my forehead. Then, he picks up Lola and places her on the ground. "You're not just a flower, you're the whole meadow."

Now I really am melting. Forget being a plain old marshmallow—I'm a s'more, squished between Oliver's golden graham cracker biceps and rich, chocolatey kiss. Without limitation, our lips, hands, and limbs explore each other greedily like we're famished and just stumbled across an all-you-can-eat buffet. He reaches for my knotted belt, working it undone. Suddenly my robe is off and the luxurious duvet is the only thing pressing against my arched spine. He brushes my collarbones and nibbles my nipples. God, I love hotel beds. I could just vanish into these sheets and be forever content. Is there anything better than sex after you've been at the spa all day? (Rhetorical question.) We're kissing and kissing like he's trying to plant a field of wild cosmos inside of me.

Oliver pauses for a moment to readjust, placing my sprawled body higher up on the plump pillows and traveling south. It gives me a mini-moment to think about what it is that I truly want: to stay crazily in love, write to my heart's—and *Vogue*'s—content, and be deliriously happy. Of course, I'll live in Manhattan one day and I'll continue reading a vast number of novels and wearing leopard prints as often as appropriate. (It's *not* too much to ask for.) You really do have the power to live the life you want; the only person standing in your way is you. In my case, a certain *diabla* was too, but she's more dead to me now than that show with Christina Applegate.

The number one thing I've learned post-Rivera Riots is that life is so much more exquisite when you take it into your own fiercely capable hands.

And speaking of exquisite, I've got to get back to those decadent dimples.

CPSIA information can be obtained
at www.ICGtesting.com
Printed in the USA
BVHW030338211121
621549BV00004B/8/J